Prais[e] Susan Cran[dall]

Pitch Black

"Prepare to be thoroughly captivated by Crandall's *Pitch Black* world! . . . A superbly woven suspense that sucks you in and doesn't let go . . . Susan Crandall is a master storyteller whose characters never fail to touch your heart."

—Karen Rose, *New York Times* Bestselling Author

"Keep the lights on bright for *Pitch Black* . . . takes the reader on a thrill ride into the soul of a small town, a very special woman, and the sheriff who wants her even more than he wants to solve a terrible murder."

—Karen Harper, *New York Times* Bestselling Author

"Crandall brings a strong new voice to the genre."

—Romantic Times BOOKreviews Magazine

A Kiss In Winter

"Everything a contemporary romance reader wants in a book." *—Midwest Book Review*

"A very character-driven story, *A Kiss in Winter* is a tale of family expectations and disappointments."

—Romantic Times BOOKreviews Magazine

"Complex characters, intricate relationships, realistic conflicts, and a fine sense of place." *—Booklist*

more . . .

"Great characters, a touching relationship, and exciting suspense."
—*Affaire de Coeur*

"Brilliant characterization, edgy suspense . . . a tension-rich mystery."
—ContemporaryRomanceWriters.com

On Blue Falls Pond

"A powerful psychological drama . . . *On Blue Falls Pond* is a strong glimpse at how individuals react to crisis differently, with some hiding or running away while others find solace to help them cope."
—*Midwest Book Review*

"Readers who enjoy . . . fiction with a pronounced sense of place and families with strong ties will respond well to Crandall's . . . sensitive handling of the important issues of domestic violence, macular degeneration, and autism."
—*Booklist*

"Susan Crandall writes nothing but compelling tales, and this is the best yet. I'm moving her to the top of my favorite author list."
—RomanceReviewsMag.com

"Full of complex characters . . . it's a well-written story of the struggles to accept what life hands out and to continue living."
—*Romantic Times BOOKreviews Magazine*

Promises To Keep

"An appealing heroine . . . [an] unexpected plot twist . . . engaging and entertaining."
—TheRomanceReader.com

"FOUR STARS!"
—*Romantic Times BOOKreviews Magazine*

"Another fantastic story by Susan Crandall."
—RomanceReviewsMag.com

"This is one book you will want to read repeatedly."
—MyShelf.com

"One of today's most enjoyable authors."
—RoundTableReviews.com

Magnolia Sky

"Emotionally charged . . . An engrossing story."
—*BookPage*

"A wonderful story that kept surprising me as I read. Real conflicts and deep emotions make the powerful story come to life."
—*Rendezvous*

"Engaging . . . starring two scarred souls and a wonderful supporting cast . . . Fans will enjoy."
—*Midwest Book Review*

The Road Home

"A terrific story . . . a book you will want to keep to read again and again."
—RomRevToday.com

"The characters . . . stay with you long after the last page is read."
—Bookloons.com

Back Roads

"Accomplished and very satisfying . . . Add Crandall to your list of authors to watch."
—Bookloons.com

"An amazingly assured debut novel . . . expertly drawn."
—TheRomanceReadersConnection.com

"A definite all-nighter. Very highly recommended."
—RomRevToday.com

Also by Susan Crandall

Pitch Black

A Kiss in Winter

On Blue Falls Pond

Promises to Keep

Magnolia Sky

The Road Home

Back Roads

SEEING RED

SUSAN CRANDALL

FOREVER

NEW YORK BOSTON

Cover design and art by Rob Wood

Forever
Hachette Book Group
237 Park Avenue
New York, NY 10017
Visit our Web site at www.HachetteBookGroup.com

Forever is an imprint of Grand Central Publishing. The Forever name and logo is a trademark of Hachette Book Group, Inc.

Printed in the United States of America

First Printing: February 2009

10 9 8 7 6 5 4 3 2 1

In memory of Jane Henry Younce, friend, classmate, and fellow writer. You taught us all how to laugh in the face of adversity. Thank you.

Acknowledgments

It's funny the things an author will ask you to do. Luckily the folks around me are used to my peculiar questions like, "Can I come and smell your stables today?" A huge thank you to Lorrie Mahaney for indulging my senses and answering all of my horsey questions.

I want to send out a special thank you to my editor, Karen Kosztolnyik, and my agent, Annelise Robey, for all of the special guidance they provided in molding my loose idea into a story that exceeded my own expectations. You held my hand and led me when the woods were too dense for me to find my way.

As all books are truly a team effort, thanks to the rest of the wonderful people at Grand Central Publishing for putting their time and expertise into this book.

And, as always, appreciation to my fabulous critique group, IndyWITTS (Garthia, Sherry, Vicky, Brenda, Pam, and Alicia), for their eagle eyes, their sharp insights, and their continual support.

SEEING RED

Prologue

February
Charleston, SC, County Courthouse
Fifteen years ago

The long wooden bench on which Ellis Greene sat next to her father reminded her of a church pew. But there was nothing holy about what was happening in this courtroom today. For the past few minutes, she'd kept her gaze fixed on her hands in her lap. Her fingernails were chewed to the quick, the cuticles ragged and red. They hadn't been that way nine months ago.

She sighed and tried not to cry. Today was her fourteenth birthday.

Nobody remembered.

For her entire life, her dad had made such a huge deal out of "family first." No matter what he was talking about, he always managed to stick in, "Ellis, remember, friends come and go, but your family is forever," or something equally dorky. She never wanted to hurt his feelings—because growing up, he hadn't really had a family—so she always nodded before she turned away and rolled her eyes.

But now she got it. And her dad had stopped talking

about much of anything. He just looked at her with sad eyes and a frown on his face. He didn't let her go anywhere or do anything. A person would think she was six, not fourteen. Her mother said to give him time and he'd adjust. But how could somebody adjust to something as horrible as what had happened to Cousin Laura?

Although she'd never let anyone know, Ellis had always hated how boring her life was . . . how boring her family was. The thought that things would drag on forever just the same had sometimes made her depressed. Like she was caught in one of those vapor locks she'd studied in science, stuck with things being just like they were until the day she died of old age—or boredom. She used to spend hours willing something to happen.

And then it did.

Every time she went to see Laura in the rehab center, she told her how sorry she was and that she wished she could take back that wanting, the thousands of secret wishes for something big to happen. Not that *sorry* could help Laura. It was just like her daddy said: "Sorry never fixed anything."

A week ago in this courtroom, Ellis had sworn to tell the truth. It was all she could do for her cousin now. If she could do anything else to help, she would. But the doctors said there's nothing anyone can do. For a long time, Ellis hadn't believed it. For a long time, she'd hoped.

Now all she could do was tell what she'd seen the night her cousin had been kidnapped from her bedroom and left for dead on the beach. . . .

Just then, the jury filed back in. They'd been deliberating for three days. As they took their seats, Ellis's heart beat hard and fast, and her stomach felt like it was crawling up her throat. She couldn't tell by looking at them what verdict they'd come to.

Angry sleet clattered against the courthouse windows—a freakish occurrence even in February around here. It seemed Mother Nature didn't think it was right for everything to bloom when beautiful, perfect Laura lay pale and shrinking in her bed instead of finishing her senior year of high school.

Ellis shivered.

She couldn't look at Hollis Alexander, the man sitting at the defense table. After a minute, she couldn't even look at the jury. This was nothing like what she'd seen on TV.

This was the first day she'd been allowed in the courtroom, except when she'd testified. It was because she was a witness, but her dad wouldn't have let her come anyway. She'd had to beg to come today.

Her dad took her hand and squeezed it. She felt his breath on her ear when he whispered, "You should be proud of yourself, Ellis. No matter what they say, you acted bravely and did right by Laura."

Ellis didn't feel brave; just the opposite. Fear had crept into her life, and she had a feeling it had moved in permanently. She shuddered, thinking what her life would be like if the jury let Hollis Alexander go free.

The prosecutor, Mr. Buckley, had warned them that the case was thin, that the jury was going to have to believe all the circumstantial evidence. He'd tried to keep Ellis from feeling pressured as she'd testified. But she knew exactly where things stood. Without her identifying Alexander in the first place, there would have been no arrest. Without her testimony, without the jury believing her every word, he would likely go free.

Of course, everyone had been careful not to say that straight out. But she saw it in the nervous uncertainty in Mr. Buckley's eyes, in her uncle's heavy sad stare each time he looked at her. And her dad . . . He sometimes looked at her with so much fear in his eyes—like she was the one on trial, and might be hauled off to prison. He hadn't wanted her to testify at all. And if there had been any other way for the prosecutor to have made his case, Ellis was certain her father would have forbidden it. The fact that he allowed her to testify told her exactly how much of this case depended on her.

She'd told her story, just like Mr. Buckley had instructed. But what if the jury didn't believe her? The man who attacked Laura would go free, and it would be all Ellis's fault.

She closed her eyes and swallowed hard, but her stomach wouldn't go back where it belonged.

The bailiff looked serious, bordering on grouchy, when he announced the judge in a flat voice.

The courtroom was so quiet, she could hear her father breathing next to her.

She lifted her eyes and looked at the back of Aunt Jodi's head. Her hair was the same beautiful blond as Laura's; Ellis wondered if Uncle Greg felt as sad when he looked at Aunt Jodi's hair as Ellis did. She didn't think her aunt had stopped crying since the trial began. Her head was bent, and Ellis heard her sniffles. Uncle Greg put an arm around her.

At first, Uncle Greg had been certain that Nate Vance had done this horrible thing to Laura. Sometimes, even with Hollis Alexander on trial, Ellis thought her uncle still believed it, or at least that Nate was in some way responsible for Hollis Alexander finding his way to Belle Island in the first place, which was ridiculous. Uncle Greg had never liked Nate, even before; he said Nate came from trash, so he could never be anything better. Laura was too good for "the likes of Nate Vance."

Stupid. Stupid. Stupid.

Nate was great. He loved horses. He loved Laura. He would never have hurt her.

Ellis looked across the courtroom aisle. Nate sat on a bench entirely empty of anyone else, despite the crowded courtroom. His mom worked in the hospital cafeteria and couldn't get off—at least that's what Ellis wanted to think. She was pretty sure Nate's mom had never said "family first." From what Ellis had heard about the woman, she probably wouldn't be here with him anyway. Nate's dad . . . Well, Ellis didn't know anything about him, other than it had been so long since Nate had seen him that he didn't remember what he looked like. Uncle Greg said Nate's dad was in prison somewhere, but Ellis didn't believe it.

Nate was wearing a shirt and tie, just as he had each day of the trial. Ellis knew because she'd stood outside the courthouse and watched him go in every day when her dad thought she was at school. It was always the same tie; he probably had only one. She thought his daily presence was a real show of respect, because, like her, he hadn't been allowed inside the courtroom except when he'd testified.

Now, waiting for the verdict, there wasn't any shame or guilt in the way he held his head. Even though there were plenty of people who whispered behind his back and thought like Uncle Greg—that Nate still might have been involved some way in Laura's "ordeal."

Nate looked over at Uncle Greg. And Uncle Greg stared back—almost as hatefully as Hollis Alexander had stared at Ellis when she'd been on the witness stand. Nate didn't look away from her uncle, though, like she had from Alexander. Nate kept his face calm and held Uncle Greg's gaze until Uncle Greg finally turned away.

Ellis sat up straighter and tried to look as confident as Nate.

As she waited, things crept into her mind, things she tried to keep locked out. Laura's stiff fingers curled against the braces they'd put on her to keep her hands from closing. The sound of the respirator hissing in and out, in and out.

"Has the jury reached a verdict?" The judge's voice sounded like gravel hitting pavement.

One of the jurors stood up. "We have, Your Honor."

The judge ordered, "Please rise, Mr. Alexander."

Ellis looked then at the man who'd hurt Laura. She didn't want to, not after the way he'd looked at her when she'd testified, like he was a snake and she was a mouse with two broken legs. But it was the right thing to do.

She was glad he didn't turn around and look at her. She could hardly breathe as it was.

Her dad's arm went around her shoulder, and he held her close to his side. She saw he was holding her mother on his other side.

The judge asked the man in the jury box, "On the count of kidnapping, how do you find?"

"Guilty." The man in the jury box looked right at Hollis Alexander when he said it, as if he wasn't afraid.

Aunt Jodi's sob sounded over the rest of the whispers in the room.

"On the count of criminal sexual conduct in the first degree?"

"Guilty."

"On the count of assault and battery with intent to kill?"

"Guilty."

Her dad let go of her and leaned forward, wrapping his arms around Aunt Jodi and Uncle Greg. Her mother joined them, putting her forehead against Aunt Jodi's. Everyone was crying.

Ellis stood rigid, feeling like an island in a sea of movement.

Those words. Those charges. They brought pictures to her mind that she wished would disappear. They brought alive the pain and fear of Laura's "ordeal." Everyone had been so careful when they spoke about what happened when Ellis was within earshot. But she knew it had been bad—just look at what was left of her cousin. But hearing those words . . .

Her stomach rolled. She couldn't cry. She couldn't move. She couldn't speak.

Right then, Hollis Alexander turned around and looked at her with those nearly colorless eyes. His lips moved, but she couldn't figure out what he was saying.

Then, suddenly, she couldn't see him anymore. All she could see was Nate's blue tie as he stepped in front of her.

"Don't look at him, Ellis," he said. He put his hands on her shoulders. "He can't hurt you now."

She realized then what Hollis Alexander had said:

"You'll pay."

Chapter One

Sometimes, in the dark hours before dawn when sleep crept away like a scolded dog and left only unwanted restlessness behind, when memories clogged her throat and sucked the air from her room, Ellis broke her iron-clad rule and opened her balcony door. But never, never did she do it without studying the darkness three stories below to ensure there was no unfamiliar movement, no human-shaped shadows among the palmettos and overgrown azaleas.

She went through the familiar routine of shutting off the alarm, removing the safety bar, unlocking the double locks, and opening the sliding door. Then she stepped out onto the balcony.

She wanted to blame her sleeplessness on a normal thing like the disintegration of her long relationship with Rory. She knew she'd broken his heart. As soft as she'd tried to make it, she'd hurt him deeply. Dear, sweet Rory. It wore on her like windblown sand on stone.

But that wasn't the true reason for her insomnia—she wasn't a normal person, with normal issues.

Summer was coming. She could smell it in the sourness of the low tide marsh, feel it in the sluggish heaviness of the humid air. Even if she could ignore the prompt from her senses, her own internal clock would wake old terrors and bitter recollections. Since that horrible summer sixteen years ago, sleeplessness had become a living, breathing being whose presence haunted her nights.

Ellis filled her lungs with a draught of fresh air and tried to clear her mind. And still nervousness lingered, a sticky spiderweb of memory that she would never be able to completely swipe away.

Her condo was a duplex, over one other residence and a hurricane-mandated breakaway parking garage. Logic told her she was perfectly safe; she'd selected this place, inside a gated community, with great care. Still, she strained her ears for a stray footfall, sniffed the light breeze for the smell of cheap cologne.

The memory of that smell—too strong, too sharp—would taunt her for the rest of her life. If only she'd investigated when she'd been drawn from sleep, when that smell had first teased her senses. If only. The odor hadn't awakened her. She couldn't say what had roused her out of her dreams. But the odor was what she remembered of that moment. It had slipped in the bedroom window on the moist night air, distinctive and unpleasant. It had been as if the man had saturated his clothing with a drugstore knockoff of Aramis in an effort to mask his own body odor. But that had been there, too, lying just beneath the artificial fragrance—a sour-edged blade swaddled in a handful of wildflowers and cloying spice.

Ellis leaned her elbows on the balcony railing and closed her eyes, concentrating on the scent medley of broken pine needles underscored with jasmine and brackish water. The humidity amplified everything, making all smells more pungent, as if decaying South Carolina vegetation, brackish water, and pluff mud weren't pungent enough.

She'd moved to this side of town, the marsh and river side, away from the beach that had been her childhood home. Away from the house that sat side by side with Laura's. It hadn't seemed to make a difference. Maybe she should have left the island altogether. She'd toyed with the idea. And yet, trading the scant security of what was familiar for the complete vulnerability of a place wholly new seemed like trading one fatal disease for another.

Here she had her routine. Here she knew her limitations, had structured her life so she could live within them. *Here* was better than some unknown there.

Her inability to face living in unfamiliar surroundings had cost her two extra semesters in completing her elementary ed degree. She had commuted to the College of Charleston and had always structured her class schedule so she would be back in Belle Island, behind the safety of closed doors, by dark.

Teaching fourth grade in her small hometown had worked out well. No one here questioned when she scheduled all of her parent meetings during daylight hours.

Ellis stood on her balcony, turning her mind away from summer's arrival, toward next fall's class. Preparation for the next school year is what had gotten her through the past few summers. Maybe this year she'd add a field trip to—

The ring of her telephone bit into the silence. Ellis jerked away from the railing with her heart rocketing up her throat.

As she hurried back into the bedroom, she looked at

the clock. It was nearly five a.m. Pretty late for pranksters. Too early for everything else. That left bad news.

She snatched up the phone. "Hello?"

"I figured you'd be awake."

"Dad? Is everything all right? Mom . . . ?"

"We're fine, baby. I know you can't sleep either this time of year, and since misery loves company, I thought I'd take a chance and call."

"You know me too well." She heard the *tappity-tap* of her father's keyboard and knew he'd been passing his sleepless hours poking around on the Internet.

"When are you leaving for Martha's Vineyard?" he asked.

"Dad, I told you. Rory and I need some time apart." Rory's Grandma Ginny had a place in Martha's Vineyard. Over the past four years, the annual trip north had been a welcome escape from the demons that rode in on the South Carolina summer humidity.

Her dad sighed. She knew he loved Rory like a son; they sailed and fished together. This was hard on her dad in ways that reached beyond her relationship with Rory. And that made Ellis feel even worse.

Her relationship with Rory had always been like a favorite sweater—warm, comfortable, uncomplicated. But two weeks ago, things had changed. He'd taken the step she'd thought she'd silently and sufficiently discouraged.

When Rory proposed, Ellis had been blindsided by raw panic. Her lungs had seized. She'd broken out in a cold sweat. Her heart skittered with the same fear she'd felt the time she'd come close to a head-on collision on the bridge over the estuary. She couldn't decipher why her reaction was so severe, so extreme, let alone explain it to poor Rory.

He was a good man. He loved her, although their differing ideals of love had often been a subject of near-contentious discussion. Rory was a romantic in the extreme. She couldn't count the times they'd debated whether van Gogh's self-amputation of his ear was a measure of his instability or his devotion. Rory was a true heart and saw only love in grand romantic gestures.

It should be easy for her to open herself up to a sentimental and loving man like Rory. And yet she held back.

Maybe there was something missing inside her, some deficiency that prevented her from feeling the depth of emotions that other people do.

Even so, cutting him loose frightened her only slightly less than his proposal. What if this was her one chance at happiness? She didn't want to make a mistake. And, if she was totally honest with herself, giving up on Rory felt like she was giving up the hope that somewhere buried deep inside of her, there were those passions, those emotions that inspired poets' verse and made ordinary men and women sacrifice all for love—well, short of cutting off a body part.

Of course, Rory didn't understand the dark hole that dwelt in the place that love should light. Her parents didn't understand it. How could they? They were all normal.

"You can still go north," her dad said.

"And you can still fish with Rory."

"You know I can't stand to look into those sad puppy eyes when he asks about you." His words were punctuated by mouse clicks in the background. He went on. "Maybe the trip will be a good opportunity for you and Rory to work on your problems." He paused. "I just don't think you should spend your entire summer here."

"I'll have to be here in August." Then she added, as if her father would ever forget, "It'll be time for another hearing."

"Sweetie . . ." His sigh rode heavily across the telephone line. "You don't have to do it. Uncle Greg and I—"

"Save your breath, Dad. You know as well as I do that I have to do this. For Laura."

"You've already done right by your cousin. Laura wouldn't want you to put yourself through all of this again and again."

"Okay, maybe I'm doing it for me, then." She'd never taken the option of videoconferencing her testimony at Hollis Alexander's parole hearings. It was important for him to see her, to know her conviction to this cause. And she needed to stare the bastard down, to make up for her inability to do it as a teenager.

"It's not that I don't think you and Uncle Greg can make our case," she said. "I just *have* to be there."

After a few seconds of stone silence, she thought maybe she'd lost the connection. "Dad?"

"Goddamnsonofabitch."

His tone knocked the bottom out of her stomach.

Something thudded, like books falling off the desktop.

"Dad! What's wrong? Are you okay?" Was he having a heart attack?

Finally, her father's clipped words came through. "He's out. Paroled."

"No." The word was no more than a breath filled with

dread and childlike fear. Shaking her head in denial, she said, "That's impossible. His hearing wasn't even on the schedule last time I checked."

"Well, I'm on the Department of Probation, Parole and Pardon Services Web site, and it says right here in black and white that Hollis Alexander was paroled two days ago. Two days ago!"

"It has to be a mistake." The fist that had clamped around her lungs and stolen her breath when she'd opened the sliding door once again squeezed tight.

"Let's hope," her father said. "It says he was paroled with 'conditions.' I'll call Lorne Buckley as soon as the prosecutor's office opens. We'll get this cleared up."

Lorne Buckley had led the case that put Alexander away fifteen years ago. He'd been patient and kind as he'd coached Ellis through the nightmare of her testimony. She'd been frightened to the point of nausea as she'd sat on that witness stand. Looking into Buckley's kind eyes and not those of Hollis Alexander had been the only thing that had held her together.

"Victim Services is supposed to give Uncle Greg thirty days' notice before a hearing." As she said the words, she realized she sounded like a whining child. That notification was a courtesy, not a law.

"I'll have Greg check with their office too. Ellis, until we know for certain what's going on, I want you to stay home with the doors locked and your alarm on."

Any normal grown woman would scoff at the suggestion as overly dramatic. Right now she didn't feel like a normal woman. She felt like a sitting duck.

Ellis watched the sky brighten outside her locked condo, feeling as if she were the prisoner. The sensation had started the instant she'd closed that sliding glass door and reset the alarm. She paced her small living room, stretching legs that demanded to run, trying to fill lungs that wouldn't expand.

She needed to be outside. Running. Sweating out the fear.

This world was totally upside down, a place where victims were prisoners of the past and criminals went free to threaten innocents' futures. At moments like this, she was glad Laura had finally let go of life. It had taken nearly four years after the attack, but her tremendous suffering was over; she didn't have to face her fears anew.

Ellis went to her bedroom and changed into running shorts and a tank top. Even if she couldn't find the courage to actually go out and run, the act of preparation gave her something to do.

Besides, if Alexander was out of prison, she couldn't stay behind locked doors forever.

A locked door didn't keep him from Laura.

But she wasn't like Laura, young and innocent. Ellis knew what kind of dangers lurked out there, and she was prepared to protect herself in ways Laura had never even imagined. Thanks mostly to the insistence and encouragement of Nate Vance. In a time of vulnerability and fear, he'd given her a sense of power, of control.

But that had been before he'd dropped off the face of the earth.

As diffuse shafts of light from the rising sun poked through the pines, she looked outside again. Her neighborhood was populated mostly with retirees and vacation homes. Her downstairs neighbors were off visiting their new grandchild in Oregon. On an ordinary day, there wasn't a lot of early morning activity. Today the street seemed to have an unusual air of desolation.

Once, on cable TV, Ellis had seen a person whose body was completely covered in bees—head to toe, fingertip to fingertip, one big undulating, humming mass. That's how she felt, as if hundreds of thousands of tiny legs walked on her skin, and she had to fight the urge to flail, knowing that any movement would spell disaster.

Her legs twitched. She shifted her gaze to her running shoes sitting by the front door. She was tempted to go out just to prove to herself that she could. Dad would totally flip out if he called and she didn't answer. And if she called him and told him she was going out, he'd worry himself sick. Even if it was overreaction, she'd give in to it—for now, for Dad.

After making herself a cup of tea, she settled on the couch with her laptop. The link for the DPPPS Web site was in her "favorites" folder. That in itself suddenly struck her as ludicrous. *Favorites?* In what twisted universe was having the state's Department of Probation, Pardons and Parole in your favorites folder a sane and reasonable thing?

With a quiver of disgust, she clicked on the link. Two selections later, she reached the Pardons and Paroles Schedule page. Clicking on the date of the most recent parole hearing, she saw for herself, right there in the middle of a list of twenty-five names, most of which had DENIED typed next to them, was HOLLIS ALEXANDER, PAROLE—COND.

It had to be an error. A clerk who'd typed in the incorrect

inmate number. A glitch in the system. Prosecutor Buckley had assured them that after what that man had done to Laura, no parole board would even consider releasing him a day before he completed his thirty-year sentence.

It struck her then that Alexander had already served half of that sentence. What had seemed an eternity to her when she'd been fourteen now loomed in the not-so-distant future. Another fifteen years. She would only be forty-four. Hardly the old woman she'd envisioned that day in the courtroom.

She looked at the screen again. PAROLE—COND. If indeed this was correct, she wondered what special conditions had been imposed. Was shackled to an immovable object too much to hope for?

Closing her eyes, she could see him as clearly as if he'd been standing before her seconds ago. The soullessness in his ice-blue eyes were the only thing that belied the choirboy façade.

You'll pay.

The threat had been made. But over fifteen years had passed. She'd been an impressionable child he'd been trying to intimidate.

Over the past four years, she'd faced him twice in parole hearings. Alexander always stared at her with an air of contempt, with loathing in his glacier eyes, but never had he repeated the threat.

As of that last parole hearing, Alexander had been moved from a Level 3, maximum-security facility, to a Level 2. According to the prison official's assessment recommendation, he'd been a model prisoner during his incarceration and had devoted himself to the facility's training program for seeing-eye dogs.

Perhaps he was the rare creature that had actually been rehabilitated by his time in prison.

If he'd really been paroled, she could only hope.

Wayne Carr finished his telephone interview with the director of the Belle Island Historical Restoration Society and clicked off his microcassette recorder. He wanted to get this article dashed off and get his ass out onto the golf course. Marie, the *Belle Island Sentinel*'s editor, seemed to have some sort of tee-time radar—it didn't matter if Wayne was golfing with the mayor, which, of course, made it a working event. She always dumped some worthless assignment on him at the last minute.

Stop the freaking presses! The historical society has decided what paint colors will be allowed on the buildings in the historic district. Now, that's news!

He reminded himself that he'd made a trade years ago. He'd given up real journalism in exchange for love. Abigail's family had lived here for generations and would, according to Abi, for generations to come (not that they'd had any luck in adding branches to the family tree, despite thousands of dollars and countless humiliations at the fertility clinic). There had been no room for compromise seventeen years ago when they'd graduated from the University of Virginia; if he wanted Abi, he had to follow her home. And Abi had some mighty fine assets to recommend he do just that.

At least he hadn't given in to his father-in-law's pressure to join the family business. Wayne *wrote* for papers; he didn't work in some smelly paper mill—even as a vice president.

He'd had a few of his freelance articles printed in low-country magazines. And the outline for his literary novel was nearly complete. Maybe soon he could quit the newspaper and not worry about being herded into the paper-making biz.

The phone on his desk rang.

He would have ignored it, but Marie was standing just outside his cubicle.

"Carr," he said.

"Wayne Carr?" the man asked.

"Yes." He opened the computer file to get his article going. If he hurried, he'd just make that tee time. The pause went on long enough that Carr stopped typing. "Hello?"

"This is Hollis Alexander."

Carr's hands froze over his keyboard. The back of his neck tingled. "What can I do for you, Mr. Alexander?" The sensational trial of Hollis Alexander had been the only ripple in the placid pond of life on Belle Island, the only opportunity for real reporting.

"Do you remember me?" Alexander asked.

"Of course," Carr said cautiously. Fifteen years. It had been fifteen years. What could the man possibly want? Carr didn't think they could just call anyone they wanted from jail. "I thought you were in prison."

"Well, now, I got good news. I got parole."

"Oh?" After a couple of seconds of expectant silence, Carr added, "Congratulations."

"Why, thank you, sir." It sounded like Alexander was drawing on a smoke, then let his breath out in a long stream. "I can almost hear your mind grindin' away from here. You're askin' yourself, 'Why is ol' Hollis callin' me?' Am I right?"

"You have to admit, it is a bit of a surprise," Carr said dryly.

Alexander gave a chuckle that shot the hairs on Carr's arms to attention. "That's what makes life interestin', ain't it, surprises? I really missed surprises while I was in prison. The only surprises a man gets there are the unpleasant kind."

"What do you want?" Carr picked up his pack of cigarettes and stuck one between his lips. He was halfway to lighting it before he caught himself; no smoking in the office.

"What, no catchin' up? No how you been these fifteen years?" There was another chuckle that felt like fingernails on a chalkboard, then a drag on a smoke. After Alexander blew it out, he said quietly, "I've called to ask a favor. I'd like you to help me clear my name."

Carr blinked and forgot all about his tee time. "After fifteen years? Why now?"

"Well, a man can't do much to prove his innocence while he's in prison, 'specially when he's got no money."

"I'm a newspaper man, Mr. Alexander, not a lawyer. I don't know what you think I can do for you."

"I read all your articles, the ones you wrote right after that girl was found. You know I didn't do it."

"I don't know any such thing."

"You were plenty vocal about the attacker bein' the girl's boyfriend—and you were right." He paused. "Listen, man, I just need someone in my corner, get public opinion in my favor, maybe even help me convince a lawyer to petition to reopen my case."

Carr's brow furrowed. "Mr. Alexander, what good will that do? You've served your time. Getting the case reopened now will be extremely difficult. I suggest you get on with your life."

"They've got more technology now. DNA testin' and whatnot."

"Well yes, but—"

"I'm also contactin' the Justice Project—they've gotten all kinds of convictions overturned on DNA evidence."

"Yes, but they don't accept many cases. The odds are against you—especially since it's been so long and you're now free."

"Free?" Alexander gave a choked chuckle. "I just thought you might be interested in gettin' the story . . . you know, for the paper. Maybe even write a book about it." Another puff on the cigarette. "There's lots of money in a book like that. You help me; I help you. Ain't that the way it works out here in the real world?"

This was just too much to process during an unexpected phone call. Carr couldn't be hasty. "Let's meet and we'll talk."

⁂

Hollis Alexander hung up the phone, pleased with how well things were falling into place. But he had to move slowly, to have patience. Patience to follow his plan, even though he burned for a swift and frightful reckoning. It wouldn't do for his retribution to fall short of complete because of his own impatience.

So many people to punish. So many sins to rectify.

He finished unpacking, laying his neatly folded socks beside his tidy stack of underwear in the cheap particle-board chest of drawers.

Too damn bad his parole required him to live in this fucking halfway house. Of course, the parole board hadn't called it a halfway house. They'd referred to it as "a supportive environment to aid him in his transition." Bullshit. Bullshit. Bullshit. It was just prison with an unlocked door.

Nothin' he could do about it, so he focused on the advantages of "transitional housing." He did have a room all to himself. And it made the powers that be feel in control. That could be a valuable asset—along with the court of public opinion.

He shook his head. All he'd had to do was mention a book and that journalist had jumped right on the bandwagon.

People were so fucking predictable.

He straightened the worn blanket that covered his twin-size bed and left his room, closing and locking the door behind him.

He was whistling as he headed to see his parole officer and report on his new job at Heidi's House of Hounds. Then he was going to make an unexpected call on an old friend.

CHAPTER TWO

Nate Vance sat in the gate area at LaGuardia, next to a young woman gently jostling a baby. She was traveling alone and had eyed him just a little suspiciously when he'd taken the seat next to her. He supposed she was right to; there were plenty of seats across the aisle. Unfortunately, she was worried about the wrong man.

Nate had noticed the guy with the shaved head had been shadowing the young mother for the past ten minutes; the man's eyes were steady on the woman's purse. Babies and diaper bags made great distractions for thieves.

Opening his newspaper, Nate smiled and gave the woman a friendly, yet not too forward nod. "Beautiful baby."

She smiled cautiously. "Thank you."

He returned his attention to his paper and didn't pursue conversation. He didn't want to frighten her off and have to figure out a way to continue watching over her without really freaking her out.

He glanced at his watch, frustrated at the amount of time he was wasting. It had been quite a while since he'd flown in anything other than a corporate jet—not since the last time he'd gone to South Carolina, over two years ago. Although he had to take care of some business in Savannah first, Charleston was his destination. And because of that, he was flying commercial, and under one of his aliases, Samuel Johns.

He didn't allow himself low-country visits often. But he'd been one of the thousands of faces in the crowd when Ellis Greene had graduated from Charleston College. He just couldn't miss that. Not when he'd known how difficult pushing through had been for her. He hadn't chanced getting too close; he'd used his binoculars to search for her black-robed figure among hundreds. But he'd found her.

She'd looked happy and hopeful . . . whole. It had made his heart swell to see it, making it worth all the contriving he'd had to do to get there.

And then, a couple of years later, he'd slipped into Belle Island and watched her teach her self-defense class in the park. His identity had been protected by the tinted windows of a rental car—and he'd never been so tempted to throw caution out the window.

She'd developed into a very striking woman—tall, athletic, with those exotic green eyes and full lips. He'd always known she'd be a knockout. But watching her instruct those girls with passion animating every feature, every action, he'd felt a deep stirring he'd not expected. The kind of stirring that makes men risk rejection and ask for women's phone numbers.

His surprise at this feeling had only been surpassed by his shock at its intensity. He'd been tempted to initiate things that would spell disaster for him—and wouldn't do her a bit of good either.

Before he weakened and revealed himself to her, he'd started the car and driven away.

He hadn't dared to go back since. Until now. With Hollis Alexander out of prison, the risk of Nate *not* going outweighed the risk of his returning to Belle Island.

The airline called his row for boarding.

Nate folded his newspaper and stood, but he remained where he was until the young mother's group was called. Then he followed her to the Jetway entrance and handed his boarding pass to the gate attendant.

⁂

With all the impotent fury of a father who had been unable to protect his child, Greg Reinhardt started dialing Victim Services five minutes before the office in the state capital was scheduled to open. On his sixteenth dial, at exactly eight-oh-one, someone picked up the phone.

"I need to speak to Valerie Scatterfield." Scatterfield had been assigned as the "liaison" for Laura's case. She'd taken over last year when Cyrus Boone had retired. Greg had never felt comfortable with the change—obviously for good reason, as things now stood.

A father of three daughters, Cyrus had taken a special interest in Laura's case, had been there from the beginning. To Valerie Scatterfield, a childless veteran of bureaucracy, Laura was simply another victim years past the crime, just another case number.

"May I tell Ms. Scatterfield who's calling and what this is regarding?"

"Tell her it's Greg." Hopefully the guard dog on the

other end of the line would hurry this along like a personal call, which it was, personal to *him* anyway.

"One moment."

When Valerie Scatterfield answered the phone, she sounded breathless, as if she'd hurried from the coffee station to take the call. "This is Valerie."

"This is Greg Reinhardt. Laura Reinhardt's father."

"What can I do for you, Mr. Reinhardt?" There was no recognition in her voice.

"You can tell me how in the hell Hollis Alexander got paroled and we weren't notified about the hearing."

He heard paper shuffling. "I'm sorry, who was the inmate again?"

"Hollis Alexander. Ridgeland Correctional. Supposed to be serving a thirty-year sentence for raping and beating my daughter to death."

"Murder or manslaughter?" *Chocolate or vanilla? Coffee or tea?*

Greg wanted to reach right through this phone line and wring her neck. Why in goddamn hell did Cyrus have to retire? "Neither. It took her four years to die."

"Oh. I'm very sorry," she said, her tone changing drastically. Apparently, that appalling fact pierced her professional armor. He heard a keyboard in the background. "We do have him listed as paroled on May twenty-third. He's in transition housing, which is good. Let's see . . . He's to meet with his parole officer this morning and is due to meet with him again next Monday, then every two weeks thereafter. As a sex offender, he has to stay away from schools, parks, and playgrounds. And, naturally, he's been ordered to have no contact with the victim's—with your family."

Greg's stomach wanted to expel the coffee he'd consumed. "So it's too late to send the bastard back to prison?"

"Unless he violates parole, sir."

Greg scoffed. "And somebody catches him."

"As with all law enforcement, I'm afraid the probation department is understaffed. I'll give you his parole officer's name and number in case you have a complaint."

With the number of offenders out there and with the understaffing problem, a parole officer keeping a real eye on Hollis Alexander would be like a man trying to watch one fiddler crab in a marsh full of them.

Greg shifted gears. "So why weren't we informed about his parole hearing? We're registered. We've been given thirty days' advance notice in the past. If we'd been there, he wouldn't have gone free."

"Mr. Reinhardt, he isn't free—"

"Let's not get into a semantics discussion. He's out. He has a life after he robbed my daughter of hers. We should have been able to present our case at the hearing."

"Let me go back and check something." More keyboard clickety-clacks followed. "Hmmm, that doesn't make sense."

"What?"

"According to my records, you've been removed from the notification list."

"That's impossible. If you're trying to cover up incompetence—"

"Oh, no, Mr. Reinhardt. This was taken out of the system before I transferred here. Besides"—her voice grew slightly testy—"our service is a courtesy to victims and their families. We have no reason to hide our mistakes."

"When was it removed?"

"Umm, looks like September before last. It's marked as requested by the next of kin."

"I *did not* request it."

"Perhaps your wife, then?"

With a muttered curse, Greg slammed down the phone.

⁂

It was eight-forty a.m. when Ellis heard footsteps coming up the outside staircase that led to her front door. Her gaze darted to the alarm control panel. The reassuring red "armed" light gazed back. She snatched up the cordless phone and tiptoed to the door. Just as she leaned close to look out the peephole, a soft knock sounded.

"Ellis? It's Dad."

As she disarmed the security system, she felt as foolish as a preacher caught in a lie. She had to get some perspective on this. If Alexander was freshly paroled, she doubted he would jeopardize his freedom so quickly. And if he *was* coming after her, he wouldn't very likely do it in the light of day—or with a knock at her front door.

She unlocked the door, then smiled over her shoulder at her dad as she headed to the kitchen. "You still like your coffee so it'll walk to the table on its own?" Putting on a brave face was an important component in managing fear.

"Only when your mother isn't in sight. She's got me on watered down decaf. Might as well drink dishwater," he said glumly. "But however you take yours will be fine."

Somehow he made the statement sound both resigned and hopeful.

As she prepared coffee, her dad went to the fridge. "Do you have any of those refrigerator cinnamon rolls, you know, the ones that have that doughboy on them?" He leaned into the refrigerator. "Criminy, you don't have anything in here. What do you live on?"

"I can make you some oatmeal."

"If I'd wanted oatmeal, I'd have eaten at home and gotten my brownie points for it."

Ellis turned around and leaned against the counter. "Does Mom know about Alexander?"

He nodded. "She went over to tell your aunt Jodi in person."

"What did Uncle Greg say when you called him?" Her aunt and uncle had divorced thirteen years ago; Ellis's mother had said it was because they dealt with their grief in such different ways.

"He's mad as a wildcat in a waterfall. I'm sure he was all over those people at Victim Services the minute they showed up to work." Her dad opened the pantry door and pulled out her one and only junk food—brown sugar cinnamon Pop-Tarts. After ripping open the silver bag and dropping two into the toaster, he turned to her. "Maybe the Web site was wrong. They've always notified us before."

"Let's hope. I mean, Prosecutor Buckley seemed pretty sure Alexander wouldn't get parole—ever."

"Well, one thing I've learned is that this world ain't what it used to be. All you hear about are overcrowded jails and criminals' rights and how they deserve a second chance, that they can't help the way they are, that they're all victims of their upbringing. I say big flippin' deal. Let 'em suffer a little for all the suffering they've caused."

Her father was firmly of the biblical eye-for-an-eye mind-set. And Ellis had to admit that what her mind said was right and humane, her heart thought was a bunch of bullshit. Laura was dead, having never awakened from her coma. Uncle Greg and Aunt Jodi were ruined people. Nate Vance's life had been marked by the shadow of this crime, driving him away from his home.

She noticed her dad was trying to pry the broken half of his Pop-Tart out of the toaster with a butter knife. "Unplug that thing before you electrocute yourself."

He kept poking.

"If you fry yourself, Mom'll know you've been sneaking junk food."

The phone rang.

"That's probably the food police right now," Ellis said as she picked up the phone.

"Send Daddy to Aunt Jodi's right away!" The panic in her mother's voice arced through Ellis's body.

"What's wrong?"

"Greg's lost his mind—" Something crashed in the background.

Ellis remembered the last time Uncle Greg had lost his mind: when the police had come with the news that Laura's naked, unconscious body had been pulled out of a breakwater.

"Maybe you should call the police."

"Just send Dad!" The line went dead.

The wild ride as Ellis's dad drove them to Aunt Jodi's felt much longer than its actual four miles.

Greg's Corvette sat in the front yard, stopped at an angle to the front steps. The car's spinning tires had kicked the St. Augustine grass out of its sandy bed, leaving a swerving outline of his route from the driveway to the porch. The driver's door stood open.

Her father was out of the car before Ellis had even reached for the passenger door handle. He sprinted toward the front door, calling for her mother. "Marsha!"

By the time Ellis got inside, her dad had joined her mother in attempting to quiet Greg. Her uncle's face was an unnatural purple, his eyes wild. He leaned forward, straining against her dad's grip on his shoulders. Ellis's mother stood between Greg and Jodi, calling his name in a voice so quiet that Ellis wondered why she bothered.

The room looked like the aftermath of a raucous teen party. Books were splayed on the floor. One of the toss pillows lay in the cold ash of the fireplace. Two lamps sat ready to topple off the edges of their tables, shades askew. The collectibles Jodi kept on her fireplace mantel lay shattered on the hearth. The bricks were littered with tiny arms and legs, porcelain hands gripping clusters of flowers, cherub faces split in half.

Jodi sat hugging herself on the sofa, withdrawn like a terrified child. Her face was wet with unnoticed tears, her eyes unfocused.

Ellis shot another glance at Greg. Her mother and father now stood shoulder to shoulder, facing him, inching him backward out of the living room.

He reached around her father and punched a finger in the air. "I will never, *never* forgive you for this!"

Ellis hurried to her aunt and knelt on the floor. "Aunt Jodi?" she said softly, her voice sliding beneath Greg's angry words: *"You have no respect for our daughter . . . goddammit . . . you went behind my back . . ."*

Jodi rocked slightly.

Greg's voice became more diffuse; her parents must have gotten him into the kitchen. Underneath Greg's rants, Ellis could hear her father's deep voice, low and lulling. It reminded her of how, when she'd been a child, he used to coax her back from a nightmare. Somewhere in the mix were the light strains of her mother's voice, urging her brother away from hysteria.

Slowly, Ellis reached out and laid her hand on Jodi's knee. "Aunt Jodi," she said softly, "it's me, Ellis."

Jodi blinked.

"Are you hurt?" Ellis asked.

She couldn't tell if Jodi shivered or shook her head. Her aunt kept her arms wrapped around herself.

The voices in the kitchen dropped another notch.

"Are you hurt?" Ellis asked again.

Jodi's voice was shaking when she said softly, "He didn't touch me. Just"—she waved her hand around the room—"did this." Her forehead furrowed and her mouth twisted. She sobbed, "He doesn't understand what it's like f-f-for me. He doesn't know . . . I h-had to do it. I couldn't bear to hear that man's name ever again."

"Had to do what, Aunt Jodi?"

Jodi unfolded a crumpled tissue in her hand and blew her nose.

"What did you have to do?" Ellis asked. "Why is Uncle Greg so mad?"

"I had us taken off the list."

"What list?" Even as she asked it, Ellis began to assemble the pieces.

"For notification of the parole hearing." Fresh tears slipped from her eyes. "I just want to f-forget." The last words rode out on a choked sob.

After all they'd been through, how could Jodi have done such a thing? Ellis felt a fraction of her uncle's rage. It took all of her compassion, all of her self-control, not to leap to her feet and carry on just as Greg had.

Right then, her mother entered the room with a tall glass of water. She held it in front of Jodi's face and said gently, "Drink this."

"Did you know?" Ellis asked her mother.

"Not until now."

As Ellis watched her mom sit down beside Jodi and slide a comforting arm around her, it struck her—maybe for the first time—the unusual nature of the relationship between these two women. They hadn't been friends before Greg and Jodi were married; their relationship had been born solely of that marital bond. Even though Greg was Marsha's brother, Marsha had somehow managed to balance that fact with her sustained friendship with his ex-wife.

Momma's words when she had told Ellis her aunt and uncle were getting a divorce came back to her: *"It's not Aunt Jodi's fault, and it's not Uncle Greg's. Their marriage is another of Hollis Alexander's victims—he killed it just the same as he took away our poor Laura. Greg and Jodi both need our love and support."*

And her mother lived up to that commitment, even now.

Ellis looked at the aftermath of this most recent storm, at the shattered belongings, the broken woman.

Alexander was still hurting his victims, even without setting foot on Belle Island.

❧

Hollis Alexander stood on a Charleston sidewalk that had been broken and heaved by the gnarled roots of the live oak that grew between it and Logan Street. He took a satisfied breath of free air and studied the black lacquered six-panel door and the four steps that led up to it.

There had been a recent repair where the edge of a concrete step had chipped—smooth and white, bleached bone against weather-pitted gray.

The brass knocker had dulled. The windows were clouded with rain spots and dust. Vegetation threatened to swallow up the house.

Hollis pulled a comb from his pocket and ran it through his hair. Then he climbed the steps and sounded the heavy knocker.

Even though fifteen years locked up like an animal had marked his soul, his body had weathered it well; the image in the mirror told him he hadn't changed all that much on the outside. Good. She would see him as she always had, as the boy who had befriended her, the boy she trusted.

It was taking a long time for her to answer. But that was to be expected.

Finally, the door opened. Justine Adams looked up at him from her wheelchair.

The instant her faded gray eyes met his, he knew just how easy this was going to be.

❦

Ellis's father walked her up the outside staircase and waited until she unlocked her front door.

"You sure you'll be all right?" he asked.

"Of course." Her dad had promised to drive Uncle Greg to Charleston to see Prosecutor Buckley. Greg was hoping to get some sort of electronic monitoring added to Alexander's parole. That way they'd be able to check on the DPPPS Web site at any time and know right where he was.

Ellis thought it a fool's errand. But it did give them something proactive to do.

Her dad turned to leave, then looked back over his shoulder at her.

"Seriously, Dad. Alexander has his freedom again. I doubt he'll be stupid enough to come here and risk losing it."

He gave her a look she hadn't seen in years, one full of apology for the carefree youth that had been taken from her. With a nod, he went on.

If she didn't work off some of this tension, she'd go mad. She decided to take a long, control-affirming, soul-cleansing run.

Normally she kept a moderate, steady pace, managing her cardiac rate for maximum endurance. Today she pushed herself as if she were being pursued, running blindly on familiar rural roads, lost completely in the rhythm of her footfalls and the rasp of her strained breathing.

The thick humidity clung to her like an impregnable layer of plastic. Sweat slicked her body, matting her hair against her skull. Still she ran.

Finally, light-headedness began to nibble at her vision, and her leg muscles cramped. She slowed to a walk, gasping against the suffocating grip of exhaustion.

When she looked around, she realized just how far she'd run. She was on the rural road front of Belle Creek Stables, where she and Laura had spent so much of their time—where Laura had fallen in love with Nate Vance.

Ellis stilled, staring at the shaded pastures lining the road, the red metal roofs of the stables and outbuildings. Several horses grazed lazily in the heat, swatting bothersome insects with well-groomed tails. Her feet had brought her to the place she'd patently avoided for over fifteen years. It was only a little over six miles from her house but might as well have been a continent away.

For an instant, Ellis thought she heard Laura's voice floating across the pasture, coaxing General Lee, her favorite mount, to accept the bridle. It was a scene Ellis had lived more times than she could count, and recalling it struck a fresh slash of grief across her heart.

Dizzy and nauseous, she stumbled to the fence. She slung her forearms over the top rail and laid her forehead on them, closing her eyes.

But closing her eyes was no defense against the memories that came to her like whispers and shadows. The pain was as wicked and raw as it had been years ago.

Maybe Aunt Jodi was right to want to forget. Maybe it was the only way she could stand to go on living.

Ellis and Uncle Greg had devoted the past fifteen years to making sure that no one forgot Laura and what had happened to her, that the horrible circumstances remained in the forefront of every parent's mind, keeping them vigilant against predators like Hollis Alexander. And during the past six years, they'd extended that effort to making certain Alexander remained where he belonged—locked away from everyone's innocent daughters.

But maybe that remembering was taking its own toll. Here they were all these years later, her with her locks and alarms, and teaching her yearly self-defense class, and Uncle Greg living alone, looking for happiness in shiny red Corvettes and badass speedboats.

Laura was still dead and the hole she'd left in their lives as big as ever.

Ellis squeezed her eyes tighter and willed the past to go away.

Then a hand fell heavily on her shoulder.

CHAPTER THREE

Miss—"

Ellis jerked upright, swung around, and landed a blow with her elbow in the center of the man's chest. Then she jumped out of his reach, ready to fend off further attack.

She gasped in horror when she saw the slight, elderly man lying sprawled on his back in the tall grass. His straw cowboy hat had landed in the road, revealing thinning silver-white hair. He wheezed, eyes wide, palms raised in defense.

"Oh, dear God! Mr. J!" Ellis fell to her knees next to him. When she reached for him, he flinched. "I'm so sorry!" she said.

Old as Mr. Jacobson appeared, he still didn't look a day older than when she and Laura had been girls. He still managed the stable, even though he had to be about a hundred.

He looked at her through tearing eyes.

"It's me, Ellis Greene." She saw him often enough around town that he should recognize her, but she might have knocked that recognition right out of him. "Just try to relax," she said. "Your breath should come back."

It did. Several minutes later.

He lifted himself onto one elbow. Ellis supported him from behind.

His voice was frail and thready when he said, "You got a kick like old General Lee."

"Now that's saying something." Thank God, the man was recovering.

Winded though he was, Mr. J managed to sound wistful when he said, "General Lee, I miss that old bastard." He gave a respectful pause. "That cousin of yours was the only one 'sides me that could ride him."

General Lee was nothing like the dignified, silver-haired man after whom he had been named. He was hell on hooves. Laura had been fearless when it came to riding him.

Mr. J said, "Miz Von der Embse always thought she'd work up the courage to try; that's why she kept him."

Helaina Von der Embse was the heiress whose daddy had left her this old rice plantation some forty years ago. She'd turned it into a breeding stable and visited occasionally from New York or California, or wherever the hell she lived.

Mr. J rolled onto his hip, and Ellis helped him to his feet.

"I really am sorry," she said.

"No need." The old man picked up his hat and dusted off his backside with it. "I just come out of the barn and seen you over here. I'd'a been a mite more careful, if I'd recognized it was you . . . what with your past an' all."

She looked him over. He appeared steady on his feet. Still . . . "Is Paco still around?" Paco had been the placid quarter horse she'd ridden while Laura risked life and limb on General Lee. God, how she'd loved that quiet, steady horse.

"Yes, ma'am. But we don't let no one ride him anymore. He's earned his retirement."

Unlike Mr. J, apparently.

"Can I walk back with you and see him?" She couldn't let the old guy totter around on his own until she was certain he was all right.

The smile that lit up his face made Ellis ashamed of her ulterior motive.

"I think Paco'd like that." He shoved the hat on his head and extended the crook of his arm to her, elegant as a Southern gentleman.

Ellis smiled and rested her hand on his forearm, ready to tighten her grip if his step faltered.

Although they entered the barn from the shade, it still took a moment for Ellis's eyes to adjust to the interior light. At least that's what she told herself when she stopped cold in the doorway. Sixteen years, and now here she was.

Mr. J marched on ahead and stopped in front of a stall. "Here's my boy."

Ellis forced herself to move forward.

If Mr. J had found a way to halt the progression of time, he hadn't shared it with Paco. It broke Ellis's heart to see the sunken areas of his face, his prominent poll, and his graying muzzle.

As Paco's velvet lips grazed her palm, Ellis felt the whisper of what had been a blinding passion for most of her youth. She closed her eyes, breathed in the smell of sweet hay, saddle leather, and the earthy scent of warm horseflesh.

Paco nudged her cheek with his nose.

"There now. Paco 'members you, don't you, boy?" Mr. J stroked the horse's neck.

Ellis stepped away, her pride at Paco's recognition mixed with a healthy dose of shame. Had Paco felt she'd abandoned him in the same way she had when Nate had left?

They left the barn and emerged into the bright light. Without taking a moment to consider her words, she asked, "Do you remember Nate Vance?"

Mr. J faltered slightly. Ellis moved to steady him by the elbow, but he looked straight ahead and kept moving. "'Course I do." He sounded peeved.

"I was just wondering what happened to him . . . where he ended up?"

"How would I know? That was a long time ago—and folks 'round here didn't seem partic'arly sad to see him leave." He stopped and tipped the brim of his hat. "If you'll 'scuse me, miss. I'd best get back to work."

With that abrupt change of disposition, he turned and walked away, leaving her standing in the dappled shade. For a moment, she watched his retreating back, the rigid set of his bony shoulders and the quick movement of his bandy legs.

She finally turned and walked down the tree-lined lane that led to the road. With every step, it seemed the sand beneath her feet sighed of a bittersweet past.

❧

As Hollis listened to Heidi, his new boss and the owner of the kennel, he had trouble keeping his mind on what she was saying. He just kept thinking how little her name suited her. Heidies should be little blondes with mocking blue eyes and luscious bodies that they used to their advantage—women who thought they were special. But this Heidi was built like a transvestite, with short magenta-colored hair that stood up in spikes and feet that looked three sizes bigger than his.

"That sums up the work," she said as they returned from the back rooms to the front desk. "I'm sure you'll do fine. You came highly recommended by the service-dog program at Ridgeland."

"Thank you, ma'am. I'm glad for the job. I love working with dogs." Hollis offered the look of shy gratitude he'd practiced in the mirror.

Heidi smiled in a way that said he'd hit his mark.

"Like I told you on the phone," she said, "I don't care about your past. I got a brother who served time. Everybody deserves a chance at a clean start."

Just then, the front door opened and a young woman who deserved a name like Heidi—or Gretchen or Adriana—came in holding a silky white Maltese in her arms. Hollis preferred big dogs to those bred solely for ornamental purposes, but in this case he'd make an exception.

He stepped forward with outstretched arms and a choirboy smile on his face. "What a beautiful dog," he said. "Please tell me we're going to get to keep her for a while."

He was careful to keep his attention on the dog, not the woman. But he didn't fail to notice the way she straightened her posture, enhancing the tight fit of her low-cut shirt as she handed the pooch over.

"Him," she corrected. "Beau is here for grooming." Her voice oozed seductive confidence.

"This here's Hollis," Heidi said. "He'll take Beau on back and get started. You want the usual?"

Hollis didn't hear the woman's answer. He was humming happily as he took the dog through the swinging door. He'd not considered the prospect before, but most of the folks dropping off dogs here would be women. If even half of Heidi's clientele were like Beau's momma, this job was going to be a great *resource* . . . as easy as shopping from a catalog.

❧

It was a long, silent walk back home. Ellis's emotional strength had been sapped by her long-avoided return to Belle Creek Stables even more than her physical strength had been from the ruthless pace of her run.

The narrow deserted road to the plantation and stables dead-ended at the marsh. Isolation settled heavily on her shoulders. Ghosts of the past dogged each footstep, their ethereal presence circling like a taunting crowd. The tension of their attendance strung her aching muscles as tight as bowstrings. She walked slowly, jumping like a fool at every squirrel that dashed for cover and every bird she startled into flight.

And all of those thoughts she'd been running from caught up with a vengeance.

She had to ask herself, Had she truly run this way by happenstance? Or had her inner voice guided her feet when she'd been ignoring it in her head?

Everything about that place—the smells, the sounds of the horses' gentle nickers and their hooves against soft earth and wood chips, the very feel of the air on her skin—made her acutely aware of all she had lost.

Nate Vance had been as much a part of the stable as Paco and General Lee. More than that, he'd been her and Laura's friend.

But late that spring, Nate had become more than a friend to Laura. At first, Ellis had had to stamp out a little spark of jealousy. She'd known that she was too young for Nate to think of her that way. And no one could blame any guy for going after Laura; she was perfect. But still Ellis had harbored a little ember of hope that someday . . .

In the aftermath of Laura's ordeal, Ellis remembered wishing that Laura and Nate had never started hanging out. That way she wouldn't have lost them both in a single year.

Finally, she rounded the corner onto her street and saw Rory's Mini Cooper parked in her drive. Damn. She was looking forward to a shower and a long nap. After a day like today, there would be no sleep once darkness fell.

She took a deep breath and walked on.

Rory sat in the shade, on the steps that went up the side of her building to the entrance of her third-floor condo. He stood when she approached. She studied him as she would a stranger, trying to view him with fresh eyes.

He was tan and athletic, his smile wide, his light brown hair boyishly tousled. A desirable man by anyone's standards. And kind. And intelligent.

Her stomach sank, landing in her lower regions with the grace of a deflated balloon. If a man this good and this attractive couldn't start a fire inside her belly, maybe she didn't have the fuel.

He stood, sticking his hands casually into the pockets

of his cargo shorts; but the set of his face was far from relaxed.

"I was getting worried," he said, just a little sharply. "You didn't answer your cell."

Ellis patted her pockets. "Oh! I must have forgotten it." It startled her to realize how dangerously distracted she'd been when she'd left.

"With all that's going on? Ellis!"

"So Dad's called you."

"He's worried." Rory stepped closer. The hands came out of the pockets and settled on her shoulders. "*I'm* worried."

"You're sweet and I appreciate the concern, but I'm perfectly fine."

"We think you should go up north with me."

She tilted her head and raised a brow. "We?" She thought she'd made it clear to her dad she wasn't going.

"It makes sense, Ellis. Come with me. We can stay in separate rooms if you want. If you aren't going, I'm not either."

She felt as if she'd just heard a discordant squeal of violin strings.

He's trying to be thoughtful.

"You know as well as anyone, I can take care of myself," she said more harshly than she should have. But seriously, she held a brown belt; Rory was a science teacher who couldn't bring himself to have his students dissect frogs. The thought of him offering protection seemed absurd.

For some odd reason—probably because of her unexpected visit to the stables—Nate Vance shot into her mind again. Even at her most vulnerable, she'd felt safe with him, but in an exhilarating passenger-on-a-high-speed-wave-runner kind of way.

And you were fourteen years old. Grow up.

She said, "You have to go. Your grandmother lives for your visits."

"She'll understand. I'm not leaving you, not now." His voice carried a force she rarely heard. He cradled her face and leaned down, kissing her.

It had been weeks since they'd been close. She felt the tremor in his touch, heard the longing desperation in his breathing. Leaning into his kiss, she searched for some hint of that kind of passion within herself, of the spark that said she could not live without this man's kiss.

It was nice. Pleasant. But her ears didn't ring and her heart didn't race.

You're expecting too much.

Finally, she pulled away and patted his chest. "I'll be fine. You know I don't take chances."

Rory narrowed his eyes. "You went off without your cell phone."

"And I always learn from my mistakes. It won't happen again." She smiled confidently.

He stood there looking doubtful.

"Come on, you know me better than that." She took a step backward. "Now promise me you won't change your plans." She held up a hand when he opened his mouth to interrupt her. "At least not yet. It's been a shock. We'll all get used to the idea that Alexander's out of prison." She stepped around him. "Now, I really need a shower."

"I'll call and check on you later," he called after her.

"All right."

When she got inside and looked down to the driveway

from her front sliding glass door, she saw Rory leaning on the fender of his car talking on his cell phone—no doubt reporting to her father.

What more did she want? He fit in with her family. He loved her enough that he was willing to disappoint his beloved grandmother to stay with her. He'd kissed her with desire even though she smelled like a locker room, for heaven's sake. Why had her love not grown?

Because you're not capable of more.

She stripped off her damp clothes, dropping them on her bedroom floor as she headed to the shower. As she turned on the hot water, she hoped Rory would go to Martha's Vineyard as planned. Maybe in his absence she'd be able to get herself figured out so she could stop hurting him.

Rory snapped his phone closed, a tick developing in his overstressed jaw muscle. Ellis's dad hadn't been the well of support Rory had hoped for. Although Bill had agreed in principle that Ellis should go north with Rory, he had hedged when Rory had asked him to call and talk some sense into her.

He got in his car and left Ellis's driveway. How had things gotten so far off track between them? He'd thought Ellis wanted the same things he did. They got along great. They'd been dating for over three years. Still, when he'd proposed, she'd acted like the thought had never even crossed her mind. Worse, she seemed repulsed by the idea.

A trip together would be his opportunity to get things straightened out and pointed back in the right direction.

Somebody had to make Ellis see. Somebody had to make her understand. If Bill wasn't going to help, Rory had to figure out a way to change her mind.

Chapter Four

The rain shower that had arrived just after dark had stopped. Ellis lay in her bed staring at the ceiling. She'd known sleep would elude her tonight. But she hadn't known that Nate Vance would be the reason.

She supposed it was natural to drift to the past with Alexander free, and after returning to the stables for the first time in years. She'd avoided the place fearing it would conjure only bad feelings. But the opposite had happened. The moments that played in her mind were the few good ones in a dark time. And they all centered around Nate. He'd handed her the reins of control when her life had felt like a roller coaster gone wild.

June, sixteen years ago
One week after Laura was attacked

It had been seven days, and Laura had shown no signs of waking up. Ellis's parents were keeping her locked up like a princess in a tower. She worried she might never have a drop of freedom again. Her mother cried almost as much as Aunt Jodi. Her dad had that expression, the one where his mouth was all hard and looked like it had parentheses around it, the one that said he was about to go batshit about something.

The only place they went was to the hospital. Which wouldn't be so bad if they'd let Ellis sit alone with Laura. She'd gotten over her shock of seeing her cousin with a respirator tube in her throat and needles in her arms.

The nurse said Laura could probably hear them, that they should keep talking to her. Ellis wanted to tell Laura not to pay attention to all the negative crap everyone kept saying; if they thought she could hear, why did they talk like that in her room?

After a full week of living like that, and more of the same to come according to the doctors, Ellis was as jittery as a bird with clipped wings.

She needed to be alone. She needed to *move*.

At five a.m., long before her momma and daddy were up, Ellis stepped out into the misty morning.

She could see only a short way down the beach. Mr. Coon and his dog were just shadows in the fog. Mr. Coon tossed a stick into the low surf, and Calliope chased after it. Ellis watched Calliope bring the stick back twice before she moved on. Something about it made her feel more normal.

The shell driveway crunched under her feet. The sound seemed loud in the early morning quiet. She glanced toward her parents' window but saw no movement. Then she looked at Laura's house. The curtains were drawn. Ellis knew no one was home, because both Aunt Jodi and Uncle Greg were sleeping at the hospital in Charleston.

Ellis felt as if she'd swallowed a sock, but no tears

came. She'd already cried herself dry. Maybe today would be the day Laura woke up. She filled herself with that thought, that prayer, as she began walking toward town.

Even before she started running, her heart beat fast. She knew everyone thought it was dangerous for her to be alone. But Ellis wasn't beautiful like Laura; the guy hadn't taken Ellis when she'd been sleeping in the same room. Besides, she was careful. She wasn't stupid enough to run on back roads. She stuck to where there were plenty of houses, just in case she needed to call for help.

And on top of that, she'd smell that man long before he was close enough to touch her. She'd recognize him. Even though it had been dark when she'd seen him, she'd never forget those vampire eyes as they'd caught the moonlight. Yes, she would recognize him, and then . . . then she'd scream and they'd catch him. They'd catch him and punish him for what he did to Laura.

Her anger burned hotter. She *wished* he'd come after her. She wanted him to. Then all of the ridiculous talk about Nate would go away, and the man who hurt Laura would go to jail forever.

It grew lighter as she ran; a depressing gray light because of the fog. As she passed Blue Heron Park, she saw someone sitting on top of a picnic table about twenty yards from the street.

She slowed, looking carefully. She sniffed; humidity carried scent better than dry air.

The figure moved and she froze.

Then she heard the soft whinny and looked beyond the picnic table. A horse was tied near the edge of the woods that led to the marsh.

Her momentary fear disappeared.

Nate raised his hand in a half-wave.

Ellis climbed over the knee-high chain-to-post fence that separated the park from the street, her heart lifting for the first time in a week.

Reaching the table, she climbed up and sat next to him. They sat shoulder to shoulder with their feet on the bench seat. Nate's hair was damp from the mist, making it look darker than normal.

He gave her a tired, sad smile. "Paco said to tell you hello."

Ellis smiled back, feeling just as tired as Nate looked. "Tell him I miss him." She'd bite off her tongue before she told Nate one of the reasons she hadn't been to the stables was because her parents had forbidden her to be around him.

They sat in silence for several minutes, staring toward woods swathed in gray haze. Out of the corner of her eye, she saw him swipe his wrist across his face.

"They won't let me see Laura." He sounded so alone, she wanted to take his hand. But they were folded tightly in front of him.

"This will get straightened out," she said. "And they'll have to let you see her."

He turned away and made a sound that could have been a scoff or a muffled sob.

"The police don't think it was you," she said. The entire town, on the other hand . . .

"They've had me to the station *three* times for questioning. They tried to get me to make a confession."

"That's ridiculous! I told them what I saw. They had me looking at mug shots!" She realized how loud she was being and lowered her voice. "How can they think it was you?"

"There are things you don't know, are too young to understand." He scrubbed his hands over his face.

"I'm not too young!" She was so tired of everyone saying that. "What? What don't I know?"

He shook his head. Then he looked at her. His gray eyes reminded her of mercury. "How is she?"

Ellis looked away. She couldn't lie while looking into his eyes. "I think maybe she's a little better."

He sat up straighter and grabbed her arm. "She's awake?"

"No," she admitted. Then she added, "But her eye isn't swollen completely closed any—"

He slammed his fist on the picnic table. It was so unexpected that she jumped a little and looked at him. His eyes were closed, and he looked like he might throw up.

He took a deep breath, then opened his eyes. They didn't look like mercury anymore. They looked dark, like storm clouds.

"What are your parents doing, letting you run around alone at this hour?" His voice was as angry as she'd ever heard it.

"They don't know," she said in a small voice.

"You snuck out? Ellis!"

She raised her hands. "I know. I know. But I just couldn't stand it. They're suffocating me!" She paused, then added lamely, "I left a note."

He got off the picnic table and stood in front of her. He put his hands on her shoulders. "Listen to me. Whoever did this is still out there somewhere. You have to be careful."

"I *am* careful." She was getting her bristles up, as her momma called it.

"No, you're not. No one knows where you are. And you shouldn't be out alone."

"I'm not," she said smartly. "I'm with you."

He ran a hand through his hair. It stood straight up in spikes, like a rock star. "Okay," he said. "Get up."

She stood and crossed her arms over her chest. She wasn't going home. Not yet.

"If you're gonna be so damn belligerent, I'm gonna teach you a couple of ways to defend yourself."

"If you know some, why didn't you teach Laura?" she asked before she really thought about what she was saying.

He stood there, looking like she'd just punched him in the gut. She felt terrible. "I'm sorry—"

He shook his head. "You're right. I should have."

"No," she said. "None of us knew this could happen."

Something flashed in his eye, the same look as when he'd said she was too young to understand some things. Then he took her by the shoulders and squared her in front of him. "Well, it's not going to happen again—not to you."

He showed her what to do if someone grabbed her from behind. He made her do it over and over. She got closer to getting away each time.

When they took a break, he told her this was just the first move he was going to teach her. He wanted her to be prepared.

Ellis sat next to him again, wondering at the feelings swirling inside her, at the little sparkles rushing through her blood. Even though he was just teaching her to protect herself, when he touched her, it was like . . . magic. When he touched her, she felt safe.

She realized Nate was still talking. ". . . been learning jujitsu and Grav Maga; with that one you can really hurt somebody."

"You want to hurt somebody?"

He stared at her for a minute, then said, "I want to kill whoever did that to Laura."

A little chill danced over her skin; something in his voice scared her just a little.

He blew out a long breath. "Back to work."

She shook out her cramped muscles and said, "Okay, this time I'm gonna do it."

He came at her from behind again. Just as his arms encircled her, she heard someone shouting from the street. "Hey! You! Stop!"

When Ellis looked up, she saw a woman running toward them. Her car sat on the street with the driver's door hanging open.

Nate let Ellis go.

She raised her hands. "It's okay! I'm okay!"

As the woman got closer, Ellis saw it was Dr. Kreag, her family physician.

"He was just teaching me how to defend myself," Ellis said.

Dr. Kreag didn't look convinced. "What are you two doing out here so early?" She looked past Ellis, giving Nate a nasty glare. "Aren't you a little old to be—"

"It's not like that!" Ellis said. "I was running, and Nate told me I shouldn't be out alone. He's showing me some martial arts stuff."

"Do your parents know you're out here . . . with *him*?"

Ellis glanced at Nate. Why wasn't he saying anything?

"No. They were sleeping when I left. I didn't want to wake them."

Dr. Kreag extended her arm and motioned Ellis forward with a flip of her fingers. "I think I should take you home."

"I'd rather run back."

"I *insist.*" Dr. Kreag shot Nate another hateful look.

"She's right," Nate said. "You should go."

As she got in the doctor's car, Ellis saw Nate walking to his horse. He didn't look back.

Ellis listened as the last of the rain dripped in the downspout, missing Nate more than she had in years. He couldn't have imagined, as he'd suffered scrapes and bruises from her attempts to thwart his mock attacks, how those lessons would change her life. Teaching teenage girls how to protect themselves had become a very important part of who she was.

And during her secret meetings with Nate, she'd discovered something new, something adult. His intimate closeness had awakened feelings inside her that she'd only read about in novels and seen in movies. A deep yearning that she had had no idea how to quell.

She wondered, Did he ever draw on fond memories of the time they'd spent together? Could he recall the feel of her against him as acutely as she recalled his touch? Or had she faded completely from his memory?

Foolish, foolish thoughts.

Ellis closed her eyes, and snippets of her life flashed, changing quickly from one to another, endless in their progression, relentless in their emotional toll.

The quiet, steady hum of the air conditioner usually cultivated a feeling of being safely cocooned, lulling her gently to sleep. Tonight it annoyed her like a dripping faucet.

With a frustrated sigh, she threw off the covers and got out of bed.

The moon had come out, casting shadows of furniture and houseplants, making it easy to make her way to the kitchen. She left the lights off as she poured herself a glass of milk. Then she went into the living room, her head pounding from all her overthinking.

There was an air-conditioning vent directly in front of her sliding door, making the glass cool to the touch. She leaned her forehead against it; not quite an ice pack, but much less trouble.

Rolling her forehead from temple to temple across the cool surface, she stopped when a tiny red-orange light caught her eye. There, below, beneath the old oak, just behind a curtain of Spanish moss.

She looked more carefully. It disappeared. She set the glass of milk on the table and stepped back from the door, glad she'd left her lights off.

Keeping her gaze fixed on the place where she'd seen the glow, she waited. In a few moments, it shone again. Then faded.

A cigarette. Why would someone be standing out there smoking at this hour . . . or any hour, for that matter? The humidity after that rain was heavy enough to make a cigarette nearly too damp to burn.

Thoughts of Alexander's threat bounced around in her mind. Her heart sped up.

She was overreacting. There was a guard on the gate. No one got in who shouldn't.

Rory? Security knew him; he was on an automatic approval list. And he'd seemed adamant in his conviction to protect her.

But Rory didn't smoke.

So what if someone was out there smoking.

At three a.m.? Under a dripping tree?

Maybe she should call and have security check it. Yes, that's what a rational person would do.

A rational person would just go back to bed.

She picked up the phone.

She identified herself and explained to Mr. Breese that she'd seen someone "loitering" outside her condo. She received a pleasant, although decidedly *unalarmed* assurance that he would check it out.

Then she went back and looked out the sliding door again, keeping herself deep enough in the room so as not to be seen. After several minutes without seeing the orange glow, she decided whoever it was had left—or had extinguished the cigarette.

Headlights of the complex's John Deere Gator came slowly around the corner, then stopped, its light shining in the direction of the old oak. The pavement beneath its wheels was still wet, black puddles gathering in the low places.

As Ellis watched the uniformed man climb out, it struck her as ludicrous that she was putting her faith in an aged security officer who drove something that looked more like a golf cart than a police vehicle, an officer who carried a radio and a flashlight instead of a weapon.

Ellis watched as the guard followed his flashlight beam, poking around under the tree. Then he walked deeper into the foliage, toward the marsh. She lost sight of the flashlight beam. Suddenly she was concerned for *his* safety.

Her phone rang and she nearly jumped back into last week.

With a dry throat, she picked it up.

"Ms. Greene," the guard said, his speech as slow as a turtle in the sand. "I checked all round out here—" which came out as *he-ah*— "I don't find a trace of nobody. Nobody been through the gates for hours. Musta been a resident."

She looked out the window and saw the flashlight beam bobbing toward the Gator.

"Well, thank you for checking," she said, feeling more than a little foolish.

"Happy to oblige, miss. You have a good night, now."

"You too, Mr. Breese."

She watched as he climbed onto the Gator's bright yellow seat and then puttered away.

"It's time to stop jumping at shadows, Ellis Greene." She picked up her milk, which had warmed. She went to the kitchen and poured herself another glass. As she headed back to her bedroom, she looked out the sliding door once more.

She blinked, then squinted as she leaned closer. The orange dot faded and disappeared. But there was no doubt; whoever had been out there was back.

Returning to bed with her milk in one hand and the

cordless phone in the other, she knew there would be no escape into sleep tonight.

❦

If he hadn't gotten his feet stuck in a mud bog when he'd had to move to better cover, he might have seen the humor in the old geezer with his flashlight bumbling around in the dark. Did Ellis really feel more secure now that the old guy had poked at a couple of bushes?

A sense of security could be a tenuous thing. He just had to make certain he used Ellis's—or her lack thereof—to his advantage.

He rested his hip on one of the thick low branches of the oak and looked back up at her window. She thought she was being clever, staying away from the glass like that. But the moon reflected off her white T-shirt, giving her away.

When she'd first stepped to the glass and put her head against it, he'd had a good view of her long, naked legs. He'd imagined the air-conditioning blowing on her, making her nipples tight. He'd imagined his hands slipping between those legs.

Then the old guy had come along and ruined everything.

But this wasn't the end. It was just the beginning.

Chapter Five

Jodi sat alone at her kitchen table. She'd put on a Queen CD and cranked the stereo loud enough to vibrate the floor to mask the fact that she was sitting all alone in the middle of the night. Spread before her were the bits and pieces she and Marsha had picked up from the fireplace hearth.

With tweezers, Jodi sorted the fragments into piles. After that was done, she could decide if any of the figurines could be glued back together. She'd found almost all the parts to one of her favorites, a Hummel that was a little boy handing a fistful of wildflowers to a little girl. Greg had given it to her before they were married.

They'd been so happy. And it seemed so very long ago.

Chills ran over her arms as she recalled his fury when he'd come here this morning. If only he understood. But he hadn't understood what it was like for her back then, and he didn't now. Nothing had changed. They would never be like they once were—and now all hope of becoming something new was gone too.

She shoved all but the Hummel's ceramic shards aside. Then she picked up her bottle of glue. With an intensity that blocked out all else, she began at the feet.

Two hours later, her back ached from hunching over the project, but she had all but the top of the little boy's head more or less back together.

Rotating the paper on which she'd been assembling the figure, she studied it from all sides. Not too bad. A couple of the seams would show less after she'd touched them up with colored Sharpies.

She turned the figurine so the little girl's face was toward her. A crack ran right down the middle of it; small splinters of ceramic were missing from the seam. That little girl's face would never be the same. Never.

The little face blurred before her. She blinked.

It was ridiculous the way Greg wanted to dwell on what couldn't be changed. It served no purpose. He certainly wasn't any happier because of it. Couldn't he see that the less they thought about the horror of what had happened to their daughter, the better off they were?

Couldn't he see how tearing open that wound time after time only made it deeper?

Her vision distorted further.

Couldn't he see . . . ?

With a vicious swipe, she knocked the Hummel off the table. The sharp sound of it hitting the wall and its pieces clattering onto the tile floor hit her heart like a hundred arrows.

❧

As soon as it was light, Ellis was out of bed and dressed. Early rising was one of the few advantages to sleepless nights. She'd decided to go to the stables first thing this morning to check on poor Mr. J. The man didn't have a spare ounce of flesh on him; she'd bet money he was black and blue today.

When she pulled out of her drive, she paused, looking across the street at the old oak. She put the gearshift in park and got out. Searching the ground beneath the oak, she didn't find any cigarette butts. That settled her mind somewhat; whoever had been out here must have cared enough about the place to take his trash with him. It fit well with the comfortable theory of resident or guest.

She walked all the way back to the fence that separated the marsh from the complex. There were a couple globs of mud lodged in the chain link several inches off the ground—as if someone had climbed over.

"Dear Lord, stop making an erupting volcano out of a molehill!" she muttered. Caution was one thing, a wise thing, but paranoia was quite something else. Paranoia made you stupid.

She got back in her car, grateful that the shift had changed at the guardhouse and she didn't have to see Mr. Breese.

Ten minutes later, she pulled into the lane at Belle Creek Stables. As she got out of the car, she looked around for Mr. J.

Something seemed different. Which was odd. The last time she'd been here, the lack of change had been remarkable. Pausing, she scanned all around her. What was it? Something subtle, something that niggled yet didn't stand out.

She turned in a slow circle.

When her gaze landed on the plantation house, she saw it. The windows and French doors had been covered by blinds and heavy draperies before, sealing out the slightest ray of light. But today, the windows were uncovered and the French doors all stood wide open.

"Z'at you, Ellis?"

She turned. Mr. J headed her way from the stable door.

"Good morning," she said, surreptitiously looking him over for bruises.

"What can I do f'r ya, Ellis Greene?" His voice was loud and not at all welcoming.

"I came to apologize again for—"

"Ah now, no need." His gaze flickered toward the plantation house, then back to her. There was something standoffish in his eyes. He'd cut her off yesterday. Was he angry?

"Is there anything I can do for you?" she asked, unsure what else to say.

"Nah." He swatted the air and started back toward the stable.

Unwilling to leave things like this, she grabbed blindly at a topic of conversation. "I see the house is open. Ms. Von der Embse making one of her rare visits?"

Rare was an understatement. Ellis couldn't remember the last time the woman had been to Belle Creek Plantation.

Mr. J turned to look at her. He licked his lips quickly, almost nervously, as if moistening them to pass a lie. "Nope. No Von der Embse here. Just time to air the place out."

"Jake!" a man's voice called from the river side of the house. "Need a hand here."

Familiarity danced along Ellis's nerve endings. She'd

swear she knew that voice, but when and where remained hidden in the shadows of lost memory.

Mr. J stepped around her. "Thanks for comin' by. Careful on your drive home."

"Jake!" The timbre of that man's voice thrummed along the pages of her past, teasing but never falling into place.

"Comin', boss!"

Boss?

Mr. J moved with uncharacteristic quickness as he rounded the front corner of the house.

Ellis followed him.

When she rounded the front veranda, she saw Mr. J's slight form in the front entrance, trying to help a much larger man steady a tall, four-foot-wide wooden door onto its hinges. The big guy stood just inside, his right shoulder wedged against the door edge, his face hidden from view.

"Can you reach the hinge pin and slide it in?" the larger man huffed. He lifted the door with a strap, keeping his shoulder tight on the edge.

"Dag-nabbit. You always was the most stubborn . . . I told you to wait 'til Sully come in this afternoon. Hangin' this damn door is a three-man job." Mr. J tried to keep pressure on the door while looking around on the entry floor, Ellis presumed for the hinge pin.

The top of the door started to move off center.

Ellis hurried up onto the veranda and put her hands on the door, adding just enough pressure to bring the door vertical again. "What can I do?"

"Hold it right where you are. Jake, let go nice 'n easy; walk 'round this side and put it in."

Mr. J eased away.

The man said, “As I lift, guide the hinge into place. Jake can slide in the top pin.”

“We ain’t all giants,” Mr. J said testily. “I can’t reach the top ’un.”

Ellis heard the pin hit the foyer floor.

“What the . . . Them’s slicker ’n snot,” Mr. J complained.

The man said, “Just do the middle and bottom. I’ll get the top.”

After a couple of tries, the first pin slid home.

“Good thing you greased ’em, boss. I’d never got it through.”

The man grunted. “Hurry up.”

As soon as Mr. J had the second pin in place, the man said, “Ellis, move around here and hold up on these straps.” One at a time, she took them from his hands. He ended up behind her when the handoff was finished.

Ellis. He called me by name. I must *know him.*

“There!” The man stepped away from the door.

Ellis released her straps and stood back. She got her first clear look at the man. He had dark hair and a square jaw sporting a couple days’ stubble.

It was only when she looked into his gray eyes that she realized who he was.

He smiled. “Hello, Ellis. You’ve grown up.”

Chapter Six

Nate wasn't prepared when Ellis threw herself into his arms. He managed to keep his balance by wrapping his arms around her and swinging her in a circle.

And suddenly it was as if the past sixteen years hadn't been. He was seventeen, and they'd just spent a long night helping Mr. J deliver a foal. Ellis had always jumped into his arms the minute newly delivered babies successfully struggled onto their wobbly legs. Laura had been too squeamish to attend a birthing, but Ellis had been there every time, with her nose stuck right between Nate and Mr. J.

As he settled her feet back to the ground and looked into her eyes, he realized it wasn't the same at all. There was nothing platonic about the way she felt against his chest, nothing brotherly in the way his heart raced as he looked into those incredible green eyes.

He quickly released her.

He wasn't here to romance her. She wasn't supposed to know he was here at all.

He dropped his hands to his sides and stepped a safe distance away, but her fragrance still lingered in his senses.

Exhaling strongly, he tried to rid himself of her scent as well as his inappropriate response to her closeness.

He quickly schooled his features and ordered his thoughts.

How was he going to handle this?

Immediately after Ellis squealed and threw her arms around Nate's neck, she realized she was behaving like a twelve-year-old.

She was thankful Nate's response to seeing her seemed equally unchecked; she felt just a little less foolish when he set her back down on her own two feet.

Looking into those stormy eyes, her senses began to register that this was no longer the boy she'd known but a man grown in height and breadth, mature ruggedness replacing boyish good looks.

He had a crescent-shaped scar near the corner of his left eye that hadn't been there fifteen years ago. His neck was lean and corded; she could see his pulse in the artery beneath the surface of his skin. He'd always been muscular, but the solidness under her hands had felt completely unfamiliar to her—and undeniably masculine.

However, the look in his eyes didn't match the exuberance of his initial reaction. She took a tiny step backward.

"I can't believe you're here . . . after all this time." Even as she said the words, she realized she was overstepping. She'd been so unimportant in his life that he'd disappeared without a word, had left and never sent so much as a postcard.

"Jake tells me you're an elementary teacher."

"Yes. Fourth grade." Sending a quick glance Mr. J's way, she wondered if he'd kept in touch with Nate over the years. She'd never asked after those first weeks when she'd bugged the man day and night, asking if he'd heard from Nate.

Nate's mother had moved away from Belle Island the year after Nate disappeared. As far as Ellis knew, no one had heard from her either.

"Good." Nate nodded. "That's good." In the lull that followed, he stared at her, looking rather ambivalent. Back in the day, they'd never had an awkward moment, could talk about anything. But the years had robbed them of easy conversation.

She asked the first innocuous question that popped into her mind. "How's your mother?"

Nate said softly, "She died eight years ago."

"I'm sorry to hear that." Ellis hadn't really known Nate's mother. She did know what the town had said about her: that she was "loose" (which, now that Ellis was grown, she knew could mean anything from prostitution to wearing an indecent neckline), that she was white trash and let Nate run wild. Ellis had ignored the comments. This town had also said a lot of unkind and untrue things about Nate back then.

"Laura's dead too." Only after the words were out did Ellis realize that it was an utterly insensitive way to break the news.

No surprise registered in his face. "I know."

Had he only discovered it when he'd arrived back in Belle Island? Had he maintained contact with someone in town? That idea stung, salt in a wound she thought had healed long ago. Ellis had shared his grief, had stood by him when others had not. And he'd cut her cleanly from his life.

She wanted to know everything: Why had he left so abruptly, so mysteriously? Why had he abandoned Laura before all hope was gone? And there was that small, needy voice deep inside that asked, *Why did you leave me? I needed you even more than Laura did.*

But she only asked, "When did you find out?"

He held her gaze. "The day she died."

"How?" *Tell me you were closer to someone else, someone you trusted more than you did me.*

Nate hadn't had a lot of friends. He'd started working at the stables when he was eleven years old. The few friends he did have had distanced themselves after Laura's attack. All except Ellis.

He didn't look her in the eye when he said, "I kept in touch."

"With Mr. J?" If so, why didn't Mr. J ever let her know Nate was alive and safe?

"Yeah." The look on his face said there was more he wasn't saying.

"Why didn't you come back for her funeral?" Didn't he know what people said about him when he'd disappeared right after Alexander's guilty verdict?

"Would it have made a difference?" The cynical tone in his voice was accompanied by an aggressive thrust of his chin.

"To me." She felt a flutter of panic, of raw vulnerability, as if she'd stepped onto a busy street buck naked. She wasn't an unschooled teen any longer. She couldn't just blurt out her innermost feelings to him as she'd once done.

He looked into her eyes, and her feeling of overexposure intensified. Her skin blazed with the heat of embarrassment, and she momentarily forgot to breathe. Even so, she found herself leaning closer to him, toward his solid strength, toward the memory of his protection.

Finally, he said, "For that, I'm sorry." His eyes said he meant it.

Ellis swallowed, her gaze welded to his. There were so many more questions she wanted to ask. But her voice had stopped working.

"Them horses ain't gonna let themselves out to pasture," Mr. J said, breaking the mesmerizing force field that bound Ellis to Nate. She blinked and finally drew a clear breath as she watched Mr. J walk around them and through the open door. "Some of us got work to do." He started down the broad front steps, mumbling about "sleeping dogs" and "pecks of trouble."

Ellis looked back at Nate. "He called you 'boss'?"

With a half-smile, Nate said, "Jake's idea of humor."

She nodded, even though she'd never detected a humorous bone in the old guy's body.

"When did you arrive?" she asked. It was a nice, uncomplicated question, one that she would ask any acquaintance, she assured herself. One that didn't require dredging up the past.

"Late yesterday," he said.

She waited for him to elaborate.

He didn't.

"So," she said in a tone she hoped sounded casual, "what brings you to Belle Island?"

Nate stepped out onto the porch. His gaze moved from the marshy river to pastures and the woodlands that flanked the house. His eyes shone with that contagious passion she remembered from her first days at the stables.

He gave an offhanded lift of a shoulder, dismissing the past fifteen silent years the same way she had. "Had some time off. Wanted to see Jake again." He drew a deep breath. "This place . . . it holds good memories." He shifted his gaze to her; she could feel it probing. There seemed to be the slightest edge of challenge when he said, "Glad to see you still come here. You loved it almost as much as I did."

It was true. And she'd cut this place out of her life, just as Nate had cut her from his. Up until yesterday, when she'd seen Paco again, she hadn't realized what a gaping hole it had left in her soul. But she wasn't going to admit that she'd been scared away by the very memories that had drawn him back.

It was different for Nate. This had been the one place where he'd been respected, where he'd been more than a penniless kid from the trailer park.

"How long are you staying?" she asked, wondering only briefly if she was telling a lie by not correcting Nate's misconception that she still came here regularly.

"I'm really not sure." He didn't offer more. In fact, he was retreating again.

He turned his back on her, bending down to gather up the tools lying on the porch floor.

She started toward the steps. "Well, I guess I'll be going. It was good to see you."

He lifted his chin in acknowledgment, but to her

disappointment, he didn't engage her in further conversation. It was as if he really was the stranger the change in his physical appearance said he was. That fact made Ellis strangely sad, as if he'd deserted her all over again.

She walked down the steps, loneliness gnawing at the edges of her soul. The wind gently rustled in the treetops. Why did she suddenly feel so alone?

"Ellis," Nate called.

Her falling spirit fluttered upward. She turned and looked up at him. "Yes?"

"I'd appreciate it if you didn't tell anyone I'm here."

He didn't wait for her agreement. He turned and entered the house, closing the newly hung door behind him.

She lingered there on the steps for a moment, listening to the sound of his footsteps through the open windows.

Nate sat on the broad staircase inside the plantation house and fisted his hands in his hair. He pulled until it felt his entire scalp would lift, but his scalp and the thoughts running under it remained vividly intact.

He hadn't expected this rush of—he couldn't quite name what seeing Ellis up close had done to him. She'd always been an amazing person. But now her body had caught up—and surpassed—that beautiful personality. He'd known she'd changed, had seen it two years ago when he'd watched her teach her class in the park. Still, he hadn't been prepared for the dynamic impact of facing—and touching—the whole package of the grown woman.

When she'd thrown her arms around him, it had felt as if he'd never left. He'd never measured his words with her as he did with everyone else. Of all the people he'd known, only Ellis had seen Nate's unguarded side. It had been a risk he'd taken only once. And his friendship had been detrimental to her in the end.

Ellis had been pure. After Laura had been attacked, there was no way he could remain close to Ellis and not taint her with this town's perception of him; a perception that lingered long after Hollis Alexander had been arrested for the crime. Nate supposed it had been there all along. But the quiet whispers he'd always been able to shut out became deafening shouts of accusation after Laura had been found, bloody and broken, on the beach.

It had been better for Ellis that he'd left. She would have stood by him, he knew. And she would have suffered for it.

He sat on the stairs for a long moment, eyes closed.

Who was he kidding? He dropped his head back and stared at the ornate plastered ceiling. His leaving Belle Island hadn't been that simple . . . or that noble.

He'd been a coward. A fact that was all too easy to forget when he'd seen the unabashed joy in Ellis's eyes the instant she recognized him. Which she'd done surprisingly quickly. He'd left here a boy and returned a man who'd seen too much, learned never to trust anyone, and knew things that made a peaceful night's sleep impossible. The changes in him had to be every bit as visible as those he saw in her.

Although she'd been fourteen when he'd left, she was now several inches taller—having grown into those coltish legs—and had developed curves that had felt unfamiliar when he hugged her against him. The beauty he'd seen masked by youth had emerged; she was a woman who would draw sidelong looks from every man she passed.

But the most startling change had been her eyes, even in that initial moment of delighted recognition. They were no longer the eyes of an optimistic young girl. The mossy depths were cautious, guarded. The Ellis who had thrown her full heart into everything she did, the girl who'd been led by her passions, was gone. It was evident to him, because he'd held her spirit in his memory for all these years, constant, never changing. He supposed someone who'd been by her side day after day might not even notice the change.

It made him sad to see it. Her exuberance had been the fire that lit her soul.

Even throughout those horrible months—even when she'd shunned the stables and had trouble sleeping—even then, she'd still been Ellis; sparky, vibrant Ellis. Willing to defy her parents and meet secretly with him.

How would he have survived those months without her?

Nate scrubbed his hands roughly over his face. He'd thought he could come here and approach this as he would any other operation. This onslaught of feelings was not in the plan. Feeling led to mistakes. Mistakes to disaster.

He'd risked a lot by coming to the plantation, especially now. He'd be a weak son of a bitch to let his emotions risk the outcome.

He was here for one reason only. And he'd better remember it.

The sound of Ellis's car starting came through the open windows. He kept himself planted until the crunching of her tires on the sandy lane faded completely from his hearing. Then he gathered up his tools and headed out to the main stable.

He was hanging up the hammer when he sensed Jake behind him. Nate kept about his business, ignoring the old man, wiping the hinge grease from the tools and putting each item back in its proper place. That was one of the things he liked about being here; he could always count on finding things where they should be, no last-minute scrambles, no surprises.

"You tell her?" Jake asked.

Nate drew a deep breath. Trying to ignore Jake was like a buried ham bone trying to ignore a starving hound.

"No."

Jake harrumphed.

Nate didn't turn around.

"It'd make things easier, you know."

With a glare over his shoulder, Nate said, "I know what I'm doing. No one is to know I'm here."

"Don't know if you noticed or not, but you wasn't invisible. Ellis knows you're here."

"She won't tell anyone."

"How'd you reckon that?"

"I asked her not to."

"Pssst," Jake scoffed. "You don't know women a'tall, then."

"I know her."

Jake walked out, mumbling about unnecessary carryings-on.

Nate called after him, "Gas up the boat. I'll need it tonight."

Wayne Carr drove into Charleston in the midst of rush-hour traffic. Half of him wanted to do a U-turn and head back to Belle Island. He didn't relish breathing the same air as Hollis Alexander, even in a public place. But the practical half of him knew this meeting was unavoidable.

Shortly after crossing the Cooper River, Carr exited to surface streets. He followed the directions Alexander had given him and found Beulah's Pigs 'n Grits, the hole-in-the-wall where they were to meet for breakfast. Carr's stomach rolled at the dirty-windowed sight of the place.

After parking on the street and hoping all the pieces of his Jaguar would still be there when he returned, he entered the cafe. The lighting was dim. A cursory glance at the torn vinyl floor and the yellowed walls told him he should be glad for the lack of illumination. There was a long counter with stools on the right, booths on the left. Alexander sat in the one nearest the door. He smiled, not looking a bit older than the day he was convicted.

Carr's hand went to the gray at his temples, wondering at Alexander's secret to youth.

As Carr sat down, Alexander said, "I recommend the pecan waffles."

The waitress shuffled up to the table and looked down over her considerable bosom.

Carr handed her the menu. "Just coffee." And he wasn't going to touch that.

Alexander raised a brow. "Clear you ain't ever been denied good food. That's one of the things you don't get in prison, you know—pecan waffles."

Had Alexander's eyes been this cold before? Carr looked away, drawing a sweetener packet from the holder.

"So," he prompted, anxious to get out of here. "Your proposition?"

Alexander leaned back in his seat. He pulled up the sleeve of his T-shirt. "Got me a new tattoo."

The word *justice* was written inside a lightning bolt that shot down from the crest of Alexander's left shoulder.

Carr took a deep breath.

"Got it high." Alexander smiled. "Don't like to ruin the image for the ladies."

The waitress delivered the coffee and Alexander's waffles. Alexander dug right in. Carr took his time adding cream and sweetener to his coffee and stirring it.

Finally, Alexander said, "Here's the deal. You write your stories in the paper, like the ones you did back then, the ones that told the *truth*." He hissed the word *truth* through gritted teeth. "Help me get a lawyer to prove I was sent up for somethin' I didn't do. And you can write my story—*beginning to end*."

The way he said those last words made Carr's neck hairs stand on end. He pushed his coffee cup away. "You're saying Nate Vance raped and beat Laura Reinhardt?"

"Yeah. I'd seen him plenty of nights on the beach with that girl. And *I* went to prison for the little prick."

"I don't see why you want to do this now," Carr said. "No one's seen Vance since your trial. Who knows where he is? Just move on. You won't get those years back. Don't waste your next ones chasing this."

Alexander dropped his fork. Syrup splattered and the handle clattered against the plate. "It don't matter to you what I do with my 'next ones.' Just write the damn articles."

With a shake of his head, Carr said, "I can't see what

good my articles will do. I have a responsibility to my community; opening this up will upset a lot of innocent people. And I don't have any connections with criminal attorneys. I'm sorry, but I can't help you." With a feeling of relief, he started to get up.

Alexander grabbed Carr's hand. His grip was that of a man who worked out. "Sit. Down."

The venom in Alexander's voice made Carr do just that.

After a moment, Alexander reached onto the seat next to him and brought up a large manila envelope. Without a word, he slid it across the table. Then he leaned back and rested his arm on the back of the booth.

Carr didn't like the look in the man's eyes.

Sweat beaded on Carr's forehead as he opened the flap and peeked inside.

Christ almighty.

He closed his eyes and the envelope. If this got out, he could kiss life as he knew it good-bye.

Chapter Seven

Hollis Alexander had cost Prosecutor Buckley yet another night's sleep. He sat in his office with a pounding head and burning eyes. Today he felt every day of his fifty-eight years.

He tipped his chair back as far as it would go and stared at the ceiling, trying to separate his emotions from his perspective on Hollis Alexander's newfound freedom.

Buckley had been a widower for nine years. He missed Helen every night, but none so much as last night. She'd been his sounding board and his strength when the case he'd been putting together against Alexander—the hardest and most frustrating experience of his career—hadn't seemed to have two steady legs to stand on.

In fact, she'd been the first to make him see—when he'd been having trouble making a case against the most likely suspect, Laura Reinhardt's boyfriend—that maybe, just maybe, the Greene girl was right and the perpetrator *had* been the mystery man she'd seen outside on the path that night. Not that that belief had done him much good. They had no way to ID the man, no way to compare him to the evidence found at the scene.

But shortly after that, Ellis Greene had identified him in a bizarre twist of fate.

Once they had Hollis Alexander in custody, they discovered a previous arrest for rape and several accusations of window-peeping in his past. The rape case had resulted in acquittal, so it wasn't admissible in court. But it certainly had helped cement the Reinhardt case in Buckley's mind.

Alexander had been slick and organized and patient. He'd even come up with a defense when the fingerprint and hair samples confirmed he'd been on the scene; he admitted to peeping in Laura's window but had sworn he'd done nothing else.

Buckley's case had relied on circumstantial evidence and a fourteen-year-old girl's testimony. It had been traumatic enough for Ellis Greene, losing her cousin, having been sleeping right there in the room with her the night she'd been kidnapped. How long could he expect the girl to hold up? He'd feared, when in the courtroom, Ellis would collapse under the pressure of testifying in front of Alexander, that her story would become confused and muddled under cross-examination. But she'd been strong and steady and completely believable. And so they'd won.

Helen had said they would.

Right now, Buckley would give his eyeteeth to hear Helen say Hollis Alexander was a changed man, that his soul had been cleansed by his time in prison, and he wasn't a danger to anyone's daughter.

But men with that kind of twisted sickness inside them don't recover, don't change.

Most likely, Alexander would control himself for a while, until temptation grew too great. Maybe by then he'd have moved on to less conspicuous pastures, leave teenage girls in Charleston County alone. Little consolation.

The thing that made Buckley break out in a cold sweat was his conviction that Alexander *was* going to commit another crime. It was only a matter of time.

He should never have been freed—even conditionally.

But the man had met all criteria for his parole. He'd comported himself with extraordinary decency and diligence to tasks throughout his incarceration, reinforcing his claim of innocence. With all of the glowing reports, it would be easy enough for someone to believe that perhaps Alexander was what he'd always claimed to be—a man wrongly accused, wrongly convicted.

Buckley thought it was all a means to an end. Alexander had carefully cultivated his new self. Patience had been his key to freedom.

When Greg Reinhardt and Bill Greene had been in his office yesterday, Buckley had painted an optimistic picture for them. He'd assured them that Alexander had been deemed worthy of parole and a second chance at life. Buckley had also pledged to personally keep close contact with Alexander's parole officer. It was the only thing he could offer.

Greg hadn't been fooled. He'd left here with murder in his eyes. And Buckley couldn't blame him. Hell, if he'd been Greg Reinhardt, he probably would have killed Alexander with his bare hands before the trial; no court could give a father satisfactory justice for such mistreatment of his child.

God help him if he had to prosecute Greg Reinhardt for assaulting Alexander. How in the hell could any man with a heart do that?

Buckley sat up in his chair and rubbed his hands over his face, his gut heavy with dread. Alexander had suppressed his violent tendencies for fifteen years. Buckley feared an explosion of that pent-up rage was inevitable. This man was going to do something truly horrible again—and there wasn't a damn thing Buckley could do to prevent it.

Driving to her parents' house, Ellis's thoughts were filled not with her father's mysterious telephone summons of a few minutes ago, but with Nate Vance.

A part of her wished she hadn't returned to the plantation today. Then Nate could have remained a shadow of a memory, and she could have continued on with her youthful perception and adolescent imaginings. He'd certainly grown into the ruggedly handsome man she'd expected him to. But the shock of actually seeing him with all of the boy stripped away had left her rattled. It had taken hours for her heart to settle back into a slow, steady rhythm and her hands to stop trembling. Her mind, however, still hadn't calmed.

No matter what she'd tried to do to distract herself, memories of him kept popping up, mingling with the reality of the man he now appeared to be. And the same questions—some new, some fifteen years old—kept nagging: Why had he left without a good-bye? Why hadn't he ever contacted her? Why hadn't he come back for Laura's funeral? Why was he back in Belle Island after all these years? Why had he seemed so happy to see her at first, then withdrawn? And why in God's name had he asked her not to tell anyone he was here?

All of these answerless questions were brewing a monster headache.

She pulled up in front of her parents' house and shut off the car. Rubbing her temples, she sat for a moment. As always, she had mixed feelings about being here, which only added to her tension.

The house was a typical story-and-a-half Carolina house, with a metal roof, dormers, deep eves, and a wraparound porch. Its first story was raised five feet above the sand. And it was a mirror image of Laura's house next door. Ellis's bedroom window had faced Laura's.

Uncle Greg and Aunt Jodi sold their house soon after Laura had been moved into long-term care. But Ellis's parents remained in the house they'd lived in all of their married lives.

Apparently, they'd done a better job of disassociating the place from the crime next door than Ellis had. Or, she thought, maybe it was easier if you didn't have to look at the dark eye of Laura's bedroom window the last thing every night and the first thing every morning.

The two houses were separated by a narrow beach access pathway that rose over the low dune and cut through the sea oats. The wraparound porches had steps on all four sides, which had made them perfect for games of flashlight tag and hide-and-seek.

When she and Laura had been little, they'd used their flashlights to send their own secret code from one bedroom window to the other long after they were supposed to be asleep. And when they'd gotten older, Ellis would watch for Laura's bedroom light to come on at eleven-thirty—Laura's curfew. Then Ellis would wait. Laura always signaled good night with her flashlight before she went to bed.

And after that awful night, what had once been the best part of living there had become the worst. Ellis never returned home without a knot in her stomach.

Her uncle's Corvette sat in her parents' drive. The knot tightened.

She could hear her uncle's raised voice as she approached the front door. Quietly, she let herself in.

Ellis's parents were seated in the living room, watching with tired, drawn faces as Uncle Greg paced in front of them.

No one noticed she was here. She remained where she was, watching.

"I'm going to find him," Greg said, slamming a fist into his palm. "I'm going to drive up and down every street in Charleston. I'm going to question every lowlife, and I'm going to find him."

"And do what?" her mother asked.

Uncle Greg blinked at her as if she were slow-witted. "He needs to know *someone's* watching him. He needs to remember." After a pause, he said, "Maybe I can provoke him into doing something that'll violate his parole. Send his ass back to prison where he belongs."

However wrong of her it was, part of Ellis wished he'd just do that.

"Damn Jodi!" Greg turned and stalked back across the living room.

Ellis's dad said, "It's not Jodi's fault—"

Greg spun and glared at her father. "Did they let the bastard out the last two times? No! Because we were there to put a face on the crime. If we'd been there . . ." He exhaled strongly through his nose and shook his head.

"It might not have made any difference. You heard what the prosecutor said; Alexander's been a model prisoner—"

"How can you believe that?" Greg shouted. "You *saw* her. You saw what he did to my little girl! He's a monster. It may not be tomorrow, but he'll do it again—and again and again."

Ellis shivered at the thought of Alexander stalking some unsuspecting teenage girl.

"We can't do anything except what we've been doing." Ellis's dad stood and faced her uncle. "Make certain people don't forget, don't let down their guard. He'll have to be in the sex offender registry—"

"I don't know why I hadn't thought of that." A light shone in her uncle's eye. "Thank you, Bill." He snatched his keys off the coffee table.

Her father grabbed his arm. "You can't go after him! The law protects him. You could end up in jail yourself."

Ellis stood there looking at the two men. Their anger was so strong, she could almost taste its bitterness in the air. Hollis Alexander was still destroying her family.

Her mother looked up and saw her.

Ellis moved into the living room.

Her dad and uncle continued to stare at each other.

After a moment, her father took a deep breath, let go of her uncle, and said softly, "Laura is gone. Why go out there and drag trouble back to our doorstep? The man is miles away." He flung an arm wide, and for the first time glanced at Ellis. "I want him to stay that way."

"I want him dead." Greg's voice was flat.

When Ellis glanced at her uncle's face, her breath hitched in her chest. She'd only seen such brittle hatred once before in her life—when Hollis Alexander had looked at her in the courtroom on the day of his verdict.

Greg turned around and stomped out of the house, slamming the door behind him.

"Bill, do something!" Her mother jumped up from the sofa.

Her dad stared at the door for a moment. Then he blew out a long breath and scrubbed his hands over his face. "What would you have me do? He's a grown man."

That's when Ellis saw it, and she only recognized it in her father's eyes because she'd been feeling the same thing. Underneath his rational thoughts, his realistic arguments, a primal part of him *wanted* Greg to go after the man, to do whatever was necessary to take that vile creature off the streets.

Her mother said, "*Talk* to him."

That primeval look faded from her dad's eyes. He gestured in the direction of the doorway. "I've been trying to talk to him. You see the results I've gotten!"

Greg's Corvette roared out of the drive, sand spray and crushed shells clattering against the house like hail.

"Well, now it's too late." Her mother's tone was accusing. "What if he does something foolish?"

Her dad went to put an arm around her mother. "This has taken its toll on all of us. He'll come to his senses."

In a rare show of temper, her mother shook him off and stepped away. The deep lines in her forehead said she would not be placated.

Her dad tried anyway. "Even if Greg does find out his address from the Web site, Alexander is in a halfway house. There are plenty of people around. Greg'll calm down by the time he gets there."

Ellis's mother pulled her lips to the side, narrowing her eyes as she looked at him. After a beat, she headed for the door. "*I'm* not going to wait for a catastrophe. I'm going to his house, talk some sense into him before he finds out that address."

"Marsha!"

She picked up her car keys and kept going.

Her father looked torn for a moment; then he hurried into his study. When he came back, he had a .38 revolver in his hand. He held it out to Ellis. "I asked you here to give you this. Take it. You know how to handle it."

"Dad! No." Ellis stuck her hands in her shorts pockets. She knew how to handle it all right; her father had taken her to a firing range on a regular basis ever since Laura's attack. But she never liked it. The weight of it in her hands made her stomach roll. The kick as a bullet shot out into irretrievable space made her break out in a sweat. She'd refused to keep a gun in her house.

"Take it."

"I don't need a gun. Alexander goes after defenseless teenage girls. I'm neither defenseless nor young." *No, not defenseless, but afraid, always afraid. Afraid of someone like Alexander making a mockery of all of my precautions, all of my training.*

"It would make me sleep better. In fact," he said, "maybe you should move back in here with us. Just for a while."

As if she wasn't struggling enough with her memories these days. She shook her head.

"Please"—his eyes were pleading—"take the gun with you . . . for me. I have to go after your mother."

Reluctantly, she took the weapon from his outstretched hand and felt the familiar roll in her belly.

He hurried to the door and said, "Be careful."

Ellis looked at the blue-black metal resting in her palm. She was tempted to put it back in her father's desk drawer. But if it gave her dad a measure of ease . . . She tucked it inside her purse.

After she left her parents' house, she drove past her uncle's, just to make sure everyone was there and not racing down the road toward disaster in Charleston.

All three vehicles were in the drive; her mother and father's cars effectively blocking in Uncle Greg's Corvette.

She considered going in but realized she might serve as the spark to ignite the anger between her uncle and her father again. It was clear that her dad didn't want Uncle Greg to do anything that would draw Alexander's attention back to their family.

Besides, it would soon be dark.

She rolled on past and headed home.

When Ellis got inside her condo, the first thing she did after locking the door behind her was to shove the gun deep in her desk drawer.

❦

Hollis sat at Justine's long, polished dining room table, eating the best piece of beef he'd ever tasted. Justine sat at the head in her wheelchair, Hollis at her left-hand side. It had been so long since he'd dined here that he'd had to pause in order to recall what each piece of silverware was used for.

"It's so good to have you back home," Justine said, her gray eyes looking at him as if he was a long-lost son. "And so lovely of you to take your time to visit with an old woman."

He reached out and clasped her hand resting on the tabletop. "You aren't old." He smiled. He did the math. She'd been forty-two when they'd met; she was only fifty-nine. But the truth was, Justine was a homely woman, at any age—and she didn't work at overcoming it. "And *you're* the lovely one." He lowered his eyes, appearing self-conscious. "Not everyone welcomes an ex-con into their home." He bit his lower lip and kept his gaze on his plate.

"Oh, Hollis, I regret every day that I didn't testify for you at your trial. I could have told them it was a mistake. I know you were trying to protect me, but I could have told them the kind of person you are. You were a victim of circumstance, paying for a crime you didn't commit. Lord knows you shouldn't have been looking in a young lady's window, but we all make mistakes, especially in our youth. Look at me, locked in this wheelchair for the rest of my life for one little mistake I made. It happens. You've proven to me you're a thoughtful and caring young man. We'll not discuss this topic ever again. You hear?"

He blinked, as if battling tears, and smiled at her. He used his softest voice when he said, "Yes, ma'am. God bless you." After a pause, he added, "And I'd like to help you again, make it like it used to be, just me and you. You don't need strangers doing for you now that I'm here."

She gave a brisk nod of dismissal and patted his hand.

"All right, then. How about some coconut cream pie? I remember it's your favorite."

He jumped up. "Let me clear the dishes."

She wheeled backward. "I'll start the coffee."

As Hollis stacked the china, he wondered if the gamble of telling his defense attorney about Justine would have paid off. Would her testimony have swayed the jury from the circumstantial evidence? Or would it have led the police to search the woman's house? That would have been disaster for certain.

No. He'd done the right thing.

He took the dishes into the kitchen and began rinsing them in the sink, set low and accessible. Justine's little mistake—driving with a blood alcohol level double the legal limit and crashing into a two-hundred-year-old tree—had left her legs paralyzed. But it had also brought her to Hollis. At seventeen, he'd been working as a helper to the contractor who revamped this house to accommodate Justine's new limitations.

By the time the job was done, Hollis had made himself indispensable to her—errands, odd jobs, and the like. Plus, her limited mobility only compounded her already introverted behavior; she'd been hungry for his friendship. And that friendship had given him the ability to expand his hobby.

If the police had found what was in Justine's basement . . . well, things would have been a whole lot worse than fifteen years in prison.

Chapter Eight

Although memories had stolen her sleep, Ellis looked out on the early morning with a sense of purpose. It was time to put thoughts of Laura and Nate and Hollis Alexander away. Today she would be proactive, focus on something that would protect girls from the Hollis Alexanders of this world. It was the first day of the self-defense class she taught each summer, a class that mothers who remembered Laura's attack insisted their daughters take.

Before bed last night, she'd dutifully set the gun on her nightstand. On her way to the shower, Ellis looked at it sitting there with all of its deadly little bullets tucked in their chambers. She wanted to bury the damn thing in the back of her desk drawer again. But she'd promised her dad. She picked it up and tucked it inside her purse before she finished her morning routine.

At nine o'clock, she stood waiting in the shady area in Blue Heron Park. It sat at the very edge of downtown Belle Island, allowing most of her students to arrive on bicycles and on foot. In this community, twelve-year-old girls weren't afraid to walk or bike wherever they needed to go. Ellis envied them.

The girls gathered around her, sitting in a semicircle

on the coarse grass. She'd had all of them in her fourth-grade class at one time, and the way most of them were looking up at her said they still thought she was young-new-teacher cool. Good. That gave her a fighting chance to make what she taught here stick.

None of these girls had been born yet when Laura had been attacked. Time and forgetfulness led to complacency. Most of these kids felt as she had at their age; they lived in a world cocooned from the evils that dwelt beyond the long bridge across the estuary. And that somehow those evils did not even think to cross that bridge.

"It's good to see all of you again," she began. "We'll be meeting here for three weeks. This class is going to be pretty physical, so I want you to make sure you wear old clothes from here on out." She picked up the stacks of two pamphlets she'd created, *Predators* and *Self-Defense Common Sense,* and handed them to the girls. "Pass these around. Feel free to take some for friends who aren't joining us. I want you to share what you learn here with every girl you know. It could save her life.

"Lots of what we discuss will be common sense, but don't take it lightly. The best way to survive an attack is to avoid it in the first place. Criminals look for weak or distracted victims. You're going to learn to project an air of confidence and to be aware of your surroundings."

"Miss Greene." Jessie Baker raised her hand as if they were in school. "My momma said your cousin was kidnapped from her bedroom—right here in Belle Island. Is that true?"

"Yes, Jessie, it's true. Sometimes, no matter how careful you are, trouble still finds you." Ellis kept right on talking, discouraging specific questions about that crime. "In dangerous situations, I want your *first* instincts to be the right ones. For instance, if someone tells you, 'Don't scream, or I'll kill you,' I want you to immediately start making as much noise and attention-getting ruckus as you can. The guy has just told you what will foil his plan—use it."

Ellis had always wondered why Laura hadn't called for help. Ellis had been right there, sleeping in the bunk above her cousin. Laura had only to yell. What threat had Alexander made that had prevented it? He'd gotten in by cutting the window screen. But there hadn't been any sign of a struggle. . . .

Ellis realized the girls were all sitting there with expectant looks on their faces. She brought her mind back on task. "I want you to be able to protect yourselves. In addition to making sure y'all make smart choices, we're going to learn a few defensive martial arts moves. A friend of mine taught me my first moves when I was just a little older than you."

Right on cue, Rory's nephew, Daniel, sprinted from behind a thick tree.

He grabbed Ellis from behind, and in two swift moves, she had him lying on the ground struggling for breath.

She'd enlisted Daniel because he was a defensive lineman at UNC, a good eight inches taller than her, with a neck the size of her thigh. She hadn't given him a heads-up on her skills. He was simply to try and take her down, or drag her off to his waiting car.

Gasps and murmurs came from the girls, who hadn't been expecting the demonstration.

"See," Ellis said, barely breathing hard herself, "it's not going to matter if someone is bigger than you, stronger. With what I'm going to teach you, it won't matter." She reached down and offered Daniel a hand up.

He hesitated taking it, his eyes wide. "Damn . . . I mean, dang, Ms. Greene." His breath was short and his words choppy. "You coulda warned me."

She laughed. "Wouldn't have mattered, Daniel. You never stood a chance."

The girls sent up a cheer, clapping and shouting:

"Way to go, Ms. Greene!"

"I wanna do that!"

"Show us!"

"Oh, I will. You're all going to be kick-butt women. And at the end of the program, I'm going to give you some real live football players of your own to take down to prove it."

Ellis saw the light in their eyes. She was giving them what they wanted most in this world—power. Nate had given it to her; now it was her turn to pass it on.

At the end of the class, Ellis waited until all the girls were safely on their way home before she picked up her backpack and walked the forty yards to her car. It felt good, doing something positive instead of dwelling on things she couldn't change. After this class, even though Hollis Alexander was back among the general population, she felt just a little more in control.

That had been Nate's gift to her, the sense that she could defend herself, that she was more than a helpless victim. And that most precious gift resonated in her soul every day.

When she reached her car, there was a single long-stemmed red rose tucked under the windshield wiper.

She looked around.

The park was empty except for a minivan and a mother with two young children heading toward the playground.

The rose had a black satin ribbon tied around the stem with a note:

Some things are worth waiting for.

Although it was unsigned, it had to have been Rory. Why couldn't he just leave things alone?

Shame quickly swept over her. He knew this was a rough time for her. He was trying to be supportive.

It would be rude not to respond.

But she had to stay firm.

Rory's summer job was house painting. He was currently working on a Victorian over on Pinckney Avenue. She drove there and parked on the street. Rory was high on a ladder, painting the fish-scale shingles in the front gable. He looked down at the sound of her car door closing.

By the time she'd reached the ladder, he was on the ground.

"Hey, there. This is a pleasant surprise," he said, smiling.

"So was the rose."

"What rose?" Something flashed in his eyes, something that made Ellis uneasy.

"The one you left on my car while I was teaching class."

With a shake of his head, he said, "I got here at five-thirty this morning."

"Oh." She waved a hand in the air. "It must have been Daniel. I had him help with my demonstration today."

"Doesn't sound like Daniel; he never even gives his girlfriends flowers—says they're a waste of money." There was just a hint of jealous challenge in Rory's expression.

"Hmm. Must have been Dad," she lied. That note didn't contain something her dad would say.

Rory looked at her for a long moment with disapproval in his eyes and a frown on his face. Then he said, in the tone he would use with a student suspected of cheating on a test, "Is there anything you want to tell me?"

"No." Like she'd come prancing over here telling him about getting a rose from an anonymous gifter if she was seeing someone else. She turned and started toward her car.

Stopping and turning back to him, she said, "On second thought, there is something I want to say to you. We're taking a break. As in, *not dating*. If I'm getting flowers from some other guy, it's really nothing for you to disapprove of." She hurried on toward her car.

"Ellis!"

She ignored him. As she drove away, he was still standing there staring at her with his hands on his hips.

It took the entire drive home for her to stop grinding her teeth.

She picked up the rose off the passenger seat and stared at the card.

Some things are worth waiting for. It was typed, not handwritten.

Nate? No. Not after the way they'd parted yesterday.

Maybe Rory was messing with her.

"I got here at five-thirty this morning."

He hadn't said he hadn't left. That had been her own mental leap.

When she'd first told him she wanted them to stop seeing each other, Rory's first assumption was that she'd found someone else. Although she'd always been truthful with him, he didn't look convinced when she assured him he was wrong. Was he so suspicious of her that he was trying to trick her into confessing to seeing someone else?

As much as she didn't want to believe it, she couldn't think of any other explanation.

She stopped at the trash can and dropped the rose inside before she headed up to her condo.

Greg slumped low in the seat of his Corvette, even though the windows were tinted far too dark for anyone to see him from across the street in the daylight. He'd been sitting outside the big old house on St. Phillip Street—the halfway house that was Hollis Alexander's new, no doubt tax-dollar subsidized, home—since four a.m.

Greg was thankful that Bill and Marsha had delayed his coming to Charleston. He'd been so blinded by rage that he would likely have ended up in jail. Now he felt calm—like the green sky before a tornado.

He'd cast out the possibility of forcing Alexander to do something to break parole. The way the system worked, the man would be back out in no time.

Lorne Buckley hadn't said it, but Greg could tell by the look in the prosecutor's eyes that he thought Alexander would attack another girl. It was only a matter of when. Someone had to take matters in hand and prevent that from happening.

Over the past few hours, Greg's thoughts had turned to thinking of ways to do Alexander in, ways that would appear accidental. But all of his dreamed-up scenarios were flawed.

He decided the best thing to do was study the man and his habits. Then maybe he could figure out a way for Hollis Alexander to simply disappear. Parolees took off all the time in order to resume feeding their sick need for violence.

The front door of the house opened. A figure emerged from the shadow of the porch.

Alexander climbed into an old blue cargo minivan.

When Alexander pulled away from the curb, Greg started his car and followed.

❦

Hollis noticed the car tailing him right away. The Vette hung back a couple of cars, as if it wasn't too conspicuous to hide in the flow of traffic. It didn't take a genius to figure out who was driving it.

Hollis parked at the curb a block before he reached Heidi's House of Hounds. He jumped out of the van and waited for the Vette to catch up. Then he stepped directly in front of it.

Unfortunately, the car stopped short of making contact with Hollis's legs. Two more feet and he could have thrown himself on the ground and called 911.

The street was fairly narrow, with parking on both sides. Several cars stopped behind the Corvette.

Hollis raised his hand, walked to the driver's side window, and tapped on the glass.

After a moment, the window went down.

"Mr. Reinhardt"—Hollis looked down at the man behind the wheel, pleased that he looked so thoroughly haunted—"I'm going to have to request that you stop harassing me."

In a heartbeat, Hollis was shoved backward by the driver's door.

He raised his hands in front of his chest. "I only made a civil—"

Greg Reinhardt's face was mottled a satisfying red as he poked Hollis in the chest. "You filthy, depraved animal! I'm going to do more than harass you, you dirty son of a bitch!"

Hollis backed away, looking frightened and calling for help.

A man jumped out of the car behind Reinhardt's and rushed forward. "Here, now! I'm calling the police!" He held his cell phone high.

Reinhardt shoved Hollis in the center of his chest. Hollis made the most of the attack and sprawled on his backside in the street. The Good Samaritan rushed to help him up.

Reinhardt got back in his car, slammed the door closed, and took off with a squeal of tires.

Once Hollis had finished taking the Good Samaritan's information as a witness, he thanked his rescuer profusely. Then he walked the last block to work, his heart singing with his good fortune.

He entered wearing his brightest smile. "Good morning, Miss Heidi."

She looked up from the schedule book, gazing over half-glasses and smiled back. "You look like the cat that got the cream."

He headed past the front counter. "What can I say? I

love my job." *And with any luck, I'll be long gone in a week.*

"You might not think so when you see who's first for a bath this morning. Beatrice is a Great Dane with an aversion to water and people who don't belong to her. You're going to have your hands full."

"Bring her on." If there's one thing he could do, it was handle a bitch.

He paused before pushing the swinging door open. "Mind if I make a phone call first?"

"Of course not. Use this one. I'm going back to feed the hungry hordes."

Hollis waited until he heard the dogs start yowling and barking at Heidi's entry into the kennel; then he pulled a slip of paper out of his pocket and dialed.

The phone was picked up on the third ring. "Yeah?" The man sounded sleepy.

"Is this Curtis?"

"Yeah."

"Franklin B. gave me your number. I'm in need of your services."

"Huh. He tell you anything else?"

"He said you blew up the chemistry lab at St. Simon's High School, and your sister's name is Sheila."

Curtis gave a gruff laugh. "What can I do you for?"

"Social. Birth certificate. Driver's license."

"Six hundred."

"I need it next week."

"Seven hundred."

Hollis didn't respond. The man was gouging him. Franklin had said five hundred would get it done.

Curtis said, "Ticktock, my man. You need it fast, time's movin' on."

Hollis finished the deal and hung up. Seven hundred. He should have made a stink. But when it came time to split, he needed to have everything ready. He didn't have time to find another source. Besides, he was in too good of a mood to let a greedy piece of shit like Curtis ruin it.

His key to Justine's exterior basement door still worked. Everything in his secret room was just as he'd left it. His meeting with Wayne Carr had gone according to plan. And now Greg Reinhardt had just handed Hollis another weapon.

It was becoming clear; God was on his side. Those who deserved it would receive their just punishment. Each one carefully planned. He just had to take his time and do it right.

Chapter Nine

At five o'clock, Ellis had just finished drying her hair after her shower when she heard a knock at her front door.

For one foolish moment, her heart leapt at the thought it might be Nate.

But the gate hadn't called. It had to be someone already on the approved list, her family . . . or Rory.

God, don't let it be Rory.

Looking out the peephole, she saw it was her uncle.

She let him in.

He handed her a neatly folded newspaper. "This was in your paper box."

He was unshaven—a first that she could recall. Uncle Greg was meticulous about his appearance. His bloodshot eyes were sunken into bluish pools of flesh.

"Are you okay?" she asked.

Instead of answering, he flung his arms around her and pulled her into a fierce hug. She didn't realize he was crying until she felt his breath hitch and a scalding tear fall on her shoulder.

Ellis kicked the door closed and kept very still, her arms wrapped lightly around her uncle's waist.

After a few minutes, he whispered, "I miss her. After all this time, I still miss her so much."

At that moment, it became so clear. As a child, she'd thought all grief was the same, that she and everyone around her hurt equally. She'd had no idea that there were degrees of grief—like burns on the heart. Some, like hers, were painful but eventually healed, leaving an ugly scar as a reminder. But her aunt and uncle, their grief, a parent's grief, seared deep. They'd been left with bloody wounds that would never close and scar. Time could only reduce the amount of blood flow, but the wounds remained forever fresh.

"I know," she whispered back. She didn't try to placate him or trivialize his raw emotion by saying she missed Laura too. Nothing she felt could ever match his heartache.

Finally, he pulled away and wiped his face with the palms of his hands. "I'm sorry to barge in here like this. . . ." He didn't look her in the eye.

She didn't want him be embarrassed or regret coming to her.

"I'm starved," she said, wondering when he'd eaten last. "Come into the kitchen and I'll make us omelets."

The fact that he followed her without comment spoke volumes about his emotional state.

After he'd eaten, he began to look a little less like the walking dead. She'd been quiet, letting him lead the conversation. They hadn't talked about Laura—or Hollis Alexander.

Ellis was surprised when he asked, "Have you talked to Jodi?" He kept his gaze on his empty plate.

She started to raise a brow, then schooled her features. "Yes." She waited, gauging his mood.

He pushed a stray chunk of mushroom around on his plate. "How is she?"

Ellis wanted to tell him that he should call her and find out himself. She finally said, "Unhappy."

Greg's eyes rose to meet hers. "Why? She has what she wants—a life where Laura never existed." He sounded more drained than bitter.

Although Ellis had spent most of the past years with that very perception of her aunt, she now wondered if Jodi's trying to forget had only made the hole in her life that much larger. Her efforts might be no more than turning her back on a leaking dam; sooner or later, the flood would come and sweep her away.

"Maybe you should talk to her."

Surprisingly, he didn't respond, negatively or otherwise.

After a moment, Ellis picked up their plates and took them to the sink.

As she rinsed them, he said, "I'd better go."

He didn't sound like he wanted to.

She thought of her parents and their after-dinner routine. She grabbed her newspaper off the counter and handed it to him. "Why don't you read me the horoscopes and funnies while I load the dishwasher? I'll put on some coffee."

The grateful look he gave her broke her heart.

As she opened the dishwasher, she heard the pages rustle behind her.

"*Marmaduke* is my favorite," she said. "Save that one for last."

He was quiet for so long that she turned around to look at him.

He stared at the paper with his lips pinched and the muscle in his jaw clenching and unclenching.

"What?" she asked, moving closer.

When he didn't respond, she looked over his shoulder. Before she could read anything, he crumpled the paper and tossed it on the table. "That son of a bitch."

"Okay, now that you've killed my paper, you're going to have to tell me."

"Wayne Carr."

Carr had been writing for the paper for twenty years. He tended to think of himself as a big-city reporter who gave up the glamour of high-profile journalism to marry a woman who would not leave Belle Island. He'd managed to piss off almost everyone in town at least once.

Ellis's personal hatred of the man had been born when Carr had had Laura's case completely solved within the first twenty-four hours; Nate Vance was guilty. And he'd never completely let that notion die, even after Alexander had been arrested.

"What'd he do this time?" she asked.

"He's helping Alexander."

"What!" She snatched the crumpled paper from the table and opened it.

AN INNOCENT MAN CONVICTED?

by Wayne Carr
wayne_carr@BISentinel.com

It's the stuff of nightmares. Being in the wrong place at the wrong time and having your life forever altered. Being young and poor, and having no defense against a system set against you. According to Hollis Alexander, this is exactly the nightmare he found himself living fifteen years ago when he was convicted of a crime he says he did not commit.

Sixteen years ago, Laura Reinhardt, a Belle Island High senior and honor student, was kidnapped from her bedroom and assaulted. She never regained consciousness and died four years later.

Nathaniel Vance, the victim's boyfriend, was initially suspected of the attack. But Mr. Alexander was soon added to the suspects list. There was little evidence, and DNA examination was in its infancy, rarely used and unreliable.

Alexander was convicted on circumstantial evidence alone. Nathaniel Vance disappeared from Belle Island, his longtime home, the day after the verdict and has never returned.

Alexander said, "The person who attacked this girl is still out there—probably claiming new victims. It's not just for me that I'm doing this. I've served the time already. But now that I'm free, I plan to find the true criminal and save countless women from a fate like that poor girl, and maybe keep another guy like me from paying for someone else's crime."

Mr. Alexander is in the process of securing an attorney to petition the court to reexamine the evidence with new technology.

When I asked Mr. Alexander how he managed to come out of his unjust incarceration without bitterness, he said, "I've always believed in God's plan. He has a purpose for me."

As a member of this community, I plan to do all I can to support Mr. Alexander in his search for justice. We never want to lose another young woman like we did Laura Reinhardt.

Ellis slammed the paper down. "Hollis Alexander wouldn't know God if he walked up to him on the street and shook his hand!"

Greg stared at the table, the muscle in his jaw still working.

Ellis's angry words flowed. "*Nate* was young and poor, and *he* didn't get railroaded into prison! What in the hell is Carr thinking? Supporting Alexander! My God!"

She threw the paper in the trash. "This is bullshit! No one will listen."

She hoped. Nate was back in town. A panic she'd thought she'd never have to face again clawed up her windpipe—the same panic she'd felt when they'd come close to arresting Nate sixteen years ago.

Several hours later, Ellis sat in her living room, her feet tucked beneath her on the sofa. She couldn't seem to make herself do anything other than stare into empty space. Poor Uncle Greg. It was difficult enough, going through the things he had, but now to have this thrown at him. She hoped this wouldn't be the straw that would end up breaking him.

And what about Carr and his nasty little article? What kind of hornet's nest would that stir up?

An even more alarming thought struck: What if Carr discovered Nate was back in town?

This could be the excuse she'd been looking for to head out to the stables and see Nate again. It had taken all her willpower not to go out there today. She longed to see him again, to fill in the blanks of the years they'd been apart, to ask him why he left in the first place. But he'd been so remote, so distant. He probably wouldn't want to see her.

Now, however, she had a good reason.

It would have to wait until tomorrow. It was already dark.

As she sat there, exhaustion jumbled her thoughts and tinged her memories. After Nate had left town, she'd missed him so much her bones ached. Now the images of Nate the boy bled into the reality of the man he'd become. When he'd lifted her off her feet and swung her around, her heart had felt lighter than it had in years. The elation of reunion eclipsed all thought. In that instant, she'd been a fourteen-year-old girl, thrilled by the sensations he set off inside.

But she wasn't fourteen. And she and Nate had lived lives completely separate from each other—lives that numbered more years than those they'd spent sharing friendship and a love for horses.

Who knew, he might have a wife and family.

She frowned.

Why did the idea of him being happy and fulfilled in a life away from here sit like a spider on her shoulder? If she was the good friend she imagined herself to be, she'd want nothing more than to hear his life had been filled with love and joy and fulfillment from the day he'd left Belle Island.

Maybe she wasn't the person she'd always considered herself to be.

For a long time, she sat there contemplating that thought. She knew she possessed an emotional void, that she was incapable of commitment, unable to bare her soul. She was an incomplete person. Her relationship with Rory had confirmed that. But she'd always thought of herself as a steadfast friend.

About three a.m., she decided to go to bed. She shut off the lights and headed toward her bedroom.

As she passed the sliding glass door, a shadow of movement caught her eye. Under that same oak.

Her heart rate kicked up as she strained to see in the dark. The more she concentrated, it seemed the less she could trust her eyesight.

Nothing. No movement. No cigarette glow.

But something had been there; something had moved.

With Alexander out of prison, there was a chance it was him. And if it was, catching him outside her condo would violate his parole. If she called security, their approach would only scare him off again.

She stood there looking out into the night. She shivered at the thought of going out there. Open darkness slid across her skin like a cold dead hand. But she couldn't ignore this.

Concentrate on the light, not the darkness, she told herself.

There were plenty of low-voltage lights dotting the landscaping near the buildings. It wasn't completely dark.

The landscaped area across the street led to the marsh. That's where the huge old oak stood sentinel. Its twisting, Spanish moss–draped branches reached low to the ground, providing cover without completely obstructing the view of the person beneath it.

Her condo was on the deepest loop in the complex. The main entrance to her unit, her front door, was on a third-story porch on the side of the building. Her bedroom window and living room balcony faced the street. Anyone standing under that oak wouldn't be able to see her leave her condo.

She could skirt around back and get a better look, unseen.

Ellis picked up the phone and called security at the front gate. Then she pulled the gun out of her purse and hurried to the door.

As she undid the lock, her fingers started to shake.

This is no different than opening the sliding door at night. He won't know I'm outside. I can do this.

She had to know if someone was out there . . . and if that someone was Hollis Alexander. It might save an innocent girl, and if he was here in Belle Island, it could be one of *her* girls.

He'd threatened her. But she wasn't weak and unprepared. If she could catch him, he'd go back to prison.

That thought made her push on.

Pulling her door quietly closed behind her, she paused and forced herself to draw a deep breath. Her chest felt like it housed a dozen hamsters running frantically in wheels.

With soft steps, she descended three stories. Just as she'd taught her girls in self-defense, she kept all her senses trained on her surroundings. Her ears alert for a soft footfall or movement in the shrubbery. Her gaze moving, searching all angles as she descended.

And she concentrated on the faint light.

Once on the ground, she slipped behind the building instead of following the walk to the front. The security guard and his Gator would be here soon. She needed to hurry, before the headlights scared the person off.

Could it have been her imagination?

No. Hundreds of nights she'd walked past that sliding door in the dark. Before this week, she'd never seen so much as a raccoon moving out there.

Someone was under that tree.

Holding the gun against the side of her thigh to keep it from shaking, she tiptoed through the pine straw along the back of her building. She would ease around the side of the building opposite her door and stairs, concealing herself in the tall shrubs that lined the garage. From her vantage point at the front corner, she could get a clear view beneath the oak across the street.

And whoever was there wouldn't be able to see her.

As she moved, she prayed it *was* Alexander. She could hold him at gunpoint until the real police arrived.

And if he ran?

She paused and shifted the gun in her grip.

If he ran . . . she'd shoot him. She'd shoot him and not feel a moment of remorse.

She moved ahead, a mix of fear, dread, and anticipation pounding through her body.

Pressing her shoulder against the building, she slipped around the corner.

Suddenly, the dark bulk of a man in black was directly in front of her.

She whipped her gun up, supporting it with both hands, and pointed it at the center of his chest.

Her heart bucked.

His hand shot out and grabbed her gun hand, bending the fingers backward. With his other hand, he wrenched the gun from her grasp.

Stupid! Stupid! Stupid!

Training kicked in. She leaned away and twisted to deliver a sidekick to his knee.

He was a half beat ahead of her. He rushed forward, using her lack of balance and her captured wrist to send her backward onto the ground. The impact was soft, rolling.

Before she could react, he was on her, pinning her shoulders to the ground with his knees.

She fought the blind terror, the instinct to dig in her heels and struggle. She went limp. If he relaxed, she stood a chance of getting free.

"Ellis, Ellis. Never hesitate. If you feel threatened enough to raise that gun, pull the trigger."

She stared at his face. *Nate?*

He got up and offered her a hand.

"What in the goddamn hell are you doing out here?" She rolled onto her knees and got to her feet on her own, keeping some distance between them.

He smiled, his teeth flashing white in the moonlight. "Protecting you."

❧

When he heard the boat motor stop close by in the marsh, he'd climbed up into the big old tree and discovered a vantage point into Ellis's condo nearly as good as if he was standing on her balcony. He couldn't believe he hadn't thought of climbing up there before. He'd waited an hour or so, enjoying the close proximity to her and watching for anyone on the grounds. But the motor didn't start back up, and he didn't see anyone come from the direction of the marsh fence.

He dismissed it as someone doing some night fishing and climbed back down.

Then her living room lights went out. But her bedroom lights didn't come on.

A short time later, the living room lights came back on. That's when he saw the man with her.

The cheating bitch.

His heart beat faster as he scrambled back up the tree.

Ellis went into the kitchen. The man stood with his hands on his hips facing the sliding glass door.

Nate Vance. God*damn* it.

Gritting his teeth and digging his fingernails into the tree trunk, he cursed again.

Nate Fucking Vance.

This changed everything.

Chapter Ten

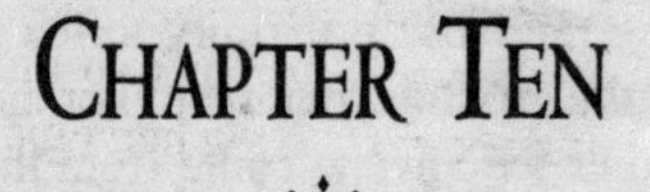

This was supposed to be simple, Nate thought as he followed Ellis up the stairs to her condo. He'd come and go, unnoticed and undetected.

His plan had been to watch for a few days, wait to see if Alexander came here. If Alexander stayed away, Nate was going to spend some time shadowing the man, just to make sure he wasn't taking up his old bad habits.

If Alexander stayed away from Ellis and didn't stalk any new females, Nate would then have to weigh his options. He couldn't stay away from his responsibilities forever—not without consequences.

Now there were new consequences that bothered him about staying too long. In those few minutes he'd spent with Ellis at the plantation, he'd realized that same spark, that deep connection that had linked them years ago, was still as vibrant as ever. And yet, it held a new and distinctly different aspect, a sexuality that was wholly new.

Seeing her tonight in that skimpy top and shorts, well, the brotherly feelings he'd counted on to help him keep his distance had gone up in a puff of red-hot steam. Watching her sweet little tush sway in front of his eyes as he climbed the stairs behind her made him imagine all sorts of things.

If he stayed too long, he feared he would give in to the temptation that right at this very moment was making his mouth dry and his hands tremble with need.

He couldn't allow it. He had nothing to offer a woman like Ellis.

He reluctantly moved his gaze from her backside to the ground below as they climbed the last few steps.

She opened the door, seemingly unaware of the things she was doing to him.

He took a deep breath and followed her into the dark condo.

She flipped on the lights.

The first thing he noticed was the security alarm. He pointed to it with the little .38 he'd taken from her. "You should have set this."

She cast a green-eyed glare over her shoulder. He was pretty sure she meant it to be reproving, but it was sexy as hell. "I was only out for a moment . . . and I *had* a gun." Her glower moved to the .38 in his hand.

"Someone could have slipped in while you were down there snooping around."

She made a dismissive sound through her teeth. "Am I really to believe you were out there in the middle of the night, all dressed in black, to protect me? From what, may I ask?"

"I'm parched. Do you have anything to drink?" He was parched, his mouth as dry as dryer lint, but it was for a reason he could never let her know. Why hadn't he anticipated the possibility that she could do this to him?

It appeared she was gritting her teeth as she went into the kitchen.

While she was out of the room, he stood in front of the sliding glass door and took a moment to collect himself. He was glad to see a safety bar in the tracks of the door.

He moved away from the door and looked around the rest of the room. He paused at the long narrow table behind the sofa. It was lined with framed snapshots.

A nostalgic smile came to his lips when he looked at one with her and Laura leaning on the fence at the stables. God, they were so young.

Then he noticed the photo of Ellis and a young man Nate assumed was the boyfriend, Rory. Their arms were around each other as they stood on a beach. A gray sky blended with the gray surf behind them. The wind was blowing Ellis's hair.

Nate realized he was frowning.

He turned away from the photos and sat down.

Ellis snuck furtive glances from the kitchen to where Nate sat on her sofa, looking entirely too big for the room. It wasn't just his physical size, even though his muscular bulk did remind her of one of those guys on a marine recruitment commercial. He also had a presence, a commanding authority that crowded everything around him. He fit in her room like a regular man bunking with Santa's elves.

Despite his size, Nate was cobra-fast. Yes, she had hesitated pulling the trigger, but that didn't fully account for what had happened. In less than the blink of an eye, Nate had gone for—and gotten—her gun. A normal person wouldn't have even registered its presence in that instant.

Obviously, Nate wasn't a normal person.

She pondered that as she studied him. All dressed in black, he looked like a commando on a night raid.

There were only so many things a man could be doing that would require skills honed as sharply as his. The odds of it being on the right side of the law were about fifty-fifty.

Ellis wasn't a gambler. She had to ask herself why she felt so certain that he was in the right 50 percent.

She shook away those thoughts and poured them both a glass of sweet tea. It was time to ask some very pointed questions.

Her phone rang, making her jump. Tea sloshed over the side of one of the glasses, onto the counter.

She snatched the handset up with her heart beating too fast. "Yes?"

Nate came into the kitchen and stood just behind her, so close she could feel his body heat.

"Miz Greene." Mr. Breese drawled the two words into the span of a normal person's full sentence.

She'd almost forgotten she'd called the front gate.

She grabbed a paper towel and mopped up the tea mess, trying to put a little more distance between her and Nate.

He stuck to her like summer flies on a horse.

The security man went on. "I didn't see nobody down here—again." He used the same tone he might have if she'd asked him to investigate an alien landing in her front yard.

Looking over her shoulder, she waved Nate away, nodding that everything was fine.

He stepped back maybe six inches, still close enough that the small hairs on her skin registered his closeness.

"I'm sorry to have bothered you," she said. "I appreciate your checking. Good night."

"'Night, miss."

She hung up the phone and turned.

Nate stood there with his hands on his hips. She had to tilt her face up to look him in the eye, which set off an unexpected rush of sparks along her nerve endings.

She shifted and picked the tea glasses up off the counter, then shouldered past him.

He was on her heels all the way to the coffee table. "Who was that?" he asked.

"No one of concern." She set the glasses on coasters and took a seat in the chair, sitting at a ninety-degree angle to the sofa. She wanted to look him in the eye when he explained what he was doing sneaking around her place in the dead of night.

"It's almost four in the morning," he said, still standing over her. "Nobody calls at four in the morning."

Leaning forward, she picked up her tea. She kept her eyes fixed on the table when she said, "It was my backup. I called security before I went down there."

He choked out a laugh. "Backup? You mean the old guy in the Gator?"

Her cheeks warmed; she worked very hard not to look at him. "I was being *cautious.*"

"*Cautious* wouldn't have unlocked that door." His voice was harshly scolding.

He finally stopped looming over her and sat down on the sofa.

She shoved a glass of sweet tea toward him. "No turning this around and getting me on the defensive. You promised me an explanation." She put out her open palm. "And my gun back."

He picked up his tea and took a long drink. With a shake of his head, he said, "No gun. Not yet."

"Afraid I'll shoot you?"

"You had your chance." The way he said it sounded like he thought she might regret not taking advantage of it.

A truly cautious woman wouldn't be sitting here alone with a man she hadn't seen for fifteen years, one she'd caught creeping in the dark like a thief and wouldn't return her weapon. But if Nate had meant her harm, he'd already had plenty of opportunity to do it.

"Tell me what's going on," she said. "Why are you here?"

He looked around as if he hadn't heard her question. "So where's the dog?"

"What?"

"The beast that belongs to that big honkin' spiked collar and leash with 'Killer' branded on it, hanging just outside." He gestured toward her front door.

"Oh, I don't have a dog." Again, not prudent. She was never this reckless. She should have said he slept under her bed, awaiting an attacker. This man was not the boy she'd known years ago; she really had to start thinking before words tumbled out of her mouth.

A slow smile spread across his face. It made her chest feel peculiar, and the room was suddenly too warm. She took a drink of tea.

"Good strategy." Then his voice lost its praise. "A real dog would be better."

After a calming breath, she said, "Hey, I'm not putting some poor doggie at risk to protect me. A person who breaks in knowing there's a dog is willing to kill it. Besides, a dog has to be walked after dark."

"Maybe you should think about a bird," he said.

"A bird?" She was so surprised that she forgot and looked into his eyes again. "An attack bird?" Her voice sounded tight, excited. She cleared her throat.

The side of his mouth lifted into a half-smile. Dear Lord, he really did look like a movie commando—handsome, daring, dangerous.

"To go with the leash and collar. A macaw or something. Down in South America, I saw some amazing birds. If you take them around a dog, they can learn to bark. That way—"

"I'll have the audio to back up the props."

He pointed at her and nodded, like she was a prize pupil. She glowed in the praise.

"Still," he said, "Alexander does his homework. He's a watcher, patient in his planning. You won't fool him—or someone like him."

So, she thought, this "protection" was about Alexander.

It was time to stop dancing around the rosebush and dive into the thorns. "So you just happened to be here visiting for the first time in fifteen years a few days after Alexander got parole."

"I'm here *because* he's out." He held her gaze, but his eyes were steely, unreadable.

"And how did you know he got parole?" she asked.

"I checked the Web site."

She stared at him for a long moment, her heart beating too fast. "Why?"

His gaze cut away. He leaned forward, resting his elbows on his knees. Then his gray eyes pried so deeply into hers that she felt stripped bare. "Ellis, I remember Alexander's threat. I take it very seriously. I owe you my life. They would have locked me up instead of him if it hadn't been for you."

"No," she said. "They didn't have any evidence. You were just a convenient target."

"They didn't have much more evidence on Alexander than they did on me. They would have convicted me; I know it."

She thought about the things she *hadn't* told the police. Would it have changed the outcome? Back then, she and Nate had never talked about the details of that night. But she knew he'd withheld some things, just as she had.

"You did it, Ellis," he said, reaching out and taking her hand. "You saved me."

Looking into his eyes, she suddenly felt like she was falling, tumbling into their gray depths. She curled her fingers around his and held tight. It took a conscious effort not to go over and climb into his lap. It startled her to realize a part of her wanted him to protect her, to be there so she could let down her guard, at least a little.

He brought her fingers to his lips and brushed a kiss across them. Certainly an act of fealty, not romance. "You gave me my life. The least I can do is protect yours."

She sat transfixed, relishing the feel of his warm breath on her fingers.

Then she blinked and rationality edged back into her thoughts. His sentiments were noble, tempting even. But she couldn't afford to get used to someone else looking out for her—especially not someone who was going to be gone in a few days.

She reclaimed her hand. "Are you going to hang around protecting me forever?"

She meant it to sound facetious, a call back to reality. But the look in his eye remained dead serious.

"Until I know he's no longer a threat to you, yes."

"And you think he's a threat to me?"

He raised a dark brow. "Why are you running around in the dark with a gun if *you* don't?"

"I'm always careful. It doesn't have anything to do with Alexander being on parole."

"Good to hear. But, if I may point out, tonight you could have been in real trouble."

"I wouldn't have been out there at all if you'd let me know what you were doing instead of sneaking around in the dark."

He tilted his head and drilled her with a pointed stare. "But you *thought* it was Alexander."

Hard to argue that one. She redirected, "What is it you do, Nate Vance, that you can pick up and come here to protect me indefinitely?"

"I have lots of flexibility in my work." He didn't offer further explanation.

"I see." Then she realized she hadn't asked the most pertinent question yet. "How did you get inside the complex?"

He grinned. "Boat down the river and through the marsh. That little fence is only good for keeping gators out."

"Where are you staying, with Mr. J?"

"Part of the flexibility in my work depends on discretion, on no one knowing much about me or where I happen to be. So the less anyone knows the better—for everyone." He slid forward in his seat, reaching out to run a fingcr down her cheek. "So, please, no more questions. Just let me make sure you're safe."

She closed her eyes, soaking in the feel of his finger against her skin, wanting to draw so much more from his simple touch of friendship.

When she realized what she was doing, her eyes snapped open and she leaned away from his touch.

With a dismissive chuckle, she said, "Well you don't have to stand around out there all night long smoking in the dark to do it."

He sat up straighter and glanced toward the sliding door. "Smoking?"

"Yeah, I saw your cigarette last night."

"I wasn't in Belle Island until very early this morning."

"You weren't?" Her skin felt clammy all of a sudden.

He looked grim when he turned off the lamp and got up. "You're sure you saw someone out there?"

"Yes." The taste the tea left in her mouth turned cloyingly sweet. "I called security, but they didn't find anyone."

Keeping himself to the side, out of sight, he looked out the sliding glass door. He pointed. "There, under the big tree?"

"Yes," she said. "Right where I saw you tonight."

His voice was tight when he said, "I wasn't under the tree."

Chapter Eleven

Nate kept to the deepest shadows as he searched the grounds around Ellis's condo. He supposed he should feel some satisfaction in predicting Alexander's move correctly. In normal circumstances—in his job—he would. Eliminating the threat would be that much easier. But the fact that Ellis was the target tweaked something inside him.

The way he felt when close to her had taken him by surprise. Of course, he'd known she'd grown up. He'd seen it for himself. But, sweet Jesus, he'd had no idea he'd find himself this drawn to her. He'd given in to the urge to kiss her cool, trembling fingers. And he hadn't wanted to stop there.

They'd been friends before. In fact, she hadn't known it, but she'd been the closest friend he had in Belle Island. And the way he'd left . . . Well, he'd expected his departure to kill any fondness she held for him—and certainly to obliterate her unshakable trust in him.

But when he'd looked in her eyes, he'd seen it, there behind the maturity, beyond the distance time had put between them. The trust, the fondness was all still there.

Unfortunately, he didn't deserve one iota of her trust,

and certainly not a scrap of affection—not after what his life had turned into.

He lived in a shadow world populated with liars and thieves, misfits and outcasts. It was a world that was dangerous and cruel.

He'd lived with liars for so long, he hardly knew how to deal with the truth. And he'd learned to lie with the best of them. Truth, he'd discovered, was an overrated commodity, one that had no value in his world.

He'd never given himself over to long, soul-searching thought about the lies and their purposes. Life was what it was, certainly not what he'd intended it to be. The essence of the peculiar dance his existence had become boiled down to two things: power and money. Since money bought power, it trumped all else. Truth never got so much as a fingernail hold in the equation.

But Ellis, sweet Ellis. Her spirit was pure and true. She taught children. She gentled horses. She worked to keep young girls safe. Her life was honesty and goodness. He could not let his life follow him here. He could not sully her goodness with his tainted touch or the dark stain of his affection.

He looked up at her living room door. He'd left her there holding her gun, with orders to shoot anything that came through a door or window while he was gone. She handled the weapon like someone trained, but her revulsion to it was clear. Another testament to her innate goodness; even when threatened, her humanity won out.

The lights in her condo remained off, the sliding glass door nothing but a reflective panel of black. But he could sense her there, feel her looking out into the night, searching for him. Her champion.

He couldn't fail her the way he'd failed Laura.

He moved on. *Focus,* he thought. Focus on what he'd come here to do.

Underneath the oak where Ellis had seen the movement that had drawn her out earlier, he searched the ground with his penlight. There were no discarded cigarette butts. But there was evidence someone had indeed spent a good amount of time there. The few sprouts of weeds were flattened and broken. Feet had shuffled in the pine straw until there was a bare spot. This sandy, loamy soil didn't hold an impression, so he couldn't tell anything about the size of the person.

It didn't really matter. Only one person would have any reason to be sneaking around here two nights in a row.

The question was, had Alexander fled? Or was he still hanging around?

Nate kept himself concealed as much as possible as he systematically searched the area. He hoped that if Alexander was here, he could still surprise him.

An hour later, he completed his circuit. He hadn't turned up any other signs of the man. Nate's opinion that the "security" in this place was a joke had intensified when he'd poked around the gatehouse for at least five minutes and never aroused so much as a glance up from the guard reading the newspaper.

Alexander had most likely entered the complex the same way Nate had, over the fence somewhere on the perimeter bordering the wetlands. But truthfully, it wouldn't have taken much to get through the front gate unseen.

Had Alexander been scared off? Or had he still been out here watching when Nate was in Ellis's living room?

That question bred another. Would Alexander recognize him? Not likely. It'd be best if the man didn't put two and two together.

Nate needed to remain a ghost in this town.

After Greg left Ellis's, he'd driven to the beach and waited for darkness. She hadn't let him leave until he'd had himself under control. He was grateful for her patience. But now, as he sat in the lonely dark many hours later, the avalanche of pain once again overtook him.

How was it that the years did nothing to dull his grief? He vacillated between resentment and envy over Jodi's ability to close off that part of her life, to lose herself in the bliss of denial. How would it feel to close his eyes at night and *not* see Laura's broken and unconscious body caught in that breakwater? To not see her wet hair tangled and matted over her bruised and swollen face?

To not have rage continually simmering just beneath the surface of his skin?

People thought he chased risk for pleasure. No one knew the dark truth; he did the dangerous in secret hope that it would end the pain.

Finally, he started the Corvette and drove slowly past the old house, the place that held the last happy moments of his life—and the most horrific. It had been Jodi's idea to move. She'd made the decision the day they'd moved Laura to Garden Grove, a place where human beings who'd lost everything that made them human were stored—where they waited for death to complete its course.

For a long while, he sat on the street in front of the house. He tried to bathe himself in the good memories, the birthdays and Christmases. But his mind always circled back around to the morning his world was slung out of its orbit, shooting into vapid darkness, away from all light and warmth.

He started the car and drove out of town. It was late enough that the roads were deserted. He wound the engine too tight, never shifting until well into the red line. He pushed the Corvette too fast around curves, driving without purpose through the night.

After some time, a plan started to form in his mind.

He drove home, and for the first time in days, he slept.

Ellis kept watch out the windows as Nate searched outside. He was good. Even with the knowledge he was out there, she couldn't see him moving around.

Just another nugget to make her wonder what he'd been up to these past years. He'd been in South America. South America always brought drug cartels to mind. That fact shifted the odds from fifty-fifty to eighty-twenty in favor of Nate being on the wrong side of the law.

Try as she might, she just couldn't see him in a ruthless, lawless role. Was she being totally naïve, still seeing him through the trusting eyes of a besotted teen?

She'd like to think she was more clearheaded than that. Besides, she was a firm believer that a person didn't change his basic makeup. A good person didn't turn evil. Circumstances could harden him, life choices could shift his outlook, but what was deep inside remained the same.

Going into the kitchen, she looked out the window at

the grounds on the back side of the building. She studied the shadows and contours until her vision blurred. No sign of Nate.

The weight of the gun in her hand didn't give her much security.

Nate had been right. Never pull a gun if you don't intend to fire. It was one of the first things she'd learned in her self-defense class at the shooting range—and the reason she'd never kept a gun in her possession. The sensation of a bullet exploding from the chamber was so violent, she'd barely been able to pull the trigger when aiming at a paper target. She certainly couldn't count on herself to do better against a living, breathing being, aggressor or not. That being the case, the risk of handing over the weapon to the attacker outweighed the benefit—and it was exactly what she'd done with Nate a short while ago.

Of course, she'd justified her hesitation; what if it had been Mr. Breese? She couldn't shoot first and identify the person later. And, of course, Nate's superior skill at disarming her had made that hesitation seem much greater than it was. In the end, that's all it had been, justification.

She went back to the living room, shifting the gun from one hand to the other, wiping her palms on her shorts. As she looked back at the tree across the street, a thought occurred to her. Rory had vowed to protect her. Security would let him enter without question. Had it been him beneath that tree?

She thought of the rose and his ambiguous denial. If it had been, had his purpose been to protect? Or to frighten her into thinking she needed him?

No. She was being ridiculous. For one thing, Rory had

quit smoking after his dad had been diagnosed with lung cancer over two years ago—

A knock sounded at her door, and she nearly dropped the revolver.

"It's Nate."

She checked the peephole before opening up and letting him in.

He stopped her as she reached for the light switch. "Leave it off."

"Find anything?" she asked.

He shook his head. "But you were right. Somebody has been under that tree recently. We have to assume it was Alexander."

She nearly mentioned her wild thought that it could have been Rory, but she didn't want to open the subject of her relationship with him. Nate was right; they had to assume it was Alexander. If it had been Rory, there wouldn't be any danger anyway.

"Now what?" she asked.

He looked down at her. Her eyes were well adjusted to the dim moonlight in the room. It was easy to see the transformation as the hard, determined look on his face softened.

Gently, he removed the gun from her hand. She let it go, glad to be rid of it.

"Now," he said. "You go to bed."

Her heart dropped a little in her chest. "Okay, then." She licked her lips, half searching for a reason to keep him here.

She put on an appreciative expression to hide her unwarranted disappointment. "Thank you for your concern."

She reached for the doorknob with her right hand and held her left out to him. "I'd like to have my gun back."

He looked oddly amused as he tucked the gun into the back of his waistband. Then he took her hand from the doorknob and held it in his. "Oh, I'm not leaving."

"Oh?" She swallowed hard, her mouth unexpectedly dry.

"You need to sleep. I doubt you'll be able to knowing Alexander was standing under your window an hour ago." He took her by the shoulders, turning her to face the short hall to her bedroom. He held her with her back to his chest. Leaning close enough that she felt his breath on her ear, he said, "Go. Sleep. I'll be right out here."

A little chill traveled from her ear, down her neck, and pooled at the base of her spine. She tried to dismiss her very sexual response as gratitude. That's all it was. Gratitude and exhaustion. She never knew it could feel so good to have someone else in charge. She'd never *wanted* anyone else in charge. That thought scared her just a little bit.

She half turned and kissed his cheek. Then she hurried into her bedroom and closed the door.

She didn't sleep.

CHAPTER TWELVE

Ellis felt the crawl of every protracted minute until the sky began to lighten in the east. She was thankful when it was time to drag her tired bones out of bed and get ready to teach her class in the park. It beat lying here wondering about the man who was on the other side of her bedroom door.

She'd dressed and finished washing her face and brushing her teeth when the doorbell rang three times in rapid succession.

When she hurried into the living room, Nate was already looking out the peephole.

"Shit," he said under his breath.

"Ellis!" Her uncle's shout was followed by a firm knock.

Her heart slid back down to its proper place as she moved to open the door.

Nate grabbed her wrist. "It'd be best if he doesn't know I'm here."

"He's obviously upset. I can't just not answer the door."

"Ellis," her uncle called through the door. "I hear you talking to someone in there. Are you all right?"

She shot Nate a look of determination. "I'm fine." She

yanked her wrist free and disarmed the alarm, then opened the door.

Lucky for Nate, he didn't try to stop her.

For an instant after the door opened, Greg stood there, looking confused. His gaze skittered from her to Nate and back again. "Um . . . sorry. I didn't know you had—" His eyes suddenly narrowed. For a brief moment, he studied Nate's face. "It's you!" He stepped into the room and stood toe-to-toe with Nate. "What in the hell are you doing here with my niece?"

Her uncle had always treated her with the protectiveness of a father. The loss of Laura had magnified it beyond reason.

Ellis put a hand on her uncle's arm. "Nate's here to help."

"Does Rory know about this?" Her uncle looked at her with accusing eyes.

She nearly laughed. It had taken Greg nearly a year to dismiss his concerns over Rory's intentions. "It's not like that," she said.

Greg was so focused on giving Nate the stink-eye that Ellis wasn't sure he even heard her.

Nate didn't move, didn't speak. She noticed a muscle tick in his jaw.

"Dear Lord!" She motioned toward the kitchen. "Let's go sit down."

Greg looked at her. "You're sure you're all right?"

"Perfectly." She closed her eyes and shook her head, then headed to the kitchen. "I need coffee."

She didn't wait. The men would follow or start swinging. Either way, she needed caffeine and Tylenol.

They followed.

Greg took a seat at the kitchen table. Nate leaned up against the counter with his ankles and arms crossed. He still hadn't said a word.

Drumming his fingers on the tabletop, Greg said, "What, exactly, is going on here?"

Ellis filled and started the coffeemaker. "It's a long story." She heard his intake of breath and headed off his next comment. "Which I'll be happy to explain fully in a minute. First, tell me why on earth you're here at this hour thinking I'm in some sort of trouble?"

"I got a call a few minutes ago from security here at the complex saying you'd reported a prowler, and they'd been unsuccessful in trying to reach you this morning."

"No one tried to reach me." Ellis's skin suddenly felt too small.

Nate spoke for the first time. "Didn't you think it odd that security contacted you and not Ellis's parents?"

"I was half asleep. I just threw on my clothes and rushed over here."

Nate looked at her. "Is your uncle even on your emergency contact list?"

She shook her head, her stomach feeling like a bag of snakes. "No. Only my parents' home and cell numbers."

Ellis's last fingerhold of denial crumbled away. Her skin crawled, thinking of Alexander out there watching her. That was his thing, after all, watching women—before he took his game to the next level.

"Who would have called me, then?" Greg asked. His voice held a suspicious tone, his gaze directing that suspicion toward Nate.

Ellis sat down with her uncle. After a quick glance at

Nate, she said, "We think Hollis Alexander has been watching my house."

Greg remained so still, she thought he might have stopped breathing.

Finally, he asked, "You saw him?"

"I saw someone. Two nights in a row. Who else could it be?"

Greg's voice rose in anger when he said, "You mean he was out there and you didn't call anyone to report it? You didn't even call your dad or me to let us know? We could have caught the bastard! He'd be back in prison."

"I did call security. They didn't find anyone. I dismissed it as being someone from the complex. But when it happened again last night, I began to suspect . . ." She poured the coffee.

If she told him how she'd discovered Nate, Greg was sure to blow a gasket. He'd hated Nate from the moment he'd set foot in the Reinhardt house. He'd never seen Nate's presence as anything but suspicious, a guy from the wrong side of the tracks sure to ruin Laura.

She handed a mug to Nate and set another in front of her uncle.

"You still haven't explained why *he's* here," Greg said.

She sipped her coffee, scrambling for a way to present the situation in an undamning light.

Nate saved her by saying, "I came by to check on her. Apparently, I frightened him off. He must have called you."

"Why would he call me?" Greg asked.

That was a very good question. One Ellis had no answer for.

Nate said, "I'm sure he had a reason. I just don't know what it is yet."

Greg cut a glance toward Nate. "What the hell are you even doing in Belle Island? I thought you were long gone."

"I was." Nate didn't move from his spot against the counter. "I came back when I learned Alexander had been paroled."

"Why?" her uncle challenged.

"Because I owe Ellis."

In a low tone, Greg said, "Ellis is none of your concern."

"With all respect," Nate said evenly, "I beg to differ."

"I don't want you around my niece." Greg stood, his voice dropping even more. "Laura was fine until you started hanging around. If not for you, someone like Alexander would never have found her."

"That's enough!" Ellis shouted, stepping close. "Uncle Greg," she said, her tone matching her uncle's, "Nate is here as my friend, my guest."

She knew it was useless to try to change her uncle's opinion of Nate, so she didn't. "I'm a grown woman, and you know as well as anyone I can take care of myself. We all want the same thing here—for Alexander to be put back in prison where he belongs."

There was a flash in Nate's eyes, a flash that said prison wasn't what he had in mind for Hollis Alexander. Again she was struck with how little she knew about this man and what he'd been doing for the past fifteen years.

"Now," she said, drawing a breath, "let's figure out a way to work together to make that happen."

Greg said, "Nate left here fifteen years ago without a thought for you, or Laura. You don't even *know* him. This is not the time to put your trust in a stranger."

It frightened her a little that he'd just put to words her own thoughts.

He grabbed her hands. "If Alexander is hanging around here, the best thing you can do is what your dad wants you to—leave. Please"—he paused—"leave. It won't have to be for long."

Something in his eyes set off a new fear. "You aren't going to do anything rash."

"I think you're the one who needs to worry about doing something rash." His eyes were hard when he said to Nate, "Go away. Leave Ellis alone."

"I can't do that. Not while she's in danger."

"Just make sure you aren't the one to hurt her," Greg said firmly, then headed toward the door.

In the silence that followed, Nate's breathing told her he was working to keep himself in check.

"What?" she prompted.

After a moment, he said, "Everyone is going to know I'm here."

"So?" That was the least of their problems at the moment. "What difference can it possibly make? Alexander already knows you're here."

He closed his eyes briefly. "Forget it."

"No, I won't. What is it that makes people knowing you're here a problem?"

"It has nothing to do with any of this, so don't worry about it."

She didn't push. Deep down, a little voice said it was because she was afraid of the answer she might get. She ignored that voice.

"What did Uncle Greg mean when he said Alexander

wouldn't have found Laura?" she asked. "How can he blame you for that?"

After Laura had been attacked, Greg had said that she'd changed when she began seeing Nate, had started keeping secrets. But Ellis had dismissed it as her uncle looking for logic and reason in a random, violent act.

She thought back to that summer. True, occasionally she'd seen Laura sneaking back in her bedroom window in the wee hours. A couple of times, she'd seen Nate walking her up from the beach. They'd had their arms around each other. But what on earth could that have to do with Alexander finding her?

"He just needs someone to blame," Nate said with a shrug. "Might as well be me." He stepped closer and took her by the shoulders. "I am here for *you*. Nothing else matters."

He looked into her eyes, and for a moment, she couldn't move. The floor undulated beneath her feet. Only the strength of his hands maintained her balance. She felt each heartbeat surge her blood, and her vision closed off everything except his face.

They stood there, looking into each other's eyes. Ellis searched for any hint of duplicity, the slightest indication of deceit, but there wasn't a shadow of anything treacherous. She saw only strength and caring . . . and something more. Longing? Passion?

The room was suddenly too warm. She continued to stare into his smoky eyes; their gazes locked in an intimate dance that drew her closer to him.

Swallowing dryly, she asked, "Is that really why you came back? For me?" The words left her lips in a whisper.

He cupped her face in his hands. "For you."

He leaned slightly closer.

Ellis's lips tingled in anticipation. She stopped breathing, feeling as if she was cresting the first long incline of a roller coaster.

Instead of taking the stomach-dropping plunge, her car stuck at the top when Nate pressed his lips to the center of her forehead—not her oh-so-ready mouth.

When he released her, she looked everywhere except into his eyes. If she looked there, he'd see how mistaken she'd been, how she'd misread his intentions. She would die of embarrassment.

This was a lesson she wouldn't forget.

He was only here because he *owed* her.

❧

Lorne Buckley arrived at the O.T. Wallace County Office Building in a bad mood. The fact that he found Wayne Carr sitting in the anteroom of his office knocked it down yet another notch.

When Lorne entered, Carr rose from his seat. As usual, he was dressed in his own version of hip reporter: three-hundred-dollar shoes that worked at looking casual and scruffy, jeans, and an open-neck collared shirt under a ridiculously expensive sport coat. Naturally, his ensemble was completed with sunglasses and an ultracool three-day growth of beard. All but the beard no doubt supplied by his wife's inherited money.

Lorne said good morning to his secretary and walked past Carr without as much as a nod of recognition. What did the man expect after his article in the paper? The *Belle Island Sentinel* was a small paper, but plenty of people read it—and more than one had called to read it aloud to Lorne.

Wayne Carr had been a major thorn in Lorne's side during the Reinhardt investigation and had remained so throughout the trial. Lorne had been damn lucky that Carr's articles hadn't completely tainted the jury pool.

Once behind the closed door of his private office, Buckley took a few minutes to cool off.

He poured himself a cup of coffee and made a phone call. Finally, he keyed the intercom and told his secretary to send the man in.

Being raised in the South, Buckley followed proper etiquette and stood to shake Carr's hand. The difficult part was not wiping it on his pant leg afterward.

"What can I do for you, Mr. Carr?"

"I've been contacted by Hollis Alexander. He's asked me to assist him in clearing his name." Carr sat in the chair on the other side of the desk and crossed an ankle over his knee.

"And this concerns me in what way?"

"I just thought you'd be interested to know, in case you need to prepare yourself."

"For what, exactly?"

"For the case to be reopened," Carr said, as if it was a done deal. "For evidence to be reexamined. Alexander swears he was wrongly convicted. He's also contacted the Justice Project."

"Funny," Buckley said, "that he waited until he'd served so much time before he pursued such avenues, don't you think?"

"He told me he was preparing to contact them before his parole was granted. DNA testing has come a long way."

Buckley leaned back in his chair. "Of course, he has every right to pursue this. But it'll take a compelling reason for a judge to order evidence to be reexamined. I don't think Alexander has one. He admitted to being on the scene—*after* the fingerprint placed him there. There was an eyewitness. DNA testing won't change any of that."

Carr seemed to consider this for a moment.

Buckley said, "I know how hard it is to admit your initial position was wrong, especially after making such public statements immediately after the crime, but I can't believe you'd allow yourself to be pulled into this quagmire again."

"The man says he's innocent," Carr said. "Why else would he be spending his time, now that he's free, to prove it? Why not just move on?"

"Could be lots of reasons. As long as he's got a felony conviction and has to register as a sex offender, it's going to be that much harder for him to get back into his old pastimes—peeping, rape. Not to mention parole can be revoked. He could go back for another fifteen. He's pond scum. I'd distance myself from him if I were you."

"Justice means more to me than avoiding confrontation and disapproval." Carr gave a self-righteous tilt of the chin that begged to have an uppercut delivered to it.

"Alexander is blowing smoke up your ass. Although, I can't say I can figure out the exact plan for his game, but you can bet he has one."

"His *game* is justice." Carr leaned forward. "Our legal system is not designed to reveal and repair its mistakes; you know that as well as I do. If dozens of people are proven innocent after the fact, how much harder will it be for you guys to get a jury to convict? Everyone will be too afraid to make the call."

"You know what side I'm on. That's not going to change."

Lorne was ready to be done with this. "So again, I ask, what do you want from me?"

"I'm just giving you a heads-up, an opportunity to save face—to come forward with things that will look much worse if they're dragged out of the dark by a defense lawyer or the Justice Project. If your office reveals mistakes willingly, it'll play that much better all 'round. I can help you do that."

Bullshit. You're fishing, trying to get me to say something you can misquote in your newspaper.

"I stand by my case," Buckley said. "If a defense attorney can convince a judge to have the evidence reexamined, there isn't anything I can do about it."

Carr straightened and his eyes probed. "So, there are things that DNA examination might alter?"

"I really can't say. Now, if you'll excuse me, I have another appointment."

Carr stood. "If you change your mind, if there's anything I can do to help present your side, just let me know."

"I'll be sure to do that."

Carr walked out, closing the door softly behind him.

Buckley opened his desk drawer and pulled out a bottle of Tums. As he chewed two of them, he thought about that physical evidence. DNA testing *had* come a very long way in fifteen years. But it still couldn't create something that was not there.

Alexander was a pervert and a rapist. So what if the Reinhardt case had been thin? A jury had convicted.

There wasn't any reason for Carr's visit to unnerve him.

But it did.

Chapter Thirteen

Greg had only gotten halfway through reporting to his brother-in-law what was going on at Ellis's place when Bill's line indicated there was a call waiting. Bill had signed off, saying it was Ellis. Greg's last words had been to make sure she told him about both Alexander *and* Nate Vance.

That kid. Why had he shown up after all these years? He was sure to bring trouble to Ellis, just as he had to Laura.

Laura had changed in those last months, after Nate Vance had started hanging around. There had been secrets and lies; they were subtle, shadowed and misty. Although Greg had turned away, closed his eyes to the signs, he'd known. He'd known and delayed acting. Why hadn't he forbidden Laura from seeing the kid?

Because you couldn't deny her anything.

Jodi had defended Nate, had said Greg was looking for someone besides himself to blame for not keeping their daughter safe. That he wanted someone to point the finger at to ease his own guilt.

But it wasn't that. It was simple logic. Nate Vance had lived in a place where people actively looked for trouble—drugs and who knew what went on there. One of them might even have been connected to Alexander in some way. Why else would a lowlife from Charleston come all this way?

That same logic said Nate was guilty of *something*. He did disappear the day after the guilty verdict.

Regardless of whether Nate had led Alexander to Laura, the clear fact was that he brought trouble.

Ellis was too blindly trusting when it came to Nate Vance, always had been. No good would come of the man's return to Belle Island. Greg wasn't going to stand by and watch Ellis be hurt.

When he stopped for a red light, he dialed the cell phone of the kid who detailed cars at the dealership. Bradley wasn't supposed to have his cell on while working, but Greg knew better than to assume the kid followed the rules. He was rewarded for his thinking when Bradley picked up on the third ring.

"Yo, master-salesman-dude, thought you were supposed to be here working today. Z'up?"

"Something came up," Greg said. Car sales had been so flat; it didn't really matter if he went in to work or not. "I need some of your investigative skills."

"Cool."

Bradley was a whiz with computers. He had a growing side business, some of which Greg was pretty certain involved illegal hacking.

"I need some information on a guy. This might require some serious law bending."

Bradley chuckled as if he was rubbing his hands together. "All riiiiight."

Greg explained the details. Bradley was practically drooling by the time they ended the call.

In his aimless driving as he'd spoken to Bradley, Greg found himself on the road in front of Jodi's house. He slowed to a crawl.

It was midmorning. She'd most likely be there, working at her sewing machine, doing the alterations that paid her bills.

He nearly pulled into her drive.

Over the years, they'd managed to build a bridge over the mudflat of their divorce. Unfortunately, the last time he was here, he'd blasted the supports right out from under it. And he didn't have the emotional energy to try and rebuild it right now.

Although he hated the idea of his empty house, he drove home. He had to get some sleep. Tonight, if Hollis Alexander showed up outside Ellis's condo, he was going to get an unexpected surprise.

❦

Ellis tried to ignore Nate sitting on a nearby picnic table while she taught her class—which proved near impossible because the girls continually looked his way and whispered to one another. She'd heard the word *hot* more than once. Plus the fact that she could actually *feel it* when he looked at her, as if his gaze possessed a physical presence, warm and weighty. No, there was no way to pretend he wasn't here.

She went through the class more self-consciously than she wanted to admit.

Finally, the hour was up. "Okay, I'll see you girls

tomorrow. And don't forget what I told you. This isn't a game. Buddy up. Use your common sense. And remember that face in the photo I showed you."

There was a chorus of "yes, ma'am" and "okay."

Once the last girl had gone, Nate left his perch and walked over to her.

"That was pretty impressive," he said.

"Thanks. I told you I can take care of myself." She was unable to keep the pride out of her voice.

He gave her a cautionary glance. "It's one thing to know how to defend yourself, and another entirely to execute it without hesitation when a threat presents itself."

"I know that."

"You didn't pull the trigger last night."

"And you're complaining?" She tried to deflect the truth of her vulnerability.

"Like you just told the girls, this is serious, Ellis. You have to do exactly what you asked of them today. No more running around alone in the dark. You cannot let your guard down for a minute, and you can't hesitate because you're afraid to hurt someone." The cold hardness of his words suggested he spoke from experience.

She crossed her arms and stared into his eyes. It was a mistake. Whenever she looked into them, her heart closed to questions she might not want to hear the answer to.

Her gaze shifted to his throat. Not much better. She forced herself to ask, "What is it you do that makes you such an expert?"

He hesitated long enough that she could tell he was selecting his words carefully. "I'm in security."

"Not good enough. Be more specific."

She looked toward the woods, at the place Nate had

tied his horse the day he'd given her that first self-defense lesson.

Don't think of that. He's not that boy. He's a man living an unknown life.

When he didn't say anything, she chanced looking into his face again. His eyes were closed, so she wasn't sucked into their good-sense-eradicating depths, but looking at those lips had nearly the same effect.

Finally, he opened his eyes and said, "I can't."

His refusal shot through her like a shard of hot glass. "So you are involved in something illegal."

His stormy gaze held hers. "No, I'm not."

She edged closer to him and poked him in the center of his chest. "You *demand* my trust, but *you* don't trust me. You hide behind half answers and—"

He took her by the shoulders, probably more roughly than he'd intended, and he leaned over, his nose close to hers.

She felt the magnetic pull of that silver gaze, was intensely aware of the trembling of restraint in his grip. All of that barely controlled power set off something alarming inside her—not fear, which logic dictated, but a desire to flush all caution down the toilet and kiss him.

And, she realized with a start, his eyes mirrored that desire.

It should have frightened her. But instead she found herself excited, ready to step off a high cliff.

Her heart sped up. She moistened her lips.

His gaze followed the path of her tongue.

Then he blinked and straightened, putting more distance between their faces. "My answers don't have anything to do with not trusting you. My work is not something I can talk about . . . to anyone." His hands lessened their grip and moved up and down her arms, a caress of apology.

He sighed and took his hands off her.

She wished he hadn't.

"Believe me," he said, "it's as frustrating for me as it is you. It would be dangerous for both of us if I said more. But I assure you, what I do isn't criminal."

She wanted that to be enough. But it wasn't. "Not criminal?"

"No."

"But dangerous?"

He pressed his lips together and huffed through his nose.

She pressed. "FBI? CIA? DEA? Any of the other letter-designated good-guy organizations?"

"Stop it, Ellis," he said softly. "I can't tell you. If that's something that you have trouble dealing with, I'm sorry. It's the way things have to be." There was true apology in his voice, and he looked at her with a steady gaze that didn't appear in the least duplicitous.

She felt her good sense again dissolving. God, what was wrong with her? She was never this imprudent.

She stooped to grab her backpack. "All right, then." Without looking at him, she started walking toward her car.

After a moment, she heard him fall into step behind her. By the time she was halfway to the parking lot, he'd caught up.

She couldn't believe she'd conceded so easily. Not like her at all. She decided to take another tack. "What about the rest of your life—your *personal* life?"

She hadn't seriously considered that he might be married with a houseful of kids. Although the thought tied her stomach in an unpleasant knot, it would make her feel a little better about the kiss on the forehead this morning.

"Personal life," he echoed. "I don't have one."

The knot loosened a bit. But she wondered, was he dedicated to his job? Or emotionally unavailable?

"Married?"

"No."

"Any kids?"

He looked at her like that was the most ridiculous question she could have asked. "No."

"Man, you can be a real pain in the ass. I get it, work's off limits, but I'd like to be able to have a conversation. Do I have to pry everything out of you with a nut pick?"

"Why so curious?" he asked, making a show of looking down his nose at her.

She decided to be truthful. Looking directly into his eyes, she said, "Because we're friends."

A slow smile came to his lips. It looked both seductive and dangerous, a pirate's smile. "Yes, we are."

A man with a smile like that hadn't lived a life of celibacy. It made Ellis want to jump his bones right here and now.

Her voice squeaked slightly when she asked, "*Ever* married?"

"No."

She realized she was smiling. She looked away and asked, "Why not?"

"That's far too complicated a question."

"Girlfriend?"

He raised an eyebrow. His knowing grin set off

fireworks in her belly and made her embarrassed she'd asked. "Not at the moment."

"Anyone ever tell you what a sparkling conversationalist you are?" She hoped her glib response disguised her disappointment that their easy way with each other had been buried under the debris of fifteen years of living.

"Sorry. I don't spend a lot of time *sharing* these days."

"Don't make sharing sound like a dirty word. We used to share a lot."

"Yeah." That one syllable held more longing than four letters should have to carry.

After a moment, the nostalgic silence got to her. "Okay, you're off the hook. Turnabout's fair play. You can ask me stuff I won't want to answer."

They'd reached her Mustang. He opened the driver's door for her, and that pirate's smile appeared again. "I don't need to."

"Oh." She wished she could suck back that single word. It sounded hurt and defeated, pathetic. All of which were accurate and true.

She tossed her backpack into the backseat, and then tried to duck into the car.

His next words stopped her. "You graduated sixth in your high school class. You commuted to Charleston College for five years and got a degree in elementary ed. You've been teaching at the grade school here ever since. The kids all love you. You occasionally help your dad during the summers with his historical restoration business. You've dated Rory Bales—a junior high science teacher—for the past three years. You usually go to Martha's Vineyard for three weeks during the summer." He took a deep breath. "You want me to go on?"

She realized her mouth was hanging open and closed it. "How? Why?"

"Because you're important to me." He put his hands on her shoulders. "Because you're one of the few truly good things that has ever been in my life."

She looked up at him. For a long time, neither one of them moved. Ellis didn't think she could. His touch felt so right, so natural. And it kindled little fires all over her body.

Afraid he'd see the yearning in her eyes, she rested her forehead on his chest, breathing in the scent of him.

He put a finger beneath her chin and raised her face to his. He kissed her lightly on the lips. Then he let her go and stepped away.

"Why didn't you say good-bye?" she asked.

He looked at the ground. "Because I couldn't find the right words."

"Why didn't you ever contact me?"

"Because nothing good could ever come of it." He started around the front of the car to the passenger side. "We need to get the boat back to the plantation."

"Wait." The word was drowned out by the blaring siren of a passing ambulance.

Lucky thing, she realized. Kept her from making a complete fool out of herself.

She got into the driver's seat and started the car, feeling like a balloon that had been overinflated and then, just before it burst, all the air let out of it in a rush.

Chapter Fourteen

Just as Ellis and Nate were pulling into her driveway, her cell phone rang.

"Oh, crap." She braked and lifted herself in her seat to dig her phone from her back pocket. Just as she taught her students, whenever possible, she kept her phone on her body and not buried in some purse or backpack where it would do little good in an emergency. "I forgot I was supposed to call Dad back."

When she'd spoken to him after her uncle's surprise visit this morning, she'd explained everything to him—Nate's return, the man under the tree. He'd once again campaigned for her to leave town. Once she'd explained that if Alexander was stalking her, he'd most likely just follow, her dad had said he'd take time off work to stay with her.

Her dad did architectural historical restoration and worked pretty much alone. He'd just started a project at the local movie theater that had significant penalties for not meeting deadlines. He couldn't afford to take time off. So she'd assured him, rightly or not, that Nate would be with her at all times until they figured out what was going on with Alexander.

Luckily, her dad had never seen Nate in the same shadowy light that Uncle Greg had. Still, she was to call and report in regularly. One of those times was supposed to be as soon as she'd finished teaching her class.

She flipped open her phone. "Sorry, Dad, I forgot. Not to worry, I'm fine."

"Ellis." Her mother's voice sounded shaky.

Ellis's heart dropped like a rock in a river. "What's wrong?"

"I'm at Beachcrest Hospital. Your dad's had an accident."

"What kind of accident?" *Oh, God, the ambulance.*

"The scaffolding he was working on collapsed."

"How is he?" Ellis threw the car in reverse and backed out of the drive.

Her mother sniffed. "They're going to operate on his right leg, but they want the orthopedic specialist from Charleston to do it. He's got some cuts; they're doing more X-rays. . . ."

"I'm on my way." She turned to Nate as she closed her phone. She stopped the car and shifted into drive. "Get out. I have to get to the hospital."

"Your dad?" he asked.

"Scaffolding he was on collapsed."

"Then let's go."

"You said you had to get the boat back—"

"You're wasting time," he said. "Drive."

Ellis saw her mother through the wide glass doors that led to the emergency waiting room. Her arms were folded across her middle, and she was pacing slowly back and forth in front of a section of empty chairs. She looked small and alone.

Ellis was moving so quickly, the automatic doors had not opened when she reached the threshold. Nate snagged her elbow, keeping her from slamming into them. She waited a half second and the doors slid open with a swish.

Her mother looked up. The gratitude on her face made Ellis's heart turn inside out.

"How is he?" Ellis asked, wrapping her mom in a quick, fierce hug.

"He's going to be okay. But he needs surgery on his leg. . . ." She picked at the tissue in her hand. "He's in radiology again. They're supposed to call me when he's back down here."

Her mother's gaze shifted over Ellis's shoulder, looking at Nate.

"Mom, you remember Nate."

A thousand questions flashed in her mother's eyes, but Ellis maneuvered her toward a chair. "How did this happen?"

Nate hung back near the entrance.

"I'm not sure," her mother said. "Howie said they'd been using the scaffolding in that same place for two days. He had no idea what made it give way."

"Was Howie up there too? Is he hurt?" Howie was a kid just out of high school who had been working with her dad for the past six months.

Ellis glanced at Nate. He was surveying every entrance to the waiting room like a . . . a bodyguard. Maybe that's what he did. Maybe he guarded a celebrity or a political figure. . . .

Her mother's voice drew her from her suppositions. "No, thank goodness. He was still unloading the truck."

"Where is he?" Ellis looked around. The waiting area held only two other people, an elderly man and woman. The man had his finger wrapped in a bloody dishtowel.

"I asked him to stay at the site and pick up the tools and lock them in Bill's truck. He needed something to do, other than pace around and worry me to death."

Her mother was her practical self. How reassuring that was. Ellis supposed no matter how old she got, she'd always look to her mother for a steadying hand.

That feeling made her think of Nate. Had he ever had a person he could count on no matter what? Someone who would hold it together for him when everything fell apart? It certainly hadn't been in Belle Island as he'd grown up. He'd stood alone when the sheriff and the entire town had thought he'd hurt Laura. His mother hadn't even stopped him when he'd dropped out of school three months before graduation—right after Alexander's trial.

At that time, Ellis had seen Nate as a man already. But he'd been no more than a boy—younger than Howie, even. And Ellis couldn't imagine Howie living on his own, let alone taking off to places unknown by himself.

She wished she could go back. Go back and find the courage to defy her parents openly, to stand up in front of the whole town as Nate's friend. Maybe then he wouldn't have left.

How different would both their lives have been if he'd stayed? It was a question with no answer.

An hour passed while they awaited her father's return

from radiology. Nate kept a polite distance. Yet he was never out of Ellis's peripheral vision. Her adrenaline-fueled panic had receded. Still, something inside her vibrated with awareness when Nate's gaze moved in her direction. It was as if his gaze, his attention, bore a physical property of its own—one only she seemed aware of.

Her mother had grown quiet, allowing Ellis's mind to wander.

She realized this was the first time she'd been in this building since Laura had been moved to the rehab facility. The distinctive smell of the hospital blurred the lines between past and present, triggering feelings Ellis thought she'd beaten into submission long ago.

She sat thinking, running her finger over the faint ridge of scar under her chin.

Beachcrest Hospital, July, sixteen years ago
Two weeks after Laura was attacked

Ellis's family had begun to treat *her* like she was in a coma. She'd become invisible, a nonperson. Just another fixture in the room.

Not that she minded. It gave her better opportunity to listen to things she wouldn't be able to otherwise. Nobody wanted to tell her anything about the investigation or the details of what happened to Laura. Ellis picked up what she could and tried to piece it together so she could tell Nate later.

She was sitting in the chair in the corner of Laura's

hospital room, where she'd been reading for the past two hours. The phone on Laura's bedside table rang.

Uncle Greg answered it.

"Hello, Detective." This was followed by several short "Uh-huhs" and "I sees" and Uncle Greg's face growing red.

Ellis sat as still as a rabbit caught in the open.

He hung up and stood there for a few seconds with his hands on his hips, staring at the phone like he'd like nothing better than to rip it from the wall and slam it onto the floor.

Aunt Jodi started to cry again, even before she knew what the call was about.

Finally, Uncle Greg said, "Looks like there's not much hope of any DNA or blood evidence. The salt water—" He pressed his lips together and brought a hand to his eyes. Then he turned his back.

Ellis expected her aunt to go to him. But she didn't. She stood planted right where she was, between Ellis's mom and dad. She kept repeating, "What does that mean? What does it mean?"

Uncle Greg spun back around and shouted, "It means it's gonna be that much harder to nail that little bastard's hide to the wall."

Ellis flinched. He was talking about Nate.

Her dad asked, "What about fingerprints?"

The police had taken Ellis's fingerprints, as well as the rest of the family and Laura's friends, in order to isolate ones that could belong to the person who cut the screen to her room.

They'd taken Nate's. Somehow, Ellis didn't think they were using his for elimination.

Uncle Greg said, "Still processing them."

If the police arrested Nate and stopped looking, they'd

never find the guy Ellis saw between the houses that night.

If only she'd yelled when she'd seen him. Dear God, if only she'd hung her head over the edge of the top bunk to look for Laura, she'd have known her cousin was gone. If only . . . Those two words had been eating her alive.

Her dad asked, "What about the nylon stocking they found in the path?"

"He said they've sent it to the state lab but not to hold our breath."

"What about"—her dad paused—"semen?"

Now she knew they'd forgotten she was here.

Uncle Greg said, "Must have used a condom."

Aunt Jodi ran into the tiny bathroom and closed the door.

If Nate had wanted to have sex with Laura, he wouldn't have had to beat her up to do it. Ellis wasn't completely dense. She'd seen them sneaking around, Nate walking Laura up from the beach and helping her back in her window plenty of nights.

But Ellis wasn't about to tell her uncle that. It wouldn't help Nate.

"Nate Vance raped and beat my little girl," her uncle said through clenched teeth. "He's got to pay—DNA or no DNA."

Ellis felt like she was going to throw up.

She jumped up. "It wasn't Nate!"

Uncle Greg and Daddy both turned to her, looking startled.

"I told them what I saw!" she said.

"Sweetie," Daddy said, coming toward her. "Let's go to the cafeteria—"

"I don't understand why nobody will listen to me!" Ellis stood rigid, with her hands fisted at her sides.

"The police know what they're doing," Daddy said.

"But I saw him. I *smelled* him. It wasn't Nate!"

Uncle Greg said, "I don't get this *smelling him*." She could tell he was trying not to yell. "How could you smell him when he was outside, fifteen feet from the house?"

"You know Momma says I've got a dog's sense of smell. And maybe he'd been *closer* to the window and was moving away."

"The police know what you said. They'll handle it." Uncle Greg sounded mad.

Daddy put a hand on her shoulder. "We know you like Nate. But you're just a child. There are things . . ." He sighed. "It was dark, Ellis. People use that path all the time. You didn't see this man *with* Laura; you were sleepy—"

"Dad! Stop!" She turned around and ran out of the room.

Now she knew she could never tell the rest of it.

She went past the nurse's station and the elevators. For a few minutes, she hung out in the little lounge, staring at a wall-mounted TV with muted sound, not really seeing it. She heard the nurses talking at their station and the elevator *ding* as the doors opened and closed.

She had to calm down. She wouldn't do Nate any good by yelling and running away.

After a few minutes, she headed back to Laura's room. She had to convince them to *listen* to her.

She rounded the corner.

That's when she smelled it.

Her head snapped up. She stopped dead and sniffed.

It was that same too-strong cologne and sour-sweat smell.

A light-haired guy wearing a baseball cap was turning away from Laura's door, as if he'd been peeking through the sliver of a crack.

Ellis ran toward him. "Hey!" she called, trying to get him to turn around.

He moved faster.

As she ran past Laura's room, she slammed her palm against the door. "Dad! Dad! It's him!"

The guy sprinted toward the stairwell at the end of the hall.

Ellis ran after him.

She heard her dad call, "Ellis!"

"It's him!" she shouted, running.

The guy disappeared through the door to the stairs.

Her uncle passed her.

Ellis heard her dad calling for her to stop.

She hit the stairs at a run.

She saw her uncle a half flight down.

A door slammed below.

She caught her heel on a step and pitched forward. Lightning struck her chin as she fell onto the landing.

Before she could get up, her dad was there. He knelt next to her and held her down. "You're bleeding."

She struggled to get up. "It's him! The man I saw!"

"You're *sure* you recognized him?"

"It was him. I smelled him." She got to her feet, but her dad held her arm, preventing her from taking off. "Why else would he run?"

"Uncle Greg will get him. Let's get you back up to the nurse's station. Your chin is bleeding."

She nodded.

The second her dad's grip lessened, she broke free and took off down the stairs.

"Ellis!"

She heard her dad's thudding footsteps behind her.

The ground-level door opened into the lobby area.

People were pointing and staring at the front doors. She jumped over a little kid putting a puzzle together on the floor and sprinted for the entrance.

Once on the curb, she scanned the parking lot.

She heard tires squealing and metal crunching off to the right.

Her uncle was running after a white Taurus. He finally stopped, bending over with his hands on his knees.

Ellis caught up. "He got away."

Her uncle raised his face. "I got the license plate number."

"Thank God!" Ellis looked down at her shirtfront. No wonder her dad was freaked. "I guess I'd better . . ." She took a step and everything faded to black.

In sixteen years, the memory hadn't dimmed.

Ellis stopped rubbing the scar on her chin. How different things would have turned out if that call hadn't come exactly when it had, if she hadn't gotten in an argument with her family. The police might never have found a match to that fingerprint on the outside of Laura's window.

Nate stood near the emergency room door, blending

into the background, keeping sentinel over her. He was right. It could so easily have been him on trial.

She closed her eyes and suppressed a shiver.

"You okay?" her mother asked.

How could she admit she'd been sitting here thinking of Nate and not her father? "Just worried about Dad."

Her mother patted her hand. "He'll be fine. He was lucky he didn't land on his head." She leaned closer and lowered her voice. "It's not as hard as I always tell him it is."

Ellis chuckled.

The door opened to the emergency area. A nurse wearing blue scrubs and a stethoscope said, "Mrs. Greene?"

Ellis and her mother stood.

"Y'all can come back now."

Ellis was halfway to the door when she looked over her shoulder. Nate was right behind her.

He said quietly, "I'll wait just outside his exam area." He held the door, then followed her in.

Ellis didn't know what she expected when she stepped through the curtain into the small examination room that held her dad's gurney—his usual cheery hello? The reality of his condition slammed into her like a baseball bat to the chest.

His eyes were hooded and cloudy. His constant fidgeting attested to the strength of his pain. One side of his face was scraped raw from cheekbone to chin. His right arm was in a sling. His right leg was wrapped, the dressing soaked through with blood.

His gaze ran briefly across her, but he didn't speak.

Her mother moved to his side.

Ellis stood rooted in place. She swayed. Her vision

tunneled. The color bled from everything, leaving only dimming shades of gray.

She had to get out of here before she fell flat.

Turning, she batted the curtain away.

When she took that first step, her knees buckled.

Arms went around her.

Nate's voice seemed so far away. "I've got you."

She was hot, so hot.

"Here," someone said. "Breathe this. Open your eyes for me now."

The sharp scent of ammonia jabbed her nose and sinuses. She tried to turn away from the odor.

"Come on, baby, just one more sniff," Nate said against her ear.

She mumbled, "I don't faint. I'm not a fainter."

"We know," Nate said softly.

Her body began to return to her. "I'm okay now."

Although Ellis was beginning to feel steady enough to walk on her own, she leaned heavily against Nate's side. Hot only a moment ago, the air-conditioning now chilled her skin, and she welcomed his warmth. At least that was the basis of her justification. In truth, she longed to be wrapped in his arms, to rest her head on his shoulder, and pretend they were in some other place, brought together by different circumstances.

They went through the waiting area and out the same automatic doors they'd entered earlier.

"There's a bench over there." She pointed to a shaded area tucked between two wings of the building. It was a "meditation garden" donated by the local Kiwanis a few years ago. It seemed purely ornamental; each time Ellis had driven by on her way to a doctor's appointment, she'd wondered if anyone ever used it. Now she knew. It was the perfect place to hide from the ugly reality of what went on inside the hospital walls.

A breeze whispered through the trees, making the temperature in the shade comfortable. Nate sat down with her, keeping his arm firmly around her shoulders.

They sat in silence for a while. Finally, she said, "I really don't faint. I don't know what's wrong with me. It's just I've never seen him so . . ." She shook her head.

"Why do you do that?" he asked.

"What?" She looked over at his profile.

He turned toward her, their faces inches apart. She couldn't help but watch his lips as he spoke. "Not allow yourself to be like the rest of us mortals."

"I don't know what you mean," she lied. She couldn't tell him that she feared if she let go of her control, even for a moment, she would never regain it.

When she would have looked away, he took her chin between a bent finger and his thumb, holding her still. "You don't have to be the strong one. Not while I'm here."

He leaned closer, that steady silver gaze halting the breath in her lungs and the blood in her veins. His lips brushed hers, once, twice, in a feathery light touch.

Her hand moved to the side of his neck and felt his strong, rapid pulse. When she opened her mouth to his questioning kiss, his arm tightened around her, and he tasted her like a man starved.

"I assume you discovered who left you that rose." Rory's voice came from behind her.

She jerked guiltily away from Nate. "Rory . . ."

He stood at the entrance to the garden. His tone had been even, but his face was deep red.

She rolled her lips inward, as if she could draw Nate's kiss inside where Rory couldn't see it.

Nate stood, leaving a hand on her shoulder.

"I ran into Howie downtown," Rory said, his words clipped. "Why didn't you call me about your dad?"

She should have. Rory and her dad were close. But calling Rory hadn't even crossed her mind.

She couldn't tell him that. "I was waiting to see when they're going to do the surgery."

"I see." His gaze lingered on Nate.

"Um, this is Nate Vance, an old friend."

Rory stepped forward and offered his hand. "Rory Bales." His eyes were not friendly, but his tone was cordial.

There was something about Rory's nonreaction that made Ellis feel insignificant, cheated. Would she have felt better if he had punched Nate in the nose?

Of course not; that would be childish. Still . . .

It struck her that she'd never been so swept away by Rory's kiss, even in the beginning.

Blushing, she told Rory, "Go on in. I'll be there in a second."

He turned and left without another word.

She waited until he was long out of sight before turning back to Nate.

"Does he always do whatever you tell him to do?" Nate asked coolly.

Ellis's defenses came up. "He's being considerate and a gentleman."

Nate looked at her, his eyes snapping. "If you were mine, I sure as hell wouldn't slink away without a fight."

His tone sent shivers down her body—excited shivers.

Shame prompted her next words. "Luckily, I don't *belong* to anyone. Rory's giving me the space I asked for; we're taking a break."

Nate stepped closer and ran the back of his fingers down her cheek. The look in his eyes held her in place; the feel of his touch reached much deeper than the surface of her skin. "He's a fool." The low-spoken words whispered across her nerve endings.

The power of the moment left her temporarily stunned. She fought the compulsion to say things that couldn't be recalled—foolish, fanciful, romantic things. Things with no foundation in reality.

She swallowed dryly and said, "I-I'd better go back in."

She turned and started away, guilt nipping at her heels. She'd let her guard down with Nate in a way she never had with Rory. She *trusted* Nate. Nate who'd deserted her years ago and had just blown in on the wind, not Rory who'd patiently worked to earn the trust she stingily withheld.

"Ellis," Nate called after her.

She turned.

"What was that about discovering who left the rose?" He hadn't moved to follow her.

She'd forgotten. "There was a rose on my car when I finished teaching class yesterday." *Some things are worth waiting for.* "I thought Rory had left it. . . ." She didn't finish; she wasn't about to admit that she thought Rory had misled her when she'd asked him.

"And you don't know who did?"

"No." She turned and hurried away, trying to deny what she saw in Nate's eyes.

The idea that it had been Rory's attempt to manipulate her was only slightly less unsettling than the thought that the rose had been left by Alexander.

Nate let Ellis return to the hospital emergency room ahead of him, trailing behind yet keeping her in his line of sight.

He should be ashamed of himself. He'd wanted her boyfriend to think they were lovers. He'd stood there with an air of possession of something that didn't belong to him—no matter how much he was beginning to want it.

Instead of following Ellis through the double doors that led to the treatment area, Nate lingered in the waiting room. Too agitated to sit, he stood, leaning his back against the wall with his arms crossed over his chest. He stared at the television, but the only image in his mind was Ellis's face.

He had no right to come here and insinuate himself into her life. Not only was his future not his own, but his presence also brought additional risk. There were people in his world who wouldn't hesitate to use her. That's why he never got close to anyone . . . and why he'd buried his connection to this town. He hoped someday he could return and live a normal life—if that day didn't come, he'd need a place to hide.

Chapter Fifteen

Hollis walked quietly in the dark night. He kept to the shadows created by the tall shrubbery bordering the deep, narrow lot on which Justine's house sat. He needed supplies for tonight's project, things he couldn't keep at the halfway house, things he couldn't risk keeping in his van.

He'd been hinting around to Justine about how much he'd love a digital camera. With a digital camera, he wouldn't even need a darkroom any longer.

He'd told her about the Nikon SLR with the telescopic lens that would be perfect for his wildlife photography. *Wildlife.* Wild life. Too true. He sniggered at his own play on words. A camera like that cost serious money. And his cash was going for more urgent needs at the moment.

Her eyes had lit up when he'd talked of his passion for photography and his dream camera. He hoped she gifted him soon, or she was going to miss her chance.

He thought of the technological advances he'd been denied while in prison. Digital cameras . . . what a miracle. And just one of many things he'd missed out on. The Internet opened a whole world of opportunity.

Not for the first time, he damned his infatuation with

Laura Reinhardt. She'd muddled his judgment, made him take risks he never would have considered for another woman. He hadn't been able to resist going to the hospital; the need to look at her broken and bruised had burned like a fever. It should have been safe. And it would have been, if not for that screaming kid.

Well, she'd pay. No good deed went unpunished.

He sniggered again as he dug in his pocket for the key.

Turning on his flashlight, he slipped in through the basement door.

The basement was safe. There was no lift to bring Justine to this level, and the outside door was down in a well of five steep steps.

He went to the coal-bin door and unlocked the padlock.

Humming softly to himself, he gathered what he needed: compact binoculars, latex gloves (another wonderful improvement, latex gloves available at every drugstore), stolen license plate, knife—

"Hollis?" Justine's strained voice called from the door on the first floor. "Are you down there?"

He froze, holding his breath. Damn woman was always upstairs by this time in the evening.

"Is anybody there?" she called again, with less conviction.

Hollis waited.

Finally, he heard her mumble, "Must be my imagination."

The door at the top of the stairs closed. He heard the lock—which was never engaged—slide home.

Oh, yes, can't be too careful. He barely suppressed a chuckle.

After a minute, he heard the drone of the lift carrying her to the second story, and he got on with his business.

❦

At eleven-thirty, Nate and Ellis walked across the hospital parking lot toward her car. The specialist from Charleston had finished surgery on her dad around five in the afternoon. It had gone well.

Shortly after the surgery, Ellis and Rory had had a private conversation. Ellis had returned without him and in an unreadable mood. Questions about their relationship had gnawed at Nate as he'd watched them throughout the afternoon. It didn't matter that it was none of his business.

As he and Ellis walked through the muggy night, he held out his hand. "I'll drive."

She looked like she was going to argue, then handed over the keys. "How is it you're still so chipper? You don't even have dark circles under your eyes."

"I'm used to going without sleep." He unlocked the Mustang and opened the passenger door for her. "You know," he said, "your choice of cars surprised me."

"Why?" She stopped in front of him and looked up.

His heart sort of stumbled in his chest when she looked up at him like that, her green eyes sparkling, her lips slightly parted as if inviting a kiss.

And he wanted to. Kiss her until Rory disappeared completely from her mind and her heart.

She isn't yours to kiss.

He took a slight step back, and she got in the car. "You

always were all about the environment. I expected a nice earth-friendly hybrid, not a muscle machine."

"You'll note it's even a GT. I want some power when I step on the gas."

Nate easily read between the lines. Ellis lived her life with a constant eye to personal safety. She wanted a car that could outrun, or run over, anyone who threatened her.

As they drove, he decided the decent thing to do was apologize for stepping across a line and making a problem for her with Rory. He didn't really want to. He wanted to make his air of possession something more than a mirage. But it was wrong. He was leaving, and Rory was a safe, stable guy who could give her a future.

As he turned to speak, her head, already leaning against the passenger window, bobbed. Her eyes were closed.

He was glad not to deal with the subject. The less he thought about Ellis with another man, the better.

He pulled her car into the garage.

She roused as soon as he shut off the engine, blinking sleepily. "Sorry, I dozed off."

He nearly reached out to brush the hair from her face but stopped himself. He wasn't going to take any more advantage of her emotional state, no matter how much he wanted to carry her upstairs and crawl into bed next to her. The mere thought of curling himself against her bare back and holding her throughout the night made him shift uncomfortably in his seat.

He smiled, hoping she hadn't read the carnal look in his eye. "Hospitals are exhausting. Let's get you upstairs." He opened the door and got out before he gave in to the weakness he was quickly developing for her.

After closing the garage door, he followed her on the walk around the corner of the building to the stairs, trying not to notice the graceful sway of her hips.

He put the key in the lock and opened the door.

He entered first and then allowed her to step around him and shut off the alarm.

After closing the door and locking it, he started a systematic search of the condo. "I need to get the boat out of here before the tide goes out. I should only be gone a couple of hours."

Ellis followed along behind him as he checked the condo. She was so tired; he didn't think she realized what she was doing.

Once he'd inspected under the bed, behind the shower curtain, and in every closet, he returned to the front door. "Try to get some sleep while I'm gone. And keep the gun on your nightstand. Remember, shoot first, ask questions later. Lock the door and set the alarm behind me. You have my cell number if you need me. Don't answer the door. I'll call you when I'm back. And be sure to check the peephole before you open up."

"Now if a bedtime lecture like that won't lull a girl into a restful night's sleep, I don't know what will."

Even dog-tired the girl showed spunk. He grinned and slipped his hands into his jeans pockets to keep from touching her.

She smiled an exhausted smile and let him out.

He stood outside until he heard the dead bolt slide home and the *beep-beep-beep-beep* of her alarm.

After checking for, and not finding, Alexander anywhere on the grounds, Nate climbed the fence by the marsh and untied the aluminum johnboat. The tide was already going out; he had to push it into water deep enough to start the motor.

There were a few things stashed at the plantation that he needed, things Ellis didn't need to know about. It was time to go on the offensive.

Once out into the water, he climbed in, slick with mud and wet to the waist. He pushed the little motor to its limits as he navigated through the marsh to the river. He looked up into the clear night sky. He knew how to navigate by the stars, but it took him a few minutes to reorient himself to the northern hemisphere.

When this was all done, he would go back to his life. He'd thought he was content with his choices. Now . . .

One thing was certain—he had to get back to that life, before it came looking for him.

❧

Ellis roused from sleep and blinked to focus her eyes on the digital time readout on the cable box beneath her TV. Four-thirty.

Why wasn't Nate back?

Tip-tap.

The sound was barely audible under the hum of her air conditioner.

Tap.

She sat up on the sofa where she'd fallen asleep with the light on.

Holding very still, she listened. She could hear the soft buffet of the breeze against her windows, the hushed murmur as it rounded the corner of her building, and the tinkle of the wind chime on her downstairs neighbor's balcony.

She switched off the lamp and moved to the sliding glass door.

She'd never installed window coverings on the slider; there was no traffic this deep in the complex and nothing but trees and marshland across the street. That was one of the things she'd liked about this place; she could always keep an eye on what was going on outside. But now, with Alexander out there, she realized how exposed she'd left herself.

Keeping a foot or so back from the glass, she studied the darkness outside. The black outline of treetops moved against the cloudy night sky.

She concentrated on the area beneath the old oak where she'd seen the cigarette glow but saw nothing.

Tip-tap.

She spun around. The sound was coming from her front door, or near it. Faint, yet definitely there.

Digging in her pocket, she pulled out her cell phone and dialed Nate's number.

As it rang, she inched closer to the entry.

"The phone you are trying to reach is not in service."

"Damn," she whispered. Where was he?

Tiptoeing over to her thermostat, she shut off the AC. There wasn't anything she could do to quiet the wind.

Turning her head so one ear was toward the door, she waited.

Finally, *tap.* It was so soft this time that she almost didn't hear it.

Scriiiitch. Tip-tap.

Moving as if approaching a sleeping tiger, she neared the door and leaned to look out the peephole.

The fish-eyed view showed her porch to be clear.

Tap.

Was something up against the door, too low for her to see?

There was no way she was opening it to find out.

She waited for several minutes in silence. Just as she turned away from the door, *tap.*

It had to be something to do with the wind.

Moving quickly through the darkness, she retrieved the gun, just in case she was wrong.

Then she sat on her sofa and stared at the white outline of her front door.

Where in the hell was Nate? Had he run into Alexander? With the way Nate had disarmed her the other night, she assured herself, he could handle Hollis Alexander.

Worry continued to stir in her mind. Maybe Alexander had been waiting out there by the boat. Maybe he'd ambushed Nate.

Her stomach churned.

There was nothing to do but wait for dawn.

A sharp noise jerked Ellis awake. With a quick, startled breath, she grabbed the gun and sat up straight.

Blinking, she realized it was the telephone—and that it was daylight.

Pain stabbed in her neck from having fallen asleep slumped in the corner of her sofa.

She snatched up the phone. "Nate?"

"I'm on my way. I ran into a little snag," he said. "Don't leave there without me."

"Thank God you're all right." Her insides quivered with relief.

"Has something happened?" Alarm colored his voice.

With a tension-relieving sigh, she said, "No. But you said you'd only be gone a short while. And I tried to call. . . ." Her voice trembled. Now that she knew he was safe, she realized just how terrified of losing him she'd been.

"Sorry. The boat motor cut out, and my flashlight went dead, so I couldn't find the damn screwdriver to fix it. It's a freakin' long way to paddle against the outgoing tide."

"Why didn't you call?" Anxiety channeled quickly over to irritation.

"While I was groping around trying to find the screwdriver in the dark, my phone fell out of my pocket into the water."

"What are you calling on now?"

"I have another one; it wasn't with me." Before she could question him, he said, "Listen, I'm almost to the gate. Call security and tell them to let me in. I'm driving a black Hummer."

What kind of person has more than one cell phone? "Why didn't you call me as soon as you got to the plantation?"

"I didn't want to wake you."

She shot to her feet. "Goddammit! You think I could go to bed when you were out there possibly in trouble?"

"You were supposed to be asleep long before you would have even considered I was in trouble."

She gritted her teeth and growled. Then she hung up on him.

After she called the gate, she stood at the sliding glass door and waited.

When he stepped out of that shiny black Hummer, her heart took a skipping lap around her chest.

He looked up and saw her watching. He grinned. Dear Lord in heaven, what that smile did to her. It cooled her anger and warmed her heart. The hours away from him and the worry that he'd been hurt had acted as a crucible, burning away everything except the purest of emotions. It was startling to realize just how much she wanted him.

She reminded herself that not only was she pissed at him, but also that he'd been her cousin's boyfriend. Sure, it had been a lifetime ago, but something still felt just a little taboo about lusting after him.

She used those feelings to mask what was in her heart. She could not open that door with her desire for him running wild. Nate was far too perceptive not to notice.

Standing at the door, she waited. When she saw him through the peephole, she jerked it open. "You're lucky I don't shoot you —"

The look on his face dried her words in her throat. Following his gaze, her breath stopped when she saw what had been tapping against her front door.

Chapter Sixteen

Nate's throat was tight when he said, "Are these like the one you found on your car?"

Revulsion shone in Ellis's eyes as she stared at the cluster of long-stemmed roses. They hung from her door knocker by a length of black ribbon. Their petals were bruised and withered, darkening their color to that of dried blood.

A note dangled from the ribbon. Nate knelt to read it.

Still waiting . . .

"Yes." Her answer was a low whisper. She wrapped her arms around her middle. "I thought . . ." She bit her lip.

Nate reached out, pulled her into his arms, and held her shaking body tight against him. She buried her face against his shoulder and sighed, the warmth of her breath reaching the skin beneath his shirt.

Stroking her hair, he wished he could make all of her hurt, all of her fear, go away.

"I shouldn't have left you alone." God, what if Alexander had wanted to do more than leave a disturbing message? A dark sickness the color of those battered roses welled in Nate's gut.

She pulled away. "I was safe . . . the alarm . . . the

gun. He wouldn't have hurt me." Her trembling had stopped. The inner strength that had always amazed Nate reemerged; it shone in her eyes and was written in her posture.

As much as he admired her strength, a little part of him wanted her to *need* him.

He gave a quick nod. "Call the police. Let's see if he left us anything useful."

As Ellis made the call, Nate studied the rose and the door knocker more closely. The brass knocker was a horseshoe; he wondered if Ellis had chosen it because of her love for horses or for good luck.

Ellis doesn't count on luck.

He nudged the door closed with his foot and joined her in the kitchen.

"They're sending someone right away," she said. Her fingers lingered near her lips. It looked like she was going to speak again.

"What?" he prompted.

"Nothing." She turned away and started making coffee.

Nate watched her carefully. She was tired. Maybe he wasn't reading her right. Still, something seemed hidden in those eyes, as if there was something she wasn't telling him.

Fifteen minutes later, a Belle Island police officer arrived and took Ellis's statement. The man seemed distracted, in a hurry. It was clear he didn't view two mysterious appearances of roses as a threat to person or property—even after they explained Hollis Alexander to him.

He bagged the roses and took several fingerprints from

the knocker and the doorknob. He left with a reminder for Ellis to be cautious and the air of a man who wanted to be someplace else.

Ellis crossed her arms over her chest and watched him descend the stairs. "Well, that was a waste of time."

Nate lifted a shoulder. "Maybe, maybe not. Maybe we'll get lucky with one of those fingerprints."

Ellis scoffed.

"We're not any worse off than if we hadn't called them," Nate said. "At least now it's on record."

"Uh-huh." Ellis didn't sound convinced. "I've got to get ready for class."

⁂

Greg was in the shower, washing off the fatigue of his long night, when his cell phone rang. He reached out, wiped his hand on a towel, and picked the phone off the top of the toilet tank. Looking at the ID, he saw it was Bradley.

Greg answered, "What do you have for me?"

"More than you can guess."

Greg shut off the water.

"Some stuff with this guy isn't matching up." Excitement built in Bradley's voice. "On the surface, everything is legit. He was in the marines and now works security for an international shipping and courier company. But, when you scratch just a little deeper, the guy has some serious money, too much tucked away in too many holding companies and offshore accounts for a man in his position."

"And?" Greg prompted.

"And?" Bradley mocked. "Dude, *international ship-*

ping. Big money in moving illegal crap—drugs, weapons, stolen goods, people. Very lucrative. Why else hide the money?" Bradley paused, as if letting Greg catch up with his line of thinking. Then he said, "If this guy isn't being investigated by the government, he needs to be."

Greg had never been so glad he'd followed his gut instinct. He'd ignored it once, and the result had cost him everything. Never again.

He had to get Nate Vance away from Ellis.

⁂

As Nate drove Ellis to the park, he seemed to be retreating further from her with each rotation of the wheels. His hands gripped the wheel just a little too tightly. His attention cut to the rearview mirror a little too often. The steady hum of the all-terrain tires was the only noise in the car. The drone faded and returned with every stop sign, each time emphasizing the lack of conversation just a little more.

Not that she wanted to talk. It would be hard to discuss what was going on and not expose her underlying worry that Rory was behind the roses. Right now, she was too tired to think clearly, let alone decipher a mystery. She had to save what energy she had to help her girls.

She watched out of the passenger window as they drove through downtown. People around here drove nice mid-priced sedans, minivans, and pickup trucks. This wide-stanced black Hummer stood out like a combat helmet on a beauty queen.

Nate pulled into the park's gravel parking lot. It was shaded by the wide reach of the live oaks. Some of these trees were well over three hundred years old and had branches larger than most tree trunks. Ellis always felt insignificant, a tiny speck in the vastness of time, when she stood beneath their boughs.

Nate had been the first to make her see the oaks that way. She looked over at him and wondered if he still felt that way about them. Maybe later, when his face didn't look so stony, she'd ask.

Looking around the lot, Ellis noticed a couple of cars parked a bit farther down with drivers sitting behind the wheel. She recognized the closest one as Chelsea Obermeir's mother. She was glad to see parents being extra vigilant; her warnings about Hollis Alexander had made an impact.

She gathered her backpack from the floorboard and climbed down out of the Hummer. Chelsea's mom lifted a hand in a rather tentative wave. Ellis waved back as she headed for the spot where the girls had already gathered for class.

She'd gone about ten feet when she turned to see Nate climbing up to sit on the hood of his vehicle. Even though he was wearing sunglasses, she could tell he was scanning the area. He paid particular attention to the dense woods at the edge of the park.

She looked in that direction. The thought that Alexander could be hidden there watching sent an icy finger of revulsion down her spine. For some reason, even though it was daylight, the thought of him skulking around when she was out in the open was much more disturbing than him looking through her windows in the dead of night.

As soon as she got near the girls, they all started talking at once.

"You were right, Ms. Greene!"

"Oh, my God, did you hear?"

"It was on the news, but my mom already knew because—"

Ellis held up her hands. "Whoa! Slow down."

Jessie Baker stepped up as spokeswoman. "You were right about us needing to be careful. A girl was attacked and killed last night." Her eyes were huge and her face grave. "It was on the morning news."

Ellis went cold; her skin felt the stab of a thousand tiny needles. The distraction of the police officer now made sense.

It was impossible to think this attack was unrelated to Alexander. If he left the roses, he was definitely in Belle Island last night.

Chelsea Obermeir added, "My uncle's a cop, and he called my mom this morning. The girl's roommate found her on the beach at Seaside Apartments this morning."

With numb lips, Ellis asked, "Did your uncle say if they had any idea who did it?"

"He just told my mom not to let me go anywhere by myself."

"He's right. None of you girls should." Ellis quickly reorganized today's lesson in her mind. What would be the most valuable defense tactic she could give these girls? "I see some of your mothers brought you. Did anyone walk here alone?"

They chorused, "No way!"

"Good. Good." She set down her bag. "Listen, I want you all to pair up and practice your defense of an attack from behind, like we did yesterday. I'll be right back."

She trotted over to Nate.

He slid off the hood and stood, removing his sunglasses. His gray eyes were as sharp as a surgical blade and his body rigidly tense.

"Did you know a woman was killed last night?" she asked.

She could see the muscles in his jaw tighten as he clenched his teeth.

"Where?" he asked.

"Seaside Apartments. She was found on the beach this morning."

He scanned three-hundred-sixty degrees. "Okay. You should be all right here for a while. I'm going to go see what I can find out. I'll be back before your class is finished."

"Okay."

He made her double-check to make certain she had his new cell number in her phone.

She started away, then stopped and looked back at him. She finally voiced the question that she'd pushed from her mind the instant the girls had shared the news. "Why someone else and not me?"

He stepped closer. "Maybe because you're making it too difficult for him . . ." He blinked slowly and shook his head. Then he gently cupped her cheek. "I really can't say for sure—but I'm damned thankful."

The fierce caring she saw in his eyes made her lightheaded. She'd waited her whole life for someone to look at her like that, as if he'd willingly lay down his life for her.

She swallowed, but her mouth was so dry the muscles in her throat bunched into a knot.

Instead of making a fool of herself by wrapping her

arms around his waist and pressing her ear to his chest to hear if his heart was beating as fast as hers, she whispered, "We have to catch him."

Nate held her gaze and her body responded; heat pooled in some places while shivers ran over others, breathing became an effort. It was becoming an automatic reaction when he looked at her, like Pavlov's dogs.

After a moment, he blinked and said, "We will. I promise you. We will."

Ellis normally saved the lesson about techniques that could leave lasting injuries or be fatal to an attacker until near the end of the course. She bumped that lesson up. She covered blows to the throat and eyes, carefully explaining what areas of those targets were most vulnerable and how to inflict the most damage. She emphasized that when someone means you harm, it's imperative to do the same to them—immediately, while they still think they've taken you by surprise.

The girls nodded and watched with serious eyes as she demonstrated the defense moves. Then she had them pair up and practice the motions.

Ellis had just stepped in to correct one girl's technique when she heard someone pulling into the parking lot much too quickly. She looked up and saw her uncle's Corvette. He braked hard enough that the tires slid in the loose sand and stone. He quickly got out, slammed the door, and stalked toward her.

"Where is he?" he asked from twenty-five feet away.

"Nate?" She told the girls to continue their practice,

then hurried to meet her uncle. Whatever had him worked up, the girls didn't need to hear it.

"Yeah, Nate."

"We heard about the murder. He went to see what he could find out."

"Murder?"

"A woman at Seaside Apartments."

"God*dammit*!" Greg jammed his hands on his hips and turned his head, looking off toward the street. Then he turned back to her. "Alexander?"

"Who else? Let's hope he left evidence."

"I spent the night looking for him. Guess I was in the wrong goddamn place."

Ellis nearly cautioned her uncle that running around alone at night looking for Alexander could be dangerous, but it wouldn't make any difference. In the past week, she'd seen the uncle she'd known vanish, replaced by this hollow-eyed, revenge-seeking wraith.

"Has anyone checked on Aunt Jodi?" Ellis asked.

"I'll have her stay at my place until we know what's what here."

"Uncle Greg, you can't go over there and bully her—"

He raised a hand. "Save it. If she won't stay with me, I'll convince her to stay with Marsha."

"If you didn't know about the murder, why are you here?" She knew her mother had left several messages for him late yesterday, telling him about her father's accident and surgery. She figured he'd be at the hospital this morning.

Greg glanced over his shoulder, toward the parking lot, as if to assure himself no one was within earshot. "I have something important to tell you."

Her scalp prickled with dread. "Oh?"

"Nate Vance is using his job to cover the fact that he's a smuggler."

"What!" She looked around and lowered her voice. "Where in the hell did you get an idea like that?"

Her uncle's eyes looked as if he hadn't slept in days. He probably hadn't. "I *told* you not to trust him."

She didn't say what was on her mind—that her uncle hadn't been exhibiting the kind of judgment she was particularly inclined to rely on of late. This was just another overreaction brought on by stress and fatigue.

"What makes you think he's involved in something illegal?" she asked.

"We're still digging for details. He works for an international shipping corporation. He's got way too much money, and he's trying to hide it."

"What corporation?" This was a detail she wanted to hear.

His gaze shifted away. "I'm not sure."

She closed her eyes and tried to be patient. "So how do you know about his financial status?" Greg had hated Nate from the beginning; all of this crap with Alexander was making her uncle completely crazy.

"I've hired someone to investigate him," he said.

"Who?"

"A private investigator."

There was something in Greg's body language that said he wanted to sidestep this issue, so she pressed. "Where did you come up with this investigator?"

"He works at the dealership, a real whiz with computers. He locates deadbeat dads all the time."

"Bradley Thompson!" she nearly shouted. "You're

using *Bradley Thompson,* the car-wash kid, as a private investigator?" As far as Ellis could tell, Bradley Thompson had a hard time telling reality from the computer games he immersed himself in. She pressed her lips together and shook her head. "Seriously, Uncle Greg! You have to stop this here and now. You can't go around spreading rumors based on Bradley Thompson's perceptions."

"*You're* trusting Nate on *his* word!" The desperation that colored her uncle's voice had her truly concerned. He needed sleep; he was coming apart at the seams. "You can't trust a man like that to protect you. He's got his own agenda; you can bet on it. I'm going to find out what it is."

She rubbed her temple. "Uncle Greg—"

"I don't have documentation yet. I came straight here to warn you."

Outrageous as his actions currently were, her uncle did have her well-being at heart. She took a second to calm herself. "Thank you. I'll be sure to ask him about it when he gets back."

Greg's eyes widened. "Like he's going to admit anything! You need to stay the hell away from him."

"Why do you hate him so much?"

With his mouth pinched tight, he said, "Because he *changed* her. If not for him, Laura would never have crossed paths with a man like Alexander."

"How can you blame Nate? He didn't know Alexander!"

"I don't believe it. It all changed when *he* started hanging around. The secrets. She *changed*."

Ellis hadn't seen any such change. But pity tore at her heart. She put a hand on her uncle's weary-looking shoulder. "Nate told me he works in security. If it's for an international firm, don't you suppose there could be a lot of money in it?"

"He's a criminal. All the signs are there. He was bad news as a kid; he's worse now." A new light dawned in his bloodshot eyes. "I'm going to call the FBI, DEA, and ATF. Maybe they're looking for him."

"Don't let Bradley Thompson make a fool out of you," she said. "Your livelihood depends on your reputation in this town." He'd said as much for as long as she could remember: *I'm a salesman; my best tools are my name and my word.*

She went on, "There's no need to jump to the most incriminating conclusion, even if Bradley isn't inventing all of this to make a buck. Think about it. If Nate's *hiding* from law enforcement, why would he still be hanging around when so many people know he's here?"

She could see a glimmer of rationality surface in her uncle's eyes.

"I don't want you hurt," he said stubbornly.

"I know. And I appreciate it. I *will* talk to him," she said. "If I don't like what I hear, then I'll take the appropriate action."

"With your dad's accident," Greg said with a deeply creased brow, "I'm responsible for you."

"I *am not* a child. I don't need someone to look out for me or to make my decisions for me. I'll take care of this."

Jesus, had he not seen the way she lived her life? She was so damned careful that she barely *had* a life.

Ellis looked around. Mrs. Obermeir was staring at them. "Please go. There's no need to make a huge scene."

He followed her gaze. The Obermeirs were good customers of his.

He took a deep breath, then said quietly, "I promised your mom I'd meet her at the hospital. Come with me."

"Uncle Greg, I'm twenty-nine. I'm currently teaching these girls how to take out a man's eye. I think I can take care of myself."

"I know," he said reluctantly. "If Alexander . . . He threatened you. . . ."

There was no way she was going to tell him about the roses.

"Go on," she said as if placating a child. "Tell Mom I'll be there as soon as my class is finished."

Not giving him an opportunity to argue further, she turned around and returned to her girls. She heard his car start and leave the parking lot.

Twenty minutes later, Nate returned. She was picking up her bag, having just finished talking with Mrs. Obermeir.

He waited for her by the Hummer.

"So," she said as she approached, "what did you find out?"

"The crime scene and the location of the body are still blocked off. The victim was a nineteen-year-old named Kimberly Potter. You know her?"

She shook her head. Had this girl died because Ellis was making herself an impossible target? God, what an awful thought.

Nate said, "The newsfolk milling around say someone heard a loud voice around twelve forty-five that may or may not have been associated with the attack. Her car door was left open, her keys and purse inside. The police aren't releasing any more details at the moment."

"Did you talk to the police yourself?"

"No. Just neighbors and the reporters. Her roommate said Kimberly had been out to some party last night. She didn't know that Kimberly hadn't come home until this morning. She saw Kimberly's car and started looking. She found the body in the dunes."

"Surely, with our reports about Alexander, the police will make the connection."

"You should call again, just to make sure."

She nodded. Maybe this nightmare would be over soon. *And then Nate will be gone.* It was inevitable. But that didn't mean she didn't dread the loss.

After a moment to fortify herself, she said, "My uncle came by a few minutes ago."

He raised a brow.

"I have some questions."

"All right." He took off his sunglasses and looked her in the eyes.

"Uncle Greg's had someone digging for information about you. He says parts of your life don't add up, insists you're involved in something criminal."

"I've told you before; I'm not a criminal," he said coolly.

"That's all? That's all you have to say?" She crossed her arms and glared at him.

"I'm a security consultant for an international company that transports valuable commodities—antiquities, high-dollar collectibles, jewelry, museum pieces, that kind of thing. It's a job that's best done if no one knows who you are or too many details about what you're moving and when you're moving it."

"From countries like South America?" *Where the drugs come from.*

"For one."

"So what is this company's name?"

"Intelliguard. Does that mean anything to you?"

She gave a solemn shake of her head.

"I didn't think so," he said.

"So what you do is legit? No smuggling? No secret bank accounts?"

Something closed off behind his eyes. "I've told you that I'm not a criminal and that I can't discuss the specifics of my work. What more do you want?"

"I just thought you trusted me."

He stared into her eyes for so long, Ellis forgot to breathe. Then he reached out and took her hand in his.

"I trust you more than any other person in my life," he said solemnly. "But that doesn't change the rules of my work." He rubbed the back of her hand lightly with his thumb. "I know your uncle doesn't trust me. He never did. But I swear to you—my life out there has nothing to do with what's going on here. I won't let it touch you. I can keep you safe. Trust me."

She felt herself being pulled into his steady gray gaze. She could see the truth in his soul, the promise in his heart.

For the first time in fifteen years, she took an incautious, uncalculated leap, heedless of where she might land. "I trust you."

Chapter Seventeen

Lorne Buckley received the news of last night's murder in Belle Island the same way most everyone else did—on the morning news. He'd known in his gut that Alexander would go after another victim, but he was stunned the man had done it this soon. It sickened Lorne to think they'd deliberately set him free.

Before he left his house, he called the Belle Island police. He told them of his suspicions and made certain they had a recent photo of Hollis Alexander to work with.

The local authorities were still in the early stages of the crime-scene investigation; the medical examiner had been on scene for only a short time. Officers were conducting interviews and searching for witnesses. They weren't able to give him much beyond what he'd seen on the news. And he supposed until he had a case to construct, the details didn't matter. A young woman had been violated; someone's daughter was dead.

Forty minutes later, he walked into his office. His secretary handed him a sealed envelope. "This came for you a few minutes ago."

He took it. It was blank, no address or postmark, no return address. "Hand-delivered?"

"Yes. One of the girls from Craig Mahoney's office."

Mahoney was a defense attorney, an adversary in the courtroom but a friend in life. They often joked that they would spark a good sitcom. *The Proscutor and the Defense Attorney*, the lawyerly version of *The Odd Couple.*

Lorne went into his office and closed the door. Inside the envelope was a handwritten note.

Lorne,

Heard something you might want to check out. A newspaper reporter from Belle Island named Carr is making the rounds, trying to get someone to present a petition to the court on behalf of Hollis Alexander for new DNA analysis and access to evidence. Can't imagine anyone will take it on. But he's making nonspecific accusations about misconduct and withheld information during discovery.

Doubt anyone will listen to him but thought you should have a heads-up.

Craig

Why in God's name did Wayne Carr keep after this? It was clear after this morning that Alexander was a pervert *and* a murderer.

Lorne crumpled the paper in his hand. He squeezed it as if he could crush the life out of the words.

Then he spread it back out and ran it through the shredder beside his desk.

❦

Nate stood in the hospital corridor, just outside Bill Greene's room. Ellis had gone in alone. Knowing Greg Reinhardt was in there, Nate felt it prudent to stay on this side of the door.

Besides, he needed some time to himself. He'd been concerned about outside complications interfering with this situation with Ellis. But he'd never expected those complications to be initiated by someone in Belle Island.

Nate had invested too much to let his world unravel now. No matter what, no one here could know the truth of what he did.

His cover was solid; the likes of Greg Reinhardt certainly didn't have the sophistication to break through it. But, damn, Nate had hated the look in Ellis's eyes when he'd refused to explain.

He leaned against the wall. Closing his eyes, he let his head fall back.

Ellis had said she trusted him. He had to protect that trust. She'd always looked at him with eyes that said she thought he could do anything. He liked the idea of being her knight in shining armor. But he couldn't allow her to lift that visor and see the man beneath the metal.

For a single moment this morning, she'd eyed him like a threat. God, that had cut deep. But the truth was he lived in a world of liars and thieves, killers and outcasts. He *was* a threat to her—only in ways neither she nor her uncle could ever imagine.

"Nate?" Ellis's voice was soft, concerned.

His eyes snapped open.

"Are you all right?" she asked, laying a hand lightly on his arm. "You look funny."

"I'm fine," he said. "How's your dad?"

"In pain. Grouchy. Uncle Greg is driving him crazy. Mom wants us all to leave for a while so he can get some rest."

They headed toward the elevators. Nate started to settle his hand on the small of Ellis's back—a gesture of possession.

Then he remembered what he was and withdrew it.

Ellis sat in the passenger seat of the Hummer, guilt nibbling at the edges of her consciousness. She'd been shamefully relieved when her mother had asked them all to leave the hospital.

Even though Ellis's dad hadn't been swayed by Greg's accusations concerning Nate, it hadn't kept her uncle from making the occasional stab at trying to convince him. Even with Nate remaining outside in the hall, there had been enough tension in the room that even the nurses seemed to notice it when they'd come in to record her father's vitals and administer medication.

Lulled by the vibration of the passenger window against her temple, Ellis was nearly asleep when she heard Nate open the driver's window.

Rousing, she was surprised to see they were already at the gate to her complex. She looked past Nate and waved to the security guard.

Sam, the day security man—boy, really—smiled at her. "Ms. Greene."

She suspected Sam had a crush on her. Or perhaps he seemed to straighten his shoulders to display his pecs when she saw him, because she was one of the few women under sixty who passed through this gate on a regular basis.

It had never made sense to her that young and beefy Sam was the day guard and the old guy took the graveyard shift.

Nate said, "Would you please call Ms. Greene to inform her if there are any repair vehicles or deliveries that come through?"

Sam leaned closer, looking at Ellis across the wide expanse of the Hummer's interior for confirmation. Apparently, Nate didn't have the proper authority to make such a request.

"Yes, please do. With the murder and all . . ."

Sam nodded. "Good thinking, ma'am." Then he looked at Nate again. "We only allow nonresidents through, even deliveries and repairs, once they've been cleared by a resident."

Nate said, "Just the same, please notify her."

Sam stiffened.

Ooh, a pissing match. Just what she needed.

Ellis leaned across and smiled. "I *really* appreciate it, Sam. I know I'm probably being overly nervous. . . ." She offered up a weak and defenseless woman to his big strong security man. "I feel so much better with you on duty, especially now, with all that's happening."

Sam looked somber when he said, "Thank you, ma'am."

Nate closed the window and pulled away from the gate. "Dear Lord, I didn't know you had it in you."

She tilted her head and batted her lashes.

He muttered, "I hope you didn't strain yourself with that act."

"I have to admit, it wasn't easy."

He laughed. It sounded like something he didn't do often.

Ellis looked at her door knocker; she would replace it as soon as possible. The thought of Alexander's perverted hands touching it made her sick. Had he killed that girl before or after he'd tied the roses on her door?

Her stomach heaved. She swallowed down the bile.

Had he chosen a victim in this town to send her a message?

Her hand shook and the key missed the slit in the lock. If so, would one of *her* girls be next?

She tried the key a second time and missed.

Wordlessly, Nate reached around her, took it from her hand, and unlocked the door.

Once they were inside, he set down the large black duffel bag he'd brought up from the Hummer.

Ellis eyed it curiously.

He noticed her interest. "Tools," he said.

She inched closer to the bag.

"Don't. Touch."

She kept her eye on it. "What kind of tools?"

"The kind that would make your security boy weep with envy."

She backed away and tried to crack the tension by quipping, "I thought maybe it was your shaving kit and jammies, since you said you're going to be staying here for the next couple of days."

He started for the living room. Without looking back, he said, "I don't wear jammies."

A little ripple of giddiness cascaded over her. Now there was a picture she'd no doubt spend a great deal of time contemplating.

As she locked the door, she asked, "Are you hungry?" They'd gotten a quick bite in the hospital cafeteria a couple hours earlier.

"No. I'm going to catch some sleep. Once it's dark, I'm going hunting."

His words evoked an ominous picture, one that involved those serious and no doubt deadly "tools" in his bag. The reality that Nate was about to hunt down a brutal rapist and killer hit her hard.

She opened her mouth to tell him not to go, to stay here with her and let the authorities catch Alexander. But she stopped. Ellis believed with all her heart that Nate could get the job done more quickly than the police—preferably before Alexander claimed another victim.

She pointed toward her bedroom. "You take the bed."

He started to argue, but she cut him off. "I can sleep tonight, while you're . . . out."

For a moment, he stood there looking at her, his expression unreadable.

"Something you want to say?" She stepped closer to him and waited, trying not to notice that he smelled like a man who'd bathed in a fresh mountain waterfall.

"Yeah, there is." His tone was grave enough that she almost backed away from him, away from whatever he had to say.

"While you were teaching your class, I also went past the Aragon Theater and checked out that metal scaffolding your dad was on. It's clear someone used a hacksaw to weaken several of the supports; they didn't even try to conceal it."

Her hand went to the base of her throat, and her heart tried to jump out of her mouth. Someone . . . Alexander.

Nate said, "I called the police."

"Then they can arrest him," she said quickly. "If he's been around any one of us, he'll go back to prison."

"Not without proof. Maybe the investigation will somehow reveal he was here. Or maybe they can get some evidence from the scene."

Damn, why couldn't they arrest him and then investigate?

Of course, she knew that wasn't how things worked. She said, "You know Dad went with me to every parole board hearing."

Nate nodded. "Alexander obviously has a plan, and he's had a long time to work out the details. I need to figure out exactly what he's got in mind and what his end game is so I can be a step ahead of him. It's clear he wants revenge. But what does he think will even the scales?"

"You think he's not done with Dad?" She could barely utter the words.

"I don't know. I've arranged for a twenty-four-hour guard for both your parents. I've already called your dad. We thought it'd be best if he informed your mother."

Ellis was impressed, both with Nate's protection of her parents and his understanding of how to keep her mother's anxiety to a minimum. And he'd done it all with absolutely no input from her. Truthfully, that part did rankle. But under the circumstances, she would forgive him.

"What about Uncle Greg?" she asked. "He was at all of

those hearings too." She thought of him out there blundering around, fueled by reckless anger, looking for a cunning and calculating criminal.

"Yes, well . . . It's impossible to guard an adult who doesn't want to be guarded. Your dad is supposed to get your mother to work on him. I have a guy I can call in if we get Greg's consent. I suggested your folks tell him that the police arranged it."

She gave a nod of admiration.

"So," she asked, "who are these guys you've got guarding my parents?"

"Good reliable people who owe me a favor or two."

"That was half an answer."

"Their names are Charlie and Ben. And that's all you're going to get." He looked into her eyes. "You said you trust me."

"Me trusting you is one thing. This is about my parents."

"These guys are professionals. Your parents are in the best hands possible. The other choices are leaving them vulnerable or sending them away. With your dad's condition, moving them will be more difficult, but I'll arrange it if you want me to."

"No." She paused. "No. I'm just not used to having someone come in and steamroll—"

"I *am not* steamrolling." He said it firmly but without a hint of defensiveness. "Time was short. A job needed to be done. I thought you'd be relieved your parents are safe."

"Are they?" She studied him closely. "Are they safe?"

He reached out and rested his hand on the side of her neck. "They're as safe as they can be in the current circumstances." He pulled her a little closer and stared deep into her eyes. His voice dropped when he said, "But I don't think Alexander's going to risk getting caught to go after them. He drew attention to himself with this girl's murder, which bothers me because I can't yet figure out why he'd do it. But since he has, he's going to concentrate on his major goals first."

"Major goals," she whispered. "Me."

His other hand slipped behind her neck, and his thumb caressed her cheek. "Horrible as that sounds, we can work it to our advantage."

"Bait?" The word stuck and stuttered across her dry tongue like bare thighs across a plastic seat. "Bait," she repeated. The idea made perfect sense. She squared her shoulders. "If it gets him caught, put me on the hook and cast the line."

His grip on the back of her neck tightened. "I would *never*"—he gave her a firm little shake—"do anything to increase your risk."

The depth of emotion she saw in his expression made her heart stumble. She reminded herself that although he cared about her, it wasn't in the way that was setting off little solar flares all over her body.

"Never," he repeated the word; it was no more than a breath. And then he pressed his lips to hers. Softly. With reverence.

A supernova overpowered the sun, eclipsing the solar flares with a blinding pure white light.

Still, she held back, returning his kiss with the same wariness she would use to approach a wounded bird. Any movement too quick, any response too strong, might expose the depth of her true feelings and cause him to startle and fly.

It took all of her willpower. Her hands itched to bury themselves in his hair. Her tongue yearned to seek his. Her body ached to feel his pressed firmly against it.

She gently slid her hand to the side of his neck and was surprised to find his pulse tripped along as fast as hers.

His hand left her neck. The backs of his fingers ran so lightly across her collarbone that her knees quivered.

His tongue traced her lower lip, and every cell in her body responded. When his fingertips traced the edge of her knit top's scooped neck, her breasts tingled, her nipples contracted as if touched by icy water.

She shifted, moving so his fingers slid beneath the fabric. When he grazed her nipple, she nearly cried out.

Need thrummed along her nerve endings, a need so strong, so overpowering, she shuddered. Her body seemed to move of its own accord, her pelvis seeking his.

Suddenly, something seemed to snap inside him. The trembling tension she'd felt under her hands stopped. His arms circled around her, pulling her hard against him.

As her arms went around his neck and her mouth opened fully to his, she realized that all of those years ago, she hadn't imagined herself with a man *like* Nate; she'd imagined herself with him, and him alone.

When he lifted his head, his eyelids were heavy with passion, and his smoky eyes burned with heat. That look alone nearly sent her into an orgasm.

She wanted him to make love to her, and she didn't want him to be gentle about it.

He blinked slowly, then again.

The primal look eased from his face, yet he still held her.

"Ellis . . ." Nate's voice sounded as if he stood across an empty gymnasium, not right next to her. "My beautiful Ellis."

"Don't stop." Her voice was no more than a raspy whisper.

But she could see it was over.

"God, I don't want to." His voice quivered. He kissed her again, but it was a gesture of retreat.

He held her close and spoke against her temple. "I have to leave soon. . . ."

"I don't care," she said.

He put a little space between them and looked down at her. "I do. I won't make love to you and then go away."

She truly didn't know how she was going to survive his leaving. But she did know that feeling this way and *never* being with him wasn't going to make it better.

Just when she opened her mouth to try changing his mind, he said, "That would make me the creep your uncle thinks I am."

Well, hell. This was going to take some time to work around.

She kissed him lightly. "Never in a million years."

His smile was grateful. It broke her heart all over again to think of how he'd lived his youth with this entire town looking down on him.

He pulled her arms from around him and held her hands in his. "I'm a loner. Always was, always will be. I'm not the man for you."

She smiled. *Oh, buddy, this isn't over yet.*

He let go of her hands and stepped back. "We have to focus on stopping Alexander."

"Yes, we do," she agreed.

It happened right before her eyes; the shift in his thoughts was reflected in every aspect of his body. Nate the lover disappeared. Nate the professional—the hunter—took over.

She hated for this moment to end, but there would be another. Never had she felt this electrically alive. She wasn't about to give it up without a fight.

She followed his lead and asked, "How are we going to do it?"

He paced as he spoke. "We have to use what we know about Alexander to his detriment. He's organized. He plans. He's patient." He rubbed his forehead. "I can't figure where this murdered girl fits in. It draws unnecessary attention to him. It's counterproductive to what I can see as his goal."

As Ellis watched him, she had to work to stop thinking of his hands on her. She put her mind to a more productive task. After a moment, she said, "Maybe the girl wasn't part of his plan," she suggested. "Maybe it was like his attack on Laura—random."

Nate fixed his gaze on her in a way that turned her insides to water. "Ellis"—he paused—"Laura's attack wasn't as random as everyone believes."

CHAPTER EIGHTEEN

Ellis stared at Nate. How could Laura's attack *not* have been random? Alexander was a twenty-one-year-old Peeping Tom living miles away in a run-down section of Charleston. What possible connection could there have been between him and Laura?

Her breath caught. Had Uncle Greg been right? Had Nate somehow led the man to Laura?

As much as she feared the answer, she forced herself to say, "Explain."

Nate took her gently by the arm and led her to the couch.

She was still burning from that kiss. His hand on her bare arm flamed the embers she was trying to stamp out. When they reached the couch, she pressed herself into the far corner.

"You were young," he said. "You couldn't see things for what they were. And everyone else . . . Well, everyone else only saw what they wanted to. Or maybe they saw what *Laura* wanted them to." He paused, as if choosing his words wisely. "She was working so hard to maintain that image of perfection and to have *everyone* love her; she was like a leaking vessel, and no matter how much love and adoration you poured in, it would never fill her."

"That's absurd," Ellis snapped. "Laura was always happy. She was beautiful and popular. Everyone did love her."

"That's how you saw it—because she wanted you to."

Ellis crossed her arms and shook her head. "No. We grew up together. I would have known something was off."

"You were thirteen, Ellis," he said patiently. "Think about the perspective of the kids you teach."

Ellis knew that a person's brain wasn't fully able to process emotions and make intelligent decisions until after their teen years. That's why teenagers did such illogical and obviously stupid things. But she'd never thought of herself that way. At thirteen, although she'd been mature for her age, she supposed she'd been the same hormone-charged mess that every other thirteen-year-old girl was. And she *had* idolized Laura.

Ellis tried to view Laura from this alternate perspective as she nodded for Nate to continue.

"I know you—and everyone else, for that matter—thought I was her boyfriend. But my relationship with Laura was much more complicated. *She* was much more complicated."

"But you loved each other." Ellis realized her voice sounded like that of a child hanging on to her belief in Santa Claus.

"I did love her," he said solemnly. "But Laura didn't love me, not in the way you imagine. She sort of needed me; sometimes I think she even hated me. But now I realize what she hated most was herself."

Ellis frowned and shook her head. "She and I were close; I would have seen it. She was *happy*."

He sighed and appeared to weigh what he was about to say. After a moment, he said, "She *appeared* to be happy. She was a chameleon, showing everyone exactly what they wanted to see—and it was eating her alive."

Ellis struggled to look beyond the memory of the brilliant smile, the memory of the coolest girl in school, the memory of the fearless horsewoman. But she still could not see what Nate claimed to be the truth.

Her disbelief must have shown.

Nate scrubbed a hand over his face. "Okay. Here's the truth of it. Laura was drinking. Not just party drinking. She had a serious problem. I saw the signs, because I'd lived with an alcoholic all my life."

Ellis shook her head. "I would have known."

"She was expert at disguising it." He furrowed his brow. "And you were only a kid. Would you have known if she'd been anything short of falling-down drunk?"

Ellis couldn't deny it. At thirteen, her idea of a drunk had been fashioned from television characters with grossly slurred speech and comedic physical impairments.

"But she was the president of Students Against Drunk Driving." Ellis just couldn't make this work in her mind. "She worked with the local police in their substance abuse prevention program in the grade school."

Looking straight into her eyes, he said, "How better to keep people from looking too closely, even if their suspicions were there? Laura's life was all about creating the image."

Ellis tried to reconcile the picture he was painting with the cousin she'd known. They *had* been close—best friends, like sisters. She'd thought Laura shared everything with her. Had she been completely blind?

What about her aunt and uncle? Had they had any idea?

He continued. "I thought I could help her. And she needed me to help maintain her illusion of perfection, to clean up her messes. She wanted me to *try* to save her, even though I don't think she really wanted to be saved."

"That's what you were doing when you brought her back to her bedroom window at night," Ellis said, her disbelief beginning to fade. "I always thought you two were . . . you know, fooling around."

"We never slept together." He looked her square in the eye when he said it. "A few weeks before she was attacked, I discovered she was sneaking out to the beach in the middle of the night—alone. I started checking nearly every night to make sure she wasn't out there too drunk to get back to her room." He ran a hand over his head and rubbed the back of his neck. "I was just a dumb kid. I thought I had a handle on it. I thought I could save her, that I was strong enough, smart enough to fix it. Maybe I was selfish in wanting to believe that." He closed his eyes and swallowed hard. "I should have gone to her parents. I should have. But then it was too late."

Ellis searched his face, looking for the lie. Nate had been a teenage boy. Every teenage boy Ellis had ever known had only one thing on his mind. If what he said was true and Laura was drunk on her ass so often, how could he not have taken advantage of the opportunity? If Laura had been drinking . . .

Memories broke free, coming fast and furious, flipping past like the thumbed pages of a picture book. The pages stopped falling, and the book opened fully on one particular spring evening.

March, sixteen years ago
Three months before Laura was attacked

If it wasn't for Laura, Ellis decided, she'd *never* get to do *anything*. Ellis's mother (the Fun Killer) didn't even let her see R-rated movies. She was thirteen, for crying out loud. Did her mom think that seeing R-rated movies was going to make her have sex with boys or rip up her school with an automatic weapon? Seriously!

It was Friday night. The night Mom and Dad always went out to dinner with Aunt Jodi and Uncle Greg. When they'd been little, Ellis and Laura had shared a babysitter. When Laura had gotten old enough, she babysat Ellis. But now Ellis was old enough to stay alone. Every week, she worried that Laura would abandon their Friday nights at Laura's house for something more interesting with her high school friends. But Laura stuck with her, surprising as that was.

Laura was the coolest girl in the whole high school, even though she was only a junior. Ellis hoped that next year, when she finally got to high school, some of that popularity would spill over onto her. She also hoped that she'd "bloom," as her mother called it, and be even half as beautiful as Laura. Of course, there was no way Ellis would have Laura's long legs and great hair, but at least the mousy brown could be fixed with a box of Clairol—if the Fun Killer would relent.

Laura came into the living room with two videos in one hand and a huge bowl of popcorn wrapped in her other arm. "Sex?" she asked. "Or sex and violence?"

"Hmmm," Ellis said, trying to sound cool and sophisticated. "Be more specific."

Laura set down the popcorn and held up the videos. "*Sliver* or *Romeo Is Bleeding*?"

The cover of *Sliver* looked almost like a porn movie—not that Ellis had ever seen a porn movie. But that cover was way hot.

"*Sliver*," she said.

Laura handed her the movie. "Pop it in the VCR. I'll go get the Cokes."

About halfway through the movie, when Ellis couldn't tear her eyes away from what Sharon Stone and William Baldwin were doing, she reached blindly toward the coffee table for her Coke. She was too hot to breathe and too self-conscious to look to see if Laura's face was as red as Ellis's felt.

She had the glass nearly to her lips when Laura's hand clamped around her wrist.

"That's mine." Laura's voice sounded odd.

She didn't release Ellis's wrist until she'd taken the glass away from her.

"Oh, sorry," Ellis said, feeling like a total dork about this sex-scene business.

Laura handed her the other glass. "No problem." She picked up the remote. "Want me to rewind?"

"No!" Ellis took a sip of Coke, then added more offhandedly, "Not necessary."

Laura paused the movie, grabbed her glass, and stood up. "I'm getting a refill. Want one?"

Ellis thought of her thick waist—the Fun Killer wouldn't let her drink diet because of the chemicals. "No, thanks."

While Laura was in the kitchen, Ellis heard a car outside. Her guilty eyes cut to the door. It was too early for the parents to be back.

She went to the window and looked out. Her uncle's car was in the drive.

"Laura! They're home!" Ellis hurried back to the sofa, casting a panicked eye toward the nasty activity frozen on the TV screen.

Crap! She couldn't find the remote.

In the kitchen, she heard the *thunk* of a glass on the counter and a cabinet door slam.

"Where's the remote?" Ellis called.

She had her hand shoved deep in the cushions when the front door opened.

"Girls?" Uncle Greg was in the living room before Ellis could straighten up. She raised her eyes and waited for the reprimand.

Laura came back into the room. "Daddy. You're home early." She didn't even sound worried.

"Your mother and Aunt Marsha want to take a walk down the beach . . . full moon, you know. I came in to get Mom's sweatshirt." Then he headed upstairs to the master bedroom without a word about what was on TV.

Ellis finally found the remote on the floor and flipped the TV off before he came back. "Holy crap," she whispered to Laura. "You think he saw?"

Uncle Greg's voice preceded him down the stairs. "Of

course I saw." He came trotting down the steps with Aunt Jodi's sweatshirt in his hand. "You girls might want to put that away before your mothers come in, especially if you want to go to the stables tomorrow morning."

He disappeared out the front door without another word.

Ellis's knees felt like rubber. Not going to the stables would be the worst punishment ever. She looked at Laura.

Laura tilted her head, raised an eyebrow, and shrugged. Then she ejected the tape from the VCR.

Holy cow. If that had been Ellis's mom (or even her dad), there would have been an hour-long lecture about trust and making good "choices." But Uncle Greg had been totally cool.

Why can't the Fun Killer be more like her brother?

Looking back on it, Ellis realized she'd asked herself that question many times throughout her childhood. Uncle Greg had been all about fun—without a bunch of lectures about the responsibility that went along with it.

Now Ellis suddenly saw that entire evening in a whole new light. It was possible that Laura had something in that Coke.

Even so . . .

"You're saying it was *Laura's fault* she was attacked?" Ellis asked, tight-lipped with blooming anger. "Her bedroom screen was cut. He came in and got her."

And I was right there. I could have saved her.

Why hadn't Laura made a noise? Why hadn't she

called for help? If Laura had fought him, Ellis surely would have heard.

"Of course not," Nate said. "Don't twist this around. I'm telling you Laura was in trouble. Her judgment was clouded. She took risks she couldn't even see *were* risks. If anyone is to blame, it's me. I knew and didn't tell anyone. More than once, she'd promised she'd stop. I was young and foolish and believed she could. I thought I could help her all by myself."

Viewing her cousin from this new perspective, Ellis realized that perhaps the signs had been there. She'd just been too naïve to see them.

But her uncle? Had his paternal adoration blinded him to his daughter's faults?

Or had her uncle known Laura was drinking and ignored it, just as he'd ignored Ellis's viewing of contraband videos? Had he known and thought it was a simple teenage rite of passage, justified that it was safer for Laura to be drinking at home?

Perhaps Nate was right; Uncle Greg hated him because he needed someone to blame, someone other than himself.

"What did you mean," Ellis asked, "when you said she needed you to clean up her messes?"

Nate waved his hand dismissively. "You know, cover her tracks, make sure she was where she was supposed to be when the sun came up."

"So what does that have to do with her not being a random victim?"

Nate clasped his hands together between his knees and drew his mouth to the side, as if deciding. The action made the crescent-shaped scar by his eye more noticeable. "She used to get older . . . people to buy her liquor, people who could get it legally."

Ellis caught his hesitation. "By *people,* you mean guys."

Laura having a drinking problem was one thing. What Nate was insinuating here was something more. Had she simply used her beauty to coax guys to purchase her booze?

As much as she wanted to cling to that idea, it didn't really wash. There had to be more. Why else would Nate have been so hesitant?

He looked incredibly sad as he nodded. "I figure Alexander was probably one of them. Sometimes she went into Charleston, near the colleges. Maybe she came across him there."

"She traded sex for alcohol?" She nearly choked on the words. How could her beautiful cousin, a girl with everything, have valued herself so little?

"I never wanted any of you to know," he said quietly. "It wouldn't bring her back. It would only hurt you."

The irony of this entire thing twisted her heart. The only guy who wasn't having sex with her was the one who'd cared the most. The one who shouldered the blame in silence. The one who'd taken the wrath of a grieving father and kept the ugliest part of the truth to himself. He protected the family that vilified him.

Nate said, "She'd make promises that she'd stop drinking. But there was no keeping Laura from doing what she was determined to do. She was sick. She needed professional help. I know that now. I should have known it then."

He buried his face in his hands, and Ellis could see

the emotional toll living with the guilt of failing Laura had taken.

And now he feels responsible for me.

She didn't want to be the cause of more guilt weighing on his soul.

She wanted to comfort him. But she could tell he wasn't in any frame of mind to accept comfort. And, to be honest, she was still trying to digest all of this, still searching her memories for signs that she'd missed.

After a moment, he got up and left the room.

She didn't stop him.

She heard the bedroom door close.

Curling on her side, she grabbed the TV remote and turned on the twenty-four-hour local news channel. She tuned the volume low so she wouldn't disturb Nate. After four minutes of commercials, Ellis's eyes were drifting closed. Then the news anchor returned.

"And now our top story. Nineteen-year-old Kimberly Potter was found brutally murdered in the normally peaceful coastal town of Belle Island."

Ellis's eyes snapped open.

A photograph flashed on the screen over the anchorman's right shoulder. "Her body was discovered near the Seaside Apartments around dawn this morning. . . ."

Ellis's hearing faded as all of her senses honed in on that photograph.

Suddenly, Hollis Alexander's most recent attack lost all appearances of being random.

⁂

The drone of Justine's washing machine vibrated the floor over Hollis's head, hiding the small noises he might inadvertently make. Time and again, Providence worked in his favor.

He didn't normally sneak into the basement during the day, but he couldn't risk leaving certain things in his van while he was at work in the kennel. The door locks didn't work.

Everything he'd used last night had been disposed of, except the camera. He was anxious to develop his film, but he couldn't be late to work. He placed the camera precisely on the shelf, folding the strap just so and tucking it behind.

He was proud of his work space. Every single thing had a place and a purpose. It was neat. Ordered.

He was going to hate to leave it.

But, he thought, he wouldn't be leaving his precious things behind. They would go with him. It would be like moving a museum.

He looked at the photograph he'd thumbtacked to the back of the door. Laura Reinhardt had been everything he looked for—she knew she was good-looking, and she used it to get what she wanted. Hollis had known she was special the instant he'd laid eyes on her, giving head to some dude behind a liquor store near campus. She was to be his crown jewel and therefore deserved extra attention.

Oh, how he'd savored the anticipation of their time together. He'd drawn out his preparations, each day his excitement growing stronger. Each time he watched her, his anger grew until it was a driving need that nothing but dominating her would sate. He'd lain awake night after night, thinking of how she would beg.

But nothing had worked out as he'd planned. He'd drawn his game out too long.

He wouldn't repeat the mistake. Ellis Greene was going to receive her just reward sooner rather than later.

CHAPTER NINETEEN

Nate awakened as he always did, fully alert and functional. There was no moment of temporary disorientation. He knew right where he was. In Ellis's bed. Alone.

It was nearly time for him to leave, but he remained on the bed for a long while, tormenting himself with a false sense of closeness.

He'd slept on top of the covers, fully clothed except for his shoes. Her pillow was his only intimate contact with her bed. He rolled over and breathed in the scent of her shampoo. It was light, a combination of citrus and fresh-cut grass. Pure. Beautiful. And it highlighted, once again, the vast difference between them, between their adult lives.

Finally, he forced himself to stop lingering in thoughts of the impossible and swing his legs over the side of the bed. It was time to face what had to be done.

When he entered the living room, the sofa where he'd left Ellis was empty. He heard rustling in the kitchen.

He found her sitting at the table, holding a newspaper in front of her.

It was a few moments before she noticed he was there.

He sank back into a small fantasy where he arose every day to Ellis looking at the newspaper.

When she looked up, saw him, and smiled, his heart actually hurt.

"Did you rest?" she asked.

"Yeah, thanks for letting me use the bed."

"I made jambalaya. You hungry?" She folded the paper and set it on an empty chair.

"Starved," he lied. He had no appetite. Not when he thought of what lay ahead in the dark of the night.

"Sit," she said.

While she moved around the kitchen, he allowed himself to pretend that this was the first of many meals they would share. In reality, if all went as he planned tonight, it would be the last.

His eye fell on the newspaper Ellis had set on the chair beside him. It was folded through the center of a photograph. His mouth went dry.

Ellis leaned over his shoulder, placing a plate in front of him. She paused there, close enough that he could feel her magnetic pull, as if she were a satellite to his soul.

She asked, "Did you know what she looked like?"

He shook his head and picked up the paper. He unfolded the face of a girl who looked so much like Laura that he felt as if someone had put an ice cube down his back.

As he read of the crime and of the life taken, his stomach burned and his hands gripped the paper so tightly they trembled.

He realized he'd underestimated Hollis Alexander's sharp, yet twisted mind. Apparently, he was capable of multitasking his crimes, creating new ones while cleaning up business from the past. This nightmare had to end.

Nate turned the paper over to skim the lower half of the front page. There, in the lower-left-hand quarter, was an editorial by Wayne Carr—the man who had relentlessly beat the dead horse of the case surrounding Laura's attack until it had putrefied and completely poisoned Nate's life here.

As a staff journalist, I rarely request the privilege of writing an editorial. But I have taken an exception in order to do my part in preventing future crimes against our young women.

Belle Island is a community that relishes the values and peaceful life of bygone days. It's why those born here stay and why young couples disgruntled with city life come to raise their children here.

So how, I ask, can it be possible that Belle Island has become a hunting ground for crimes against defenseless women? Where young women once walked the night streets without fear, they now huddle behind locked doors.

Although these heinous attacks on Kimberly Potter and Laura Reinhardt (the only brutal crimes our fair town has suffered in its recorded history) have come sixteen years apart, there are so many similarities between them that one has to suspect one villain is responsible for both.

We know that the man convicted of attacking Laura Reinhardt sixteen years ago is out of prison. He's also working to clear his name, to find justice he claims has been long denied. Statistics prove in cases where convicted criminals are exonerated by DNA evidence that eyewitness identification—the mitigating factor in the Reinhardt case's conviction—is wrong 75 percent of the time. It's an astounding figure of inaccuracy, especially when you're talking about a person's life and liberty.

The truth of the matter is, there are other suspects from that original crime who have recently returned to our community.

Let's all keep our minds and our eyes open. We do not want to lose another young life.

Let us keep both Kimberly and Laura, as well as their families, in our hearts.

Ellis took the paper from his hands and threw it in the trash. "The man is a broken record. No one will listen," she said with conviction.

Unfortunately, Nate had experience that proved otherwise.

⁂

Ellis watched Nate as he readied himself to go "hunting." He'd been polite and eaten the food she'd set in front of him. But she could tell he had forced his consumption.

He was unloading the black duffel onto her coffee table when he glanced up and caught her staring at him.

"Let me take you to stay with your mom."

This was an argument they'd already had more than once this evening.

"If you're hunting for Hollis, I need to be here," she

said, returning his determined gaze. "I won't take a chance of leading him to my mother."

"She has protection."

"Yes, but all of us are safer if I stay here," Ellis said crossly. When was he going to get it through his head she wasn't going?

He left what he was doing and walked over to her. Looking down into her eyes, he put his index finger beneath her chin. "Please."

His nearness was making it difficult to breathe.

Straightening her spine and narrowing her eyes, she said, "I was fine alone last night. I'm perfectly capable of protecting myself."

When it looked as if he was going to argue, she put a finger against his mouth. She'd intended only to shush him, but she let her finger stay there, resting against the warmth of his lower lip.

"You said it yourself; we have to go on the offensive," she said softly. "We can't sit around and wait for him to hurt someone else." She realized how seductive her voice sounded, even with the not-so-romantic subject matter. She pulled her hand away, cleared her throat, and continued in a no-nonsense tone. "If I suspect he's here in the complex, I'll call the police right away—the real police. We have to catch him doing what he isn't supposed to. You do your part and I'll do mine."

He reached down to her side and captured the hand she'd just taken from his lips. Opening it, he brought it to his mouth and pressed a kiss in the center of her palm. The look in his eyes was more than obligation, more than concern. He looked almost hungry for her. She'd felt it in his kiss, but that had been a physical need. This hunger shone from his soul. It reached out and touched her own, caressing the core of her vulnerability. And for the first time in her adult life, she didn't shy away.

Then he said, "You are one amazingly brave woman."

With a blush of shame, she pulled her hand from his and turned away. "No. I'm not. I'm a coward."

Taking her by the shoulders, he turned her to face him again. "How can you say that?" Now that steely gaze probed deeply. And this time she flinched.

She looked away. "Because I live every night hiding behind locks and alarms. Because I structure my whole life based on my limitations. Because I can't let go of the fear." Her throat tightened. "I can't let go of the guilt. I could have saved her."

Her eyes snapped back to meet his at the startling impact of what she'd revealed. She wanted a way to recall her words.

But as she continued looking into his eyes, the panic ebbed. Relief flowed into her like the trickle of a pure mountain stream.

For the first time, she'd admitted what her life had become. Everyone saw her as strong, controlled—exactly the image she'd cultivated. The bare-assed truth was that she was neither. She'd sold everyone, including herself, a false storefront. And people had let her hide behind that façade, because they felt sorry for her.

Nate captured her hands and placed her palms over his heart. He seemed to understand the significance of this moment for her, and he waited in silence. She was so glad he hadn't come back with a contradiction, with manufactured excuses for her.

Blinking away tears, she said, "How could I *not* have

heard? I was *right there,* less than four feet from her. I heard other things. I heard Alexander when he was cutting back to the road. Why didn't I wake up and help her?"

Tears now flowed down her face.

Nate kept her hands pressed against his chest when he leaned close and kissed the wet trail on her cheek. He whispered against her skin, "I don't know why." He kissed her cheek again, near her ear. "But I do understand how you feel. I failed her too."

Ellis leaned her forehead against his shoulder and, for the first time in years, allowed herself to cry from the center of her aching soul.

He released her hands and wrapped his arms around her. He held her tight, rubbing her back, but he never tried to halt her tears.

After a while, she cried herself out. She lifted her face from his shoulder and looked up with a sniff. Framing his face in her hands, she said, "Thank you."

His own eyes looked misted when he replied, "Better?"

She managed a smile. "Not as good as I'm gonna be when we catch him."

Nate smiled back, the scar at the corner of his eye crinkling.

She traced it with the tip of her finger. "I don't remember this," she said.

"I got it in the marines. Wasn't enough to earn a medal . . ." He winked and took a step away. "Let's catch us a bad guy."

"Let's." She graciously accepted his back-to-business turn.

Nate rubbed the tracks of her tears dry with the pads of

his thumbs. Then he kissed her forehead and headed back to the black duffel. The moment had passed. The warrior had returned.

"I'm going to trade the Hummer for Jake's truck—less conspicuous."

He started laying his gear out on her coffee table. His face bore a look of steely concentration, his eyes so distant that it gave her a little shiver.

Ellis looked at the equipment. There were a pair of night-vision goggles (she recognized them from TV), a couple of gadgets she couldn't begin to identify, a belt with pockets and hooks, and a knife sheathed in leather.

He had two magazine clips that he loaded from a box of ammunition. Ellis flinched at every click as each bullet snapped into place.

It looked like he was heading to a shootout.

"You really need all that?" she asked.

His hands continued their deadly task as he gave her a cold, quick glance. "You don't go hunting underarmed." His voice was so matter-of-fact that she wished she'd kept her mouth shut.

She wondered about this job of his. What kind of stuff was he responsible for protecting—and from who?

When he pulled out his handgun, she averted her eyes. It was a monster that made her little revolver look like a child's toy.

As she watched Nate strap on the belt and holster the gun, the thing that struck her was what he *wasn't* taking with him.

"Don't you have handcuffs in your bag of tricks there?" she finally asked. "How are you going to deliver him to the police?"

His gaze snapped up. The truth was written in his eyes before he uttered the lie. "I'll pick up some plastic wire ties."

She should have called him on it. She should have insisted he promise that Hollis Alexander would be delivered in one unharmed piece to the police for the justice system to do its work.

But she kept her mouth shut.

With Nate's connections, it hadn't been difficult to find out where Alexander worked. A quick call to Heidi's House of Hounds confirmed his work hours. Nate parked Jake's truck across the street from the kennel just before seven. There were only two vehicles left in the lot at Heidi's—a newish bright red crew-cab pickup and an old light blue cargo minivan with rust craters around the wheel wells and at the base of the rear doors. It didn't take a genius to figure out which one was Alexander's.

Ten minutes later, Alexander emerged and got into the van.

Nate followed him to the halfway house, slightly disappointed that the man had gone straight home. But the night was young, still early for slime like Alexander to crawl out from under his rock and engage in his perverted pursuits.

If Nate was very lucky, he'd catch the man in the act of something that violated his parole. If he was luckier, Alexander would give him a good reason to shoot him.

Sometimes Nate wished he was a baser human being, a man like so many of those he dealt with in his job—a man with no conscience. Then he wouldn't hesitate to blow Alexander away on general principle alone. But he wasn't a man without the burden of a conscience. Besides, such an action would screw him right out of his job. He had a lot of leeway, but hunting Alexander down and shooting him without provocation would definitely cross the line. Nate would be done. Forever.

No matter how frustrating, he had to get Alexander back behind bars using the proper channels—or shoot him in the act of a crime.

Thirty minutes later, Alexander came out of the halfway house. His hair was wet and he'd changed his clothes.

He got in the old van and pulled away.

Following at a safe distance, Nate's nerves started to thrum with anticipation. *Come on, man, do something corrupt.*

He was on high alert when Alexander parked on a residential street and got out.

Peek in one window. Nate turned on his camera and entered 911 into his cell phone. He was ready.

Disappointment dampened his enthusiasm when Alexander walked up to the front door of the largest house on the block and rang the doorbell.

He was quickly let in.

Nate hunkered down to wait.

Within a half hour, it was fully dark. Nate got out of the truck and walked closer to the house. Every room on the first floor was lit, making it easy to see inside. The room facing the street, what appeared to be a formal living room, was empty. He crept along the tall hedges that lined the property at the side of the house.

A brick walkway lay between the hedge on Nate's right and the house. About fifteen feet from the front of the house was a set of narrow steps that led to an exterior basement door.

Nate moved deeper into the narrow lot.

He finally found Alexander. He was seated at the dining room table with a woman who looked old enough to be his mother. But Alexander's mother was long dead.

A relative?

Nate's research hadn't turned up any, other than a sister in Sumter who had disowned Alexander long before he attacked Laura. She'd been Nate's first call when he'd learned Alexander had been paroled. She hadn't sounded happy to hear her brother had been released.

Nate studied the two in the dining room for a moment. It seemed aboveboard, nothing more than a friendly dinner.

Returning to the truck, he jotted down the address. He'd find out who this woman was and how she was associated with Alexander.

It was after eleven when Alexander emerged through the front door. He waited on the front walk as the lights on the first floor went out. Then he walked around the side of the house.

Nate started the truck and inched forward with the lights off. Using the night-vision goggles, he saw Alexander descend the steps and let himself into the basement door.

"What are you up to?" Nate whispered.

This could be it.

Nate was just getting out of the truck to get closer when Alexander reemerged and locked the door behind him.

He hurried to his van, got in, and drove away.

Nate followed at a discreet distance.

Alexander drove directly to the halfway house.

The residence had only one entrance at the front for normal use. The others were emergency exits wired with alarms. If Alexander left again, he'd have to come back out that front door.

Dawn colored the sky violet, then pink, and Nate was still sitting there waiting.

Alexander was scheduled to work from eleven to seven. His employer was to call and report to Alexander's parole officer if he didn't show up to work. No sense in sitting here any longer.

He stretched the kinks out of his neck and rubbed his eyes. Then he started the truck.

"I *am* gonna get you," he muttered as he drove away, back to Belle Island.

Back to Ellis.

CHAPTER TWENTY

Hollis cleared his throat, then made a couple of practice passes at his excuse. Once he was happy with his performance, he dialed the number for Heidi's House of Hounds.

"Hello, this is Heidi."

"Hello," he said in a rasping croak, "this is Hollis. I'm sick and won't be in today. Got a fever and all."

"Oh, poor dear." Heidi's sympathy was no surprise. He couldn't believe his luck in finding this particular employer. "You just take care of yourself and get well, y'hear?"

"I hate to leave you"—he wheezed—"shorthanded." He finished off with a chest-rattling coughing fit.

"You sound just awful, bless your heart. Don't you worry about us. I've got high school help coming in over the weekend, so you just plan on taking off until Monday."

"Thank you, ma'am. But if I'm better tomorrow, I'll be there."

"Don't push yourself. We'll get by 'til Monday."

"Yes, ma'am." Hollis hung up and rolled back onto

his mattress with a loud laugh. He wouldn't even have to think about covering his tracks until Monday.

By then, his work would be done.

Ellis was jerked out of a fitful sleep by a loud knocking on her door. Her body was moving before her mind caught up. As her feet moved, her mind scrabbled for orientation like a mountain goat on a landslide.

What day was it? Why was she sleeping in her clothes?

By the time she reached the living room, her mind began to clear.

Nate was at the door. Had he caught Alexander?

"Ms. Greene, this is the police. Please open up."

Her heart nearly slid to flatline. Oh, God. Nate. Had Alexander robbed her of another person?

Her fingertip was on the first number on her alarm system pad before she stopped herself.

"Just a minute," she called through the door. Then she went to look out the sliding door. Two squad cars were parked in front. One from the Belle Island Police Department. The other was a Charleston County Sheriff's vehicle.

Her body turned as cold as if she'd been thrown naked into the winter surf. Horrified thoughts fought for dominance, tangling, twisting, each worse than the last. Something had happened to Nate. Or her parents. Or Uncle Greg.

Returning to the door, she checked the peephole. Three officers stood on her threshold. She recognized one from the local police, Les Winkler. She'd taught his son last year.

With trembling hands, she disarmed the alarm and jerked open the door.

"What's going on?" She could barely get the words out of a mouth as dry as chalk dust.

"We need to speak with Nathaniel Vance," Les said. "We understand he's here."

Safe. They were all safe. Her legs felt as if they'd collapse under the weight of her relief.

"No," she said. "He isn't. Why are you looking for him?"

Les looked uncomfortable. He took off his hat and asked, "May we come in?"

She opened the door fully. "Of course."

One of the deputy sheriffs followed Les inside. The other remained on the porch. His hand rested on his holstered gun, his gaze roaming the grounds below.

Once the officers were inside, Ellis noticed the sharp-eyed way they looked over her condo. Unspoken accusation was in every sweep of their gazes.

Thank God, Nate's black bag of tools had gone with him.

Les's nervous fingers rotated his hat by the brim. "Do you know where Mr. Vance is?" Les must have drawn the short straw because he knew her.

"No, I don't," she said. "I'd like to help you, but I have no idea what this is about." *And why in the hell are there three of you here?*

Out of the corner of her eye, she saw the deputy edge closer to the kitchen, leaning to get a better look around the doorjamb.

"Excuse me," she said sweetly, with raised brows. "Can I get you something?"

He straightened and folded his hands in front of him. "No, ma'am."

She turned back to Les and smiled. More flies with honey than vinegar. "Like I said, I'd like to help in any way I can."

Les asked, "May we search the premises?"

Keeping her smile, she said, "No, you may not. Not until you tell me why you're here."

"We need to ask Mr. Vance some questions."

"And it takes three officers to do that?"

Ellis noticed the deputy was now easing his way toward her bedroom.

Les shifted his weight. "We need to question him regarding the murder of Kimberly Potter."

Dear God, this can't be happening. Not again.

"I can tell you who killed that poor girl," Ellis said sharply.

"Oh?" Les lifted a brow, giving her the same expression his son had when she'd explained math story problems.

"Hollis Alexander—the man who raped and beat my cousin sixteen years ago. He's been paroled. Kimberly Potter looks uncannily like Laura. And I've seen him hanging around my condo a couple of nights—"

"You can give a positive ID?" Les said.

"Well, no. But I'm sure it was him. He left a bunch of roses on my door last night." Her suspicion that it could possibly have been Rory stayed locked in her throat. "There was an officer here this morning; he took them to the lab."

"On the occasion that you *think* you saw him, did you call and report his presence to the department?" he asked.

"I called complex security."

"And did they find him?"

After a pause, she said, "No." Then she added, "But Nate inspected the scaffolding that collapsed with my father. He said it had been tampered with. He reported that to the police too. All you have to do is find Alexander and you've solved your murder and my father's accident."

Les didn't respond.

"If you want to question Nate on Alexander's whereabouts," she said, "I'm sure he'll share whatever information he has with you."

Les looked at her as if she'd suddenly turned from an intelligent teacher to the most pathetically gullible woman on Earth. "Ms. Greene, for your own safety, it's important for us to find Mr. Vance."

"Nate didn't kill Kimberly Potter. I can't imagine why you'd even think that with Hollis Alexander skulking around here. Besides," she rushed on, "it's impossible, because Nate was with me that night. All night." The lie was out before she thought it through. Panic had driven her tongue, and now there was no way to take it back.

Les looked at her with that same disappointment in his eyes. "That's not what your uncle said."

"How would my uncle know?"

"He said he saw Nate Vance leave here at eleven-thirty and that he hadn't returned by sunrise."

She furrowed her brow. "I don't know how he'd be able to say such a thing." Uncle Greg had said he'd been out looking for Alexander, but in the wrong place. Had he been watching her place all night long?

With a dismissive shake of her head, she added, "My uncle is under terrible stress. He hasn't been sleeping. Since Alexander made threats against me, my uncle is very worried for me and my family's safety. I'm sure he's confused. Nate's been staying with me in case Alexander decides to make good on those threats."

"Then where is he now?" the sheriff's deputy asked from behind her.

"I don't know." The less said the better. She'd already screwed herself big-time. "Y'all feel free to search the place if you really think I have him stashed under my bed or in a closet."

With a look that said he'd like to slap handcuffs on her and haul her ass to county lockup, the deputy went into the kitchen.

"When do you expect him back?" Les asked.

"I have no idea." If they hauled Nate in for questioning, it would be that much longer before anyone found Alexander.

The deputy came out of the kitchen, looked at Les, and gave a slight shake of his head. Then he disappeared into her bedroom.

When he came out, he said, "Doesn't look to me like a man's been staying here—no dirty underwear, no shaving stuff."

"He's neat," she said curtly. "And I don't think he's shaved since he got here."

Les said, "When he gets back, please call and let us know."

"Oh, I will. I'm sure he'll want to talk to you—to get this all cleared up as soon as possible."

That much was true.

"Can you tell me," she asked, "what makes you think Nate had anything to do with this crime in the first place?"

The deputy spoke up. "No, ma'am. But I can tell you, you should be concerned for your own safety."

Les turned to the deputy and said, "I'll meet you outside, Bruce."

The deputy let himself out the front door.

Les hesitated only a moment, looking at her with a mix of regret and concern. "Vance's fingerprints are on the murder weapon."

"It's a mistake."

"No mistake. Prints match or they don't. No gray area. His were the only ones on the weapon. Please, stay away from this guy."

He handed her a card. "Here's my number. Call me the minute you see him." He started to the door, then stopped. "Bruce is right; you should be extremely careful."

She managed a mute nod. All of her words had been stripped from her, lies or otherwise.

❧

For a long moment, Ellis stood still in the middle of her living room. Her belly felt as if it were full of worms eating their way to the outside.

Nate's fingerprints were on the murder weapon. How in the hell could Alexander have accomplished that? It didn't seem possible.

And if it wasn't . . .

Nate *hadn't* been with her. In fact, he'd been gone much longer than he'd said he would be.

She dialed the first three digits of Nate's cell number, then froze. She couldn't be stupid. She had to organize what she was going to say.

Looking out the sliding glass door, she saw the officers were still standing in her driveway. It looked like they were planning their next move. One of them was talking on a radio.

If she let Nate walk into a trap, she'd never get her answers.

She dialed his cell.

He answered on the second ring. "I have to stop by and trade vehicles with Jake; then I'll be there."

She had time. "So, did you catch Alexander last night?" Had he even been looking?

Stop it. You know Nate didn't kill that girl.

"No. He had dinner with an older woman at a seemingly respectable home, then went back to the halfway house at eleven-thirty. He didn't leave the rest of the night. But I'll catch him doing something he shouldn't."

"Where was the house?" Her laptop sat on the desk. She opened it and woke it up.

"What?"

"Where he had dinner?"

"In Charleston."

"Where specifically?"

"On Logan Street." He sounded curious. "Why?"

"I thought maybe I could help figure out whose house it is." It wasn't exactly a lie.

"Good idea. I wrote the address down."

When he gave it to her, she entered it in cyberhomes.com. It came up immediately with a legit address.

"What kind of house was it?"

"The usual for the city, single house with a piazza."

That matched. She began to feel a little foolish for doubting him. Still, she'd proceed cautiously.

"The police were just here," she said.

"Did they find something on those roses?" Hope colored his voice.

"They were looking for you." She let it hang there.

For a moment, the line lay silent. Ellis's heart rate bumped up.

"What did they say?" he finally asked.

"They think you murdered Kimberly Potter."

"I didn't." It was a surprisingly unemotional statement.

"Your fingerprints are on the murder weapon." The words tasted bitter on her tongue.

"I don't know how he did it, but we both know who's responsible for that girl's death."

"You said he's got a plan. Why frame you?" she pressed. "You didn't have anything to do with him going to jail."

She heard him release a long breath. "I don't know. Maybe because he hoped I'd take the blame for Laura and didn't."

She remained silent. Nate said Alexander was balancing the scales; killing that girl seemed extreme.

"Ellis," Nate said. "I'll catch him."

"Not if you're in jail."

"I won't be."

"Are you leaving?" she asked, ignoring the stone in her stomach.

"What?" He sounded surprised for the first time in their conversation.

"Are you leaving Belle Island?"

"No, of course not. I won't leave you vulnerable."

She nearly let loose a hysterical, insane kind of laugh.

She hadn't felt this vulnerable since the day they'd found Laura on the beach.

"Stay put," Nate said. "I'll be in touch." He disconnected the call.

Ellis stood for a long while with the phone still to her ear. That insane laughter again threatened to break loose.

Good God, Nate's fingerprints. How had Alexander done it? And why?

The bigger question was, What next? They had to get one step ahead. If they weren't very careful, Alexander would win this time—and they'd all pay the price.

Greg poured himself another glass and recapped the bottle of scotch.

Wouldn't Jodi have a fit over this? Scotch before noon.

Well, Jodi didn't have any say in his life. It still rubbed him raw, her decision to stay with Marsha instead of him.

He knocked back a burning swallow of scotch. If he drank enough, maybe he'd get some sleep today.

When his doorbell rang, he nearly ignored it.

What if it was the police about the murder? The instant he'd seen the photo of the Potter girl, he'd called and reported his suspicions. He'd seen Nate Vance slip out of Ellis's condo that night and disappear into the marsh. Why sneak out if he wasn't up to no good? And if it wasn't Vance, the murderer was likely Alexander.

Greg walked to the front window and looked out.

A Charleston County Sheriff's vehicle sat in his drive.

He set down his drink and went to the door.

When he opened it, the deputy on his doorstep held up an envelope. "Mr. Gregory Reinhardt?"

"Yes."

"I'm here to serve you with this restraining order." He handed Greg the envelope.

"What? From who?"

"The magistrate of Charleston County has ordered you to cease harassing Hollis Alexander. You are to have no contact whatsoever with him. And you are to remain a minimum of five hundred yards from his person at all times."

"You've got to be kidding!" Greg's face grew hot, and it wasn't from the scotch.

"No, sir. The details are in the order." The deputy returned to his car.

Greg slammed the front door closed and flipped the envelope like a Frisbee. It hit the wall with a snap. Then he retrieved his glass and refilled it to the brim.

Court protection for scum like Alexander! Had the entire world gone mad?

Ellis had always mocked clichés. She considered them a lazy and unimaginative way of expressing oneself. But as she looked at the crushed path she'd made in her carpet as she'd paced the hours away, the phrase "the walls were closing in" kept popping into her mind.

It was nearing noon, and she still hadn't heard from Nate. She decided it was high time she stopped sitting around waiting for him to take care of her problems as well as his and do something about them herself.

With the focus of Kimberly Potter's murder investigation turning toward Nate, she had to get out there and see what she could uncover. Who knew how long before the flimsy foundation of her alibi for Nate would completely erode?

He risked everything by staying here. If he hadn't come back to protect her in the first place, he wouldn't be under suspicion for murder right now.

Her first task was to find out what evidence the police had. What was this murder weapon with Nate's prints? There had to be some logical explanation.

As she was sitting on her bed putting on her shoes, her home phone rang. She dove across the mattress to pick it up.

"Nate?"

For a moment, she heard only the hiss of an open line. Thinking it was a telemarketer, she was just taking it away from her ear to hang up when she heard a raspy whisper.

"Elllliiisssssss."

She went cold and clammy. "Who is this?" She didn't need to ask.

"Oh, Elllllliiissss, you're making things difficult. But I do sssoooo love a challenge." The voice sounded like a serpent, scales rasping across sand, tongue hissing in the air.

"What do you want?" She went from window to window, checking outside. She didn't see him hiding in the foliage.

"Why, I want you, Ellliiisssss." The voice slid through the phone line and snaked down her spine. "I told you I'd come."

She listened as if she had no choice.

He went on, "So much work to do. Daddy. Uncle Greg. Nate. I'm saving you for last." He smacked his lips.

Ellis barely suppressed the urge to vomit.

"What did you do to Nate and Greg?" Her voice rose as her fear spiked.

"You have no imagination, my dear. I didn't do anything *to* Nate. I didn't have to. Now he'll get what he should have gotten fifteen years ago, plus some. As for dear Uncle Greg, he's doing it to himself. All it takes is a little nudge now and again."

After a pause, he said, "You have another day—or two. I don't want to rush. A couple of things still have to play out and then . . ." He smacked his lips again. "I want you to anticipate our time together as much as I am—"

She tore the phone away from her ear, disconnected the call, and threw the handset across the room.

It hit the carpet, then slid, hitting the woodwork with a crack that sent shock waves to the marrow of her bones.

Over and over, she swiped her hands across the belly of her T-shirt, wanting to rid herself of the feeling of filth that had oozed through the phone.

She dashed from window to door, checking again to make sure everything was locked.

This had to stop. *She* had to stop it.

Chapter Twenty-One

Everything Ellis knew about rapists told her Alexander got off on bullying and intimidation. Like Nate said, Alexander was organized. He was patient. This was all a game to him, a game he'd had fifteen years to perfect. And part of his big payoff was having her locked up like a prisoner in her own home. Then he'd prove just how vulnerable her safe haven was.

Clearly he wouldn't have made that call if he didn't think he could get to her here, behind locked doors and alarm systems.

She retrieved her gun from the nightstand and put it in her purse. For a moment, she held it in her hand with her eyes closed, praying for the strength to do what she must. The thought of being out there, exposed, sickened her. And yet, that phone call had made her feel nearly as vulnerable here in her own home.

Nate was right. The offensive. Stop sitting here waiting for Alexander to make his move against her. That's exactly what he wanted. He was counting on her hiding, sitting by in fear while his plan played out.

She took a deep breath and opened her eyes. Then she called Sam at the front gate.

"This is Ellis Greene." She cleared her throat, trying to stop the quivering in her voice. "I just received a threatening phone call, and I need to leave here. Would you please come and walk me to my car?"

"I'm on my way." He sounded angry, protective.

She double-checked the revolver. All cylinders were loaded.

If Alexander came after her, it would be over. She'd shoot him. He'd never hurt another woman.

She called Les Winkler.

"Officer Winkler."

"It's Ellis Greene. Hollis Alexander just called me and as much as admitted he killed Kimberly Potter in order to frame Nate. He's also made threats against me, Nate, my dad, and my uncle, Greg Reinhardt."

"I see." He didn't sound overly alarmed. Ellis thought of the look of disappointment on his face when he'd sensed her lie. "Did he call your cell or your home phone?"

"Home—so you can check the records. My point is, you need to stop wasting your time chasing Nate Vance and arrest Alexander. At the very least, his contacting me should be a violation of his parole."

"Yes, ma'am. Of course we're checking into Hollis Alexander too."

She ground her teeth. "*Please* tell me you'll check the phone records. You have my permission, if that's what you need."

"Yes, ma'am."

She hung up, feeling like she'd wasted her time.

Sam arrived at her door, chest puffed like a rooster.

"Thanks for coming," she said as she reset the alarm and locked the door.

"Glad to help." He put a protective hand on her upper arm as they walked down the outside stairs and to the garage.

When she opened the overhead garage door, he escorted her to the car, opened the door, checked the backseat, then assisted her in. Before he closed the car door, he said, "Are you sure you should be out running around?"

She slipped the key into the ignition. "I'm not safe *anywhere* right now."

It was true. And yet hearing herself say the words aloud frightened her more than she cared to admit. The vindictive confidence that had gotten her out the door wavered.

Looking up at Sam, she said, "I appreciate your help. I'll probably ask you to come back here with me when I get home . . . if you don't mind."

A smile crossed his square face. "I'm doing a double shift today, so I'll be right here when you need me."

She smiled her appreciation as he closed the door. Not wanting to wait for the doors to lock themselves when she started moving, she hit the auto-lock button. Sometimes overkill just made sense.

Sam waited in the drive until she'd backed out and closed the garage door.

As she put her car in drive, her gaze searched the area beneath the old oak, where Alexander had no doubt watched her in the night. A little shiver caused the hair to stand up on her arms.

She turned away and drove on.

Keeping an eye on her rearview mirror in case Alexander or the police were following her, she made a circuitous route to Seaside Apartments. She drove past the complex twice, turned around, and came back.

No one followed.

Finally, she pulled into the parking lot. The complex consisted of two 2-story buildings laid out in an L-shape. They were made of cinder block and stucco and had been erected in the late fifties as a motel. Sometime in the early eighties, they'd been converted into apartments. This was one of the few beachside apartment buildings to have survived Hurricane Hugo. And it was no doubt the ugliest.

Natural disasters were odd in the way they picked and chose which buildings to destroy. Beautiful examples of architecture succumbed, while ugly testaments to man's lack of architectural imagination lived on. Charleston and the surrounding low country was a perfect cross-section of that kind of selective devastation.

Earthquakes tumbled one structure yet spared the one across the street. Wildfires completely consumed one house and leapt over the one next door.

Ellis supposed all of life was like that. Her family had been wrecked by tragedy while others remained untouched. What, she wondered, had made Laura be the one? What twist of fate had led her to Alexander's iniquitous path?

According to Nate, it hadn't been pure fate. Even so, something had brought Laura and Alexander together in the same place at the same time.

Ellis drove slowly through the small parking lot. Beneath the windswept loblolly pines, leggy azalea and crepe myrtle had overgrown the perimeter of the lot, blocking it from street view. Tall grasses and tangled vine took over on the ocean side of the aged and broken pavement. Fingers of sand reached across the asphalt, like clawing hands trying to reclaim what had once been dunes covered in sea oats and sweetgrass.

Ellis had planned on looking at names on the group mailboxes in each building to find Kimberly Potter's apartment. Now it was clear she wouldn't have to. There was a parking space piled with flowers, balloons, teddy bears, and angels. That parking space and the one next to it had the number 1555 F stenciled on the asphalt in faded yellow paint.

There was a car parked in the other space allocated to Kimberly Potter's apartment.

Ellis parked in a space marked VISITOR. Apartment 1555 F was on the second floor. She climbed the stairs and stood outside the door. Mournful Celtic music played softly inside the apartment. Normally, kids' apartment walls thrummed with bass when their stereos were on. But what had happened to this girl's roommate had knocked normal right off its axis.

Ellis knocked on the door.

The music stopped.

After a moment, she knocked again. "Hello," she said softly against the closed door. "This is Ellis Greene. I think I know who murdered your roommate, and I want to ask you a couple of questions."

After a moment, she heard footsteps. The sheer curtain on the window beside the door moved slightly. Then the dead bolt clicked. The door opened as far as the flimsy security chain would allow. Half of a young woman's face appeared in the crack, its one brown eye red and swollen from crying.

"May I speak with you?" Ellis said.

The eye blinked. The door closed. The chain scraped, then clattered against the jamb.

When the door opened fully, Ellis was shocked to realize she knew Kimberly Potter's roommate. Ava Robinson was the girlfriend of Rory's nephew Daniel.

Ellis said, "Do you remember me? Ellis Greene. I used to date Daniel's uncle, Rory. We met once at a family picnic."

A thin smile curved the girl's pale, washed-out mouth. "Yes, of course. Otherwise, I wouldn't have opened the door."

"I'm very glad to hear that." Ellis couldn't help herself when she added, "You know that chain won't keep anyone out."

Ava held up her cell phone; 911 showed on the lighted screen. Her finger was on the SEND button. "I know." She stepped back. "Come on in."

Once Ellis was inside, Ava closed and locked the door, slipping the safety chain on once again. She said, "I haven't been out of this apartment since I found—"

She pressed a crumpled tissue to her mouth.

"Are you here alone?" Ellis asked.

"Mom's flying in this afternoon. I'm moving back to Omaha. I leave Tuesday after the funeral."

"I see." Why wasn't Daniel here with her?

As if she'd read Ellis's thoughts, Ava said, "Daniel and I broke up a month ago. So, you see, there's no reason for me to stay here."

Ellis gave a sympathetic nod. Ava had moved here and found a job after meeting Daniel at USC, Columbia, some eighteen months or so ago. She'd been visiting a cousin going to school there.

Ava motioned for Ellis to have a seat. Then the girl just sat there looking at her with those wounded brown eyes.

There was no way to ease into this, so Ellis stated it plain and simple. "I think I know who killed Kimberly."

"Who?" She sat up a little straighter.

"The same man who attacked my cousin."

"Oh!" Ava's hand went to her throat. "I didn't know there had been another . . ."

"My cousin was attacked several years ago. The man who did it is now out of prison."

Ava said, "Then the police know who it is."

"I don't know that they're making the connection. That's why I need to know the details, so I can go to them and press the issue, make them see the attacks are related. Can you answer some questions for me?"

"Sure, if it'll help catch this guy."

"Where had Kimberly been that night?" Ellis asked.

"At a birthday party for someone she worked with. I think she said they were meeting at the Palmetto Grill. They're all older, I mean married and stuff, so I don't know if she went anywhere after that."

"You were home all evening?"

Ava nodded. "I went to bed around eleven."

"I know it's hard, but can you go over how you found her?"

Ava's throat worked as she swallowed so dryly that Ellis could hear the girl's tissues rasping against one another. Her eyes were wide and haunted. Her chin puckered in a way that said she was struggling not to cry.

Ellis hated herself for putting the girl through this. She knew all too well what it was like to have to go over and over something that you wanted to forget.

She prompted, "What time, and what made you go looking?"

"It was around five forty-five. I got up and saw her car out there with the door open. Kim can come home pretty wasted, but never so far gone that she'd leave the car door open like that. She wasn't in her room. I went out to her car and saw her purse on the passenger seat and keys still in the ignition.

"That's when I really freaked. I started calling her name. I'm not sure why I headed to the beach." Ava drew a shuddering breath. "But that's where I found her."

Ava's eyes squeezed closed. Ellis knew the futility of such an action. That image would always be there, day and night, burned into her memory.

"Can you describe what you saw when you found her?" Ellis asked.

Ava's eyes snapped open. She looked at Ellis like she was some freakish ghoul.

Ellis said softly, "I really need to know. It's the only way I can find the truth."

After a moment, Ava nodded and drew in a deep breath. After she released it, she continued. "I found one of her sandals at the start of the boardwalk that goes over the dunes to the beach." A pitiful smile curved the corners of her mouth, as if relishing a fond memory. "She'd just gotten those shoes. Had waited for them to go on sale. I don't know why she liked them. They were this god-awful green. . . ." She paused. "I kept calling her name, hoping to hear her answer or call for help.

"I saw her other sandal about halfway down the boardwalk. I walked out to that shoe . . . and then I saw her." Ava's eyes squeezed closed and her lips pressed together.

Her voice was a mere breathy squeak when she said, "I knew right away it was too late." Tears slipped from her closed eyes, and her hand covered her mouth.

Ellis felt tears welling in her own eyes. She hadn't seen Laura when they found her on the beach; her mother had made her stay in the house. But she'd created the picture in her mind often enough to understand how it could rob a person of their ability to speak.

After a sniffle, Ava said, "She was in the weeds, lying between two dunes. Her clothes had been cut." She ran her hand from collarbone to hips. "Split open down the middle." She shuddered. "Her panties were stuffed in her mouth."

Ava kept her gaze on the floor, as if too embarrassed for her friend to look Ellis in the face.

"What about her injuries?" Ellis prompted softly.

"Her skin . . . her skin was blue-gray, like an oyster. And there was"—she swallowed convulsively—"there was a screwdriver stuck in her throat." Ava touched the hollow at the base of her own throat.

Ellis stopped breathing. The murder weapon with Nate's prints. A screwdriver.

Alexander would have known that Nate's prints had been processed in the crime investigation sixteen years ago. Where had he gotten the screwdriver with Nate's prints? From the stables?

The boat motor cut out, and my flashlight went dead, so I couldn't find the damn screwdriver to fix it. . . .

Had Alexander taken it while the boat was tied up in the marsh near Ellis's condo?

Why, if the killer had used a knife or something to cut Kimberly's clothes, would he have stabbed her with a screwdriver? Surely the police had seen that as odd. Of course, the more obvious question was, Why would a murderer with half a brain have left that screwdriver at the scene? This entire thing screamed "setup."

Ellis wanted to spring from her chair and run to the police. But she couldn't dash out of here without a thought for Ava.

The girl was clenching her hands so tightly in her lap the knuckles were white. Ellis reached out and put her hand on Ava's. "I know how horribly difficult this has been for you."

Ava kept her eyes averted and gave a jerky nod.

"Is there anything else you can tell me?"

Ava shook her head and sniffled, but then said, "Just that somebody said they'd seen a black Hummer in the lot. Maybe that's what the guy was driving."

Ellis's heart skipped a beat. "Who? Who saw it?"

Lifting a shoulder, Ava said, "I guess one of the people living here. I just heard that someone said they'd seen it. It stuck out in a place like this, you know."

"Could it have been that *morning* that they saw the Hummer? There had to have been lots of confusion."

Ava seemed to be shrinking right before Ellis's eyes. She curled deeper into her chair. "I really don't know. I'm so tired. Everything is running together."

"I can't thank you enough for talking with me. You've been a huge help. Is there anything I can do for you before I leave?"

Ava raised her eyes to meet Ellis's. "You can make sure that bastard pays."

Ellis nodded. She knew how the violation of someone

close to you, someone you shared your home and your life with, left you feeling vulnerable and violated as well.

⁂

Hollis loved the way Wayne Carr's voice trembled whenever they spoke on the phone. Carr was one of those guys Hollis's father had called a secret faggot, married because he wasn't man enough to admit he was a queer—all clothes and shoes, prancing around with manicured hands and hair just so. Weak, for all his self-important bluster. Of course, that self-importance was currently serving Hollis well.

"Nice job on the newspaper articles," Hollis said. "But we're not done yet."

"Oh?" Carr's tone said he was scared shitless—as he should be. Hollis had yet to decide how Carr's part in this little game would end.

"We have the book to discuss," Hollis said.

"Oh, yes."

"And I want a list of the lawyers you've talked to about my case. I'd like to do a little follow-up."

Carr hesitated just long enough that Hollis thought perhaps the man hadn't carried through with his end of their bargain. "You have contacted them, haven't you? I'd hate for these photographs to come to light—might tarnish my reputation. Oh, what was I thinking? I won't be able to take credit for them. Still . . ."

"I've done everything you asked!"

"Then the names will be no problem."

There was the sound of rustling papers. Then Carr gave Hollis the names of several very good defense attorneys.

"I'm impressed," Hollis said. "Anyone showing interest?"

"A couple. I should be hearing back today or tomorrow."

"Excellent."

"What assurance do I have that once I do what you want, you won't still expose those photos?"

"Why, none. But you can be certain that if you don't, or if I get the slightest hint that you're betraying our agreement, you can kiss your cushy life good-bye." Hollis hung up. Depending on the outcome of one of his future errands, the decision about Carr's fate might take care of itself.

Hollis decided he'd settle in as a spectator for the next few hours.

Although she hadn't felt her phone vibrate in her pocket while she'd been talking to Ava, Ellis checked for missed calls as soon as she stepped out of the apartment.

There were none.

Come on, Nate. She pushed away the possibility he might well be in police custody at this very moment.

She decided to knock on a few doors and see if anyone knew exactly who had mentioned the Hummer.

The first four doors went unanswered. With the fifth, she hit some luck. It was answered by a guy who looked to be about the same age as Kimberly and Ava. He was barefooted and shirtless, wearing khaki cargo shorts with boxers showing at the waist. His hair stood on end, and he had one of those scruffy four-day beards that really wasn't working for him; he looked like a bum, not a movie star. He also looked like she'd awakened him.

She told him she was investigating the murder (misleading and yet still true). Once she'd established he hadn't seen or heard anything that night, she asked about the black Hummer.

He ran a hand over his messy hair. "I do remember somebody saying something about it."

"Was it someone you recognized?" she asked.

His mouth screwed to the side. "There were lots of people out there that morning. . . ." Finally, he shook his head. "I can't remember who said it, so I guess not. If I'd known the person, I would have remembered. Maybe I just overheard someone saying it. Everybody was talking, trying to figure out what was going on."

She thanked him and went on. She knocked on twenty doors. Only two more were answered. No one had a more definite answer than the first guy. They all remembered hearing it. No one remembered who said it, or exactly when.

Ellis returned to her car. She locked the doors and started it, getting the air-conditioning going. She decided to wait to call the police with her theory—at least until she'd spoken to Nate. This whole Hummer thing added another stone in the basket that could sink him.

Did Alexander hope to prove his innocence by making Nate look like a murderer? Nate killed Kimberly Potter, so he must have killed Laura too? Could Alexander actually think it would play out like that?

Kimberly Potter's murder wasn't a spur-of-the-moment act of insanity, not with that screwdriver from Nate's boat used in the crime. Not with the striking similarity between Laura and Kimberly. It, like everything else going on, had been planned. Alexander had watched and studied and capitalized on his opportunities.

Had pinning a murder on Nate been part of Alexander's original plan for revenge? If so, what was Nate's sin against Alexander? As far as Ellis knew, Nate hadn't offered any damning testimony that contributed to Alexander's conviction. It had been Ellis's testimony alone that had done that.

Hadn't it?

It hit her then that she didn't really know the details of what had transpired in the courtroom, other than during her own testimony and the reading of the verdict. There could be clues in those court documents.

She looked at her watch. Eleven-fifteen. She could be at the courthouse in forty minutes.

She pulled out of the parking spot and headed toward Charleston.

Chapter Twenty-two

Most of our court transcripts and records are in a database. We're very proud of our system," Pamela, the woman assisting Ellis in the Charleston County Clerk of Courts office, said. "We have transcriptions of most of our criminal cases and judgments as far back as 1991 now. The cases that haven't been transcribed yet will only have the main identification page listing the arrest, the charge, and the judgment."

Ellis followed her to a computer terminal in a small semiprivate carrel near the front of the office.

Pamela continued. "Some of them are scanned pdf files. Just click on the document icon to bring those up. You can search by defendant's name or by case number. As long as the file hasn't been sealed by the court, it should be here. Print out anything you want. There is a charge of ten cents per page."

"Do these files include the statements police used in building the case?" Ellis asked.

"No," Pamela said. "Those are kept with the case evidence by the investigating police department."

"Thank you." Ellis took a seat, excitement and dread mixing like a deadly cocktail in her stomach.

"Let me know if you need anything," Pamela said as she stepped away. "We close at four-thirty."

Ellis set her hands on the keyboard. She waited until the woman was back behind the counter before she typed even the first letter to initiate the search. She felt as though she were opening a personal diary or a secret family album.

Her first task was to choose a month and year, or specify a span of time to search using a drop-down menu. Out of curiosity, she expanded the search to five years prior to Laura's case.

Ellis typed the first letter of Hollis Alexander's name in the defendant's name box. Then she lifted her hands from the keyboard and flexed her fingers. Tension had all of her muscles at strained attention. She felt like she'd consumed a truckload of caffeine.

She was so anxious that she mistyped Hollis Alexander's name three times.

She paused momentarily, feeling as if she was opening a box that could hold a precious treasure . . . or a collection of venomous snakes. The she hit the SEARCH button.

The computer pulled up all relevant cases. Much to her surprise, there were four. She double-checked to confirm they were all the same offender. Of course they were; how many Hollis Alexanders could there be in Charleston County?

Two of the cases were sealed—juvenile records. She wondered if Lorne Buckley could enlighten her. There was a Charleston County Clerk of Courts notepad sitting next to the keyboard. She started her list of questions to ask the prosecutor. Tops on that list was whether or not

Buckley bought into this theory that Nate murdered Kimberly Potter.

The third case was a trial several months before Laura had been attacked.

Ellis opened that transcript. It was one of those with only the identification page listing the arrest, charge, and judgment. Alexander had been arrested and charged with aggravated sexual assault—and acquitted.

She jotted another question for Buckley. Why had Alexander walked?

Now she was left with only the trial for Laura's attack.

After fortifying herself mentally, realizing this would be the first time she would face all of the horrible, gritty details of Laura's case, she opened the file she'd come here to see.

She noted that Alexander had been represented by a public defender. No surprise, although she'd never thought about such things at the time. So many things fell into that category. So many gaps she'd either filled in with her imagination or ignored completely. So many things her family had kept in the shadows.

Like an emaciated person rescued from starvation, she wanted to gobble up every scrap of detail, while at the same time she was sickened at the very thought of them.

Swallowing the bile creeping up her throat, she pressed on.

She was stunned when she saw the transcript was over three hundred pages long.

As she read the first part, she realized how much of it was courtroom information, instructions given by the judge, things other than the words out of the witnesses' mouths.

Neither of the opening statements, by the prosecution or defense, held any bright flashes of discovery. Both were long-winded, laying out in vague and evocative speech why their view of Hollis Alexander's guilt/innocence was right and just.

What did surprise her was the fact that the defense attorney had admitted right up front that Alexander had been outside Laura's house that night. He painted a picture of a young man smitten, who'd made the shameful mistake of looking in her window. But that did not make him a brutal rapist. Especially when Laura's bed had been empty when he'd looked in her room at three that morning. He insisted that Laura Reinhardt suffered her fate at someone else's hand. Someone who was out there now, mocking our justice system.

She supposed contesting the fact that he'd been there, in light of the fingerprint and Ellis's seeing him, would make Alexander's story of innocence that much less credible.

Ellis scrolled down to the witness testimony for the prosecution.

At first, she couldn't find any rhythm to what she was reading. It was like looking at halting, jerky dialogue in a book, or the bare bones of a script for a play.

Words sitting alone on the page seemed grossly inadequate to transmit what had transpired inside that courtroom. Words had been stripped of their emotional delivery by a court reporter who had reduced disturbing testimony to an impersonal dictation.

Ellis skimmed over testimony whose sole purpose

appeared to be establishing Laura's position in the community, the admiration of friends and loved ones.

As she read Dr. Kreag's testimony, Ellis got her first taste of the reality of what had happened to her cousin. The doctor began by listing Laura's grievous injuries and hopeless prognosis.

The doctor explained the details of how, although no semen had been found, they'd determined that Laura had been raped.

She had multiple bruises and lacerations from the beating she'd received. Photographs had been shown to the jury as exhibits.

Ellis wondered where those photos were.

Laura had suffered a traumatic brain injury from blunt-force trauma to the head, which they suspect occurred when her head was repeatedly slammed into the ground. Her throat exhibited injuries consistent with manual strangulation. She'd also inhaled and swallowed moderate amounts of salt water.

All of these things combined had left Laura in an unresponsive, vegetative state.

Even with the dispassionate delivery, by the time Ellis had finished Dr. Kreag's testimony, her face was wet with tears. She'd vividly imagined every blow, every indignity her cousin had suffered.

How had her aunt and uncle been able to sit through this testimony?

Ellis no longer had any appetite for what was in this file. Still, she forced herself to chew and swallow every detail.

In his cross-examination, the defense attorney ignored the listing of injuries and the fact that Laura's brain had been irreparably damaged. His only question was to establish that, from her medical findings, Dr. Kreag had no way at all to identify who had delivered the beating and rape.

Ellis's testimony was next.

Simple black-and-white letters certainly didn't convey what it had *felt like* sitting on that witness stand, the sensation of being naked and afraid as Hollis Alexander stared at her with his hateful, colorless eyes.

The feel of the weight of that accusing stare was as fresh now as when she'd been on the stand.

February, eight months after Laura was attacked
Charleston County Courthouse

Ellis walked the aisle from the back of the courtroom toward the witness stand. Her breathing came shallow and fast. She was so dizzy that the floor felt odd under her feet, as if she were walking on thick foam rubber.

Mr. Buckley had told her it was important to breathe and to keep her eyes on him. He stood behind the railing, his eyes encouraging her.

This felt like one of those dreams where you're out in public, doing regular stuff, but you're naked and you can't find anything to cover up with. She could feel everyone looking at her.

It was so quiet that the sound of the heels of her shoes echoed with each step.

She made it to the railing. Mr. Buckley opened the little gate for her.

Eight steps more and she'd made it to the witness stand.

The bailiff stood before her and had her swear to tell the truth.

Suddenly she couldn't remember anything straight. All of Mr. Buckley's instructions were mixed up in her head. All the words she was supposed to use had hidden in places where she couldn't find them.

Her body flashed hot. All the spit in her mouth dried up. What if she couldn't do this?

You have to. For Laura.

Mr. Buckley had her tell the jury who she was and where she lived. The answers to those simple questions helped cool the heat of her rising panic.

"Tell us about that night, the night your cousin was attacked."

She licked her lips, but her tongue was so dry it didn't do any good. "I was sleeping on the top bunk in Laura's room. She was on the bottom. We turned out the lights around midnight."

"Was the bedroom window open at that time?"

"Yes. I went to sleep pretty much right away." She wasn't going to tell how as she'd been falling asleep, she'd heard Laura's soft laugh and whispers as she'd talked to Nate through the window. She hadn't told the police either. It would only confuse things. "It was around three-fifteen or so when I woke up. I'm not sure why. Then I heard a soft thump on the porch outside the window. And I smelled something; my mom says I have the most sensitive nose in the county." It startled her when a few people in the room chuckled.

Mr. Buckley nodded. "Go on. You're doing fine."

Ellis kept her eyes on him. "You know how you can smell camellias in the fall even when you're several feet away? It was like that. But not sweet. It was like really strong spicy cologne mixed with the way the bus smells the morning after it's been used to take the football team to an away game." There, those were the right words, the ones that had made Mr. Buckley clap his hands when she'd said them the first time.

She felt a little better.

"There's a path from the road to the beach between Laura's house and mine. I leaned over the edge of the bed and looked out the window. I saw a guy with light-colored hair that was kind of long on top; it hung down onto his eyebrows. He looked like he was searching for something, like he'd dropped something in the sand."

"Did you get a clear look at his face?"

"Yes. I remember especially because it was a full moon, and the color of his eyes was so light; they looked really strange." *Vampire eyes.*

"How far away was he from your cousin's window?"

"About fifteen feet or so."

"How long did you watch him?"

"A minute or so. I was curious about what he'd dropped, so I waited. He didn't find it. All of a sudden, he just gave up and walked toward the road."

"How fast was he moving when he walked away?"

"A little faster than a normal walk. He wasn't running."

"What did you do then?"

"I went back to sleep." She felt so guilty admitting that. Laura had needed her and she'd gone back to sleep. "I thought he was just somebody cutting through, coming up from a beach party. Kids do it sometimes. Usually not that late, though."

"Is that man in the courtroom?"

"Yes." Her heart sped up again. She'd been able to avoid looking at Hollis Alexander until now. When she turned toward him, he stared at her with those ice-colored eyes, and her skin shrank against her bones. He looked like he wanted to eat her alive. She thought she might pee her pants. "He's there." She pointed like Mr. Buckley had told her to.

"Had you ever seen this man before that night?"

"No."

"And did you see this man after that night?"

"Yes. He was outside Laura's hospital room a couple weeks later, peeking in the door. I called to him but he ran. My uncle chased him out into the parking lot."

"He *ran*?"

"Yes."

"Thank you. That's all." Mr. Buckley went and sat at his table.

Ellis looked at her hands in her lap. Her fingernails blurred; she realized she was starting to cry.

The judge called the defense attorney.

He had red hair and freckles, and looked like he was still in high school. She guessed that was impossible. He was a lawyer, after all. Maybe he was like a Doogie Howser kind of lawyer.

He stood in front of her so that when she looked at him, she couldn't help but see Alexander.

The Doogie lawyer asked, "You'd been sleeping just before you saw my client?"

"Yes. But I was completely awake when I looked out."

"Mmm-hmm. Were there any lights on outside?"

"No. It was sea turtle nesting season. Nobody had outside lights on."

"So you'd been asleep *and* it was completely dark outside."

"Not completely. The moon was bright. And my eyes were used to the dark." She wanted to say that she'd smelled him before she saw him. But Mr. Buckley had warned her not to do more than answer the question. He would have her clarify things if he thought they needed to be.

"And when you say you saw Mr. Alexander, did you see anyone else?"

At one point, Ellis had thought she'd seen a shadow near the corner of the house, but no one ever appeared. Mr. Buckley had been adamant there was no reason to mention it, as she hadn't seen anyone. "No."

"Mr. Alexander was *alone*? Your cousin wasn't with him?"

"No."

"At any time that night, did you hear a struggle? A noise? Anyone calling out for help?" His tone was condescending. Doogie wasn't nearly as nice as he looked.

"No. But when I woke up, I figure he'd already taken her to the beach by then. He was heading toward the road."

"Let's keep our statements to the facts, Ms. Greene. You did not hear any sort of struggle?"

"No." She wanted to crawl under her chair.

"At the time you claim to have seen Mr. Alexander, did you then check to see if your cousin was in her bed—

since I assume you could not see her in the bottom bunk from where you were on the top?"

"No."

"When did you first realize your cousin was gone?"

"The next morning, around nine."

"I see." He looked at the jury.

Ellis started to open her mouth, explain further, but Mr. Buckley caught her eye and shook his head. She gritted her teeth instead.

"You and your cousin were close?"

"Yes. More like sisters than cousins."

"Had she ever mentioned Hollis Alexander? Had you *ever* seen your cousin with Mr. Alexander?"

"No. And no."

"Have you ever seen your cousin in the company of any other young man?"

"Sure. But—"

"How many?"

"That's a stupid question." As soon as she said it, she wanted to clamp her hand over her mouth. She didn't dare look at Mr. Buckley now.

With a smile that made her feel totally stupid, Doogie said, "Be that as it may, you're obliged to answer."

"Laura knows everybody. She went to parties and ball games and school dances. I guess I've *seen her* with dozens of guys. But being popular isn't—"

"But never with my client?"

"No."

"Did Laura have a boyfriend?"

"Yes, she *does.*"

"Who was he?"

"Please stop talking about her like she's dead."

"My apologies. Does she have a boyfriend?"

"Yes."

"Do you know his name?"

"Nate Vance. We know him from the stables."

"You've seen Laura with lots of boys, other than her boyfriend?"

"I guess so." Hot panic eddied in the pit of her stomach.

"And did Nate Vance ever come to visit your cousin at her house?"

"Sure. But—"

The lawyer held up his hand and said, "Thank you, Ms. Greene. That's all."

Ellis sent a panicked look at Mr. Buckley. This guy made it sound like Nate was the guilty one.

Mr. Buckley stood.

Good, he was going to straighten this all out.

Ellis waited.

Mr. Buckley said, "The prosecution has no further questions."

Ellis remembered how hollow she'd felt as she'd left that courtroom. She needed absolution . . . from Nate and Nate alone. But she didn't see him again until the verdict was read.

She read on, anxious to get to Nate's testimony.

Mr. Coon testified about how he'd found Laura on the rocks of the breakwater at six the next morning when he'd been walking his dog. His description of Laura made Ellis's intestines twist and cramp.

Then the forensic testimony began.

Laura's clothing was never found. None of Alexander's hair or bodily fluids had been found on her. The expert stated he'd found vaginal traces of a spermicide commonly used in certain condoms.

Hollis Alexander's fingerprint was on the outside frame of her bedroom window. Two hairs had been collected from the screen in that window. Those hairs had been matched to Alexander.

They had also recovered a nylon stocking in the pathway beside Laura's house. It also had Alexander's hair in it.

Ellis paused. So that was what he'd been looking for.

She made a note to ask Buckley if Alexander had used a stocking over his head in the previous rape.

Ellis couldn't believe she'd reached the end of the prosecution's witnesses and Nate hadn't been called.

The first two people called by the defense testified that they had been with Alexander from ten p.m. until one a.m. on the night of the attack. A third person testified that he'd seen Alexander and his two friends at the twenty-four-hour Scotchman convenience store in Mt. Pleasant at twelve-thirty a.m.

Mr. Buckley chose only to cross-examine the convenience-store clerk. Mr. Buckley asked what the attendant had sold Alexander. The attendant listed cigarettes, a *Hustler* magazine, and a box of condoms.

Ellis was surprised when the *defense* called Nate. She quickly saw how her testimony could have buried him. Nate admitted that he and Laura had had an argument in the parking lot of the drugstore in Belle Island at nine o'clock that evening.

Ellis hadn't known this. Is that why Laura and Nate had been talking at her window later? Were they making up?

She read on with increased interest.

Defense Counsel: And what was that argument about?

Nathaniel Vance: We were supposed to hang out. She'd decided to do something else.

Defense Counsel: What?

Nathaniel Vance: She didn't say specifically.

Defense Counsel: Did this make you angry?

Nathaniel Vance: I was used to it. She did it a lot.

Defense Counsel: What did you do then?

Nathaniel Vance: Nothing. I went home.

Defense Counsel: You just went home?

Nathaniel Vance: Yes.

Defense Counsel: So she made a habit out of dumping you at the last minute? That can be very frustrating.

Prosecuting Attorney: Objection.

Judge: Sustained. The jury will disregard that last statement by the defense counsel.

Defense Counsel: Let me restate. Did Laura make a habit out of canceling your plans at the last minute?

Nathaniel Vance: Not often enough that it would make me want to hurt her, if that's what you're getting at.

Defense Counsel: Yes or no, Mr. Vance.

Nathaniel Vance: Yes.

Defense Counsel: Were you and Ms. Reinhardt sexually intimate?

Nathaniel Vance: No.

Defense Counsel: What was the nature of your relationship, then?

Nathaniel Vance: We were friends.

Defense Counsel: Was your relationship romantic in any way?

Nathaniel Vance: I said we were friends.

Judge: Please answer the question posed, Mr. Vance.

Nathaniel Vance: No.

Defense Counsel: Did you want there to be a romantic relationship between you and Ms. Reinhardt?

Ellis found herself wanting to ask her own questions. All of these bare-bones answers were driving her crazy.

Nathaniel Vance: I care about her.

Defense Counsel: I see, unrequited love.

Prosecuting Attorney: Objection.

Judge: Sustained. Get on with your defense, Mr. Murdock.

Defense Counsel: In any of your time with Ms. Reinhardt, as her friend, did you ever see her in the company of my client?

Nathaniel Vance: No.

Defense Counsel: Did you ever see her in the company of other young men?

Nathaniel Vance: Yes.

Defense Counsel: And when you saw her with

other young men, were they ever in romantic situations?

Nathaniel Vance: Yes.

Defense Counsel: How did it make you feel, when you saw her with other young men?

Defense Counsel: Do I need to repeat the question, Mr. Vance?

Judge: Please answer the question.

Nathaniel Vance: It made me sick.

Defense Counsel: Let's get back to the night of the attack on Ms. Reinhardt. Did you see her again after you left her in the parking lot of the drugstore?

Nathaniel Vance: No. That was the last time I saw her.

Ellis stopped breathing.

Nate had lied. Outright. Under oath.

Chapter Twenty-Three

Nate had had to break every speed limit in order to make it to Savannah in time. After all, his contacts thought he was staying there. No way could he let those people get so much as a whiff about Belle Island. So he'd pretended a short-notice meeting was no problem.

He'd thought he'd had everything taken care of. Apparently, there were new faces in the game. Faces that demanded to see him in person. There was too much at stake, and he'd spent too long nursing this deal for it to go south now.

Once he'd given adequate assurance to all parties, he headed back the way he'd come, back to Ellis and an entirely different set of problems.

As he drove, his mind quickly disengaged from work matters and refocused on protecting Ellis.

Too many things weren't fitting what he'd imagined Alexander's game to be. Revenge. Balancing the scales.

Nate wondered how killing that girl and framing him served Alexander's plan. Nate supposed Alexander's twisted sense of justice could see the logic—if Alexander had been counting on Nate taking the blame for Laura.

Still, something didn't add up. It hovered on the fringes of his mind, but he couldn't bring it to the fore.

Alexander was all about dominance and violation. Was part of his game manipulating Ellis by using her fear? Is that why he risked being caught to leave those roses? It seemed an awfully big chance to take for something that could be achieved in so many other, less dicey, ways.

Another question came to mind. Nate and Ellis had immediately assumed Alexander had left the flowers. But there was nothing to indicate it had been him. If he wanted to intimidate Ellis, why not sign the notes so she knew for certain?

Then there was the symbolic intimation of red roses—love.

Ellis had said the first note had said "some things are worth waiting for." Could be Alexander. He thought of the cold glare in Rory's eyes when he'd caught Ellis kissing Nate.

The second note: *Still waiting . . .*

Rory wasn't man enough to step up and confront Nate. Was he hiding behind that accepting façade? Was his technique to get Ellis back more covert?

Or am I just looking at him because I'm jealous?

He'd had plenty of practice suppressing his personal feelings in order to get a job done. He had to apply that same practice here—remove his emotions from the equation.

But could he? Where Ellis was concerned, he couldn't seem to get a grip on those emotions.

He assured himself, despite his feelings for her, something still felt off.

❦

Ellis stepped out of the judicial center onto Broad Street, squinting against the glare of late afternoon sun. Her efforts in the clerk's office had added more questions about Hollis Alexander than it had answered. Not to mention a new one about Nate Vance. Why had he lied?

For some reason, his outright lie about not seeing Laura later that night seemed so much more damning than Ellis's *nonmention* of hearing them talk as she'd been falling asleep.

Until she spoke to Nate, she would have no answer to that particular question. However, Lorne Buckley could possibly clear up her questions about Alexander. If she hurried, she might be able to catch him as he left his office. While she was talking to him, she could probe a little and see where he stood on the subject of Kimberly Potter's murder.

Ellis would also make certain Buckley was aware of Alexander's lurking outside her condo, his leaving those roses, his call to her home this morning, and her suspicion that he'd sabotaged her father's scaffolding. With any luck, that would be enough for the prosecutor to have Alexander arrested on parole violation. At least that would get him off the streets while they built their case for the Potter murder.

As Ellis headed toward the solicitor's office in the O. T. Wallace Building, excitement thrummed a chord in her chest. For the first time in days, she felt as if she had a hand on the reins of her life. Soon this would be over, for her, for Nate—

And then Nate would leave and go back to his mysterious life.

That thought settled like a damp fog on her mood. Mysterious life. He'd lied under oath.

She didn't know him at all.

A commotion down Broad Street caught Ellis's attention.

Shouts rose. Several people ran toward the center of the street. Traffic stopped.

She heard someone yelling for a doctor. Without another moment's hesitation, she hurried toward the crowd. She wasn't a doctor, but she was well trained in first aid.

As she shouldered her way through the group of people, she said, "I have some training—"

The instant she saw the unconscious man lying on the pavement, her words died and her heart jumped in her chest.

Oh, dear God.

She fell to her knees next to Lorne Buckley. He was older, his hair now silver, but it was definitely him.

She realized she was staring at his face, not assessing his injuries.

Someone took off a suit jacket and laid it over Buckley's chest. The pavement was very warm. Good for shock.

"Mr. Buckley? Can you hear me?" she asked. Even as she did, she noted the blood trickling from his left ear and his nose. It was clear his leg and possibly his arm were broken.

She leaned over his nose, listening for breathing.

There was so much noise around her that she couldn't tell. She checked his carotid pulse with shaking fingers. Slow. Weak.

Airway. Make certain he has a clear airway. Don't move his neck.

Once she focused on what she needed to do, her shaking subsided. She worked quickly and confidently, instructing others in how to help.

It seemed an eternity before she heard the wail of an approaching siren. Then, within seconds, a paramedic was there and took over.

She stepped back. As she watched, her heart began beating too fast and her shaking returned.

Poor Mr. Buckley. Such a kind man.

Suddenly it felt very personal again. Ellis turned away from what the paramedics were doing, her stomach feeling like she'd swallowed broken glass.

Several people around her were describing what they'd seen. Buckley had been crossing the street in the middle of the block, and a car had hit him, throwing him several feet in the air. The car hadn't stopped.

"He landed just like a rag doll." She heard one woman's quivering voice say. "He hit his head on that truck bumper and bounced off on the way down."

Ellis backed away, bumping against the jumble of onlookers as they gave accounts of what they'd seen. *A sedan. No, it was a two-door. Beige. Silver. White. Someone was in the passenger seat. The driver was alone in the car. It was a woman. It was a long-haired man.*

The swirl of activity and noise around Ellis made her dizzy. She leaned back against a car fender to steady herself. Much to her selfish shame, the words racing through her mind were *Now there's one less voice of reason, one less person in Nate's corner.*

❦

The Friday afternoon traffic crept out of Charleston. It stacked up on entrance ramps and clogged bridges. Ellis wished she had Nate's Hummer; she could just plow her way through.

It seemed wrong, running off from Buckley's accident like she had. It felt disrespectful. Not that she had anything to offer the police; she hadn't witnessed the accident. And she couldn't afford to get tied up in Charleston, not when the police were looking for Nate.

She swallowed dryly. God, she wished she'd been able to talk to the prosecutor.

Every time she blinked, she saw Buckley sprawled on the pavement, his limbs jutting in unnatural angles. She sent up a swift prayer for Buckley's recovery.

An accident. It was just an unfortunate accident. There was no way Buckley's hit-and-run was related to what was going on with Nate and Alexander. That was just too big of a stretch.

Wasn't it?

Things were stacking up against Nate. If she could somehow put Alexander and Kimberly Potter together at the same place and time, it'd be a good start. She didn't know why she hadn't thought to take the photographs of Hollis Alexander to Seaside in the first place.

The farther she got from the city, the lighter traffic became. It was running like water over a spillway by the time she reached the bridge to Belle Island. Even so, her grip remained tight on the steering wheel, and her nerves were twisted like bomb-blasted steel.

When she reached the entrance to her neighborhood, Sam wasn't in the guardhouse. The Gator wasn't in its usual parking spot. She really wanted him to go with her to the condo. She waited for two minutes. Still no Sam.

She used her card and went through the gate. She couldn't waste any more time. It was broad daylight; she'd be cautious.

She dialed Nate's new cell number on her way into the complex. At the first ring, she disconnected. Nate hadn't called her. Maybe there was a reason. With the police looking for him and her uncle having called every governmental agency he could think of with who knows what kind of accusations, there was a possibility of someone listening to either her or Nate's calls.

She'd wait. Nate would find a way to get in touch.

When she pulled into her drive, she parked in the center of the pavement, away from places someone could be hiding and grab her as she exited the car. Before she opened the car door, she gave a good look around. She locked the doors when she got out.

As she rounded the corner of her building, heading toward the stairs, she gave the shrubbery wide berth. She studied her surroundings carefully, watching for any hint of movement.

Climbing the last flight, she debated whether or not to get out her gun.

Too risky. She might hesitate. She trusted her self-defense instincts would be quick if someone tried to attack her. If they had a gun . . . Well, she most likely didn't stand a chance either way. Not, she assured herself, that it was an issue at all. Her door was undisturbed. Her alarm wasn't screaming.

She slid her key in the lock. If the warning beep on the alarm didn't start immediately, she'd cut and run.

She swallowed dryly and turned the knob.

The door opened.

The familiar chirping started. She had thirty seconds to disarm the alarm, or it would automatically call the police.

She locked the door behind her and walked past the keypad, ignoring its high-pitched demand. Thirty seconds was plenty of time to check the condo to make certain she was alone here.

The kitchen was clear.

The living room was clear.

The hall bath's shower curtain was open as always. Bath and closet, clear.

The spare bedroom and closet were clear. Since there wasn't a bed, there was nothing to hide under.

She entered her bedroom. No one.

Closet and bathroom, clear.

She quickly poked and swatted at the shower curtain. With an extended arm, she swung it open at the end of the tub. Clear.

She took a fast glance under the bed.

Just a pair of dirty socks.

She hurried to the control pad next to her bed and shut it off just as it was beginning to dial the police. Then she sat on her bed, feeling like she'd just run a marathon.

After checking and finding no new voice mails on her home phone, she stopped in her bathroom to wash her face before she left for Seaside Apartments again. The sticky humidity had left a salty film on her skin. All of her skin.

A three-minute shower would give her the lift she needed to go out and beat the bushes again. It was after six. She thanked heaven for daylight savings time. She had a good two and a half hours before dark.

As she pulled off her sandals, she reached behind the shower curtain to get the water going.

Her phone rang. Nate?

She stripped off her top as she ran to pick it up. "Hello?"

"Ellis? What's the matter? You're out of breath."

Damn. "Oh, Rory, I was just leaving . . . had to run to catch the phone." She wished she hadn't answered.

"I was just calling to see how you are."

"I'm fine. You know me, Cautious Clara."

"Ellis, I want to see you."

"I don't think that's a good idea." This was not the time to talk about their relationship. It had taken her weeks and weeks to make the decision to break up with him. Everything was too nuts now for her to make a sound decision about the two of them.

He was silent for a moment. She could hear his frustration in his breathing. It almost made her relent.

"Your dad's in the hospital," he finally said. "There's a crazy man after you. I think you should stop being so stubborn and let me stay with you."

She stepped out of her capri pants and realized the knees were black from where she'd knelt on the city street. A little shiver ran down her arms.

"I really appreciate your worrying about me. But between my six locks, my alarm system, my pepper spray, my brown belt, and the gun my dad's making me carry, I'm perfectly safe."

"Dammit, Ellis!" Rory yelled. Then his voice slid low and as hateful as she'd ever heard it. "He's with you, isn't he?"

"No one is with me."

"You owe me better than this, Ellis."

She did. She knew she did. They'd been together for a long time. And, whether he believed it or not, she hadn't come to her decision easily. Why couldn't he see it was best for both of them to be apart? At least for a while.

"I *am* alone, Rory. And I'm fine. Now, I really have to go."

"Wait, Ellis, I'm sorry." His voice was pleading. "I didn't mean to—"

"Good-bye, Rory." She hung up, just a little thankful for his rare spate of anger. It made her see things more clearly. She had been fooling herself. She'd thought she and Rory got along because they were alike. But it wasn't that at all. Rory was like too-soft meringue. He folded and melted into himself when he should stand strong—when she *needed* him to stand strong, stand up to her.

Another thought came on the heels of that one. Had that been the reason she'd gone out with him in the first place? Because she'd known she could win a war of wills?

"Ugh." These were thoughts for another time. She threw off the rest of her clothes on the way to the bathroom.

Then she slipped inside the shower curtain and pulled it closed behind her.

She turned toward the spray . . . and screamed.

Chapter Twenty-Four

Ellis jumped backward, lost her footing, and fell, hitting her elbow on the tub edge and her head on the tile surround. Her eyes stayed fixed on the nude doll dangling from the showerhead. Its green eyes were open. Its brown hair dripped water. A small screwdriver protruded from its throat. A pair of Ellis's panties hung from the screwdriver.

This was no child's baby doll. It was a slender twenty-four-inch, anatomically correct version of a Barbie, with no detail left to the imagination. A pervert's plaything.

Ellis lay there under the pelting water, gasping. Her right arm tingled like a son of a bitch. Feeling her head with her left hand, she located a goose egg already forming.

How in the hell had he gotten in here? The alarm hadn't been tripped. The door was still locked.

Her feet slipped and slid as she pushed herself to a sitting position.

The phone rang and her heart tried to stick itself to the underside of her brain.

She shut off the water with her foot.

The phone kept ringing.

Ellis pulled herself out of the tub, dripping water everywhere. She grabbed a towel and held it to her chest, then reached for the phone.

Putting it to her ear, she didn't say anything, dread choking her. She braced herself for Alexander's disturbing distortion of her name.

"Ellis? Ellis, are you there?"

"Nate! Oh, my God, Nate! Where are you?"

"Outside your front door. Let me—"

She dropped the phone and sprinted for the door. Her wet fingers slipped on the dead bolt. When she got the door open, she hurled herself into his arms.

"He was here! He was here, *inside*."

Nate's arms came around her. He lifted her feet off the ground and stepped inside the door.

He held her with one arm and pulled his handgun. "Where?"

"Not now. He's gone." She clung to him. "I don't know how he got in. The alarm was still on."

Nate kicked the door closed behind him and put his gun away. "While you were in the shower?"

At that moment, she realized she was wet and naked. His hands were on her bare back. The towel was pressed between them.

"Oh." She released her hold on him and tried to gather the towel around her. "No, while I was gone."

He grabbed the towel ends and pulled them to meet on her back. Then he held her close again. "You were supposed to stay here."

"I had things to do," she said defensively.

He didn't pursue that topic. "You're all right?"

She nodded. Shame began to creep into the light. Oh,

yeah, she was a real kick-ass woman. She was behaving like a frightened ninny.

"You're shaking," Nate said.

"I'm wet. The air-conditioning is on." She knew that wasn't the cause.

He was kind enough not to call her on it.

He stroked her wet hair. "Okay," he said. He pressed his lips to the top of her head. "Go get dry. Then you can tell me everything."

She nodded. But neither of them moved from the embrace.

He held her for a long while, like a gentleman, his hands remaining stationary *and* on the towel. He kept assuring her, in a low, lulling voice, that she was all right, that he wouldn't let anything happen to her.

And she believed him.

So much so that she began to think of other things . . . like his hands on her bare back.

Now was not the time.

She took a step backward, making certain the towel stayed in place.

"Oh, I've soaked your shirt." She placed a hand on his chest. Were her fingertips lying, or did his heart seem to be beating too fast?

"I'm hot. It'll cool me off."

She tried to make a joke. "Not very flattering, standing naked in a man's arms and having him cool off."

He gave her a slightly crooked grin. "I didn't say I was hot when I came in the door."

She caught her lip between her teeth, for a moment tempted to test and see exactly how hot he was. But that grotesque doll was just feet away, with all of its hideous implications.

She turned away. "I'll get dressed. Then we've got a lot to talk about."

Nate clenched his teeth. What if Alexander had been waiting in here when Ellis had come in? It was a thought too horrible to contemplate.

How had the man gotten in and not tripped the alarm?

Nate realized that he hadn't asked Ellis the most obvious question—how did she know he'd been here?

Nate prowled from window to window, from entry to sliding door, with his insides twisted like a steel cable.

All of the access points to Ellis's condo were locked from the inside. All glass was intact. He scouted the windowsills—not that anyone without a very tall ladder could have accessed them. They were clean and unmarked. The sliding glass door had a sturdy safety bar, a good one that couldn't be flipped up by fishing a coat hanger between the doors.

Ellis's bedroom window opened onto the balcony too. He'd have to check that one when Ellis was finished changing; not that he hadn't already had a very nice view of her beautifully curved backside. She'd made him so hot and hard that he'd hardly been able to think.

He blew a long breath to clear his head. He had to keep his mind on deciphering Alexander in order to protect her. Not that he should even *consider* giving in to the carnal urges she set off.

Moments later, Ellis reappeared wearing a pair of jeans

and a silky sleeveless top. Her wet hair was pulled back in a ponytail that hung down between her shoulder blades.

He caught himself wishing she'd left it down.

"Figure out how he got in?" she asked. The assurance in her voice made him feel grossly inadequate to play his role as hero.

"No. I still want to look at your bedroom window."

She turned and headed back the way she'd come. "There's something else in here you need to see."

He'd spent considerable time over the past days fantasizing about getting them both into this bedroom. This particular scenario had never come to mind.

A lacy pair of black panties lay on the floor next to her bed. He averted his eyes.

She led him to the master bathroom door and motioned for him to go on in. Her posture was stiff. Whatever was in here, she wasn't anxious to see it again. No doubt Alexander's calling card.

Nate stepped around her.

There was water all over the tile floor and a bra that matched those panties lying next to the tub.

"In the shower," she said.

He pushed open the curtain.

"That son of a bitch," he muttered as he stepped closer to examine the thing hanging from the showerhead.

The doll was nasty in its own right. But what Alexander had done to it . . . Nate's hands balled into fists so tight his arms trembled. He wanted to reach out and yank it down. Tear it into pieces. But he couldn't touch it.

The screwdriver was small enough to look proportional to the doll's size. Alexander had gone to a lot of trouble in his presentation. Nate figured the panties were from

Ellis's drawer. As he looked more closely, it appeared he'd used her dental floss to hang it.

From behind him, Ellis said, "Get rid of it."

He looked over his shoulder. She still hung in the doorway, looking at everything except the doll.

"You need to call the police. This could be key evidence."

"I suppose it's a confession," she said. "He wants me to know he killed Kimberly Potter." She still didn't step into the bathroom.

He shook his head. "The doll has your hair color and green eyes. I'd lay money on those being your panties." He took her silence as an affirmative. "It's a threat, and it's personal."

"We already know Alexander—"

Nate cut her off. "I've been thinking and want you to hear me out before you say anything."

"All right," she said, her tone wary.

Nate moved her away from the bathroom. He motioned for her to sit on her bed.

"The roses and note I saw didn't have anything to name Alexander as the person who left them—no signature, nothing that would definitely ID him. And you said the previous note was equally ambiguous. And now there isn't a single thing to indicate forced entry. The alarm wasn't tripped." He looked into her eyes and could tell she didn't know where he was heading. "Who has a key and knows your alarm code?"

"Only Mom and Dad."

"*No one* else?"

"No . . ." Light dawned in her eyes—actually, more

like lightning. She shot to her feet. "Rory did not leave these things!"

Nate didn't back down. "Take a step back and look at this. First of all, there wasn't anything threatening in those roses, other than their surreptitious deliveries. You said you'd recently broken up with him. Think about the notes."

She crossed her arms over her chest, pressing her lips together and shaking her head. "No. No way."

"Ellis, all I'm trying to do is look with an open mind. We've been so focused on Alexander that we never even considered another source. The only reason for Alexander to leave them would be to let you know he's out there stalking you. Why leave doubt that he was responsible?"

"You already admitted you haven't figured out his game plan. I'm sure he had his reasons," she said stubbornly.

Nate had had plenty of experience with lies; he'd become necessarily proficient at spotting them. Ellis might not be lying, but she was suppressing something. Maybe she had already considered Rory might have left the flowers.

Or maybe she still loved him.

"Why would Rory come into my place and leave that . . . that thing?" She gestured toward the bathroom. "Rory is the most gentle soul I've ever met. He would never hurt me like that."

"The alarm, Ellis. How do you explain the alarm?"

"Maybe Alexander is some genius with electronics. I don't know! But you're way off thinking Rory had anything to do with this."

It certainly wasn't impossible for someone to disable

an alarm—a skill that would be valuable to a man like Alexander. But getting it reset . . .

Nate said, "And maybe you're blind to the truth. Maybe Rory wants you to be afraid enough to run to him."

"Ridiculous!" She got up and paced around the bedroom. Then she turned her accusing gaze on him. "What about *you*? You've seen me disarm that panel. Maybe I should ask you if you put that doll in there? You haven't been with me at any of the times my little surprises have shown up. Maybe *you* want me to be afraid."

"Ellis, you don't believe that."

She took a step toward him. "Why does that make any less sense than Rory being responsible?"

He simply stared at her, willing her to come to her senses. Of course she defended Rory. He'd been part of her life for years; it wasn't easy to admit he might do something like this to manipulate her.

After a moment, she broke eye contact and looked out the front window.

Nate stepped close behind her. His hands rose toward her shoulders; then he stopped and let them fall back to his sides. "I'm only suggesting it as a potential scenario. We can't blind ourselves to possibilities and still get a leg up on Alexander." He kept his tone soft, just short of apologetic.

Her shoulders rose and fell with a deep breath. "There are some things you don't know yet." She paused. "And once you hear it, you'll see why I'm right and that doll is an admission of murder." Nate assumed she was about to reveal something about her relationship with Rory, and he wasn't sure he wanted to hear it.

She went on but didn't turn to look at him. "Kimberly

Potter was stabbed in the throat *with a screwdriver*." Turning, she looked at him with a question in her green eyes. "That's the murder weapon with *your* fingerprints on it."

For a moment, Nate adjusted his train of thought. "My fingerprints . . ."

"Yes, *your* fingerprints. How do you explain that?"

It only took him about a half second to figure out where Alexander had gotten his murder weapon. "When I took the boat back, the motor cut out."

"So you said—and your phone fell in the water." There was a knife-edge of challenge in her voice.

"The motor did cut out. Which wasn't unusual; it's always temperamental. The flashlight was dead, and I couldn't find the screwdriver. He must have taken it from the boat while it was tied up here; it hadn't been there at all."

"You think he planned in that much detail?" she asked.

"I think the man is damned resourceful."

For a long moment, she stood there with her arms crossed, staring at him from beneath a furrowed brow.

Then she surprised him by saying, "You just said that motor is always temperamental. *Always,* as in you've had frequent, recurring experience with it. I thought you hadn't been here in fifteen years." Her mouth hardened and her eyes turned suspicious.

He rubbed his forehead. "There's something else I need to tell you." He paused. "It's important that no one else knows."

She stared at him with glittering eyes and a frown.

"I bought Belle Creek Plantation and the stables from Helaina Von der Embse. I own it. My ownership is buried under so many layers, even if someone knew what they were looking for, it would take a good long time to figure it out. It's a place separate from my life. I come here when I can, which isn't often."

She looked like he'd just slapped her. "Why keep it a secret from everyone?"

He took a step closer to her. "It's complicated. Mostly because of my work. There are people who'd use the plantation, or the people connected with it, to manipulate me. It's imperative that I keep myself distanced from that place. I want to be able to come here and not worry about someone sneaking up on me in the night."

"Sneaking up on you in the night?" She hadn't moved from her cross-armed stance.

"I don't live in a pretty world, Ellis." He was tired of sidestepping, of plying her with lies of omission. But he could not tell her the truth of what he did. Not now. Maybe not ever. "The plantation is the exception. I don't want those lines to blur."

"So you sneak in and out of town." She made it sound even dirtier than it felt.

"Yes," he admitted, holding her gaze.

"For how long?" she asked, her voice throwing down a gauntlet.

"Seven years last March."

She turned to the window again.

"Ellis—"

She jerked around and faced him. "You *left* me. Didn't even say good-bye. Never dropped a note to say you were alive and well. Just disappeared. Do you have any idea what that did to me? Do you know how worry ate my insides?

"And if that wasn't bad enough, now you tell me you've

been creeping back into town for *seven years*—seven goddamn years." She blinked and he saw that her eyes held unshed tears. "I lost sleep. I cried. I thought something awful had happened to you. I lost Laura. And I lost you."

Her weight shifted rapidly from foot to foot. Her knees flexed to lower her center of gravity. She might not be cognizant of the fact, but her body was getting ready to attack.

In the end, she only poked her index finger at him. "You *know* you could have trusted me with your secret. I kept every other secret for you! I thought we were friends."

"We were—we *are*—friends."

"Bullshit!" She took a step forward and pushed against his chest.

How in the hell had the conversation turned into this?

"Bullshit!" she said again. "I was such a stupid kid. I thought you actually cared!"

His temper flashed, hot and bright. He grabbed her by the shoulders, digging in his fingertips to get her attention. "I do care about you. I always knew what was going on in your life. You were safe. You were happy. The last thing you needed was me dragging back with a boatload of bad memories."

She leaned forward. His grip now held her back. "How can you be so incredibly, totally, utterly fucking stupid!" she shouted. "I wasn't *happy*." Her mouth twisted into a disgusted frown. "I couldn't take that kind of loss again. So I lived like a turtle in a freaking shell. And it didn't matter to you at all!"

She jerked her shoulders free and started to walk away.

He grabbed her hand. The instant he did it, he knew he'd made a mistake.

She spun and did a wrist lock turn on him. He let her twist his left hand, forcing his fingers inward toward his elbow.

Her eyes were hard, glassy with anger. Her mouth twisted with pain.

"Ellis! That hurts like a mother—"

She gritted her teeth and pressed harder.

He bent his knees, lowered his shoulder under her midsection. He sprung into a lift more quickly than she could prepare for. He flipped her over, dropping her onto the bed.

Her eyes blazed like a wildcat's. Now he'd really pissed her off.

Straightening, he took a step backward, holding his hands palms out to ward her off. "Ellis. Don't."

He could tell by the look in her eye that she was coming after him again. The girl knew how to fight. He needed to incapacitate her quickly, or she was going to get hurt.

Instead of backing away, he threw himself at her, knocking her backward onto the bed. Keeping his weight fully on her, he grabbed her wrists and pinned them over her head.

She bucked and writhed, but he was broader and managed to get his knees by her hips and keep her beneath him.

"Enough," he said through clenched teeth. "That's enough."

She wiggled and tried to twist her wrists free. Her breathing was ragged and fast.

"Stop and I'll let you go." His nose was inches from hers. "Come on. I don't want you to get hurt."

"Ha!" She nearly spat the word in his face. "Too damn late."

He knew she wasn't referring to physical wounds.

He lowered his face closer to hers and brought her hands closer to the top of her head. "I'm sorry," he said softly. "I am. I may be an inconsiderate bastard. I may have screwed up. But there isn't another person in this world who means more to me."

He could feel the tension draining from her body. A tear slipped from the corner of her eye. He made himself watch it until it disappeared into her hair. He'd done this. He'd caused this pain.

"No one." He emphasized the two words with increased pressure on her wrists. His lips were almost touching hers when he whispered, "Believe it."

He felt the rapid rise and fall of her chest beneath his—and his own body throbbing with more than exertion.

He should let her go.

He should.

He lessened his grip on her wrists but didn't move off of her.

Stop being a selfish bastard.

Then she lifted her lips to his. Her kiss was hungry and wild. And he knew it was driven by anger. Still, he allowed himself a moment. Just a moment.

Dear God in heaven, didn't she know? Didn't she know how much he cared for her?

He let go of her wrists and rolled them over, wrapping his arms tightly around her.

She straddled him, her hands on the bed on either side of his head, her mouth devouring as savagely as his.

When she started to rock her hips against him, he nearly lost all control.

Stop. This.

He reached up and took the sides of her face in his hands. It took more physical strength to lift her mouth from his than bench-pressing one-seventy.

Her ponytail had come loose, and her hair tumbled over the backs of his hands, teasing like feathers. Her breasts strained against the silky fabric of her top with each intense breath. Her mouth was parted invitingly. And her eyes, dear Lord, those eyes. The pain had been usurped by passion, the anger vanquished by lust. Every aspect of her had turned torturously erotic.

She ran her hands over his chest. "Your shirt's still damp." Her teeth captured her lower lip at the end of the last word. And her hands started to pull the fabric upward.

He pulled her against him, trapping her hands between them. He allowed himself one long, hot kiss. Then he slid her to his side and held her there, using his hand to keep her head on his shoulder.

"I'd die before I hurt you again," he said softly.

She didn't respond.

As he caressed her hair, he felt a lump on the side of her head. "What the hell?"

"I hit my head when I fell in the tub." She sounded as breathless as he still felt.

He rolled up onto his elbow, letting her head slide onto the mattress. "Let me see. Is it bleeding?"

"It's fine."

He gently parted the hair on the side of her head and

inspected the injury. Her scalp was tight and purple, but the skin wasn't broken.

"Looks painful." He wanted to wring Alexander's neck with his bare hands. He had to put an end to this before Ellis was truly hurt.

"It's not too bad."

He looked at her for a long moment, regrouping his thoughts.

"You don't know how much it pains me to say this," he said, "but there are things that need our attention." He gently stroked her temple.

She sighed in a way that clawed at his heart.

He took her chin and turned her face toward his. "I want you to know that I meant what I said."

A small smile curved her lips. "Which part, that you're an inconsiderate, sorry bastard, or that you care?"

"I care so much, I ache inside."

The intensity in Nate's steel-gray gaze closed like a trap around her heart. Her blood moved sluggishly through her veins, and she realized she'd never been so affected by just looking into someone's eyes.

Suddenly it began, a tiny orange glimmer beneath her breastbone. A tickling warmth, a flutter of emotion.

As she looked into Nate's eyes, his unwavering gaze fanned that tiny glowing ember. It grew brighter, more intense.

He slid his hand behind her neck and stroked his thumb across her throat. That slight, simple, yet oh so sensual touch was like stirring the dying coals of a night's campfire. It sent a shower of bright orange sparks throughout her body, each one hot and searing where it landed.

Then a wondrous thing happened. A tiny yellow flame licked into the darkness of Ellis's soul.

Maybe, just maybe, she wasn't so damaged inside that she couldn't love as deeply as others. Maybe she just hadn't been with the right person.

There was no way she was giving up without finding out. There may never be another opportunity. Nate was leaving, probably sooner than later. She had to know. If he was the only one who could bring her soul to life and she'd have to live without him, so be it. At least she'd know it hadn't withered and turned to dust.

She leaned over and kissed him, honing in on the utterly new sensations that rocked her body and spirit.

All of those tiny embers blazed fierce and bright.

He kissed her back, yet she could sense his restraint.

As she teased her tongue along his lips, she slid her hand across his belly, then lower, caressing him until he moaned. "Ellis," he said softly against her mouth.

"Don't talk." She nipped his lower lip and worked the buckle on his belt. "Just love me."

She held her breath, waiting for his response. If he refused, she'd scream.

He held her slightly away from him. "It's not right," he said, regret in his voice. "I'll leave you again. I *have* to leave."

"It's not the leaving that frightens me; it's the fear I'll never get to experience this . . . what's between us. Grant me this moment, please."

"God, Ellis . . ." His eyes looked like molten metal, hot, yet soft, fluid with desire.

She didn't hesitate; she kissed him, pouring out everything that welled in her heart.

With a feral growl, his reluctance vanished. His kiss answered hers in kind, and his hand slid under her top.

His mouth danced across her collarbone, then down, his hot moist breath warming her breast through the thin fabric. When his lips grazed the bare skin of her stomach, that scream almost erupted, but for an entirely different reason.

His tongue circled her navel. He whispered against her belly, "God, I want you."

She pulled off her top. "Then take me."

Nate pushed her bra strap off her shoulder, exposing her breast to his mouth, and she thought she'd fly into pieces.

He disposed of her bra. Her jeans and panties quickly followed.

Pushing him onto his back, Ellis managed to get him out of his shirt. She explored his chest with skimming fingers and tasting lips. His stomach muscles quivered beneath her touch.

His hands roamed her back, her breasts, the curve of her waist; caressing fingers becoming more urgent, more insistent in their exploration. He pulled her down on top of him, drawing her lips to his.

Ellis's emotions exploded, an outpouring of adolescent fantasy, of long-suppressed need, of love at last come to light. That tiny yellow flame in her soul burst into a blue-white fire that threatened to consume her completely.

For the first time in her life, she felt wild, untamed. Nothing mattered except what was happening at this instant, with this man.

With recklessly desperate hands, she got him out of his remaining clothes. She had to feel every inch of his skin, every curve of his body, discover every secret place that made him shiver.

Suddenly, he wrapped his arms around her and turned them so she was beneath him.

Ellis opened her body and her spirit to him . . . and lost herself in the miracle of what he offered in return.

Chapter Twenty-Five

Ellis knew the instant guilt and second thoughts began to nibble at Nate's conscience. She felt it in the increased tension in his body. She heard it in his breathing. She sensed the dampening of his unbridled emotions. He was pulling away.

"Don't," she said from where she lay with her head on his shoulder.

"Don't what?"

Propping her chin on his chest, she said, "Don't get all worried that I'm going to feel hurt and abandoned. Don't try to make me feel like we shouldn't have done this."

He remained quiet, rubbing her back, sending a new cascade of chills down her spine. Even if she suffered the loss every day of her life from now on, what she'd just experienced would be worth every minute of emotional torment.

"It was my choice," she said. "And I *was* very insistent. You're only a man, after all." She kissed his chest. "No match for my womanly wiles." She emphasized her comment by tracing his nipple with her finger.

The rumble of laughter started in his chest; she felt it before she heard it.

With his laughter came Ellis's relief. She didn't want him to regret their lovemaking nor did she want to discuss it right now. Not until she'd had some time to absorb the life-altering consequences of what she'd just discovered.

She'd spent the past fifteen years treading a tightwire of restraint, of avoiding risk, of repression. There was something in her total loss of control with Nate that had been cathartic and that raised so many more questions about her inner self and her choices.

His chuckles calmed, and he followed her lighthearted lead. "I've always been a slave to your will—you've just never known it until now. I'm afraid I've handed you a very dangerous weapon."

Sitting up, she gathered the rumpled comforter around her. "Lucky for you, I'm very careful with weapons." She started to slide off the bed, but he grabbed her arm and halted her.

"Ellis." He pulled her hand to his lips and kissed it. "We do need to talk about this—about us."

"Let's not make it complicated. I understand there is no us. Nothing else to talk about." She got off the bed and stood there, her heart wishing things were different.

In Nate's gray eyes, she saw the same useless longing. She had to get this vessel turned before it beached itself.

Forcing herself into reality mode, she said, "We've got work to do. I have to call the police about the doll, which means you need to get out of here. I'll have to change the alarm code—"

"You're not staying here."

"I've been all through this with Dad. I'm not leaving town."

"No. You're coming with me." Before she could argue,

he went on. "I can't stay here with you—not with the police looking for me. And I'm not leaving you alone. Pack a bag."

"If Alexander's so clever, he'll just follow us," she said.

"I came through the marsh. I'll leave that way while the police are here with you. Then I'll wait for you at the marina, on the dock side of the restaurant. Park and go in as if you're going to dinner. It'll be getting dark by then. Wait a minute or so and come out onto the dock. We'll go to the plantation by water."

Sounded reasonable.

"I was going back to Seaside Apartments to talk to Kimberly's roommate again, to bring photos of Alexander and see if Ava or anyone else around there has seen him."

"Good plan. But we'll go together, after the marina."

"No. I'll go on my way. It's too dangerous for you. They're still investigating the murder. Besides, then it'll be closer to dark when I get to the restaurant."

He thought it over for a minute. "I don't want you running around alone."

"I've been doing it all day long. I'm careful. Sam has been serving as my personal escort when I come and go from here."

"Good. But keep in mind, *I'm* your personal hero." He kissed her. "Don't let him get any ideas."

She smiled, suppressing the effervescent bubbles that his statement released in her belly.

"Get dressed and call the police about that doll," he said as he got off the bed.

She suddenly felt awkward gathering up her wildly

discarded clothing. She kept her back to him as she did. Once she finished dressing, she turned to him and asked, "Are you missing any other screwdrivers?"

He started toward the bedroom door. "Until today, I didn't know I was missing one." He sounded so offhand that it made her worried he might be getting reckless.

"Nate, what if Alexander planted evidence on that doll that will point directly to you?"

He paused in the doorway and shrugged. "They already have my fingerprints on a murder weapon. How much worse can it get? If there's the slightest chance he left something that we can use against him, we have to look for it."

How much worse can it get? The possibilities swam in her head until she felt a little dizzy.

Why was Alexander working so hard to frame Nate?

Too bad Mr. Buckley wouldn't be the voice of reason to the local police. Now wasn't the time; if she told him about Buckley, she'd have to go into what she discovered in the transcripts. Daylight was burning.

Nate laid his hand on the side of her neck. "Call the police. I want you at the restaurant before it's fully dark." He pulled her close and gave her a quick, hard kiss. "And be careful. Watch for anyone following your car."

"I know. I know." She nudged him toward the door. "You be careful yourself."

She waited until she saw him skirt around and disappear into the landscaping that led to the marsh. And then she called the police.

Les Winkler didn't seem in the least swayed as Ellis explained that she thought Alexander had left this doll as a confession of sorts.

"And why would he do that?" Les asked. "If he killed her, why do something to incriminate himself?"

With Nate's distracting presence gone, Ellis was able to focus on the facts more clearly. And it was becoming harder and harder to come up with logical arguments to contradict the officer's conviction that Nate Vance was guilty of multiple crimes.

"Alexander wants to frighten me," she said. "He wants me to know he can get in my place—that despite my precautions, I'm vulnerable to him here."

"Sounds contradictory to his goal, if, as you say, he wants to harm you. Why warn you? And the alarm?" Les asked. "How would Alexander have known that? Don't you think it more likely that Nate Vance noted the code when he saw you enter it?" His face softened. "Ms. Greene, this isn't at all like you. You're ignoring the facts. You're doing exactly what you warn the students of your self-defense class against. We have a murdered girl. Vance's fingerprints are on the murder weapon."

This isn't at all like you. . . . Les's words sent doubt piercing to her core.

It *wasn't* like her. Since Nate's return, she'd abandoned and compromised her own cautious nature, but only when it came to him. She'd instantly accepted things that were contradictory to reason.

Nate hadn't been with her when any of the intimidating items had been left for her.

He'd been conveniently at her door when she'd discovered the doll.

He could know the code; certainly that made more sense than Alexander somehow figuring it out, or Rory suddenly changing his nature and sneaking into her place and leaving that doll.

Why, though, would Nate want to frighten her?

There was another blinding fact. As of today, she had proof that Nate was a liar—he'd lied under oath. How much more suspect could that be?

Had she been mesmerized by infatuation? Blinded by latent teenage worship?

But why would Nate have done any of those things?

And why, if he had, would he have insisted on keeping the police involved?

The only thing for her to do was push on, dig for the truth, whatever that might be. If Nate wanted to hurt her, he'd had more than enough chances.

Still, Les's words rang in her ears. *This isn't like you. . . .*

No, it wasn't. Nothing about her was the same since Nate had returned.

❧

Les waited and followed Ellis out of the complex. Odd, she thought as she exited, Sam and the Gator were away from the gatehouse again.

Luckily, Les turned right when she went left, toward Seaside Apartments. He was just one of the people she didn't want following her.

On her way, she called to check on her parents. Just before she hung up, her mother asked Ellis if she'd seen Uncle Greg.

"No. Haven't you?" Ellis asked.

"No. But truthfully, we usually go days without talking. I just thought with your dad in the hospital . . ."

"You know how he's run himself into the ground. He's probably sleeping. Have you tried to call him?"

"Yes," her mother said. "It goes right to voice mail. His phone must be off."

"Well, if you can't get ahold of him before you leave the hospital, why don't you have either Charlie or Ben go by his house and check on him?"

"Good idea."

"Let me know if you need anything."

"You're staying in?" Her mother's tone was peremptorily reproving.

Ellis didn't tell her that "in" wasn't as safe as it should be. "Don't worry."

As before, she drove past Seaside Apartments, went around the block, drove past again, and did a U-turn. Satisfied she wasn't being followed, she pulled into the parking lot. It was nearly full now.

She started with Ava.

When the girl answered the door, Ellis said, "I brought a photo to show you." She held it up. "Did you ever see this guy? Maybe someplace when you girls were out?"

Ava studied the picture for a few seconds, then shook her head. "Nice-looking guy. I'd have remembered seeing him."

"Well, remember his face. He's the one who killed Kimberly."

"But . . . but he looks so . . . nice." She sounded like a child who'd just been betrayed by Santa Claus.

"Well, he's not. He's a monster."

Ava swallowed and handed the photo back.

Ellis then went door to door with Alexander's photograph. No one remembered seeing him. Until she reached the last apartment. A middle-aged woman dressed like a twenty-year-old and wearing a frightening amount of makeup answered the door. As she opened it, she yelled over her shoulder, "Turn down that TV!"

Ellis didn't notice any decrease in the sound level as she introduced herself as someone investigating the murder. She showed the woman the photograph.

The lady tilted her head slightly as she studied it and tapped one ridiculously long French-tipped nail against her chin. "You know . . . I think maybe . . ."

Ellis prompted, "Anything will help."

She clucked her tongue. "Well, there was so much confusion that morning. There was this guy . . ." Her brow furrowed. "He had on sunglasses and a ball cap." She tapped the photo with a long nail. "But I'm pretty sure it was him. Nice jawline."

"Where was he? What time?"

"I suppose it was 'bout seven-fifteen or so. He was just standing there with the rest of us, trying to figure out what was going on."

"Did he say anything? Talk to anyone?"

She shook her head and waved her hand, talonlike nails clawing the air. "I can't remember. Everybody was talkin' at once."

Ellis wrote her cell phone number on the back of the photo and handed it to the woman. "Maybe you can show this around. And if you happen to remember anything else, please call me."

The woman took the photo. "Can't imagine I will."

"Well, just in case," Ellis said with an encouraging smile.

As she walked to her car in the dusky light, she realized how the shadows had collected beneath the overgrown landscaping around the parking lot. The clouds had gathered, obscuring the last of the sunlight.

Remembering how easily Kimberly Potter had been snatched from here made Ellis ultra cautious as she approached her car.

That man in the crowd certainly could have been Alexander. He might have returned to get a look at the fallout from his handiwork. He was a voyeur, after all. And he had gone snooping around the hospital after Laura's attack. Maybe he'd been the one to start the rumor about the black Hummer.

If that was the case, he knew Nate drove it. Did he know it belonged to Belle Creek Plantation? If so, they weren't going to be any safer at the plantation than in her condo.

⁂

Dusk had settled and the lights had come on in the parking lot at the marina when Ellis arrived. Only one car followed her down the last stretch of narrow road. She waited and watched as it parked. Two women got out and headed toward the restaurant. Ellis grabbed her tote off the passenger seat and followed them in.

As soon as she entered, she ducked into the ladies' room. Pulling a lightweight black knit jacket from her tote, she slipped it on over her pink silk top, zipping it high enough that the pink didn't show. She'd been wearing her hair in a twist; she took out the clip and let it fall around her shoulders. She finger-combed it close to her face.

Coming out, she walked through the restaurant with her face tilted down, then went through the door that led to the outdoor dining area.

All of the tables had umbrellas whose skeletons were outlined in tiny white lights, leaving the areas between dimly lit. Luckily, it was busy enough that she didn't stand out.

She opened the little gate and walked down the steps to the public dock. There was a light mounted on a pole over the gas pump; she lingered just outside its radius and looked for Nate.

At first she thought he wasn't there. Then she heard a low whistle.

She moved forward, skirting the cone of light at the gas pump, feeling the floating dock rock beneath her footsteps.

She found Nate in the johnboat parked between two larger craft.

The instant she saw him, the tightness left her shoulders and the tension vanished from her stomach.

That reaction immediately made her doubt herself. She knew Nate didn't kill Kimberly Potter. But was she blindly ignoring warning signs of other things, as Les Winkler said?

Nate smiled and reached up for her tote. "I was getting worried."

She stood rooted in place, her tote firmly on her shoulder.

"What's wrong?" he asked.

There were things she had to say before she got into

this boat with him and went out into the dark river. Before his proximity overtook everything else.

After a deep breath, she said, "I went to the Clerk of Courts office today."

He stepped up onto the dock beside her. "Why?"

She ignored his question; she wanted to bring things out in her own order. "Did you know Alexander had been on trial for rape before he attacked Laura?"

"No." His voice was tight.

"He was acquitted. The transcripts weren't in the database, so I don't know the details."

"Goddammit."

"I know."

After a moment, he said, "You didn't answer my question—why did you go?" His tone didn't indicate he had anything to hide.

"Hoping to discover something from the trial that would give us a leg up on Alexander. And"—she paused—"I'm tired of viewing that entire event through the eyes of a sheltered thirteen-year-old. I'd already discovered I was wrong about some things."

"Like what?"

"Like your relationship with Laura—and Laura herself, for that matter." She looked him in the eyes. "Why did you and Laura fight that night?"

He closed his eyes briefly. His face contorted as if he didn't like what he was seeing behind his closed lids. "We fought about the same thing we always fought about. I caught her in some dude's car giving him a . . . *favor* in exchange for buying her booze."

The picture his words painted in her mind made her

stomach roll, brought into sharp focus what she'd been able to keep an indistinct concept.

She finally managed to find her voice again. "You didn't say that in your testimony."

"Why would I? It wasn't Hollis Alexander she was blowing. Telling that detail would have done nothing but hurt her parents and you."

"But it made you look more suspect," she said.

"I'm not saying I wouldn't have divulged those details if it had been necessary to save my own hide. But until that time came—which it didn't—there was no need to destroy her. Besides, do you think the jury would have been likely to convict Alexander on circumstantial evidence if the defense attorney had made Laura sound like a girl who'd been asking for trouble?"

That was one child's view she'd shed long ago. No matter how you sliced it, there was still a double standard. Boys who had sex with multiple partners were just being normal; girls who had sex with multiple people were whores without the pay.

"There's another question I have to ask you," she said.

"Shoot."

"Why did you lie on the witness stand?" She watched his eyes closely in the glow from the overhead light but saw no reluctance, no flash of dishonesty.

"I didn't."

"Yes. You did," she pressed. "You said you didn't see Laura again after the two of you fought in the parking lot of the drugstore."

"I didn't. I went home. My mom was having a very bad drunk. I stayed there to keep her from burning down the house or hurting herself."

"No," Ellis said, shaking her head. "I heard the two of you talking as I was falling asleep. It was a few minutes before midnight. I didn't ever tell anyone. It would have given them the wrong idea. They didn't know you came to see her lots of times after her curfew."

He reached out and took her hands. "That's what you meant earlier when you said you'd always kept my secrets? You thought you were protecting me."

She nodded.

"Oh, Ellis." He raised her hand to his lips and kissed it.

"It wasn't you?" she said weakly.

"No, baby, it wasn't."

Her throat started to swell.

He inched closer and touched her cheek. "It wouldn't have made any difference. Alexander was caught."

Closing her eyes, she thought about all she'd learned today.

With a slow shake of her head, she said, "But it wasn't Alexander talking to her. He had an alibi from ten until one in the morning."

She looked into Nate's eyes. "And if it wasn't you, it had to have been someone else."

Ellis struggled to recall that moment. She'd been just falling asleep when she heard hushed voices and Laura's quiet laughter. She remembered curling deeper into her pillow. She'd always liked to fall asleep with the sound of Laura and Nate's quiet conversations drifting in the space between her and Laura's house. Not that she ever heard much beyond the deep rumble of Nate's voice dancing with Laura's lighter one.

Ellis supposed she didn't pay particular attention that

night, because it was already set in her mind that it was Nate.

"It doesn't matter who was at the window—if there really was someone. Maybe you dreamt it. Maybe it was Alexander and his alibi was fabricated. Alexander was caught. Nothing else matters."

She supposed she *had* been very sleepy. Maybe Nate was right. Maybe it was more dream than reality.

The movement of the dock beneath her feet seemed to increase. Everything was becoming such a muddle. Why couldn't this just be over?

"Ellis," Nate said softly. "We need to go."

The words left her in a rush. "Les Winkler thinks you're not only guilty of murder, but you're also the one stalking me."

"Does he? And what do you think, Ellis?"

She squared her shoulders and faced him. "I think that if I was my rational self, I wouldn't get in this boat with you."

Chapter Twenty-six

Nate felt as if Ellis had dealt him a physical blow. Good God, could she really think . . . Anger swept hotly over him. She'd defended Rory when Nate had suggested the possibility he'd left the roses and the doll.

He stopped himself. She was right. Ellis was a cautious woman but hadn't heeded her own practices when it had come to him. He'd expected her unquestioning trust, and she'd given it.

What if he had been the bastard her uncle had thought him? Nate knew he wasn't. But there was no way that Ellis could be certain.

With a voice more calm than his racing heart, he said, "Then don't. Go to your mother's. Stay with her and Ben."

Her body tensed, as if his suggestion startled her.

He said, "You'll probably be safer there."

"I said if I was my rational self—which I obviously am not. Besides, I'm not putting my mother at more risk, not after Alexander got into my condo so easily."

"I sense a 'but' hanging in the air," he said.

"No but. I don't think you left that doll in my shower. If I did, I wouldn't have come here at all. It's just that there are so many unanswered questions. I'm so tired; I can't think straight."

Nate wondered if part of that inability to think clearly had led her to have sex with him. He turned away from the thought; it was too painful to examine.

He refrained from wrapping his arms around her and making promises he could not keep. Instead he asked, "Did you find out anything at the girl's apartment complex?"

Ellis handed him her tote. "I'll tell you when we're in the boat."

"You're sure you want to go?"

"Yes."

Before he stepped down into the boat, he held her gaze and said, "I've never lied to you, Ellis. Protecting you is the only thing that matters to me."

"Get in the damn boat," she said.

Not exactly a gush of sentiment, but it was a vote of confidence. Nate decided he would accept it as that.

After he was in the flat-bottomed boat, he helped her step down. She took a seat on the middle bench and faced forward—a sign she didn't want to talk.

Nate sat on the rearmost bench, in front of the outboard motor, and maneuvered the boat away from the dock. He kept the speed low as they moved into the channel.

He allowed Ellis her privacy while the marina slipped slowly away. The white forms of the snub-nosed shrimp boats were quickly obscured as the johnboat moved into the broad darkness of the river.

After a few minutes, Ellis turned in her seat, swung her legs over, and faced him. "Kimberly's roommate didn't recognize Alexander," she said. "But one woman at the complex thinks she saw him in the crowd the morning they found the body."

"Coming to see the fallout of his work, no doubt." Nate guided the boat to the right of a white reflective buoy.

"There was a rumor that morning that someone had seen a black Hummer in the parking lot around the time Kimberly was attacked. No one seemed to remember where they'd heard it. If Alexander started that rumor, he knows you drive the Hummer."

Nate nodded silently.

"What if he knows the Hummer and the plantation go together?" she asked, tension crackling in her voice. "He'll know to look for us there."

"It's possible," he said evenly, watching the river. *And if he does, I'll kill him without a single moment's hesitation.*

"Well," she huffed. "That makes me feel better."

He looked at her. "I don't want you to feel better. I want you to stay sharp."

Nate's words sent a chill over Ellis's entire body. She sat there for a moment, darkness pressing on her chest as if she lay at the bottom of the river.

She focused on the motor's steady putter and the calm slap of water against the aluminum hull.

It was so damn dark. And she couldn't be more out in the open.

The darkness had a physical presence, a hovering bulk that crowded so close she felt it on her skin.

She assured herself that no hands would reach out of the night and drag her to her doom.

It did no good.

The feeling of suffocation was made worse by the

weighty stillness of air that spoke of an approaching storm.

She turned away from Nate, just in case he could see the panic on her face. Stripping off her jacket, she drew a breath that felt like wet cotton.

She could not freak out. She *would* not.

Because they were traveling from the river into a webwork of creeks that laced through a pitch-black marsh, they were barely moving fast enough to keep the mosquitoes off.

She lifted her hair off her neck and secured it with the clip she'd taken out in the restaurant, hoping she wouldn't throw up all over the bottom of the johnboat.

She tried to divert her thoughts from the darkness.

But the things that rushed into her mind were worse.

She thought of her father's accident. She saw the image of Buckley's twisted body and bloody head. She recalled Ava's description of Kimberly Potter's green sandals laying a trail to her body in the dunes. That hideous doll hanging in her shower. . . .

Suddenly she wasn't hot anymore.

She jerked herself to the edge of the boat and vomited over the side.

Immediately she held up her hand. "I'm okay."

Thank God Nate spared what was left of her dignity and didn't stop.

Weakness. She hated it—most of all in herself.

Reaching down, she scooped a handful of water and splashed it on the back of her neck. It was briny, but at least it was cool. Then she dug in her bag for a piece of mint gum.

Her stomach settled and she breathed a little easier.

Soon after, Ellis noticed a flicker of lightning, lifting the tarry blackness of the sky to battleship gray. The wind came up, ruffling the tall grasses on either side of the creek.

She wondered if they'd make the plantation before the storm hit. It had been a long while since she'd seen the dot of a shoreline light. But here in the low country, light was gobbled up quickly by black water and thick vegetation.

"We'll be there in five minutes," Nate said, breaking the silence for the first time in a long while.

"Since when do you read minds?"

"You looked up at the lightning."

A gust of wind hit her in the face.

"Do we *have* five minutes?" she asked.

"If not, we're going to get wet." He didn't sound concerned.

Didn't he know the danger? They were traversing a maze in the dark. On water. In a metal boat.

Maybe he's so used to danger that it doesn't faze him anymore.

Belle Creek Plantation should be coming up on the right side. She strained to see lights.

All she saw was black.

Nate turned the boat.

Lightning flashed, and Ellis nearly jumped overboard when she saw how close they were to a long narrow pier.

Nate said, "You can't see the house from the creek unless all the lights are blazing."

Leaning forward, she reached out to grab one of the pilings as Nate cut the motor.

The wind gave another gust.

He quickly climbed onto the dock and tied up.

The first fat drops of rain hit the aluminum boat. It sounded like someone was pelting it with acorns.

She handed her tote up to Nate just as a loud crack and a brilliant flash happened simultaneously. She jerked her head down into her shoulders. Great defense against lightning strikes, she thought.

Temporarily blinded, she held perfectly still.

The rain cut loose in wild slashing sheets.

"Here," Nate called to her. "Give me your hand."

"I can't even see you."

He latched on to her arm and pulled, helping her out of the boat. Wrapping one arm around her, he started moving.

Ellis felt like a blind woman being led down the plank. She hoped she didn't step off the side of the dock. "I can't see a damn thing."

Moving them steadily ahead, Nate laughed and held her close. "And they let you drive after dark?"

"Don't you have a light in the stable yard?" She should be able to see it from here.

"Power must be out."

"Lovely." More darkness. It would be better once she was inside, she assured herself; that lancing sense of vulnerability would ease.

"Where's your sense of adventure?" he asked.

"Thanks to Hollis Alexander, I don't have one." The truth that she normally guarded slid right out of her mouth.

They climbed the steps to the covered porch. Once out of the downpour, Nate let go of her. He dug in his pocket, then inserted a key into the wide wooden door he'd been hanging when she first discovered he was back.

It seemed much longer than six days ago. "If I hadn't seen you that day," she asked, "would you have come and gone and never let me know?"

He pushed the door open but made no move to go inside. "I don't know. That had been my plan."

She stood there for a long moment, surprised at how much his admission hurt. It seemed inconceivable that she could have gone on, maybe forever, not knowing what had happened to him.

He put a hand on her arm and pulled her through the door. "Stay put," he said, closing the door on the storm. "I'll get a flashlight."

As she stood there in the stuffy darkness, she heard the wind battering the house and the *drip, drip, drip* of water falling from her onto the floor. It echoed, like water dripping in a cave.

Even though the house was oppressively warm, she shivered.

Nate returned with a flashlight. He had a towel slung around his neck and handed another one to her.

She took it and dabbed her face. It smelled like the house, musty and unused.

He ran his towel carelessly over his hair. Then he locked the front door. "Let's go upstairs. I'll open up and get some air moving."

He carried her bag up, lighting the creaking staircase with the narrow flashlight beam. The steps curved to an upper balcony that overlooked the two-story entry hall.

Ellis followed along, feeling like a kid sneaking around a haunted house.

The balcony ran across the width of the entry hall. The stairs continued up on the other side to the third floor. In the center of the balcony was a set of open double doors. When the lightning flashed, Ellis saw a large room with a fireplace and French doors that opened onto the second-story veranda facing the lane from the road. There wasn't a stick of furniture in it.

On either side of the interior balcony, hallways led to the wings containing the bedrooms.

Nate walked down one of the halls. "As you can see, the place is bare bones. So I only have one furnished bedroom."

Ellis said, "Doesn't matter. I'm not getting more than five feet away from you. This place gives me the whim-whams."

He laughed. "It's the storm. Well, and the dark. And the emptiness."

"Like I said, consider me gum on your shoe."

They reached a corner bedroom on the creek side of the house. Nate swept the light around. "See, nice and cozy. No ghosts."

"Yeah, like they'd stand still for you to shine the light and introduce them." Still, this room was a vast improvement. There was a king-size bed flanked by night tables, an overstuffed chair with an ottoman, a bookcase, and a couple of chests.

He set her bag near the bed, then went to open the French doors to the veranda and the two tall nine-over-nine windows on the room's other side. The air started to circulate immediately. It was sticky but cooler than the house.

"I'd open the rest of the house, but considering the circumstances, I don't want anything open that I can't see."

"Good idea." She shifted her weight, and water squished out of her canvas shoes.

"The bathroom is through there." He shone the light on a six-panel door. Then he lit a couple of candles—utilitarian ones, the kind a man would buy in case of a power outage.

He opened a drawer in one of the chests and pulled out some dry clothes. "You feel like eating?"

It surprised her that her stomach had completely ceased its rolling. "I might be able to eat a little something."

"Let me see what I can scrape up. You can change and dry off." His gaze traveled over her, and she realized how little wet silk concealed.

He seemed to catch himself and looked away. "I'll get the food. It'll be cooler eating up here where the windows are open." He started for the door.

"Whoa there, buddy. You just sit tight while I change. Then we'll both go down to the kitchen." She added, "That way I can see the rest of the house."

He grinned, and for the first time since he'd been back, she saw his old smile, the one that shone in his eyes and radiated from his entire loose-limbed body.

Stepping close, he slid his arms around her. "Yeah, sure." He kissed her lightly.

Leaning back, she looked into his eyes and saw the flicker of candlelight reflected in them. Tilting her head, she said, "Are you calling me a liar?"

For a long moment, he looked into her eyes. There was no humor in his expression when he said, "I think you're an incredibly brave woman." He paused. "Who's afraid of my big dark house." The corner of his mouth lifted in a teasing smile.

"Hey, I already admitted this place creeps me out," she said. "What more do you want?"

His face grew serious again, and he looked at her long enough that parts of her started to heat up. Finally, he said, "That's not a safe question to ask when your shirt is plastered to you like that."

She linked her hands behind his neck and took them a step closer to the king-size bed. "Maybe that's exactly what I had in mind."

A shuttered look flashed in his eyes, one that reminded her of his reluctance to make love to her earlier.

Damned if she cared. She wanted one more ride to ecstasy, and he was the only one who could take her there.

She kissed him, urging him past his hesitation.

When his arms remained at his sides, she said, "The cow is already out of the barn; no need to close the doors now."

With a moan that sounded of surrender, he pulled her so tightly against him that her heels came off the floor. His mouth dipped to the curve of her neck, and Ellis realized this was the only man whose intimate touch would ever move her soul. It was a bittersweet discovery. She now knew that she was capable of earth-shattering love—and that Nate would take it away with him when he left.

His mouth slid across her collarbone, wiping away everything except the sensation of his moist lips on her skin.

Was it possible to be destroyed by a man's mouth alone?

When he pulled away, he pushed the wet hair away from her face and looked at her in a way that set her on fire. "I didn't know . . . I think I've been looking for you every day since I left here."

Returning to her lips, his kiss spoke less of desperation and more of tenderness.

She peeled off his wet shirt. The candlelight made flickering shadows, defining his muscles. She ran her hands over his chest, enjoying the feel of solid muscle beneath the soft hair. It was brazen and not at all like her. But she wasn't herself when she was with him.

A startling thought hit her. Maybe all of her life, she'd been someone else. Maybe the only time she was truly herself was when she was with him.

And when he leaves, you won't find yourself ever again.

His lips once again claimed hers, and she drove away thoughts of separation. They had now. They had to make it count.

They didn't make it the additional four feet to the bed. They tore at each other like love-starved creatures. No matter how quickly they joined, or how closely intimate they were, it seemed neither of their needs could be slaked.

She wanted to meld not only their bodies, but their entire beings into one. And for one bright and shining moment, it happened. There was nothing but the supernova of their desire, the blinding purity of their mutual completion.

And afterward, when they lay on the floor in a tangle of bare limbs and discarded clothes, she felt a tear roll from the corner of her eye.

It must have fallen onto his chest, because he shifted

her so they lay facing each other. With a gentle finger, he traced the track of her tear.

She felt no awkward shyness now as she looked into his eyes.

"God, Ellis . . . if only my life was different, if only I had something to offer you." He kissed her lightly. "I don't want to leave you; you have to know that. But I won't make you promises. And I won't ask for any from you."

The naked emotion she saw in his eyes told her he meant every word. And her heart felt the double-edged sword of love; the more you cared, the more it hurt to lose.

She traced his lower lip with her finger. "My heart is already breaking—"

The last two words were obscured by a violent clap of thunder that signaled a close lightning strike. She was glad. It was the wrong thing to say; confirming Nate's fears, supporting his original stand that they should not have taken this step.

His arms had tightened around her with the thunder and stayed that way. She rested her head on his shoulder and soaked in his closeness while she had the chance.

A few minutes later, he said, "I promised you some food." He kissed the top of her head. Then he let her go and got up. He handed her her tote. "You'd better get some dry clothes on, or I'm liable to forget about feeding you."

She grinned and took the bag, clutching it to her stomach. "I'll just go into the bathroom." She stood. "You promise not to dash off with the flashlight while I'm in there."

He wrapped an arm around her waist and kissed her quickly. "I'm sending it with you."

Raising a brow, she said, "Do I need to be more specific with my question?"

He grinned and she forgot all about food. "I'm not going anywhere without my gummy shoe."

"Thank you." She went into the bathroom and dried her hair with a towel, then dressed.

When she came out, Nate looked up, slightly startled. He had one leg in a pair of shorts. "Man, that was fast. You that scared of my house?"

"Watch it, or I'll bean you with this flashlight."

He pulled up the shorts and zipped them. He didn't put on a shirt. "Come on. Maybe you'll feel less spooked after you see the rest of the place." He took the flashlight from her and led the way from the room.

"Doubt that," she muttered as she followed on his heels.

Twenty minutes later, they sat on the floor of his bedroom in front of the French doors, eating scrambled eggs and toast. He'd given Ellis a tour of the entire upstairs and the main floor of the house. She couldn't really say that it had quelled all of her unease. The place was filled with tiny curving servants' stairways hidden in the walls and high-ceilinged rooms holding nothing but dust and two-hundred-year-old memories.

But his kitchen and bedroom were little islands of comfort and hominess.

The rain continued to fall, gently now. The candles' glow lent a sense of quiet contentment.

Ellis was feeling mellow and relaxed as they ate in

companionable silence. They each leaned against the opposite jamb of the same French door; Nate's extended foot caressed the side of her leg in languid strokes.

Then Nate's cell phone rang.

As soon as he answered, he lowered his voice and got up and walked away. Thunder rumbled in the distance, working as an accomplice to conceal his conversation.

When he disconnected the call and turned to face her, she knew something was terribly wrong.

CHAPTER TWENTY-SEVEN

Nate stood in the open back door, with Ellis right behind him. He hadn't been able to convince her to wait upstairs while he dealt with this. After what Charlie had told him on the phone, Nate didn't want Ellis to see what he was delivering until Nate had had a chance to screen them.

He watched headlights approach in the hammering rain. Water was already standing in several places; here in the low country, there just wasn't anywhere for the water to go.

The car stopped as close to the wide veranda steps as it could. The driver's door popped open. Charlie jumped out and ran for the porch.

"Come on in," Nate said.

Charlie remained on the porch, swiping the water off his shaved head. "I need to get back to the hospital. Mrs. Greene'll be wanting to get home."

He handed over an envelope, which he'd wisely tucked inside a plastic bag. "I spent some time checking with the neighbors. One of them saw a light blue minivan pull up in the driveway around six this afternoon and stick the envelope in the door."

"Make? Model?" He knew it was a lot to hope for.

Charlie shook his head. "Just that it was older, boxy. And the guy who got out of it was tall. That was all she recalled. The only thing she noticed about the plates was that they were South Carolina."

He shook Charlie's hand. "Thanks, man. I appreciate all your help."

Charlie clapped him on the shoulder. "Hey, I *still* owe you."

Nate watched Charlie's footfalls splash water as he ran around the front of the car.

"Okay," Ellis said from behind Nate. "I did my part and kept my mouth shut while you took care of business. Now tell me what's going on."

He turned to her. She stood with her arms crossed and a look of stern determination on her face.

He'd avoided hurting her with these details fifteen years ago. He hated what he was about to do.

"Let's go back upstairs." He closed and locked the back door. "We'll need the extra light."

Hollis sat in the parking lot of the bar watching the rain run down his windshield. This wasn't at all what he'd had in mind when he'd followed Reinhardt when the man had left his house two hours earlier.

He'd actually expected the man to explode from his house minutes after he'd picked the envelope out of the door.

Funny, the way some people worked.

But, Hollis supposed, the more Reinhardt drank, the more likely it was he'd do something . . . exciting.

Hollis crossed his arms and slouched down in his seat. He could afford to wait. He had nothing but time.

❧

Ellis sat in the chair and watched Nate move the candles to the table closest to her. He hadn't put down that plastic-bagged envelope since Charlie handed it to him. It was now tucked beneath his arm as he collected two more candles from another room and lit them.

He set the flashlight on the table with its beam pointed to reflect off the white ceiling. Then he took a seat on the ottoman in front of her.

She bit her lip and straightened her spine, ready for whatever was making him frown so.

He took her hands and said, "You were right to send one of the guys to check on your uncle."

"Oh, no," she moaned, bracing herself for the worst.

"He wasn't there. Neither was his car. So we can't jump to conclusions. Charlie let himself in, to make sure your uncle wasn't in there needing help. He found a restraining order lying on the floor near the front door."

"Restraining order? From who?" Had he pushed Jodi too far?

Nate's jaw tensed. "Alexander."

"What!"

Nate shook his head. "We can't find out the details to-night. I'm sure it's all part of Alexander's game."

Her eyes shifted to the envelope. "And those?"

"Charlie found these photographs on the kitchen table—beside two empty scotch bottles."

She went cold. "A nudge," she whispered through numb lips.

"What?"

"Alexander said he didn't have to do anything to Uncle Greg except give him a nudge now and again."

"When?" Nate's voice rose. He leaned back and let go of her hands.

She couldn't believe she'd forgotten to tell Nate about the call. So much else had happened, it had gotten lost in the sweep of the day. "Alexander called me at home this morning." She rushed on when she saw his face cloud with anger. "He just wanted to scare me. I was so afraid he'd done something to you or Uncle Greg; that's why I listened."

"What did he say?" The cold edge in his voice sent a chill creeping across her scalp.

"He said he didn't have to do anything *to* you. And Uncle Greg only needed a nudge; he was doing it to himself."

Nate got up and walked around the room, as if suddenly filled with too much energy to be still.

She felt the opposite, as if all strength had been drained from her.

Nate came and stood in front of her, his mouth pressed into a firm frown. "And what did he say about *you*?"

That cold reptilian voice hissed through her mind. She wondered if it would haunt her dreams for years to come. "That he was saving me . . . for last. He wanted me to anticipate our time together."

He slammed his fist onto the tabletop. The candles on it flickered. "And you *forgot* to tell me this!"

"I'm telling you now. A lot of shit has been happening. Sit down and get your boxers out of a bunch."

He sat, but he looked like he wanted to break something.

She said, "I called the police. I gave them permission to do whatever was necessary to trace the phone calls. What more could you have done had you known before now?" She suddenly realized she hadn't told him about Buckley either.

After she did, he said, "Jesus, Ellis! Is there anything else you've forgotten?"

"Nope. That's all."

With an exasperated shake of his head, he pulled out his cell phone and dialed. "Hey, Raymond, it's Nate. I need you to work your magic and get me some phone records." He recited her home phone number. "Thanks." He disconnected and looked at Ellis. "If you'd told me, I could have done that hours ago."

She took a deep breath. "I can't see what good it'll do us. If it doesn't go through proper channels, the police won't be able to use it."

"Alexander's threatening you. He won't sit and wait for police procedure. Neither will I."

She looked up into his eyes, worried for his safety, worried he'd do something that would rightfully bring the law after *him*.

Even so, the protectiveness she saw in his face made her feel . . . *safe*. How could that be? She was in the most danger she'd ever been in, and he made her feel truly safe for the first time since Laura's attack.

She wanted to say something to make him understand how she felt but couldn't find the words that expressed how he'd taken the most horrific days of her life and made her feel secure.

He held her gaze, his eyes looking dangerous in the candlelight. She wanted to warn him not to do something rash, something that would risk his life or his freedom. But his flinty expression told her the words would be wasted.

Suddenly he turned and walked away, going through the bathroom's open door, taking the envelope with him.

Ellis took the time alone to settle her racing heart. Her insides felt as if they'd been churned by a whirlwind. So many emotions. So much frustration. She was furious over Alexander's arrogance. Worried about her uncle. Afraid for Nate. Confused by her sudden sense of security. Astounded to discover she wasn't made of ice. Strangled by longing for what could never be. Amazed that the seed of love—it seemed impossible, but it was there, greater than friendship, stronger than desire—could grow in such a toxic time.

Nate was in the other room long enough that she sensed he was working on reining in his own emotions.

When he returned, she'd managed to get her head closer to where it needed to be. In addition to the envelope, Nate now carried a box of tissues and a pair of tweezers.

"White cotton gloves or latex would be best, but these will have to do." He set the box on the floor, pulled a tissue out, and handed it to her. "Someone hand-delivered these photos to your uncle today. Charlie said they're very explicit, so I'd rather you let me look through them first."

Her sense of trust grew yet again; he'd held to his word and not sneaked looking at them while in the other room. "No."

He sat there on the edge of the ottoman for a moment, as if deciding whether or not to argue further. Then he said, "Touch them as little as possible. We'll use the tweezers to move them around. If you have to pick one up, make sure a tissue is between your fingers and the photo."

She managed a mute nod.

He dumped the envelope out of the baggie, then opened it using tissue-covered fingers. He gave her one last look that questioned if she was sure this was the way she wanted to handle it.

She responded with a single dip of her chin.

He knelt on the floor and slid the stack of black-and-white five-by-seven photos out onto the large ottoman where the light was best.

Ellis had to force herself not to turn away. In her mind, she'd already created a scenario for how these "explicit" photos had come to be; Alexander had had Laura pose in exchange for buying her alcohol.

But these weren't the *Playboy*-like poses she'd expected. They were worse. Much, much worse.

She'd thought she'd been prepared. But nothing could have prepared her for the shock of the total desecration of her memory of her beautiful, perfect, beloved cousin.

When she grew dizzy, she realized she wasn't breathing.

"Ellis?" Nate's voice was quiet, concerned.

She dragged in a breath. "I'm okay." She swallowed. "I'm okay." It was a lie, but in order to get to the truth, they had to press on.

She tried to block Laura out of all the photographs. This was a collection of anonymous voyeuristic pornography. It had nothing to do with Laura.

It didn't help much.

The first was taken against a pockmarked brick wall that could easily have been in a city alley somewhere. Ellis didn't recognize the guy. She couldn't decide if that made it better or worse.

She didn't recognize the next guy either. And what he and Laura were doing had nothing to do with love.

Nate pushed the photos around, spreading them out on the ottoman.

His voice was tight with anger when he said, "Some of these look like they were taken with a telephoto lens. She didn't know he was following her. *I* didn't know. . . ."

"He *was* a Peeping Tom." Ellis averted her eyes, feeling like a Peeping Tom herself. "Dear God. Uncle Greg . . ." These pictures scrambled Ellis's insides; what had they done to her uncle?

This wasn't a nudge. This was a shove over a cliff.

If the neighbor saw these being delivered at six and there were two empty scotch bottles, it was damn likely he'd crashed his too-fast car somewhere.

Nate said, "Somehow I thought Alexander was one of the guys trading alcohol for . . ." He pursed his lips. "But this paints a different picture altogether."

"Stalker. Unless he kept photos of him and Laura to himself." The words felt oily and bitter on Ellis's tongue.

Nate gave a humorless bark of laughter. "No way. He wouldn't have missed the opportunity to show your uncle that he was doing his daughter and that she was a willing participant."

"True enough." Alexander's revenge was as cruel as his other crimes.

"Besides," Nate said, "if she was voluntarily having sex with him, why rape her?"

"Rape isn't about sex," Ellis said. "Just look at these." She pointed to the photos. "He's a sick bastard. Who knows how many women he's stalked and photographed before he attacked them?" Unfortunately, Laura's behavior had given him an abundance of subject matter and opportunity.

Nate continued to study the photos, his elbow on the ottoman, rubbing the back of his hand over his mouth.

Ellis made herself look at all the photos, just in case something offered a clue. Some of the shots were taken through car windows, others through building windows, some in dirty, exposed places. All of the telephoto close-ups had a corresponding normal distance shot, as if Alexander was flaunting how far away he could be and still invade a person's most intimate privacy.

Ellis's eyes moved quickly over the rest of the pictures. One caught her eye. The guy was wearing a wedding ring. *A cheater and a prick.*

Alexander had included a regular photo to match all of his close-ups; there had to be one that went with this one.

She looked over the rest. Bingo. It was taken through a window in a brick building. The guy was leaning back on a desktop. There was a large clock on the wall in the background. It was four-fifteen.

"Oh, my God!" Ellis thrust the photo at Nate as she jumped out of her chair, the heat of fury rocketing in her veins. "Oh. My. God!" She started pacing in a tight circle. "Recognize him?"

Nate's voice was cold when he said, "Wayne Carr. Younger, yet still a bastard."

Gritting her teeth, she said, "What a duplicitous jerk!

He was the journalism advisor at the high school! I mean, how can he sit there and spout all kinds of 'protection for our young women' when he'd used Laura like that?"

"Maybe it's his guilty conscience working overtime," he said. "Atonement."

She slapped her fingers against the edge of the photo. "That son of a bitch doesn't have a conscience." She threw her head back and yelled, "God! If I had a gun—"

Nate stood up and captured her arms, stopping her frantic movement. "You do. So you need to get yourself back under some control here."

She wanted to slap him. "How can you be so calm?"

"Because anger isn't going to get the job done." He looked her in the eyes, his gaze sympathetic. "I was hoping for something incriminating toward Alexander, something we could take to the police. Unfortunately, instead of incriminating Alexander, these could be used in his appeal. Laura's behavior placed her in the path of scores of guys who could have beaten her."

She stilled. "Do you think it's possible? Someone else did beat her?"

"Unlikely . . . but possible. First thing we have to concentrate on is getting Alexander off the streets. Then we can explore that kind of prospect."

Ellis wrapped her arms around her middle. It had never, never occurred to her that anyone but Alexander had attacked Laura.

She pushed the thought away. Right now it didn't matter. Alexander killed Kimberly Potter. He had to be caught.

Nate reached out and rubbed her upper arms. "Okay?"

She nodded.

Nate let her go.

As her blind rage began to settle into a simmering anger, a question came to mind. "I wonder . . ."

"What?"

"If Alexander had these photos, why didn't he expose them at the time of his trial? It could have muddied up the waters enough for him to get off."

"Or it could have proven to the conservative jury that he was exactly the pervert they thought him to be. It would be a gamble." Nate swiped a hand over his hair. "Alexander didn't get bail, and these weren't seized when the police searched his place, so maybe they were someplace he couldn't let anyone know about. Maybe these are personal trophies he didn't really want to share with anyone. Who knows what goes on in a mind like his?"

Ellis had to admit, the inside of that man's mind was someplace she hoped to never see.

As Nate shuffled the photos back into a stack, his hands suddenly stopped. "Look at these carefully. See the dust specks? And the slightly grainy quality of the film? He could hardly have taken these to the local Photomat and had them developed."

"You think he did them himself?"

"It's possible. The bigger question is, where has he had them stashed all these years?"

She realized what he was saying. "If we can link him to the hiding place . . ." She stopped herself. "It won't matter. He's already gone to jail for Laura's attack."

"Unless there are things that can link him to other crimes; the man likes to keep his memories fresh with photos. Maybe there'll be something to link him to Kimberly Potter's murder."

"Dear God, you think he took pictures?" She shivered in disgust.

"I think if he has these, he has more." After sliding the pictures into the envelope and the envelope back into the plastic bag, he said, "I want you to take these to the police tomorrow morning."

She sighed, her stomach curling in on itself. After a moment, she asked, "What about Greg?"

"I don't think Alexander will physically attack him, not when the mental assault is so much more devastating. Remember, this is about revenge, punishment. He wouldn't have risked delivering the photos if he wanted Greg dead."

"What if Greg went after *him*?" she asked.

"I don't want to take Charlie or Ben off your parents. I can't leave you alone here tonight. Odds are, with as much alcohol as it appears he's consumed, Greg's not going to be much of a threat to anyone for quite a while."

Ellis lowered her face into her hands. "Why can't this end?" She rubbed her eyes. "I just want this to be over."

Nate took her wrists and pulled her hands away from her face. "Let's get some sleep so we can hit it fresh in the morning. I hate to say it, but I think our time's running out."

Chapter Twenty-Eight

Ellis lay in the darkness next to Nate. Her initial fear had been that she would panic when he blew out the candles and shut off the flashlight. Terrified she'd humiliate herself and insist he close the French doors and the windows.

But that hadn't been an issue at all. She'd curled up next to Nate without the slightest edge of panic, wrapped in a warm calm unlike any she could recall.

He'd made love to her so tenderly, so reverently, her heart ached.

And now she lay here, longing strangling her and keeping sleep utterly unattainable. She had to admit, she held slight resentment for the slow, even rhythm of Nate's breathing. Sleep didn't seem to be evading him.

It had finally stopped raining. There was a steady *tink-tink-tink* as the last of the water rolled from the roof and into the gutters. This empty house, those open windows, should be unsettling. But her fears had been quelled by the safe and comfortable feeling of lying next to Nate, isolated from the rest of the world.

She thought about the boy who'd stood alone all of his life and realized he'd become a man who did the same. Was he lonely? Did his heart yearn for a family? The fact that he'd purchased this place said he wanted something steady in his life.

She longed to reach across the narrow space between them. To tell him he didn't have to be alone. But there was no reason to torture them both any more tonight.

A short while later, she heard another thunderstorm rolling closer. The breeze waxed and waned through the French doors, moving across her body like feathers in the dark. There was something extremely erotic about it. She hadn't slept with an open window for sixteen years. She could hardly believe she was lying here now with the doors open to the blackness of the low-country night.

And she wasn't afraid.

Nate shifted and his breathing changed.

"You awake?" she whispered softly enough that she wouldn't wake him if he wasn't.

He turned on his side, facing her, tucking his arm under his head. "You too?"

"Mmm-hmm."

"Too spooked to sleep?" There was a teasing tone in his voice.

"No. I was just thinking."

"About?"

"You. Your life. Where did you go when you left here?"

She heard him sigh and felt the bed shake as he changed position.

"I joined the marines."

"You were only seventeen."

"Mom signed the papers."

"How could she have done it? You were so close to graduation."

"I think she was glad to see me go. Everything that had happened affected her too. She wasn't a strong woman."

Ellis snorted. "Parenthood isn't supposed to be easy."

"It worked out." There was no bitterness in his voice, no regret.

"Is that where you met Charlie and Ben, the marines?"

"Yeah."

"And after that you started doing the security thing?"

"Pretty much."

After a moment, she asked, "Do you like it? Your work, living like you do?"

"I used to. But now . . ." He let the statement hang in the darkness between them. "I never minded being alone, not having anyone close. But I think that's all changing."

A little spark of hope ignited in her soul. Was she the reason for that change?

She heard the rasp as he ran his hand over his beard-stubbled face. She got the impression that those words might not have been uttered in the light of day. But here in the darkness, isolated from the world, perhaps he was pretending as much as she that nothing else existed outside these aged walls.

They fell silent for a few minutes. The wind kicked up, and rain began to patter against the veranda. Ellis thought of the people who'd lain in this bedroom before them listening the rain. What kind of lives had they had? Had there been happy memories made here?

She waited, hoping Nate would open up further. When the silence drew on too long, she whispered, "If he goes back to jail tomorrow, will you leave right away?"

Nate was quiet long enough that she thought he might be asleep. Then he said, "I'll have to." The words were heavy, regretful. "I have responsibilities, people who count on me."

"But you don't *want* to?" The bare-naked hope in her voice made her ears burn with embarrassment.

"This isn't a job you just turn in your two weeks' notice and walk away."

"Please tell me." She laid her hand on his chest. "I want you to trust me, like I trust you."

He drew a deep breath and exhaled loudly. Ellis felt the rise and fall of his chest. Then he laid his hand over hers. "No one can know. No one outside of my task force knows."

"Task force? As in government?"

"Yes. I do covert work for Homeland Security. The shipping company job is just my cover. The records your uncle found are there to appeal to the bad guys. The reason that kid could find them is because I want them to be discovered, but not too easily. It pays to have a suspicious profile—lends credibility in certain circles."

When she feared he would stop, would tell her no more, he went on. "I deal with some horrible people, capable of unspeakable things. That's why I have to leave. Why I can't contact you after I'm gone. My situation can turn in an instant. Love is a weakness they're sure to exploit."

Love? She wanted to ask but was afraid he meant love in general, as in for friends and family, not the sort of life-altering love she was beginning to feel for him.

He sounded so lonely. Without thinking about anything but comforting him, she slid closer and moved her hand to his cheek. "Thank you for telling me." The words were inadequate for the gift he'd just given, for his utter and complete trust.

He placed his hand over hers and pressed her palm to his lips. Then he held their hands over his heart.

"If I were free to do as I choose . . . if there wouldn't be such a risk of consequences . . ." He left the sentence unfinished.

She curled against his side and rested her head on his shoulder. It took a moment, but she realized he'd just given her all that he could, at least for now. The seed of hope buried itself deep in her heart. It would take a long time before it gave up its struggle for life.

He wrapped an arm around her and squeezed the hand he held on his chest.

The storm broke and the wind lashed the ancient oaks that surrounded the house. At last, she slept.

⁂

Rory sat outside Ellis's empty condo, seething. She was with *him;* he could feel it in his gut.

Nate Vance was keeping Ellis from him, from her family. If Vance hadn't shown up back here, Rory could have gotten things ironed out with her. How could she be so blind when it came to that man?

The greater question was, what was Rory going to do about it?

⁂

Nate opened his eyes. The room was graying with the approaching dawn. Ellis was lying on her side, facing him. He studied the curve of her cheek, the sweep of her lashes, the sweet softness of her slightly parted lips. For the first time in days, all the worry was gone from her face; her brow was clear and smooth, her mouth relaxed.

As tempted as he was to kiss that mouth, he didn't. Once she awakened, he knew the anxiety, the strain, would return.

He slid carefully off the bed. In the bathroom, he flipped the light switch. The power was back on. Grabbing his cell phone and his laptop, he went in and closed the door.

Thirty minutes later, he had a name for the woman Alexander had dined with the other night. Justine Adams. Lived alone. Confined to a wheelchair after an automobile accident some nineteen years ago. What he couldn't find out was how Alexander was connected to her. But he would—today. Those two were just too odd of a combination to make sense. Alexander was certainly up to something.

When he tiptoed out of the bathroom, Ellis was still sleeping. He went out and stood on the upper veranda, just outside the bedroom's French doors. He leaned his elbows on the railing and looked toward Belle Creek. Breathing in the storm-cleansed air, he took a moment to absorb the peace of this place. Up until now, this plantation was his only weakness, his only point of vulnerability. How quickly that had changed. Risking damage to his beloved plantation was one thing. Risking Ellis's safety was something he simply could not do. He had to leave as soon as this was finished.

Then he had to stay away. Painful for him. Better for her.

Even so, now—in this fleeting moment in the dawn where light was quickly gaining hold of the day, where the freshness of the early hour gave rise to hope, to imaginings of the impossible—he allowed himself to imagine it wasn't so.

A car door slammed and he jerked upright.

Walking to the end of the porch, he looked toward the stables. Jake was here early, no doubt to check the horses after the storm.

Nate headed back toward the French doors and heard the television in the bedroom, its volume low.

Ellis sat on the bed, the remote control in her hand and shock on her face.

He looked at the TV. The news was on. Police cars and the coroner's vehicle were sitting in front of the gatehouse at Ellis's condo complex.

"Sam's dead." Her chin trembled. "Poor, poor Sam." She blinked away tears. "They found his body back near the fence at the marsh."

"Damn." Nate looked back to the newscast. Had Sam come across Alexander last night? Had the man gone after Ellis at her condo?

She put her hand over her mouth, and the tears that had pooled in her eyes flowed. "It's all because of me."

Nate sat on the bed next to her. Grasping her upper arms, he made her look him in the eyes. "It's because of Alexander—and the system that let him free. Not you."

Tears shone like dew in her moss-green eyes. He wanted to strangle Alexander for putting them there.

She drew a deep breath, let it out. Then she nodded.

"He's careful, but not perfect. We'll get him," Nate said.

Giving him a tremulous smile, she said, "Then I'd better get those photos to the police so they can start processing them."

He could see the change come over her, the soft sadness give over to hard-edged anger.

He stroked her hair and then kissed her forehead. "I'm going to check on Jake in the barn." He got up and turned toward the door. "Then I'll drive you into town."

"You're not driving me anywhere—" She stopped suddenly, staring at the TV again.

The anchorman said, *"The police are still looking for the man who murdered a young woman in Belle Island Thursday night. They haven't ruled out a possible connection with this newest murder in the usually quiet town. They have released this sketch of a suspect."*

The pencil sketch was a good one. Nate wondered who had given them his description . . . Ellis's uncle perhaps?

He looked at Ellis. Her face was so pale; her lips had even lost most of their color.

"If anyone sees this man, please contact the Belle Island Police Department at—"

Nate stepped over, took the remote from her hand, and clicked off the TV. "Let's focus on what we can do to stop this madness. I'm going to check on the horses. You get ready to go."

He wanted to climb in that bed with her and hold her until the color came back to her face and that haunted look left her eyes.

Instead, he left the room without another word.

❦

Ellis quickly showered and dressed. After putting on her shoes, she ran down the stairs and out to the stables.

Nate was just coming out. "Ready?"

"You can't drive me."

There was argument in his eyes as he opened his mouth.

She cut him off sharply. "If you're locked up while we wait for the evidence to be processed and fall one way or the other, I'll be totally alone. I need you out here."

He stood for a moment, as if deciding. Finally, he shoved his hands on his hips and said, "All right. But take Jake with you."

She rolled her eyes. "You're as bad as Dad. I don't need someone with me who is more likely to need my protection than to give it."

"And how are you going to get there?" he asked.

"Shit." She'd forgotten her car was at the marina. "I can't take the Hummer. Jake's truck?"

"Can't do without it today." There was an odd tone to his voice. Before she could push, he said, "I'll drive you to the marina in Jake's truck."

She thought for a moment. "Okay. But come back here. Don't follow me around like a superhero. I can take care of myself."

"Okay."

"Say it."

He rolled his eyes.

"I mean it. Say it," she insisted, holding his gaze.

"I promise."

"Good. Let's go."

The marina was always busy on Sunday mornings. There were plenty of people around, which made Ellis safe—and put Nate in jeopardy. She convinced him to drop her off at the parking lot entrance. Nate wore sunglasses and an old cowboy hat. The likelihood of someone recognizing him was slim. Still, she didn't want to take chances.

Just before she opened the door, Nate grabbed her left hand. "After you're done at the station, go directly to your parents' house. Ben will be expecting you."

"Where are you going?"

"To Charleston to see if this woman Justine Adams can give us any clues. Then I'm going to follow him again. Something's gotta give. He's taking too many chances; I want to be there when he screws up. I might not be back tonight."

She swallowed, her mouth and throat dry. "What if someone recognizes you?"

He squeezed her hand. "Ellis, remember what I told you I do? I'm very good at it. No one will recognize me."

"Okay." She leaned across the ragged and duct-taped seat, kissing him quickly on the cheek. "Keep in touch."

His half-smile made her just a little short of breath. "I will. You too."

She unlatched the door. When she started to let go of his hand, he held tight.

"Be careful," he said. "And *stay with your mom and Ben*." The last words were delivered with a sharp look.

With a nod, she pulled her hand from his, picked up the baggie with the photos, and got out of the truck.

She'd reached her car before Nate pulled away in Mr. J's old rattletrap truck.

For a moment, she sat there thinking through what she was about to do. Once these photos were out there, there'd be no calling them back. The very thought of other people seeing Laura like that made her sick. She'd spent her life preserving her cousin's memory; now she was about to destroy it.

Poor Uncle Greg would never get those images out of his mind.

At least they hadn't gotten word he'd been involved in an auto accident overnight. She called him, hoping he'd answer. He didn't.

She clung to the idea that Alexander's words were true. He wasn't *doing* anything to her uncle.

But had these pictures driven her uncle to do something crazy?

She started her car and plugged her cell phone into the charger. It rang before she set it down. She jumped like a startled animal.

"Hello?"

"This is Jenny Mayfield, at Seaside Apartments. You left a picture with me yesterday."

"Oh, yes." Ellis's heart leapt at the prospect of something more to offer the police.

"Well, I showed it to my older son when he got home. He says he thinks he saw the guy when he came home t'other night."

"The night of the murder?"

"Yeah. Said it was a blond guy. Looked normal. Wasn't in a hurry or nothin'. He got in a light blue minivan—one of those like repairmen use, without the windows in the back."

"Did your son tell the police this?"

"Oh, no. He won't talk to the police. That's why I called you. See, my boy, he's had a little trouble . . ."

This could be a problem, an unreliable witness—even

if she did get him to talk to the police. But she'd cross one bridge at a time. "Did he tell you anything else? What time was it? Did he know the make of the van or remember anything about the plates?" She couldn't control the anxious rush of questions. This would at least place Alexander at the scene.

"Was about one-thirty, I can tell you that. Tanner wouldn't have noticed at all if that van hadn't been parked where he usually parks. Just a minute, I'll ask him 'bout the other." It sounded like she took the phone away from her face when she yelled, "Tanner! You remember the plates or anything?"

Ellis sat with her palms sweating as she listened but couldn't make out the boy's response.

Jenny came back on. "Didn't notice the plates. Says he don't know one minivan from 'nother."

"Thanks so much. Keep my number in case he remembers something else, or you come across someone else who saw something, will you?"

"Sure. He won't have to talk to the cops, will he?"

"I don't know. But he shouldn't worry. All they're interested in is catching the man who murdered your neighbor."

As soon as she ended the call, she dialed Nate's cell and told him what she'd learned.

He said, "An eyewitness placing him there is good. Maybe not enough, though."

"We won't stop here," she said.

"Ellis, you're going to the police, then to your mother's. Sit tight until I contact you. No Nancy Drewing while I'm gone."

"Okay. Okay." She disconnected the call.

Chapter Twenty-nine

Ellis stared at the envelope on the passenger seat. Goddamn Wayne Carr. It was bad enough seeing Laura with those strangers, but at least most of them appeared to be college age.

If the ones with Laura and Carr together got out, it was going to create much more lasting gossip in Belle Island.

She sat there, contemplating taking those particular shots out. If there was evidence on the photos that could lead to Alexander, it would hardly be limited to those with Carr. What would it hurt?

"No," she said to herself. Then Carr would be scot-free to seduce another young girl. The filthy bastard deserved the bad press—but did Aunt Jodi and Uncle Greg?

Ellis left the marina. She decided at the very least, her uncle deserved advance warning that these photos were going to the police. His house was in the opposite direction from the police station. Another few minutes' delay wouldn't hurt.

When she pulled up in front of his house, the Corvette wasn't in the drive, but he usually parked it in the garage.

She got out and headed toward the front door.

"He's not home, honey," Mrs. White called from next door. She was out watering the flowers on her front porch. "He left here not an hour ago. Tore out like somethin' was wrong."

Ellis's stomach turned. "Which way did he go?"

"North. Out of town. Is everything all right?"

"Yes." Ellis trotted back to her car, hoping it was the truth.

As she jumped into the driver's seat, she glanced at the envelope.

If her uncle had sobered up, there was one place north of town he was mostly likely headed.

She hoped she'd get there before he did something that couldn't be undone.

Nate did a little canvassing of Justine Adams's neighbors, in the guise of doing a survey for a fictitious local philanthropic group interested in establishing services for citizens with disabilities.

In this churchgoing town, very few doors were answered this early on a Sunday. Nate got lucky two doors down. It was occupied by a man and his life partner, whom Nate met as the man passed through the front hall.

After a few preliminary questions, the man at the door started talking without prompts.

"It's not like we haven't offered to help her. God only knows, both Miles and I have bent over backward since we moved in."

"How long ago was that?" Nate asked.

"It'll be a year in September. Like I was saying, she just

doesn't seem to want to mix with people. Barely sticks her nose out the front door. Miles does occasional errands for her, especially if the weather's bad. But he called her last week, like he does every Monday, and she said she wouldn't be needing our help anymore—just like that." He snapped his fingers. "She has a friend who is taking care of *everything* now."

"Did she mention who this friend was?"

"No. But I have to tell you"—he looked over his shoulder, as if making certain Miles wasn't within earshot—"she really hurt poor Miles's feelings. She was very abrupt."

Nate thanked the man and left. He wondered if Justine Adams's friend was Hollis Alexander. What was his angle? And how had he insinuated himself into a recluse's life? Seemed impossible that he could have done it so quickly, considering how guarded the woman was with her neighbors.

As was common around Charleston, there was a narrow alley that ran down one side of the Adams's property. It led to two additional residences. One appeared to have originally been a carriage house for the house on the opposite side of the alley. The other was clearly a separate property, situated directly behind the Adams's residence.

Nate walked down the alley, which had a name all its own, even though it dead-ended immediately after the two houses.

No one answered at the carriage house.

At the house behind Ms. Adams's, a very tiny woman with a puff of white hair answered the door. "Are you here to fix the water heater?"

"No, ma'am."

"Well! I stayed home from Sunday service. They said they'd be here by nine."

Nate made a sympathetic noise, and then quickly launched into his survey tale.

The little woman shook her head. "Such a shame. That family's had more than their share of misery. Stanley and I moved in here when Justine and her brother were just youngsters." Her gaze drifted, as if looking into the past, her voice growing reminiscent. "You know, her brother drowned when he was eleven; Justine was never right after that. She was there, you know, saw the whole thing." She blinked and seemed to come back to the present. "Then right after her mother died, she had that awful accident that left her crippled."

"After talking to some other neighbors, it seems she keeps to herself," Nate said.

"She never did let my Stanley do a thing for her. Like I said, she's been a bit queer since her brother died. She's got no one, you know. Arranged for the construction company to fix up the house for her wheelchair all by herself." Then she paused, as if remembering something. "There was one of the young carpenters—a lovely Christian boy, so nice-looking—who did lots of things for her at first. Wonder whatever happened to him?"

Nate had a pretty damn good idea. "Do you recall his name?"

She pursed her lips and tilted her head. "Howard? No, that's not it." She looked at the floor and made *h* sounds. "Harvie . . . Hal . . . Oh, dear heavens, I don't know. But it did start with an *H;* I'm almost certain."

"Have you seen him around lately? Or anyone new, for that matter?"

"Well, I don't get out much now. My Stanley died last year and my eyes . . . can't drive myself, you know. And with the way Justine's let everything get so overgrown, I can barely see her house at all anymore. Just a shame; her father used to keep that hedge shaped as square as a brick wall."

The woman continued on while Nate shifted his feet, anxious to go. Finally, she paused, giving him the opportunity to thank her and leave.

Nate lingered in the alley, halfway to the street. If Alexander had been that "lovely Christian boy," then Justine's basement could very well be where he kept all of his incriminating evidence.

The police would need probable cause to get a warrant to search Justine Adams's place.

Nate had to get inside that basement.

Ellis drove down Bastine Road, which snaked along the river, hindering her speed. She assured herself that if Carr was home, most likely his wife would be too. Surely her uncle wouldn't do anything violent in front of her.

Slowing slightly, Ellis dialed his cell again.

No answer.

About eight miles out of town, she took a right that led down the two-mile lane to the old house. Wayne Carr, parasite that he was, lived on land that had been in his wife's family since the heyday of the rice planters—very old Carolina money.

What would Ellis do if her uncle wasn't there?

The idea of simply turning around and heading back to

town felt wrong, cowardly. At the very least, she wanted Carr to know that there was one person in this town who knew him for what he was. Sanctimonious jerk.

In that instant, Ellis realized the power she held in her hands. A plan gelled. She was going to bring him low, and if she was lucky, protect a tiny fraction of her family's peace.

As she approached the place where the drive circled in front of the house, she slowed. There were no other cars in sight.

She coasted to a stop in front of the house, put down the window, shut off the car, and listened.

Silence.

Her uncle wasn't here.

Leaning back in the seat, she gave her heart a moment to slow down.

The house looked like something out of a magazine spread—beautifully haunting in its antiquity, lushly landscaped, and artfully detailed. The garage, far off to the left of the main house, was so completely covered in close-cropped vines that it appeared to be made out of greenery. A hunting dog lazed on the porch, unfazed by her arrival. Apparently, rich dogs don't perform watchdog duties.

The house was opened to a wide screened door. She imagined Carr in there with his lovely wife, sipping coffee and reading the Sunday paper. Her heartbeat accelerated again. What if he was still porking underage girls?

She'd put a stop to it, that's what. He wasn't going to get away with it anymore.

She opened the baggie and took out the envelope. Then she slid the pictures onto the seat. With a pen from her purse, she nudged the two with Carr away from the rest. Then she put all but those two back inside the envelope.

Carr's pictures went into her purse.

Before she got out of the car, she shut off her cell phone. The last thing she wanted was a call from Nate in the middle of this and be forced to explain why she wasn't where she was supposed to be.

When she got out, the dog raised its head and gave a half wag with its tail.

She adjusted her purse on her shoulder and took a tentative step forward.

The dog laid its head back down.

"Good doggie." She climbed the steps to the white-columned porch.

She'd give Carr a break and ask to speak to him alone; threatening exposure to his wife could be great motivation.

She knocked on the door frame, then leaned close to look through the screen. The wide entry hall was empty. The only sound was the loud ticking of the grandfather clock, tucked beneath the turn in the staircase.

The silence made her realize just how isolated this place was.

Suddenly, it didn't seem peaceful. It felt desolate, remote.

Maybe she'd better just get on with her original plan, get these photos to the police.

Definitely the smart move. She'd come here in a panic for her uncle. And he wasn't here.

She turned away from the door—and nearly jumped out of her shoes.

Wayne Carr stood three feet behind her.

"Mr. Carr," she stammered, trying to slow the hummingbird flight of her heart. That's when she saw the swollen lip and the cut on his cheek. "Are you all right?" She gestured to his face.

He touched the cut on his cheek. "Oh, this . . . fine, I'm fine. I was just putting some things in the garage attic this morning, got my feet tangled up and hit the concrete floor face-first." He blotted his forehead on his long-sleeved shirt.

"Um, I'm looking for my uncle. We understood he was headed out to talk to you this morning." She emphasized the "we" to make him think people knew where she was.

She attributed her sudden skittishness to his unexpected appearance.

Carr shook his head. "No, I haven't seen him." With a furrowed brow, he added, "Why was he coming to see me?"

"Something about those articles concerning Hollis Alexander, I think," she said innocently. Then she started to step around him. "Funny, I was sure this is where he said he was coming. Sorry to have bothered you."

Carr stepped aside for her to pass.

She was halfway down the steps when she stopped. She wouldn't get this opportunity again.

"May I have a few minutes of your time?" she asked.

He held up his dirty palms. "If you'll give me a moment to wash my hands. Abi made a coffee cake; can I offer you some?"

"Oh, no thank you," she said. The very thought of eating in this man's presence made her stomach turn.

He opened the screen door for her. The interior of

the house was cool, thanks to the shade of old trees and twenty-four-inch-thick brick walls.

Gesturing toward the sitting room on the right, he said, "If you'll have a seat, I'll be right in."

Ellis went into the room and sat in one of the wing chairs that flanked the fireplace. She arranged herself so her bag was on the seat next to her, the photos within easy reach. She wasn't afraid of Wayne Carr, slinking weasel that he was. He was slight of build and at least fifty. Even if he reacted badly, she could take him down easily.

Her heart skipped along quickly. Maybe that'd be a good thing. She could call the cops, and Carr would have to explain to his wife why he'd attacked a woman in his own living room.

She heard him returning, his shoes tapping on the polished wood floor.

When he stepped into the room, he stopped at the small liquor cart. "May I offer you something to drink? Bloody Mary, perhaps?" He spoke casually, relaxed, but there was a skittishness in his eyes that gave away his unease.

He didn't want to talk about those articles.

"No, thank you."

"Do you mind?" he asked, raising a glass.

"Of course not. Is Mrs. Carr at home?"

He looked surprised. "Why, no. She's away for the day."

He sat down in a chair between her and the door.

For an instant, Ellis felt trapped with him between her and the way out. It passed when he leaned back, crossed his legs, and took a sip of his drink.

"Is there something specific you wanted to discuss?"

"As a matter of a fact, there is. Something very specific." She looked sharply at him. "About you and my cousin, Laura."

With a tilt of his head, he raised a curious brow; his body remained relaxed, his face composed.

"I know you were seeing her."

He gave an elegant bark of laughter. "Oh, my dear, I have no idea where you got such a misguided notion."

"You took special interest in her case."

"I'm a journalist. This is a small, close-knit community. Of course I did."

Ellis sighed. "I didn't come here to dance around this issue. I want you to know that you haven't fooled everyone."

His mouth tightened. He uncrossed his legs and recrossed them the other way.

She plunged ahead. "You're a lying, cheating bastard who took advantage of a troubled teenage girl."

"I wasn't involved with your cousin—"

She pulled the photos out of her purse and held them up in front of her. "These photos say otherwise."

For a moment, his mouth hung open. Then he uncrossed his legs and leaned forward, setting his drink on the table. "Where did you get those?"

"Doesn't matter. She was *seventeen*!" She shook the photos. "Seventeen! God! You were a married adult—her journalism advisor, for Christ's sake. She needed help. And you exploited that fact."

He pressed his lips together and looked out the window for a moment. "It was a long time ago."

He continued to stare out the window, his rapid, shallow breathing belying his calm posture.

"Your wife is a lovely person. I don't want her hurt any more than you do."

"Blackmail?" He looked to her and raised a dark brow. "From the schoolteacher? I never would have thought it."

She gave him a hard smile. "Anyone is capable of just about anything—given the proper motivation."

Something in his eyes lit up at that statement. It gave her the creeps.

"You've got a lot of nerve," she said, "supporting an animal like Hollis Alexander. I want you to stop campaigning for his exoneration and stop writing those horrible pieces that allude to Nate Vance being a murderer. In exchange, I'll be very happy for these photos to remain our little secret." She paused. "Oh, and if I ever get wind of you and an underage girl, everyone in Belle Island will see these." She smiled. "Nothing more complicated or dubious than that."

He sat there for a long moment, studying her as if she were an alien species.

Then he got to his feet and stood in front of her. "Give them to me." His nostrils flared with every rough intake of breath.

She was getting edgy, but she'd come this far. "I'll just hang on to them; wouldn't want your wife stumbling across them lying around the house. Of course, these are just copies." With feigned calmness, she put the photos in her lap.

One of them slid off and onto the floor.

When she bent over to retrieve it, a glint of silver caught her eye. There, under the other wing chair flanking the fireplace.

Her heart nearly stopped when she realized it was her

uncle's monogrammed pocketknife. She'd given it to him last Christmas.

Why had Carr lied about his being here?

There was only one reason. He'd done something to her uncle.

She couldn't breathe. Dizziness fogged her thinking.

She had to get a hold of herself. Appear calm. Get out of here.

With a wild fluttering in her chest and trembling fingers, she reached for the picture.

She had to continue as if her deal was concluding just as she'd planned. She forced herself to keep talking and slowly picked up the photo.

"Just your word. That's all I want." She'd go ahead and hand him the photos and get the hell out of here. "You'll stay away from teenage girls and stop with the shit-stirring—"

She slowly sat up.

Wayne Carr stood there pointing a very large handgun at her head.

Chapter Thirty

There was a six-foot-high brick wall between Justine Adams's yard and the alley. On the other side, that once-neat hedge had turned into a ten-foot-tall, who-knew-how-thick tangle of vegetation. Nate stood in the alley for a few moments, deciding his best approach to that basement door. There was no way he could wait for dark. He had to get in, get out, and get the police on their way with a search warrant.

He looked up and down the alley, and then grabbed the top of the brick wall and jumped. Hoisting himself up, he threw one leg over, then the other. He lowered himself through the hedge to the ground. He hit the dirt, his skin stinging where branches had poked and scraped on the way down.

Kneeling there, he edged forward until he had a decent view of the yard. The still humidity pressed on him as tiny insects swarmed around his face. He felt as if he'd stepped into a South American tropical forest.

The lot was narrow and deep. What had at one time probably been a neatly laid out garden surrounded by and bisected in both directions with a brick walkway was now a conglomeration of overgrown bougainvillea and boxwoods—plenty of cover for his trek toward the house. In the center of the yard, where the narrow brick walks met, were the ruins of a circular fountain. The statue in the center was missing its head. Vines crisscrossed the rest of the body, looking like an odd sort of plantlife jumpsuit.

Once he'd made it to the corner of the house, he waited to see if there was any response from inside. As he listened, he slipped on the pair of latex gloves he'd grabbed from the stables and shoved in his pocket this morning. Then he dropped down into the little well that housed the basement door.

Nothing indicated the house had an alarm.

The lock was ancient. It took him two seconds to pick it.

Once inside the basement, he dabbed the perspiration from his forehead with his sleeve, pausing to listen for any indication that Justine had heard him. He also needed a moment for his eyes to adjust to the low light. Even though this was a raised basement with windows high on the walls, vegetation crowded close, blocking out a good deal of the daylight.

The damp interior smelled of old cardboard and mildew. Cobwebs draped the floor joists over his head like Spanish moss.

The upstairs remained quiet. He pulled a small flashlight out of his pocket and shone its narrow beam around the room. Nothing but normal basement clutter—a furnace that looked like it predated the first moon walk, boxes, and shelves crammed with old tools. Nothing appeared to have been recently disturbed.

Disappointment thickened in his throat. He'd really thought he'd been onto something.

He took a deep breath that he quickly regretted. He pressed his wrist firmly beneath his nose to suppress a sneeze.

As he blinked away the tingling tears, he spotted it. An old wooden door with a hasp and a padlock. Why would anyone lock a crappy wooden door in a basement full of junk?

This lock was a bit more of a challenge, but Nate was soon inside the windowless room. He found the pull-chain light. He closed the door behind him before turning it on.

Unlike the basement in general, this room was neatly ordered. Huge sheets of thick plastic had been stapled to the floor joists overhead and draped all four walls. It took Nate a moment to recognize the equipment sitting on the workbench. Alexander had set up a dark room to process and print his own film.

Stacked tidily on shelves were boxes, both plastic and cardboard, labeled with black marker. The lettering was precise and evenly spaced. Some containers were marked just by date. Some, like the one on top, had only initials:

E. C. G.

Ellis Christine Greene.

With his gut in a knot and fury burning in his chest, Nate reached for that box.

He pulled it out and placed it on the worktable.

Although he'd known what he would find when he opened it, the sight of that first photo sent spiders down his spine. The sensation was so acute, he flexed his shoulder blades trying to shake it off.

The first photos were of Ellis teaching her class in the park. They had been taken from the stand of trees that led to the marsh. Then came those of Ellis taken through her living room window—some of them looked as if he'd been standing two feet from her when he'd taken them. And it was clear that it would have been easy enough to see Ellis enter her alarm code through the telescopic lens.

Nate fisted his hand and spun in a circle looking for something to hit. He caught himself before he slammed it into the door and made enough racket to draw attention from upstairs. Instead, he squeezed both fists against his forehead and gritted his teeth, counting his ragged and furious breaths until the urge finally passed.

He pulled another box down from the next shelf. More photos. Nate didn't recognize any of the women. It was clear Alexander had been stalking them—just as he had Laura, peeking in their windows, following them to work.

Next, Nate picked up an opaque plastic box marked MEMENTOS.

When he opened it, his heart sped up. He stared at the trophies of brutality, the memory box of a madman, feeling as if he were being spun into a spiderweb.

Broken necklaces. A cluster of silver and gold, pearl and stone; single earrings without mates. A watch with a blood-spattered face. A hammered-silver barrette. Things of beauty, bent and broken as they'd been torn from his victims.

Nate took a gloved finger and spread the jewelry out.

There it was, the proof that would nail this bastard's skin to the wall. A necklace with an intertwined *K* and *P*—the necklace Kimberly Potter was wearing in the photo that had run in the newspaper. The chain was broken, the two ends knotted to keep the initials from sliding off.

Nate felt a perverse sense of elation in this discovery. There was enough evidence in this box to solve mysteries for a lot of victims, finally put to rest the question of justice.

Unfortunately, unless the police came in here with a warrant, it would all be for naught.

Nate looked through everything again but didn't find anything that he remembered seeing Laura wear. Maybe he was missing it.

He repacked everything as it had been and closed up the boxes. When he returned them to their shelves, he noticed something tucked between the back of the boxes and the wall. He pulled out a bulging manila envelope. It wasn't dusty or brittle with age.

Taking it to the table, he slid the contents out onto the table: a current New Mexico driver's license with Alexander's picture and the name John David Woods; a birth certificate and a social security card with the same name; several stacks of cash, rubber-banded together. And then, the one thing that took him by surprise—a thick business envelope. Filled with cash.

Where would Alexander get his hands on so much money? There had to be tens of thousands of dollars.

Thievery or blackmail.

Blackmail.

Carr.

I should have thought of it the second I saw the pictures.

There could be others. Maybe that was one of the reasons Alexander had kept all those photos. If he'd taken them of the right people, the pictures were a cash crop.

For a person like Alexander, there would be no honor among thieves. It didn't matter that he'd collected money from Carr and still showed those photos to Greg. Alexander had his payoff. In a day or so, he'd be off to his new life as a citizen of New Mexico.

Nate put the envelopes back in their hiding places. Everything had to be back in their original order. He was just sliding the hateful box of mementos onto the shelf when he heard a metallic slide and click.

He spun, reaching for the gun tucked in the back of his pants, under his shirt.

Alexander stood in the low doorway, aiming a dusty hunting rifle at Nate's chest. He gave a serpent's smile. "You certainly have a way of fucking up my plans."

❧

The antique clock in Carr's foyer ticked away the seconds while Ellis stared at the gun.

She couldn't breathe. She couldn't think.

She managed to shift her gaze to Carr's face. Gone was the self-confident arrogance. His eyes looked like those of a cornered animal. And he was sweating.

She didn't have to fake her fear. "If you want the photos that badly, take them." She held them out to him.

Her best bet was for him to become confident in his control.

"I'm afraid it's too late for that." He gestured with the gun. "Get up."

Ellis moved slowly, and started to put the photos back in her bag. If she could get her hands on her gun.

"Ah-ah!" The muscles in the hand holding the gun tightened. "Keep your hands out here where I can see them."

Lifting her hands in front of her, she said, "Okay, okay. What do you want?"

"You can't give me what I want." Carr's eyes had begun to lose some of their panic. But he was still sweating profusely; maybe killing wouldn't come easy for him.

"I don't understand." Buy some time. Think.

"Stand up."

She stood slowly, carefully. Which put her farther away from her gun. "My uncle paid you a call . . . after he saw these." She lifted the photos. "*He* gave you that split lip."

"Shut up and start walking. Front door. Leave the bag."

"What have you done to him?" She stayed where she was. If she could get Carr to reach for her, to urge her into motion . . .

He didn't. Instead he yelled, "Now!"

"If I don't? I doubt you're going to shoot me right here in your living room."

He fired. The sound tore through her head. The bullet missed her by inches and hit the inside of the fireplace. "I do know how to handle this gun."

Once the rigidness of shock left her limbs, Ellis started toward the front door.

Reaching the bottom of the porch steps, he directed her toward the garage.

Ellis counted the steps, each one leading her closer to

her death. She had to get Carr within reach; her only hope was to disarm him.

"I'm really not interested in dying for those photos," she said as she walked as slowly as she dared. "It's not worth it, for either of us."

"Those damn photos. First Alexander, for those fucking articles. Now you."

An avalanche of thoughts started to drop into place.

"Alexander was blackmailing you. That's why you wrote those articles." Had it been solely to present a picture of Alexander's innocence, to enhance the appearance of Nate's guilt?

Alexander was on a crusade of revenge.

She asked, "Why help Alexander frame Nate for the Potter murder?"

Carr's voice was hard when he said, "Because he thinks he went to prison for Nate Vance's crime fifteen years ago."

Nate's crime?

"Nate didn't do—"

Oh, dear God! Alexander *didn't* beat Laura.

The voices that night. *Carr* and Laura.

That's why there had been no sign of struggle, no cry for help—because Laura had gone with him willingly.

"Ah, now you see." There was a sneer in Carr's tone. "You're not quite as smart as you thought you were. And neither is Hollis. He's grossly misjudged his situation. He should have just moved on. Then we all could have continued with our lives. But he couldn't let it go." Carr's face twisted with fury. "If only it had been just the money. But he insisted on pushing for a reopening of his case. I got a call yesterday from a lawyer willing to petition to reopen the case. That just can't happen."

It was clear Carr was going to do whatever he thought he must to preserve his freedom and his life.

He was ten feet away from her. Too far for her to charge and not get shot in the process.

If she could piss him off, maybe he'd get close and she'd have a chance to get the gun from him.

But how? *Think.*

Carr had been the only one not photographed outside or through a car window. It had been through the window of his office, a personal space. He was different.

Laura had gone with him that night.

"So what was the deal with you and Laura?" she said with as much mockery as she could muster. "You bring her booze that night? Sex for booze, that was her game, right? She was *using* you."

Carr's hand started to tremble as he squeezed the gun. "I *loved* her. I loved her and she"—he gritted his teeth—"she cheated." He said the word as if it carried a horrible taste.

Cheated? The adulterer just accused his teenage lover of cheating.

Ellis pushed. "She used you, just like all the others—"

"Shut up and open the door!" He gestured with the gun toward the back of a large SUV sitting just inside the open garage doors.

There was no way she could let him get her inside this vehicle. But she couldn't do anything until she got him closer. That was the shortfall in her defense tactics; if a guy had a gun and knew what you could do, he wasn't likely to get within striking distance.

"You loved her." It was her only shot. Get his emotions to overcome his caution. "You loved her, risked your marriage, and she didn't care."

He didn't take as much as one step closer to her.

He fired a shot that hit the ground right next to her foot. "Open the fucking door!"

Slowly, she turned and put her hand on the cargo door latch.

How could she—

The pain barely registered before everything went black.

Chapter Thirty-One

Nate left his gun hidden in his waistband and put his hands where Alexander could see them. The man already had the rifle aimed and a bullet in the chamber. The odds were against outdrawing him.

"You might as well give it up, Hollis," Nate said calmly. "It's over."

After the hideous collection Nate had just seen, it took all of his restraint not to lunge for the bastard's throat.

Alexander's slimy smile widened. "You seem to have missed the fact that I have the gun."

Nate forced a smile of his own. "That thing hasn't been fired in fifty years. I wouldn't count on it working. Might misfire and take off your head."

He saw a flicker of unease in those ice-blue eyes.

"Besides," Nate continued, "how are you going to explain shooting a man in your benefactress's basement? The woman's crippled, not deaf."

"You think you're so fucking slick." Alexander's self-assured expression evolved into an ugly sneer. "This may not be how I'd planned it, but you're gonna pay anyway." He took a step backward. "Let's go."

"No."

"Don't fuck with me!" Alexander hissed in a harsh whisper. "I'd be perfectly justified in shooting you here and now. You're breaking and entering."

Nate worked to keep a relaxed posture while he waited for his opportunity to attack. "Ah, but how are you going to explain all of this when they come to haul my body away?" He motioned to the boxes and leaned against the workbench holding the darkroom equipment. Then he crossed his arms over his chest. He had to get Alexander to relax that trigger finger.

"I'm curious," Nate said. "Why set me up for murder? I mean, I get your other games—Buckley, Greg, Bill, Ellis. I even have to admire the poetic justice in them." He nearly choked on the praise. "But I can't figure out why you're trying to frame me for murder. Is it just because I didn't take the blame for what you did to Laura?"

"What I did! You damn well know I never got my chance at her." Those cold eyes grew malevolently curious. "Tell me, was she your first? Once you got a taste"—Alexander's voice slid low and disturbing—"were you hooked? How many more have you done? Maybe we can compare notes before I kill you."

Nate studied the man for a moment. Was Alexander just screwing with him?

That gleam of curiosity said it all. Alexander thought Nate had attacked Laura and left her on the beach for dead.

That meant someone else did it. And Alexander really had gone to prison for a crime he hadn't committed.

The realization nearly sucked the breath from his lungs.

Buy some time. Figure this out.

The question kept ringing in his mind, Who *had* attacked Laura?

Later. He had to get out of this first.

Nate offered what he hoped appeared a sadist's grin as he rested his hands on the edge of the bench behind him, maneuvering his hands into a better position to reach his gun. "Well, now, trade secrets—"

He heard a door open.

"Hollis? Hollis, are you down there?" Justine called loudly.

"Son of a bitch," Alexander muttered. "Yeah," he yelled. "I'll be up in a minute."

"What are you doing down there?" she called.

Irritation flashed across Alexander's face. His gaze shifted for an instant.

Nate pulled his gun and fired in one quick motion.

The sound of his handgun was eclipsed by the sharp crack of the rifle.

Nate's left arm burned like a branding iron.

Alexander's eyes widened.

Justine screamed, "What's going on! What's happening down there?"

Alexander's stunned gaze moved to the rapidly spreading bloodstain in the center of his chest.

His grip loosened on the rifle, and it slipped from his hands.

"Hollis! Hollis! Are you all right? Hollllllisssss!"

It was two full seconds before the man fell.

❧

The first thing that registered in Ellis's consciousness was the throbbing pain and the fire on the right side of her forehead.

The second was that she couldn't move her arms.

The third was that she wasn't in back of this SUV alone.

She tried to open her mouth but realized it was taped.

A shot of adrenaline brought her fully conscious. She opened her eyes. It was dark.

No, not dark. There was something covering her, lightweight and opaque. Sweat trickled across the back of her neck.

She was on her side, her knees bent behind her.

She lay on carpet. The carpet was vibrating.

They must be moving.

She could hear someone's labored breathing. Behind her.

When she tried to turn over, she realized she was not only bound, but also her arms were somehow anchored into place behind her. Her ankles were tied together and similarly restricted.

Her thrashing did nothing but make her sweat more.

"Awake back there?" Carr's voice called over the drone of the tires. "Just relax, you're going to wake up your uncle."

Carr's confident arrogance was back.

And Ellis knew she was going to die.

⁂

As he checked Alexander for a pulse, Nate hoped the man would live to face justice for all the crimes he'd committed. But Alexander was stone dead. From the amount of blood on the floor, there would be no bringing him back.

Upstairs, Nate heard Justine's panicky raised voice calling the police.

All he could do now was wait for them to show up.

As Nate stared down at Alexander, his mind filled with the image of that tangle of broken jewelry, those souvenirs of brutality. He barely suppressed the urge to kick Alexander's lifeless body.

Dear God, what if he'd gotten his hands on Ellis?

Nausea rolled over him, and he broke out in a cold sweat.

Nate dialed her cell phone. He needed to hear her voice, needed to tell her the danger had passed—before the police got here and detained him up for who knows how long.

Ellis didn't answer.

He called the Greenes' house.

Charlie answered, which meant Bill must be home from the hospital.

Nate didn't mince words. "Let me talk to Ellis."

"She isn't here. But you might want to know some lawyer called for her, wanted to interview her in Alexander's case, said he was reopening it."

"She hasn't been there at all?" Nate tensed.

"No. She called earlier and said she'd be a while."

"Did she say why?"

"No."

"Why didn't you call me?"

"Hey, I figured she was still with you."

Nate disconnected. That's probably just what Ellis had wanted Charlie to think.

Where was she—and what in the hell was she up to?

He dialed the Belle Island Police Department's non-emergency number.

"Hello, this is Bill Greene," Nate said when the phone was answered. "Has my daughter, Ellis, been there this morning?"

"Sorry, but, no, Mr. Greene," the woman said. "I've been on since seven and no one's been in."

Nate wrapped his will around the panic that threatened to overtake his reason. Alexander was here. No danger to Ellis.

But where was she?

His mind quickly sifted through the facts. Alexander didn't attack Laura. He'd told the truth; she'd been gone when he showed up at her window.

Ellis *had* heard someone talking to Laura around midnight. Not Alexander. Not Nate.

That person was the one who'd beaten Laura.

The truth washed over him with heart-stopping iciness. Wayne Carr. He'd been the only local person with Laura in Alexander's photos.

Carr had come right out of the box with aggressive accusations against Nate after the attack—*before* Ellis had IDed Alexander.

Alexander's case was being reexamined.

Did Carr know?

Oh, God. Those photos. What had Ellis done?

Nate let loose a string of curses as he sprinted out of the basement.

Sirens approached as he floored the truck and pulled away from the curb.

As he wove through the narrow streets, he dialed Charlie's cell.

"Leave Ben there and get out to the Carr place. Ellis is in trouble."

❧

Nate pushed the truck's speed until the floorboards rattled. He flew past slower vehicles, passing in unsafe places. If the police came after him, they'd damn well have to chase him all the way to Carr's house.

His upper arm throbbed and was sticky with drying blood down to his forearm, but the bleeding had nearly stopped. The bullet had only gone a little deeper than a graze.

"Come on, Charlie," he muttered. "Come on."

The Carr place wasn't inside Belle Island town limits. Charleston County Sheriff's Department would take a while to get there, if they responded to Nate's theory at all. Wayne Carr against Nate Vance—who were they going to believe?

Charlie was his best and fastest bet. Why hadn't he called yet?

Nate decided to call the sheriff's department as a backup; to avoid a long explanation, he reported a break-in at Carr's.

By then, he was nearly there himself.

Nate swung the truck into the lane that led to the Carr place, turning so hard and fast that the rear end fishtailed.

He flew past Charlie's car, which was parked behind

a huge Magnolia whose branches reached the ground. Charlie had moved in with caution.

So why hadn't he called?

Nate drove right up to the front steps of the house and jumped out.

The front door was open.

Nate called Ellis's name as he jerked open the screen.

The house was silent.

He ran to the back door. The terrace was empty.

Maybe on the grounds. Best to search the house first.

He made a quick circuit of the downstairs. As he hurried through the front parlor, he noticed a shell casing on the hardwood floor.

Not a .38 from Ellis's gun. It wasn't from Charlie's pistol.

Sickness swelled in his belly. Scanning the room, he saw no trace of blood.

Yelling her name, he sprinted up the stairs and checked the upper floors.

He was going so fast as he came back down that he caught his heel on a step and pitched forward. One hand on the wall and the other on the rail prevented a tumbling fall to the bottom.

He exploded out the front door and looked around.

The garage doors were open.

He ran toward it, coming to his senses right before he reached it. He knew better than to run headlong, unarmed, into the unknown. The shell casing said there was a gun involved. His fear for Ellis had nearly eclipsed his training.

Moving with more caution, he pulled his gun and entered the garage. It smelled of old wood and motor oil.

There was a Jaguar parked in one of the four bays. Other than that, it was empty.

He went outside and circled around to the back.

There was a vehicle under a tarp, parked very close to the back wall.

Nate edged closer and lifted the edge of the canvas. Ellis's Mustang was under it, passenger side close to the building.

He whipped the tarp off. Her purse was on the passenger seat. So was the manila envelope she was supposed to be taking to the police.

Yanking open the driver's door, he saw her keys in the ignition.

He checked her bag. The .38 was inside. Her cell phone wasn't.

He walked to the rear of the car. There, in the small space between the passenger side and the garage, lay Charlie.

"Christ." Nate checked. Charlie was dead, a single shot to the head.

Chapter Thirty-two

With dread choking him, Nate went back to the driver's door and popped open the Mustang's trunk. With leaden feet, he walked to the rear of the car, praying he was wrong, that Ellis's body wasn't inside.

His heart stopped beating as he lifted the trunk lid.

Empty.

The rush of relief made him light-headed. His breath left him in a shuddering exhale.

There was only one way out for Carr. He had to kill Ellis and make it look like Alexander did it.

Kill her. Then Alexander would disappear or go back to jail. Carr had no idea Alexander was dead in Justine's basement.

Nate hurried back to the front of the garage. There on the ground, he saw two empty shell casings. He knelt down. No blood. One casing looked like it had been driven over, flattened and pressed deeply into the ground. They were both the same caliber as the one in the house.

Carr had driven away after he'd fired the gun. Ellis must be with him.

He kept telling himself, *There is no blood. No blood.*

Where would he take her?

It wouldn't be on his own property.

He'd want it to fit what the police knew about Alexander.

The beach?

It was daylight. A beach would be risky.

There were miles and miles of waterfront around Belle Island, acres upon acres of isolated woodlands and marsh.

How to find her?

Ellis's cell phone hadn't been in her purse.

Oh, baby, please have that thing in your pocket.

He called his techie, Raymond, and gave him Ellis's cell number and had him start working on locating it.

"It's gonna take a few minutes."

"Hurry."

Nate took the tarp and covered Charlie's body. Then he got in the Mustang and pulled carefully away from the garage; it was much faster than Jake's truck.

He drove out the lane and sat at the intersection of Bastine Road, squeezing the steering wheel, revving the engine, waiting for the call.

"Come on. Come on. Come on." He couldn't just start driving; he might head in the wrong direction and put more distance between him and Ellis.

His cell rang.

"Got it."

"Where?"

"I triangu—"

"I don't care how you got it!" Nate said. "Where is it?"

Raymond told Nate the location of Ellis's cell phone.

"You're sure?"

"Yes."

He snapped his phone closed and tore out of the drive, spinning the tires and kicking up a cloud of sand and gravel.

❧

The SUV had stopped moving several minutes ago. Before that, they'd bumped along slowly for quite a while. Ellis had heard brush scraping the sides of the vehicle.

Not good.

She wished Greg would come to, help her figure a way out of this. She could tell from his breathing that he was still alive.

Carr had gotten out. But he hadn't come around and opened the back. Wherever they were was quiet—not good either.

Sweat stung her eyes and set her wrists on fire where she'd abraded them in her efforts to free herself. She'd been able to get the duct tape on her wrists to stretch somewhat. It felt like a plastic wire tie was looped through her arms and over the tape, tying her to the floor of the van. If she could get it to start a tear in the tape . . .

The muscles in her arms trembled and cramped.

She took a deep breath and tried to relax them.

God! All of her preparation, all of her caution, and here she was as helpless as a woman ever could be.

In frustration, she gritted her teeth and, with a growl, yanked as hard as she could against her wrist restraints.

There! She heard it. The first snap as the fabric of the tape began to give way.

Slowly. Don't rush it.

Maybe Carr had left them in some remote place, waiting for nightfall. She could get herself loose and be long gone when he got back.

Suddenly the back doors of the SUV opened.

The tarp was pulled away.

Too soon. Too soon.

Ellis blinked against the light.

Behind Carr, all she could see were trees.

Carr said, "We might as well get on with this unpleasantness."

That's when she saw the knife. Wide-bladed and wicked. The top edge was serrated—a hunter's gutting tool.

Where was his gun?

There, in his waistband.

He crawled into the SUV and hovered over her. "Believe me when I tell you, I'm not going to enjoy this. But it has to look like Hollis finally got his revenge. And then he'll be next."

He slid the knife between her belly and the waistband of her jeans.

She wiggled and made as much noise as her muffled mouth would allow. She felt the bite of the knife in her skin.

"Hold still! You're just making it more painful for yourself."

With surprisingly little pressure, she heard the fabric split.

She continued to work the tape, trying not to give herself away with excessive body movement.

If he was going to assault her to make it look like Alexander had killed her, he would have to cut her legs free. She just had to wait. Be ready.

She stared at him, emitting a muffled mewling to cover any sound the tearing tape might make.

She flexed and relaxed her leg muscles, making sure there was blood flow. There would be only one opportunity to surprise him. Her legs had to work.

Then, contrary to what she'd been expecting, Carr hovered over her again.

"Goddammit, I can't do this with you watching me like that." He wrapped his hands around her neck and squeezed.

⁂

Nate disconnected the call. The police would be on their way.

The Mustang's speedometer edged over ninety. He was nearly to the turn for the road that dead-ended at Belle Creek Plantation. He supposed there was some perverse logic that had made Carr take Ellis there.

According to Raymond, she was on the river a mile northeast of the house. The old rice mill.

Nate would have to drive past the house, then take what wasn't much more than a horse trail the rest of the way.

He hoped the Mustang could make it over the rough terrain.

Dear God, don't let me be too late.

⁂

After her initial panicked struggle, Ellis regained control of her thoughts.

Fall limp. Let him think you've lost consciousness.

It took more will than she knew she possessed to stop fighting for her life.

He eased pressure almost immediately when she stopped thrashing.

She held her breath to keep from sputtering and coughing.

She felt Carr slide off to her side.

Don't move. Not until he unties your feet.

Finally, she felt him cutting the tape that bound her ankles.

Limp. Limp. Limp.

She allowed him to move her legs, setting her feet on the rear bumper.

He cut the remaining length of her jeans.

Wait. Wait. He'll have to put down the knife.

Her muscles vibrated with the need to spring.

He muttered, "It'll all be over soon."

The SUV raised slightly when he got out.

Then she heard what she'd been waiting for, the sound of his belt unfastening.

Her muscles tensed. She opened her eyes.

He was right where she needed him to be.

In one quick move, she drew her legs up, arched her back, and thrust both feet out. The blow was dead on, catching him right at the base of his breastbone, sending a shock to the solar plexus.

He fell away, out of her line of sight.

She heard him gasping.

She yanked and twisted. One hand came free.

She sat and peeled the other wrist from the tape.

Where was the gun?

She pulled the tape from her mouth, taking a good chunk of skin with it.

The gun lay on the rear bumper.

She snatched it up, her left hand supporting her right, and jumped out of the vehicle.

Carr was curled on his side, holding his middle.

"Get up." Her voice was raspy, and her lips stuck together.

"I . . . I ca-can't."

"Sure you can. Tough guy like you. Get up."

"I ca—"

She fired a shot into the ground, three feet from his head. He bent deeper into himself. A spray of dirt and sand littered his head and shoulders.

"Get. Up."

Anger tightened her grip on the gun. "Do you want to die like that, curled up like a sniveling child?" She shifted her weight from foot to foot, her energy spiking as the realization grew of her power over Carr—the man who'd taken away her cousin.

Looking up from under his brow, he said, "You . . . can't . . ."

At that second, she realized not only *could* she kill him, but she wanted to. She'd never wanted anything so much in her life as to see his blood on this sandy ground.

And she could do it justifiably. No one would punish her, not after what he'd done.

❧

Nate kept his speed up as he shot off the pavement onto the dirt track that led to the old mill. It was clear another vehicle had been through here recently.

He pressed the accelerator harder.

Please let her be alive.

Close. He was so close.

He heard a gunshot.

Oh, God, Ellis!

He cleared the trees. The ruins of the mill sat on the edge of a pond.

In front of the mill sat a Suburban.

Ellis stood behind its open cargo doors, in only her panties and shirt, holding a gun pointed at Carr's head.

Alive. The word bounced wildly around Nate's mind. She was alive.

Carr knelt on the ground in front of her. Her gaze didn't leave Carr as Nate slammed on the brakes and jumped out of the car.

"Stay back!" Ellis shouted.

Nate skidded to a stop.

"Ellis," Nate said softly. He was close enough to see the tears on her cheeks.

"Don't try to stop me."

"I won't. But you don't want to do this, baby."

Her hands trembled. "I do."

"You don't know what it's like knowing you've taken someone's life." Nate inched closer.

"He killed Laura." Her voice was raspy. "Was going to kill me." She sniffed.

"I know. But"—he put out his hand—"you don't have to do it." He paused. "I will."

Ellis's shocked gaze skittered to him and quickly back to Carr.

Nate continued closer. "Give me the gun, baby. If you want him dead, I'll do it."

Her hands shook more violently; tremors ran all the way up to her shoulders. Nate noticed the red and purple marks on her neck, and he *wanted* to kill him.

"Let me do it," he urged, inching to her side.

He reached out and slowly took the gun from her hand. He kept it pointed at Carr.

The man looked up. Snot was running from his nose, and his mouth was twisted into something between horror and relief.

Nate sent a shot whizzing past his head.

Carr squealed like a frightened toddler.

Nate could feel the fury coming off Ellis. It drew all of his body hair to attention and snapped in each of his cells; standing next to her felt very much like being close to a lightning strike. The fact that she hadn't reacted when he fired the shot told him all he needed to know.

Still, he said, "If this is what you want—"

"No." Her voice was rough, and she was shivering. "That's too easy for him. I'll take a lesson from Alexander and choose punishment that will be the most painful."

Nate took a deep breath. The disappointment he felt frightened him; maybe he was that base human being he'd once wished he was.

He kicked Carr over.

The man lay curled on his side, his cries sounding like a tortured kitten.

"Don't you think about moving," Nate said through clenched teeth.

"Un-uncle Greg's in the truck." Ellis's voice sounded like she was beginning to unravel.

Nate went to the open doors of the SUV and pulled the tarp off and checked him. Ellis stood in place, as if she didn't have the strength left to move.

"He's alive," Nate said. "The ambulance is on its way."

He turned back to her. She looked small and pale. Her hair was matted with sweat, her mascara had blackened her eyes, and there was an angry-looking rectangle of raw skin around her mouth.

But it was her trembling that completely undid him.

His insides whirled like a gyroscope set wildly into motion. His hand once again tightened on the gun; he had the almost uncontainable urge to shoot Carr anyway. Together, he and Alexander had stripped away the last precious thing Ellis had been holding on to—her sense of control. Nothing would ever repair the damage they'd done.

With his heart swelling so much he could barely swallow, Nate moved toward her, holding out his left arm.

Ellis came to his side. "Oh, my God, you're hurt!"

"A scratch." He pulled her to him, and she wrapped her arms around his waist.

He hugged her close, reassuring himself that she was safe in body, if not completely in spirit. Hot tears of relief flooded his eyes. The wail of sirens sounded in the distance.

And for the first time in over an hour, he filled his lungs with a clear breath.

Chapter Thirty-Three

It was ten o'clock that evening when Nate finally walked out of the sheriff's department interrogation room. His questioning had taken hours due to the shooting in Justine Adams's basement. In the end, his arm wound, along with Charleston PD's verification that Alexander had been armed and fired, convinced the detective that Alexander's death was self-defense.

Nate and Ellis had been separated as soon as the police arrived at the rice mill. Before parting, he'd told her of Alexander's death. Her initial reaction had mirrored his own—relief mixed with disappointment that he wouldn't stand before the families of his victims and the law.

The hours away from Ellis had been interminable. Even with the danger to her passed, his need to be near her ran through him like an electric current, making him pace the little room like an agitated animal. His entire body ached to hold her close, to breathe her scent, to feel her heart beat against his own.

Ellis was probably with her family, safe. With that thought, Nate felt like the outsider he truly was. He didn't fit in her life. She didn't fit in his. But at this moment, none of that mattered. He would go to wherever she was and wrap her in his arms, assure himself she was all right.

He walked toward the front of the station, rolling the kinks out of his shoulders. The building was nighttime quiet. As he walked through the door that led to the station's lobby, he dialed Ellis's cell.

Before he put the phone to his ear, he heard her distinct ring. He looked up and saw her sitting near the front door.

She answered her phone and stood to face him. "Hey, you."

The rest of the world became a blur, a smudge of light and color; Nate could see nothing but her face. She hurried across the lobby and hurled herself at him. He caught her and held tight.

"Oh, baby," he said against her ear. "You're safe. Safe forever."

She let out a noise that was a half-laugh, half-sob.

For a long while, they just stood there holding each other tight.

Then she looked up at him, an inviting smile on her face. "Can I interest you in a long hot coed shower?"

"You're enough to tempt the devil," he said, and then gave her a quick kiss.

"I'll take that as a yes." She linked her fingers through his, and they walked out of the police station.

⁂

Once behind the condo's closed door, Nate took Ellis in his arms and kissed her until he was the only light in her universe.

When he drew away, his eyes looked sad. "I have to leave tomorrow. And I don't know when I'll be back."

"I know that."

He sighed. "I don't want you to think I'd be going if I had a choice."

She reached out and grabbed his face, pulling him close. Against his lips, she said, "Stop talking and make love to me." She sucked teasingly on his lower lip. "And since you're leaving tomorrow, you'd better make it good."

He picked her up so swiftly that she didn't see it coming. He carried her into her bathroom and set her feet on the floor in front of the tub. Keeping one arm wrapped around her waist, he started the water.

"But I—"

He swallowed up her words with a kiss, his mouth hot, his tongue exploring. He slid his hand under her shirt, sending chills across her skin as he gently swept his fingers along the curve of her waist. His lips moved to the side of her neck, kissing and nipping the skin lightly with his teeth.

Ellis was overcome by shivers, so different from those of earlier today. If she tried to move her legs, no doubt her knees would buckle.

His breath hot and tempting against her neck, he said, "You issued the challenge. So you'd better let me do this my way."

She pulled back slightly and eyed him coyly. "All right." She grinned and winked. "Have at it."

Nate raised a brow and gave her that slow, seductive pirate's smile that had tripped her heart when she'd been questioning him about his life. It was so intense and her reaction to it so sexually primordial, that when he reached for her, she nearly backed up a step.

He slowly peeled off her shirt, keeping her bound to him with just that silver gaze. She stood trembling, anticipation setting off sparks in all of her nerve endings.

And dear God, when he touched her, gently, softly, his fingers just skimming the skin along her collarbone, she thought she might ignite like a sparkler.

His gaze grew dark as he traced the line of bruises on her neck. But he didn't ruin things by saying a word about them.

Instead, he kissed her softly and continued to draw her along a slow erotic journey as he undressed her, keeping his touch light, never venturing to the truly intimate places on her body. Lord have mercy, she feared she'd shatter like a supernova when he did.

He eased her into the tub and washed her hair, taking his time, massaging her scalp until she felt as if she had no bones left in her body.

When she let out a little moan, he leaned down and kissed her shoulder and whispered, "How am I doing so far?"

Just a little ashamed she was totally on the receiving end of this pleasure trip, she reached for the button on his shirt.

Leaning back, out of her reach, he said, "It's all about you this time, baby."

When he finished bathing her, he wrapped her in a towel and carried her to the bed. By the time he had his clothes off and slid into the sheets beside her, she was more aroused than she'd ever been in her life.

He held to his promise; the first time was all about her.

The second and the third times, however, she evened things up a bit.

❧

Ellis felt a little like pulling a Juliet arguing with Romeo about the presence of the dawn. The light of day had come much too soon. If she thought she could convince him, she'd try to persuade Nate that those rays of sun were a figment of his imagination, that it was still deep night.

But Romeo and Juliet didn't turn out so hot. So Ellis decided to face the morning with as much emotional strength as she could muster—and trust that she and Nate could create a better ending to their love story.

She kissed him, then said, "You get a shower. I'll make breakfast." She didn't want to spoil their last hour with talk of what their future may or may not be, so she started to slide out of bed.

Nate grabbed her hand. "Ellis."

She stopped and looked at him. "It's all right, Nate. I know you have to go."

"I'll be getting rid of this cell phone. I'll have to call you. But if you need me, you can contact Jake."

"Jake gets some secret code that I don't? What does he use, the Bat-Signal?"

"It's a system we've been using a long while. I won't take a chance that anyone could find out I'm tied to you."

"Are you . . . tied to me?"

He sat up and slid closer. Cupping her cheek, he said, "I think I've been more tied to you than anyone for most of my life." He kissed her lips softly.

Ellis ignored the tearing of her heart. "I know you're doing important work—"

He kissed her again. "I'll find a way to come back. But not until I'm sure I can do it safely. You've lived with fear for too long. I won't bring it back with me."

That made her afraid *for him.* "How difficult will it be for you to leave what you're doing?"

"I'm not sure. I've never considered it before."

He paused, looking all too sexy with his bare chest and the sheet pooled in his lap. Ellis wanted to shove him back onto the pillow and shut out all the talk, quiet all the uncertainty. But it was time to face reality.

He continued. "It might take some time. I'm not asking for promises from you. If you need to let go, I understand."

"For a covert-operations guy, you're not very observant." She linked her hand with his. "I've been waiting for you all my life. I'm getting good at it."

"Jake's here." Nate turned to Ellis from her balcony door.

She'd held up well through breakfast, managed rational adult conversation, but suddenly her throat was too tight to utter a sound. So she stood there looking at him, hoping he understood all the things in her heart, the things she couldn't say here and now.

Nate took her by the shoulders and rested his forehead against hers.

She closed her eyes and placed her hands on his waist. "I'll walk you down."

"No. We say good-bye here." Nate's hands slid up to her neck, his thumbs stroking the line of her jaw. He kissed her lightly. Once. Twice.

She covered his hands with her own. "Come back to me."

His sigh lanced straight through her heart.

With one last kiss, he left her. Alone and wanting.

Epilogue

Ellis stood in Paco's stall, brushing the old horse down. She breathed in the scent unique to this place and felt at peace. She'd been coming here every day since Nate left. Paco being retired, she'd started riding Mercury, the silver-white horse that Mr. J told her Nate rode when he was here.

Of course, Nate hadn't been here in a long, long time. It would soon be a year. She missed him with an ache that drove deep into the marrow of her bones.

There were days when hope was bright, and she felt his closeness in her heart. And there were days when loneliness and desperation convinced her that he was slipping further away, forgetting her, that they would never be together.

Those days made her sympathetic for what she'd put Rory through. He'd hung on to hope for several weeks after Nate had left, even though she'd made it absolutely clear they would never be together again. Last fall, he'd accepted a job in Beaufort and moved.

Today, she'd heard that Wayne Carr had accepted a long-argued-over plea agreement. As much as she wanted to see him publicly paraded as a criminal, she was glad not to have to go through a trial. The man was going to jail for a very, very long time—and there wasn't anyone to come visit him. Nor had there been anyone willing to post bail; Abigail Carr had filed for divorce even before his initial arraignment.

Ellis brushed Paco with long rhythmic strokes, losing herself in the feel of his solid flesh beneath her hands and the sweet smell of the barn. Maybe if she'd never stopped coming here, she would have healed years ago. Or maybe it was the special connection she now felt with Nate that gave this place its therapeutic power. She did feel closer to him while she was here; and she knew his love had given her the strength to deal with her fears.

While she'd been with Rory, she'd thought she was incapable of loving deeply and freely. Thanks to Nate, she now knew she wasn't an emotional cripple after all. She loved him without reservation, would wait for him until her hair grew gray and her eyesight failed.

She heard footsteps outside the stall and looked up.

Mr. J peered over the railing. "It's gettin' dark."

She gave him a smile. "Thanks. I think I'll spend a little more time with Paco."

She'd been leaving the stables later and later each evening. She'd even left her condo and run to the store after full darkness a time or two. Baby steps, she knew, but she was getting there.

"'Right, then. I gotta go up and check the house."

His footfalls faded.

Ellis bent to lift one of Paco's hooves. "Let's make sure these are clean."

She was working on the fourth hoof when she heard

footsteps stop outside the stall again. "I'm just about finished," she called. "I know you're ready to get home."

There was no response.

Jerking upright, she looked outside the stall and her breath caught.

"Hello, Ellis. You look beautiful." Nate used the same tone as when he'd first seen her on the plantation house porch.

She dropped Paco's leg and ran into Nate's waiting arms. He kissed her in a way that made her want to throw him down right here in the dirty straw and make love to him.

When he lifted his head, she asked, "Are you back for good?"

"For good." He smiled. "As of now, the most dangerous thing I'm going to be doing is disagreeing with you."

Lifting a brow, she said, "That can be pretty hazardous. Hope you're trained for it."

"Boss!" Mr. J called from the barn door. "By golly, it's good to see you."

For the first time in Ellis's memory, the man speeded up his shuffling pace. She stepped back and let the men embrace.

"How about I take my two favorite people to dinner?" Nate said.

Ellis saw the happiness flash in Mr. J's eyes. Then he glanced at Ellis and took a step back. "Oh, I believe I'll be gettin' on home."

"Don't be ridiculous." Ellis stepped close and linked her arm through Mr. J's. "I'm starving. Let's go."

Over a quiet—and for the first time in their relationship, public—meal at the marina, Ellis and Mr. J caught Nate up on what was going on in Belle Island.

Ellis noticed the servers in a little knot with their heads together; by the end of the day tomorrow, most everyone in town would know Nate Vance was back. This time there would be no shadow hanging over him, no whispers of condemnation behind his back.

That thought made Ellis feel light and free. No more hiding. No more fear. For either of them.

She realized Nate was talking to her. "Sorry, what?"

"You were looking very satisfied." He grinned in that way that emphasized the scar by his eye. It was all she could do to keep herself from leaning over and kissing it.

"Just happy," she said, leaning his way, propping her chin on her fist. "What did you ask me?"

"Buckley," he said.

"Out of rehab. It sounds like he'll make a full recovery—with time." Ellis had visited him a couple of times. It looked like one of his physical therapists was taking a very special interest in him. When Ellis had teased him about it, he'd actually blushed.

"What a waste." Nate pressed his lips together, and Ellis could see the anger gathering in his eyes, the frustrated hatred for the man who'd caused so much suffering. She knew Nate thought if he'd acted more quickly, lives would have been spared. He was wrong to blame himself, but that was part of what made him so special.

"Alexander might not have attacked Laura, but he ruined so many lives." Ellis gave a shiver. Without Nate's help, her own would probably have been one of them.

Mr. J agreed with a snort of disgust.

They sat in silence for a moment, the dark pall of the past hanging over the table.

Ellis wanted to head off the possibility of a prolonged

conversation about Alexander. She reached over and took Nate's hand. "You're just in time to be my date for the wedding."

"Whose?" Nate asked.

"Uncle Greg and Jodi's."

A slow smile spread across his face, the clouds of anger leaving him. "Good for them."

It was. Although Ellis sensed they were both far from healed. Maybe it simply wasn't possible for a parent to completely recover from the death of a child. But they did both seem happier than she'd seen them in years.

After dinner, Ellis, Nate, and Mr. J walked out into the night. Ellis and Nate had driven her Mustang to the marina; Mr. J had driven his truck.

They stopped in the parking lot, Nate keeping his arm firmly wrapped around her shoulder. Mr. J said good night and got in his truck.

Ellis looked up at Nate and smiled. "My place or yours?"

"I was hoping we could make them one and the same," he said, looking down at her.

The promise she saw in his eyes sent a waterfall of warmth over her. "You did, did you?"

He turned to face her, wrapping his arms around her waist. "Marry me."

Before she could answer, he kissed her. It was one of those fairy-tale kisses, one that changes the course of a woman's life forever—filled not just with passion, but with possibilities and hope and undying love.

When he stopped, it took her a moment to fill her lungs with enough air to speak. "Oh, yeah, I'll marry you. Want to elope right now?"

His devilish smile shot straight to her heart. "I was nice and didn't force-feed Jake to get through dinner faster. But I've waited longer than any mortal man should have to. It's time for bed. Tomorrow, we elope."

She squeezed his neck and kissed his cheek. "Good plan."

"I want to fill that plantation house with our children."

Her arms looped around his neck as she raised her brows. "Children?"

"Yeah. I was thinking maybe four or five—if it's okay with you. A big family, with lots of noise." He paused and glanced at the stars as if deciding. "Girls. I'll teach them to ride. You can teach them to kick ass."

"Four or five . . . If that's the case, we'd better get started."

Nate had come home. For the first time in his life, he would be surrounded by people who truly loved him. And it filled her heart to bursting that she could be the center of that love.

Dear Reader,

I hope you enjoyed SEEING RED as much as I enjoyed writing it. If you're looking for another fast-paced, character-driven romantic suspense, may I suggest my previous novel PITCH BLACK (Grand Central Publishing, available now). Fasten your seatbelts and lock those doors—you may want to read this one with the lights on!

Journalist Madison Wade and her newly adopted teenage son, Ethan, have just moved from Philadelphia to sleepy Buckeye, Tennessee. They're both out of their element, but Ethan needs a new start; Madison knows she must distance Ethan from the troubles of his life on the streets. Soon Ethan finds his first friend in shy and socially awkward Jordan, and Madison becomes engaged in a lively flirtation with the local sheriff, Gabe Wyatt, but then their lives are thrown out of orbit. A wilderness camping trip that Ethan takes with other teenage boys and Jordan's step-father goes horribly awry when the boys come off the mountain without their chaperone.

When it becomes clear that the step-father's death was no accident, all eyes fall on Ethan, the new kid with the troubled past. Even though he doesn't want to believe Ethan is guilty, Gabe's investigation offers evidence that leads straight to the boy. It's clear to Madison that Ethan isn't telling everything, but she can't persuade him to confide in her.

Soon another of the boys from the trip disappears. Is Ethan the next target? Or is he the villain? As Gabe and Madison try to unearth the truth, it quickly becomes clear no one is safe.

Best wishes,

Susan Crandall

THE DISH

Where authors give you the inside scoop!

♥ ♥ ♥ ♥ ♥ ♥ ♥ ♥ ♥ ♥ ♥ ♥ ♥ ♥ ♥

From the desk of Susan Crandall

Dear Reader,

Oh, how I love to write a twisted villain, preferring the play of psychological tension to physical gore. Villains are so complex, for who in this world is completely good or completely evil? Hollis Alexander in SEEING RED provided a wonderful opportunity to explore the depths of darkness that can lurk in the soul, the evil behind the mask of physical beauty and agreeability.

I always like to center my novels on what I call an "everyman" story, one that could happen to any of us (although we certainly hope it doesn't). I like to make it personal, to delve into the emotions of my antagonist and my protagonist. Therefore, I rarely venture into the arena of irredeemable evil. Hollis Alexander is the exception. He's bad and that's all there is to it. He's smart and uses mental manipulation to its fullest—this, to me, is the scariest kind of villain. And if I admit that I really enjoyed writing him, does that make you worry about my mental state?

Well, I did. I loved it, even though the idea of a *real* Hollis Alexander gives me chills and makes it difficult to sleep. Luckily, the idea of the *real* Nate Vances, our real-world heroes, makes me feel safe enough to turn out the lights and close my eyes.

Thanks for coming along with me on this journey. May our real-world heroes always be there when you need them.

Happy Reading!

Susan Crandall

www.susancrandall.net

♥ ♥ ♥ ♥ ♥ ♥ ♥ ♥ ♥ ♥ ♥ ♥ ♥ ♥ ♥

From the desk of Kate Perry

Dear Reader,

Have you ever wondered what it'd be like to have superpowers?

If someone gave me superpowers, I'd be stoked. Or would I? Gabe Sansouci, the sassy heroine in MARKED BY PASSION (on sale now), inherits an ancient Chinese scroll that does just that, only she finds out really quickly that having powers isn't all it's cracked up to be.

Don't get me wrong—if someone tapped me

with a magic wand and said I could fly, I'd *so* be soaring through the sky. But there are a few powers I'd turn down:

I Can't Go for That, No Can Do:
Three Powers Kate Doesn't Want

1. Causing earthquakes.

I'm just being practical with this one. Like Gabe, I live in San Francisco. If I made the earth tremble every time I got upset, there'd be chaos. San Francisco is beautiful; it'd be a shame if it lay at the bottom of the Pacific Ocean.

2. Reading minds.

Shudder. The idea of reading minds is so horrifying to me that I couldn't bring myself to even torture Gabe with it. Imagine your Aunt Millie thinking about sex. I rest my case.

3. Killing by touch.

Gabe has the capacity to harm people through touch, but she also has the balancing ability to heal. Um, in theory.

Of course, Gabe's not alone in this thing. With the help of Rhys Llewellyn, man of mystery and all-around hot guy, she's sure to get a handle on her new powers. Eventually.

Hope you enjoy MARKED BY PASSION! And

keep an eye out for CHOSEN BY DESIRE, the second book in the Guardians of Destiny series.

Kate Perry

www.kateperry.com

♥ ♥ ♥ ♥ ♥ ♥ ♥ ♥ ♥ ♥ ♥ ♥ ♥ ♥ ♥

From the desk of Kelley St. John

Dear Reader,

One of the best parts of writing a novel with a multitude of passionate characters is learning that your readers want to know more of their story. That's what makes it so much fun to give you the "what happened next" portion of their lives, because, as you very well know, those characters continue to live in your heart . . . and mine. Thankfully, you can revisit several of your favorites, since they tend to find their way into my other books. For example, Lettie Campbell's sister, Amy, from GOOD GIRLS DON'T, is one of Rissi Kincaid's best friends in TO CATCH A CHEAT! And—you guessed it—if Amy's there, then that means her sexy cowboy Landon is also along for the ride. So if you didn't get enough of Amy and her sex toys or Landon and his famed massage oils in GOOD GIRLS DON'T, then you can have another delicious taste in TO CATCH A CHEAT!

And if you're one of the many readers who sent the request (okay, the demand) for sexy-and-sizzling Jeff Eubanks to get together with wild hellion Babette Robinson after meeting them in REAL WOMEN DON'T WEAR SIZE 2, I promise you that FLIRTING WITH TEMPTATION (on sale now) will give you exactly what you've been asking for—and then some!

Ever true to her impulsive nature, Babette is still changing jobs, addresses, and hair colors as often as possible. (And changing men just as frequently!) Even though she can't find a man who will stick, she's finally found a job that will: Birmingham's "Love Doctor," where she heals love that's gone wrong. Her business is—*until* Kitty Carelle hires Babette to get her back with her ex—none other than Jeff Eubanks.

Jeff believes that women—not men—are the ones who can't commit, and he has the power to completely ruin Babette's new career if he refuses to take Kitty back. So Babette is determined to make him see things her way, even if it means adhering to his ridiculous challenge of no flirting for a week. She can do it. She *can*. In fact, she could do it rather easily, if the no-flirting policy only applied to beach hunks who didn't have the last name of Eubanks. Because Jeff is looking mighty good, and Babette has been a long, long time wanting . . . everything he's tempting her with.

Have mercy, seven days never seemed so long!

Happy Reading!

Kelley St. John

Kelley@kelleysbooks.com
www.kelleystjohn.com